PRAISE ... ... LES

"This is the best ur... ...ormal fantasy I have read in years. Fast paced, funny, clever, and suitably mythic, this is urban fantasy for those worn out by werewolves and vampires. Fans of Jim Butcher, Harry Connolly, Greg van Eekhout, Ben Aaronovitch, or Neil Gaiman's *American Gods* will take great pleasure . . . Highly recommended"

Grasping for the Wind

"A truly entertaining series"

SFF World

"Kevin Hearne is quickly becoming one of my favourite authors . . . I highly recommend picking up the Iron Druid Chronicles"

Fantasy Book Critic

"[The Iron Druid books] are clever, fast paced and a good escape."

Boing Boing

"If you like urban fantasy that is fun and funny, then pick up *Hounded*, *Hexed*, and *Hammered* . . . and anything else Kevin Hearne puts out in the future. You'll not be disappointed"

SciFi Mafia

SCOURGED

THE
**IRON
DRUID**
CHRONICLES

KEVIN HEARNE

orbit

www.orbitbooks.net

ORBIT

First published in Great Britain in 2018 by Orbit

1 3 5 7 9 10 8 6 4 2

A CIP catalogue record for this book
is available from the British Library.

ISBN 978-0-356-50448-3

Printed and bound by CPI Group (UK) Ltd, Croydon CR0 4YY

Papers used by Orbit are from well-managed forests
and other responsible sources.

Orbit
An imprint of
Little, Brown Book Group
Carmelite House
50 Victoria Embankment
London EC4Y 0DZ

An Hachette UK Company
www.hachette.co.uk

www.orbitbooks.net

For Tricia,
the metal editor who made all this happen

pronunciation guide

a s with other tomes, I provide this merely to help out those who want assistance with some names. You can say the names however you want as you read, of course; there will not be a test at the end, and the point is to enjoy yourself. But just in case you enjoy the flavor of names and words as I do, here are a few new names and some refreshers. . . .

polish

Andrzej Kasprowicz: AHN dray Kas PRO vich

Bartosz: BAR tohsh. Common name in Poland. Bonus points if you kinda roll the r.

Browar Szóstej Dzielnicy: BRO var SHOH-stay JYEL neet suh. Translates to Sixth District Brewery.

Chłopi: HWOH pee. Title of a Nobel Prize–winning set of novels.

Kacper Glowa: KATS per GWOH vah. The c is fun; it's pronounced like ts, so this is not quite Casper.

Maciej: MAH chay: Technically we have chee-ay for the last bit,

but it kinda blends to a single syllable the way most folks pro-
nounce it.

Piotr Skrobiszewski: PYOH ter SKROH bee SHEV ski

Władysław Reymont: VWAHD ih SWAHV RAY mont. Nobel
Prize–winning author of *Chłopi*.

Irish

Creidhne: CRAY nyah

Emhain Ablach: EV an Ah BLAH. One of the Irish planes, an isle
of apples.

Flidais: FLI dish

Goibhniu: GOV new

Scáthmhaide: SCAH wuh juh. Granuaile's staff.

Tuatha Dé Danann: TOO ah day DAN an

the story so far

atticus O'Sullivan, born in 83 B.C.E. as Siodhachan Ó Suileabháin, has spent much of his long life as a Druid on the run from Aenghus Óg, one of the Tuatha Dé Danann. Aenghus Óg seeks the return of Fragarach, a magical sword that Atticus stole in the second century, and the fact that Atticus has learned how to keep himself young and won't simply die annoys the heck out of Aenghus Óg.

When Aenghus Óg finds Atticus hiding in Tempe, Arizona, Atticus makes the fateful decision to fight instead of run, unwittingly setting off a chain of consequences that snowball on him despite his efforts to lie low.

In *Hounded,* he gains an apprentice, Granuaile MacTiernan; retrieves a necklace that serves as a focus for Laksha Kulasekaran, an Indian witch; and discovers that his cold iron aura is proof against hellfire. He defeats Aenghus Óg with an assist from the Morrigan, Brighid, and the local pack of werewolves. However, he also severely cripples a witches' coven that wasn't exactly benevolent but was protecting the Phoenix metro area from more-menacing groups of predators.

Hexed, book two, forces Atticus to deal with that, as a rival and much more deadly coven tries to take over the territory of the Sisters of the Three Auroras, and a group of Bacchants tries to establish a foothold in Scottsdale. Atticus cuts deals with Laksha Kulasekaran and Leif Helgarson, a vampire, to earn their help and rid the city of the threats.

In book three, *Hammered,* the bills come due for those deals. Both Laksha and Leif want Atticus to go to Asgard and beard the Norse in their mead halls. Putting together a team of badasses, Atticus raids Asgard twice, despite warnings from the Morrigan and Jesus Christ that this would be a terrible idea and it might be best not to keep his word. The carnage is epic, with heavy losses among the Æsir, including the Norns, Thor, and a crippled Odin. The death of the Norns, an aspect of Fate, means the old prophecies regarding Ragnarok are now unchained, and Hel can begin to work with very little opposition from the Æsir. However, a strange coincidence with the Finnish hero Väinämöinen reminds Atticus of a different prophecy, one spoken by the sirens to Odysseus long ago, and he worries that thirteen years hence, the world will burn—perhaps in some altered form of Ragnarok.

Feeling the heat for his shenanigans and needing time to train his apprentice, Atticus fakes his own death with the help of Coyote in book four, *Tricked*. Hel does indeed make an appearance, thinking Atticus might like to join her on the dark side since he has killed so many Æsir, but she is brutally rebuffed. Atticus is betrayed by Leif Helgarson and narrowly escapes death at the hands of an ancient vampire named Zdenik but ends the book with a modicum of assurance that he will be able to train Granuaile in anonymity.

In the novella *Two Ravens and One Crow,* Odin awakens from his long sleep and forges a truce of sorts with Atticus, enlisting the Druid to take on Thor's role in Ragnarok, should it come to pass, and perhaps take care of another few things along the way.

After twelve years of training, Granuaile is ready to be bound to the earth, but in book five, *Trapped,* it seems as if the Druid's enemies have been waiting for him to emerge. Atticus must deal with vampires, dark elves, faeries, and the Roman god Bacchus, and messing with one of the Olympians draws the attention of one of the world's oldest and most powerful pantheons.

Once Granuaile is a full Druid, Atticus must run across Europe to avoid the bows of Diana and Artemis, who took exception to his treatment of Bacchus and the dryads of Olympus in book five. The Morrigan sacrifices herself to give Atticus a head start, and he is *Hunted* in book six. Running and fighting his way past a coordinated attempt to bring him down, he makes it to England, where he can enlist the help of Herne the Hunter and Flidais, the Irish goddess of the hunt. There he is able to defeat the Olympians and negotiate a fragile alliance against Hel and Loki. At the end of this volume he discovers that his archdruid was frozen in time in Tír na nÓg, and when he retrieves him, his old mentor is in as foul a mood as ever.

In *Shattered*, book seven, archdruid Owen Kennedy finds a place among the Tempe Pack and assists Atticus and Granuaile in thwarting a coup attempt in Tír na nÓg against Brighid. Granuaile is sorely tested by Loki in India and is forever changed, and an emissary of the ancient vampire Theophilus strikes down one of Atticus's oldest friends.

In the novella *A Prelude to War*, Atticus consults a tyromancer in Ethiopia to discover how best to strike back at the vampires, while Granuaile meets Loki for the second time—but this time she's the one laying the ambush.

Anxious to defeat Theophilus once and for all, Atticus teams up with Leif Helgarson to make sure the ancient evil is *Staked* in book eight. Granuaile learns that Loki is making deals with dark powers around the world and is consulting an unusual seer about when to begin Ragnarok; she teams up with Perun to defeat an old foe of his and deny Loki his foresight. Owen starts a new Druid's grove in Flagstaff, receives a magical pair of brass knuckles from Creidhne, and has a distressing encounter with a troll that goes poorly for both of them. The Treaty of Rome is established wherein vampires agree to evacuate Poland and North America west of the Rocky Mountains.

After the events of *Staked*, Oberon and Atticus solve a couple of mysteries in and around Portland, detailed in *The Purloined Poodle* and *The Squirrel on the Train,* known together as Oberon's Meaty Mysteries. They befriend a man named Earnest Goggins-Smythe who winds up looking after the hounds while Atticus and Granuaile are out of town, and they also adopt a new doggie as a result of the investigations, a Boston terrier named Starbuck.

In *Besieged*, a collection of Iron Druid stories, we learn of several events that bear directly on the story to come. Flidais makes a woeful mistake by taking Perun to a "Cuddle Dungeon" in Edinburgh; Granuaile must enforce the Treaty of Rome against some rogue vampires in Krakow, led by Kacper Glowa; the Druids are called to Tasmania to save Tasmanian devils from extinction, and Owen's grove participates; and Atticus learns from the Morrigan that Loki is about to begin Ragnarok, prompting him to tell Oberon the story of what happened to his wolverine companion centuries ago.

Also, along the way, there may have been some talk of poodles and sausages.

CHAPTER 1

i had a cup of wine with Galileo once. He remains one of the greatest examples of human genius I've ever seen over my twenty-one centuries of life, and one of the bravest. Think of the giant, hairy stones he must have had to stand up to the Catholic Church back when they routinely toppled monarchs and killed people for the glory of their god (who let me buy him a shot of whiskey in Arizona once, by the way, and who did not feel particularly glorified by any murders, let alone the ones committed in his name). To look at the whole of Christendom and call bullshit on their geocentrism despite their threats took some iron guts. And he didn't give a damn that nobody wanted to believe him at first. "I have math," he told me over the rim of his cup. He gestured to it as he spoke. "And the numbers are like this fine vintage we are enjoying. Verifiable, observable, existing independent of us, and caring not one whit about human faith."

Stellar guy, that Galileo! Ha! My puns remain execrable, alas.

Eventually the Church had to admit that Galileo was right—and admit also, long after his death, that his life and work had been a fulcrum on which the world pivoted. The flourishing of the sciences that used his methods brought many wonders to humanity. Many evils too.

I am beginning to wonder now if I might not also be such a fulcrum for good and evil, even if I have labored to remain anonymous. I have endeavored for much of my long life to keep myself out of histories, all the while putting more and more history behind me. For much of my two-thousand-plus years, I did not feel I was building to some grand climax or accomplishing anything but my continued survival, but recent events have caused me to reevaluate.

According to a nightmarish visit from the Morrigan, Ragnarok will begin in the next few days, and it won't end well for anyone, because apocalypses tend not to include happy endings. Perhaps I can still do something to minimize the damage; no matter what I do, though, it cannot erase the fact that it wouldn't be happening at all had I not slain the Norns and unchained the Norse pantheon from their destinies. I am almost entirely to blame, and the guilt is already a nine-ton albatross about my neck. I don't think I'm going to get an easy gig afterward like Coleridge's Ancient Mariner did either. Telling your tale to random wedding guests is a pretty mild punishment for economy-size cockups.

It is fortunate that I have a friend able to shoulder such burdens and make me forget for a while that they are there.

<So tell me more about your plans for this meat and gravy bar, Atticus,> Oberon said as he placed his paws against a bound tree in Tasmania prior to shifting home to Oregon. My Irish wolfhound was expecting a proper feast before I went off to battle gods and monsters and assorted demons from the world's pantheons, and he'd challenged me to supply a meat bar for him, Orlaith, and Starbuck, our new Boston terrier, in the style of salad bar buffets. We'd adopted Starbuck during a stint of crime-fighting in Portland that Oberon pompously called "The Case of the Purloined Poodle." <Is it going to include all of the meats I will one day include in *The Book of Five Meats*, or are you going to just have the traditional stuff?>

"The five meat categories will be represented," I assured him.

<And the gravies? There will be more than one kind, right?>

"Of course. Didn't you have a maxim about this?"

<Oh, it's the best line from *The Communist Manifesto*, by that guy Karl you told me about. "From each according to his ability, to each according to his meat.">

"Uh . . . I think you're misquoting, Oberon. It's supposed to be 'to each according to his need.'"

<Well, I *need* that quote to be about meat, Atticus, so I fixed it.>

Choosing to keep Oberon carefully insulated from double entendres has proven to be endlessly entertaining. "An excellent job too. It can't possibly be interpreted to mean anything else but what you meant. Here we go."

I shifted us home to our cabin near the McKenzie River in the Willamette National Forest, and Oberon immediately shouted mentally to the other hounds once we arrived.

<Hey, Orlaith! Starbuck! We're home, and guess what! Atticus is going to make us a meat and gravy bar!>

Starbuck's higher-pitched voice replied immediately with his limited vocabulary. <Yes food!> he said.

<This sounds like one of the best human inventions since the sausage grinder!> Orlaith added, and both of them exploded through the doggie door to greet us, Orlaith trailing behind because she was very pregnant and close to delivering.

I had to spend a while getting slobbered on and trying to satisfy three dogs with only two hands while they demanded details on the meat and gravy bar. I confessed that I didn't have sufficient information to provide details.

Oberon was incredulous. <Okay, Atticus, wait now. What information are you lacking, exactly? Surely you are aware of the basic conditions of houndly existence? All the meats are out there, like the truth is out there, and we want to eat them all! Is that sufficient?>

"*All* the meats? Oberon, that's impossible."

<Is it, though? *Is iiiiiiit?*>

"It is. At least in the time I have allotted to me. Maybe it could be a squad goal for later. But right now we have to limit ourselves to what we can pick up in Eugene. Is Earnest here?"

Earnest Goggins-Smythe was our live-in dogsitter, whom we'd been depending on rather heavily in the past few weeks, especially as Orlaith's delivery approached. He had a standard poodle named Jack and a boxer named Algernon, or Algy for short, and they'd remained inside with him.

<Yeah, he's here,> Orlaith said.

"I should probably say hi and make sure he's okay with Jack and Algy participating in this smorgasbord. But after that, would you three like to come with me to Eugene to go shopping for the meats, so you can advise me on what to get?"

<That would be wonderful!> Orlaith said.

<Yes food!> Starbuck shouted.

<I advise you right now to get everything,> Oberon said.

"Do you want to go or not?"

<I do. My advice isn't going to change but I want to smell the wind on the ride over and slobber and shed on your upholstery.>

"Okay, give me a minute to talk to Earnest." After confirming that Jack and Algy could participate in at least some cautious meaty debauchery, my hounds piled into the blue '54 Chevy pickup I'd acquired during an escapade that Oberon had dubbed "*The Squirrel on the Train.*" Oberon looked out the back window at the truck bed.

<I'm not sure you have enough cargo space for all the meat we're gonna need, Atticus.>

"It's more than enough, Oberon."

<But leftovers, Atticus! Leftovers, for the time you'll be gone!>

"I'm not promising anything at this point beyond an assortment of meats and gravies. And maybe a story about a famous hound for the drive, since you're way too pumped up right now."

<Famous hound?> Orlaith's ears perked up.

"More of a tiny hound—a beagle, in fact."

<Oh, I like beagles!> Oberon said. <They're good at sniffing out rabbits, and then I can chase them.>

<What was the hound's name?> Orlaith asked.

"It was Bingo."

<Oh, like the song about the farmer had a dog?>

"Exactly like the song. I can tell you the true story of the actual Bingo who inspired that song."

<He had a story?> Orlaith cocked her head at me as we pulled out onto the road. It was crowded in the cab—the hounds barely fit and Starbuck had to sit on my lap, all aquiver with excitement. <The song just says that Bingo was his name-o and that's it.>

"Oh, but there were earlier versions of the song, which hint at some heroic deeds. And I know the details of that heroism."

Oberon stopped looking at the truck bed and trying to imagine it filled with meat. <Okay, Atticus, you hooked me. Tell us about Bingo.>

In the eighteenth century, just before the Agricultural and Industrial Revolutions, there was a cabbage farmer in the Southern Uplands of Scotland—that's the region closest to the border with Britain. His name was Dúghlas Mac Támhais, the Gaelic form of Douglas McTavish. In addition to his hillside of cabbages and a hayfield, he had a barnyard with some animals in there—a dairy cow, a plow horse, and, most important, a henhouse. Because chickens—those humble descendants of dinosaurs—are so delicious, they needed protection from foxes. And because cabbages are likewise delicious to some animals, they needed protection from rabbits and the like. That was where Bingo came in: Half his job was to protect the farm, and the other half was to be adorable. Bingo was outstanding at both halves of his job.

But he worried about his human. Dúghlas, you see, had taken to drinking quite a bit of ale after tragedy struck: He lost his wife as she gave birth to their first child and then lost the child soon after to fever. He was heartbroken and descending into alcoholism, and Bingo worried that he'd never recover.

One night, as Dúghlas was scowling at a potato and cabbage pie he'd made for dinner—a dish called rumbledethumps—Bingo let loose with a tremendous racket outside, and Dúghlas assumed quite rightly that they had an unwelcome visitor. He was already pickled as he grabbed up his musket, which he kept loaded and primed in case of emergencies like this one.

There was a fox trying to get into the henhouse, and Bingo was chasing him off, headed toward the property of the neighboring farm. They had a stile over the fence, for they were good neighbors, and the fox actually used the stile and Bingo leapt after him. That was the first verse of the original song: *"The farmer's dog leapt over the stile, his name was little Bingo."* The second verse had to do with the farmer's drinking habit, and that was immortalized because Dúghlas was inebriated to the point where he shouldn't be attempting things like steep steps over a fence. He managed to climb up to the top okay, but coming down was disastrous. He slipped on the first step, fired the musket into the air with a convulsive jerk of the trigger, and wound up hitting his head on the bottom step pretty badly. He was unconscious and bleeding.

Well, Bingo left off chasing that fox right away when he heard that gunshot and realized his human had stopped hollering. He ran back to Dúghlas and tried to wake him up, even slobbered on his nose, but it was no good. So he hightailed it to that other farmhouse and barked his head off until some humans came out, and then he kept running back and forth until they got the idea he wanted to show them something.

They followed Bingo to Dúghlas and brought him inside and cleaned him up, bandaged his head. These were the Mayfields, and at that time a cousin of theirs was visiting, young Kimberly Mayfield, and she thought Dúghlas handsome and Bingo adorable. She gave Bingo some sausage topped with gravy, in fact, for being such a good hound. And when Dúghlas woke up, he found Kimberly to be kind and beautiful and clearly well loved by his dog, so there was no hope for it: He fell in love again. The next verse of the old song went like this: *"The farmer loved a pretty young lass, and gave her a wedding ring-o."*

And it provides few details after that, but he also stopped drinking and became his old happy self again. So that's why Bingo got immortalized in song. He protected the delicious chickens, saved his human's life, and helped him find love once more. But much of the original story's been lost over time until we have the bare-bones song that children sing and clap to today.

Orlaith had questions. <How do you know all this? Did you know Dúghlas?>

"No, I met his son—one he had with Kimberly—years later in America. Lots of farmers came across the ocean during the Lowland Clearances, as they call it now."

<Atticus, I'm seeing some pretty significant parallels here,> Oberon said.

"You are?"

<Well, yeah! I'm good at protecting you and I'm also very handsome. Right, Orlaith?>

<He's right, Atticus. He is very handsome.>

<See? I'm just like Bingo! Except I don't have a song about me yet, and I think that's a gross oversight. Maybe we can make one!>

"Maybe. How would it go?"

<*"There was a hound named Oberon,*
And he loved sausage gravy!
G-R-A-V-Y! G-R-A-V-Y!
G-R-A-V-Y!
And he loved sausage gravy.">

<Yes food!> Starbuck said by way of applause. They amused themselves by making up additional verses and then taking turns sticking their heads out the window for the rest of the drive.

When we got into Eugene, the hounds agreed to stay in the bed of the truck while I went to get the meats and necessary gravy ingredients. I sent them mental pictures of what was available and they chose what they wanted, and I did make them choose instead of buying everything. That was for practical reasons; I didn't have all the time or sufficient kitchen space to make everything. But I did want to spend some time giving them a memorable meal, since I didn't know when I'd next be able to come home. I lost some time staring at the ground beef, packaged in red undulating waves, realizing that I might never come home and might lie somewhere beyond the aid of my soulcatcher charm to help, food for worms, packed up in some skin instead of Styrofoam and cellophane but otherwise little different from the 90 percent lean on sale. Oberon had made clear that he wanted to go with me, regardless of the danger, but I told him I couldn't bear it if he was hurt. I needed a home to come back to. I teared up at the mere thought of him living without me or me without him; we'd be so lonesome and hangdog, not to put too fine a point on it. And neither of us would be thinking of a feast like this. We'd probably not want to eat at all without the other one around to enjoy it with.

<Atticus, there may be a slight drool problem developing in the truck,> Oberon said, interrupting my maudlin reverie. <You might want to pick up a roll of those paper towels. The super-absorbent kind. Hurry up.>

<I have puppies to feed, you know,> Orlaith added. They really are the best hounds.

Earnest pitched in once we got home, and we had five hounds underfoot in the kitchen until I demanded that they vacate to the perimeter, where they could slobber and comment on the smells without tripping us up. We had a pot roast going, Cornish hens roasting, dry-cured sausages to slice, ribs on the grill, and four different gravies simmering on the stovetop. We had fish cooking in lime juice for a ceviche too, swordfish steaks sharing grill space next to the ribs, and charcuterie sliced thinly and layered on cedar planks.

When it was ready, we set it all out on the dining room table, lacking an actual bar, and put the gravies in tureens. Earnest and I had the hounds sit before it, their hungry excitement plain, and took some pictures. We then fixed each hound a plate, giving them the option to choose but knowing they'd try everything once and then come back for seconds of whatever they liked best.

<Oh, wow, Atticus, this is just the best day of food ever,> Orlaith said.

<I agree. Yes. There was that bison bonanza we had one time in South Dakota, but this even tops that.>

<Yes food!> Starbuck chimed in.

Cleanup was a major chore but Earnest and I got it done, and I managed to catch a few hours of sleep before giving them lazy belly rubs in the wee hours of the morning and kissing them on the head and telling them they were loved. I slipped out the back door, relieved to know that they were safe as I began to work on cleaning up my mess. I had a nine-ton albatross about my neck to remove.

The Morrigan had been less than specific during her visit to me; she'd said only that Loki was going to act soon but hadn't said precisely when or where. I needed more details to counter him effectively, and I knew precisely where to get them. Casting wands wasn't going to get me the specifics I needed; I needed a seer without peer who could read details in the future. Mekera the tyromancer had helped me on a couple of occasions before, and I hoped she could do so again.

She had most recently been living on Emhain Ablach—one of the nine Irish planes, and nominally ruled by Manannan Mac Lir— since I'd helped her escape from the attentions of some vampires.

That threat was over with now, the vampires in question all sent to their final deaths, and she could return to earth if she wished.

She certainly wished it. She looked a bit harried when I found her. "What's the matter?"

"There are ghosts here. I mean they've arrived recently. Very strange."

"Are they attacking you?"

"No, but they don't need to attack to creep me out."

"Hmm. It might be because Manannan Mac Lir has given up on his duties as psychopomp. The Morrigan has as well, so the dead are going wherever they can instead of where they should."

"Well, I want out."

"I've come to offer that very thing. And ask for a cheese."

Her shoulders slumped. "Of course you have. What is it you want to know this time?"

"I've been told Ragnarok is about to begin. I'd like to know precisely when and where the first attacks will occur."

"All right," she replied, her voice deadpan. "Something nice and light as usual. Where do they make great cheese these days?"

I shrugged. "Lots of places. How does France sound? Ever been there?"

Mekera's face lit up. "Ah, the *fromage* of the French! Let's go there. I think I'd like to learn from them and maybe teach them a thing or two."

I helped her gather her few belongings and we shifted to a small stand of trees outside Poitiers, in the goat-cheese region of France. Mekera might prefer a different region in the end, but I thought the area winsome and it would be a good place to find what she needed without the madness of Paris to deal with. She was used to being a hermit, after all; Poitiers would be a mighty shock to her system as it was.

"My French is somewhat rusty. Perhaps very rusty."

"It'll come back to you. And you'll be able to get along in the meantime with English."

"You think?" She looked doubtful as her gaze wandered around the streets. We were heading for a supermarket where she could purchase some basics for cheese-making. "I don't see anyone who looks like me. This might have been a bad idea."

I grinned because I'd expected her to have second thoughts. "Let's go to the store and make a cheese, at least. If you don't feel more comfortable by the end, I'll take you elsewhere."

Mekera agreed to this, her eyes darting around and her arms hugging herself. Once inside the store, however, with a basket in her hand, some of her social anxiety drained away as her professional interests took hold and she searched for ingredients. She also noted the faces of some other shoppers who weren't white, and she exchanged tight nods and smiles with them as she passed. But at the dairy case she had cause to do more than that. She had pulled a few quarts of goat milk out of the refrigerator and turned to discover a woman dressed much like her, in Eritrean fashion, wearing a light tunic with a gold-and-black embroidered neckline that then fell in a vertical line down the center to her midriff. Mekera's was embroidered in blues and blacks, but otherwise they were almost identical. Recognition flared in their eyes. The other woman, whose skin was a deep umber with cool undertones, like Mekera's, spoke first.

"Are you from Eritrea?" she asked in French.

"*Oui,*" Mekera said. "*Vous?*"

The newcomer responded affirmatively and flashed a brilliant smile, then they promptly switched to their native language, which I did not speak. I stepped away out of Mekera's sight so that she would not feel she had to introduce me. That worked perfectly; she forgot all about me, so excited to meet someone from Eritrea this far from home.

As the conversation extended and I pretended to read the ingredients of some crackers nearby, I thought I detected something in their voices and risked a peek at their auras. Yep: A touch of arousal there. They were into each other. Cool.

The other woman asked a question that startled Mekera into

remembering that she hadn't come alone. She looked around for me and I gave her a tiny wave. Somewhat abashed, she introduced me as her friend Connor Molloy. Her new acquaintance introduced herself as Fiyori.

"Pleasure to meet you," I said in French. "Please take your time chatting. I am in no hurry." I backed away again and chose to make a more thorough examination of the crackers.

Some while later Mekera found me, her face shining with joy. "Fiyori gave me her phone number! You know what this means?"

"She likes you."

"No! I mean yes, but it means I need to get a phone!"

"I agree. Let's do that and get you set up."

We took our purchases to an extended-stay hotel with a kitchenette and rented it for a month. The unspoken, understood agreement we had was that I'd get Mekera started here—or anywhere—in exchange for her tyromancy. That would give her time to get her assets transferred and find something a bit more permanent.

I did my best not to pace or look impatient as Mekera set about making a soft goat cheese. As the world's finest tyromancer, she would be able to see details of the future in the patterns of its curdling and coagulation, far more accurately than any divination I could practice. I wrote down a single question for her, though it was composed of many parts. When she was ready for it, she read it aloud: *"When and where will Loki, Hel, and Jörmungandr appear to begin Ragnarok?"* She gave a tiny shake of her head and sighed. "All right. Here we go." She squinted at the goat milk in her stainless steel pot as she added rennet and it began to posset and curd.

I had a hotel pad and pen ready to go.

"Jörmungandr first. Off a small peninsula south of Skibbereen. Near one of those fort hills."

"When?"

"Thursday morning is the best I can do."

Thursday. Thor's Day. Of course Loki would choose to begin then. That was only three days away.

"And the others?"

"Loki and Hel will appear together the same day, in midafternoon. But up in Sweden. The northern edge of a lake?"

"I know the place. Yggdrasil's root is bound there. Damn. I need to make some calls."

"And I need a phone," Mekera reminded me, "so I can make a call myself."

"Right. I'll go get you a burner phone. Be right back."

It didn't take long to find a convenience store that sold burner phones. Once I got one and activated it for her, I gave it to Mekera with my thanks and best wishes.

"Call Fiyori soon," I said.

"Why?"

"Because she likes you. And because of Thursday. I'm going to do my best, Mekera, but it might not work out well. Don't start any cheeses that need to age."

"That's not funny, my friend."

"No. No, it's not."

CHAPTER 2

if ye give the world half a chance it'll turn to shite. We knew that thousands of years ago, but Siodhachan tells me there's a fancy law about it now. Kind of like if ye have a basic cracker and ye feel okay about it, but put some fecking nasty fish eggs on top and call it caviar, now it's *fancy*.

The fancy law is the Second Law of Thermodynamics, and it says if ye have an isolated system, then entropy will increase and—gods damn it, let's just say things turn to shite and be done with it, all right? We can call it the First Law of Owen.

Except that ye can clean up the shite if ye have the heart and mind for it—call that the Second Law of Owen—and I'm proud of me apprentices right now for the work they're doing.

We're in Tasmania, saving some marsupial doglike creatures called devils. They got a strange transmissible face cancer back in the nineties and it was wiping them out, but now our job is to wipe out that cancer, finding every devil on the island and curing them, one by one. The apprentices have tasmanite spheres from Tasmania in the lockets I made them, and the elemental uses that to channel energy through them, which allows them to heal the devils even though they're far from being proper Druids yet.

Tasmania doesn't think we can wait, and I'm on board with the idea. I'm thinking these new Druids will be Gaia's healers above all else, fighting centuries of humans turning everything to shite. I wonder if they have a fancy law or name for the principle that Humans Ruin Everything for Profit. Maybe that's just capitalism. Regardless, it's going to take generations of Druids to undo all this damage.

Greta is with me and so are most of the kids' parents and we are all feeling pretty good about what we're doing to help. Watching the wee ones heal Tasmanian devils makes me think everything can be healed somehow. Perhaps there's a way to heal the breach between Fand and Brighid so we don't have to have any more war among the Fae. And maybe we can smooth things over between the Fae and Siodhachan—less likely, I figure, since he's still the fecking Iron Druid. But I'd settle for healing the breach between him and Greta.

Siodhachan is here in Tasmania too, on the same mission as we are, but somewhere else at the moment. At least Greta didn't try to kill him when we met up for a brief while. She's got more acid for him than spent coffee grounds have for me garden soil, but maybe in a season or three she will mellow out like a teacher lapping up medicinal bourbon after school. I'm going to give it time.

We've found a den with five afflicted devils in it, one of them as near death as ye can be without stepping over the line. I take care of that one, and the apprentices work on the others. We're almost finished when Greta tells me someone's coming; there is a whisper among the ferns underneath the eucalyptus. Since we're away from any settlement, I'm thinking it must be a hiker or hunter, but it's neither. It's Brighid, First among the Fae, come to find me.

She's all armored up for some reason, red hair spilling over the pauldrons, and it sets me on edge. Where's the fight she's dressed for? I hope it's not with me.

There's a faery with her, the tall, slim sort ye see in underwear advertisements, who always look bored with being so handsome and desirable and minimally dressed. Except he is dressed, all spiffy in his silver-and-green Court livery with high thread count and a powdered wig with curls on the sides of his head. Without even turning on me true vision, I can feel he's covered in magical wards, even more powerful than Brighid's.

"Well met, Eoghan Ó Cinnéide," she says, nodding once to me.

"Well met, Brighid."

The First among the Fae gestures to her right. "This is Coriander, Herald Extraordinary of the Nine Fae Planes." I'm not sure why she puts the adjective after the noun in his title; maybe it's to make him sound as fancy as he looks.

I nod at him. "How are ye, Cory? I'm Owen."

He gives me a bow dripping with excess manners and says in a mild musical lilt, "So pleased to meet ye, sir. I prefer to be called Coriander, if ye please."

If that's his preference, then I'm already suspicious we may not be the best of friends. I introduce Greta and me apprentices to Brighid and sort of wave at the parents as a group. She takes note of the apprentices and says they'll need to undergo the *Baolach Cruatan* soon.

"But I've come here on urgent business," she says. "May we draw aside and speak in private?"

"Of course." I ask Tuya, me youngest apprentice, to finish up healing the devil I'd been working on and tell them all I'll return soon. Brighid and I step into the undergrowth and the Herald Extraordinary floats about three steps behind.

"It has come to my attention," Brighid says, "that one of the Norse gods intends to begin his pantheon's version of apocalypse. They call it Ragnarok. Are you familiar with it?"

"Aye. Siodhachan caught me up on all that bollocks."

"It poses a serious threat to us. Should they harm a significant portion of our Irish population, we will suffer a similar reduction in our powers, and tethers to Tír na nÓg and the other planes may be severed."

"So it's back to defend the homeland, eh?"

"Yes. But we alone may not be sufficient. We need all the Fae to participate. We need all the Tuatha Dé Danann too."

"Ye mean we need Fand and Manannan Mac Lir."

"Correct. Siodhachan tells me she's in the Morrigan's Fen."

"Aye. I heard the same."

"It is my opinion, Owen, that only you can mend the rift between us."

"I was just thinking someone ought to be mending rifts, but I didn't think I'd have any part in it. I'm rather the sort to create rifts."

"She will not speak to me or Siodhachan. We are corrupted by iron, both in her eyes and the eyes of all the Fae who follow her. She cannot listen to us or she will lose face among them. But you are of the Old Ways and have enjoyed their hospitality in the past. You will at least gain an audience."

"Forgive me, Brighid, but I don't think so. All those Fae and the Morrigan's yewmen will cut me down before I can even flash me teeth at Fand."

"That is why I am sending Coriander with you. No one will harm him or dare touch anyone under his protection."

"*His* protection?" I glance back at the bewigged faery and wonder if he can even protect his own sack from a swift kick. Brighid catches this and smiles.

"By all means, Eoghan, feel free to test his defenses if it will ease your doubts."

"What? Ye mean punch him in the nose or something?"

"Whatever you wish." Brighid stops walking and gestures at the herald. "Do go ahead."

"Can I use me knuckles?" I asks her, and she hesitates.

"I would not recommend it. Start with your bare fists or feet."

I squint at the fancy herald. "Are ye all right with this, lad?"

"Of course, good sir. I hope you will not be injured too badly."

Their unworried confidence shakes me own, and I go ahead and check out the herald in the magical spectrum. He shimmers with layers of protective wards, among them a kinetic one of a strength and weave I've never seen before.

"Shrivel me cock, lad, who gave ye such wards?"

"Most of the Tuatha Dé Danann have contributed in one way or another. I represent a group effort. I cannot be harmed or deliver harm, except to redirect that aimed at me; I am therefore allowed everywhere in the nine planes, since I cannot be used for treacherous purposes."

"I see. And should the yewmen take it into their wee woody noggins that I'm to be skewered sideways, ye can prevent them from doing that?"

"So long as I remain between you."

"Ah, so beware me flanks, then?"

"Precisely."

I turn back to Brighid. "All right, if I go, how do ye suggest I get her to cooperate?"

"You may relay an offer I think she will find attractive, if she be not mad." And once she gives me the details, I asks when I must go.

"Now, Eoghan. I will bind this eucalyptus to Tír na nÓg while you make your farewells."

"But the devils—"

"—will still exist should we prevail. Nothing will remain if we fail."

"Ah. Thank ye for the perspective. And have ye spoken to Siodhachan about this? He's on the island somewhere."

"No longer. He heard from the Morrigan and is pursuing different objectives. We used a tree he bound to shift in and had to travel here at speed over land. You may rest assured that Granuaile will be involved as well."

"Right, then. I'll be back soon. Excuse me."

Greta waits for me, arms crossed and her neck taut with stress as she searches me face. "Damn it," she says. "You're leaving us here, aren't you? I can tell already."

"I have to, love, though I'd rather not."

"You don't have a choice?"

"Not if I want to keep me honor intact."

She growls at me, "To hell with honor! That's the kind of thinking that gets people killed. Gunnar's dead because of his sense of honor, and Hal's dead because of someone else's sense of honor. I don't want you dying for the same reason. I'd rather have *you* intact than your honor."

"Not sure if I can stay physically intact if I don't also protect me honor in this case. I have to go see Fand and convince her to help us fight off Loki. Ragnarok's coming, love. It's not the sort of thing ye sit back and watch and hope someone else takes care of it all."

She snorts in disbelief, then stops breathing. "You're serious? You're talking about the end of the world?"

"Let's hope it won't be, but yes. It's what Loki wants."

"Where are you going?"

"To the Morrigan's Fen. After that, I'm not sure. But I'll come back here to finish this job when I can. Ye can either stay here and watch over the kids—they have the knack for it now—or ye can pack up and fly back to the States. I surely don't know which is safer."

"Okay. We'll decide later."

I bid farewell to the apprentices and their parents, and tell them to keep up their fine work, and spend a little bit of time with each apprentice.

Thandi worries she'll forget everything when I'm gone, because she finds something to worry about in every situation. Her father, Sonkwe, is so patient and kind with her that I think this must be a recent behavior caused by her mother leaving them. She will see her strength soon enough.

Ozcar will be fine so long as his parents are all right. He checks on them to see how they're handling my leaving, and since they seem unconcerned, he simply tells me to be safe and they will do the same.

Tuya asks me if she's going to get to learn any more about the plants while I'm gone. Healing devils is fine, but she's really fascinated by flowers and trees and growing things.

"O' course," I says to her. "Remember that ye can talk to Tasmania anytime ye wish through your sphere there." I point to the locket around her neck. "Ask the elemental about its favorite plants and I'm sure you'll learn all ye ever wanted to know. Did ye know that there are plants here that eat bugs?"

"Really?"

"Sundews for sure, perhaps many more. Ask about them."

"I will!"

Mehdi, a solemn boy from Morocco, assures me that he and his father will pray for my safe return. "We will work hard while you're away," he adds.

Amita hears this and nods. "We will heal as many devils as we can." She's already the sort of person who works tirelessly at a goal once she's been given one. She's going to be a powerful champion of Gaia when she grows up.

Luiz, me animal lover, doesn't care at all that I'm leaving. "What? Oh. Bye," he says, then he whips his head around. "Wait. We don't have to stop healing devils while you're gone, do we?"

"No, lad. Ye can keep at it."

"Good. I love this." He flashes a gap-toothed grin at me before turning his attention back to the devil he's healing, and I'm already forgotten.

Me farewells to the apprentices finished, Greta grabs me by the face, both hands in me beard, and leans her forehead against mine. "You come back to me, Teddy Bear."

"Ye can be sure that's the plan, love." I really don't want to leave her, or any of them. This bollocks sounds like the kind of fool thing Siodhachan keeps getting involved in. Maybe this is what it's going to be like now, being one of the few Druids left instead of one of the many: Everything's an emergency. I give Greta the sort of kiss that says I want to pick up where we left off, and I promise a good run through the forest when I'm back.

Brighid is just finishing up when I rejoin them. "All right, Andy," I says to the herald. "Let's go."

"It's Coriander, sir."

I grin at him. "A four-syllable name is impractical in battle, lad, and in most poetry too, if ye care about what the bards say. I'll give ye only two syllables until ye actually save me bones from the Fae. You can pick. Cory, Ian, Andy, Gobshite, I don't care. What'll it be?"

"Coriander, sir." He shoots a pleading glance at Brighid, but she looks amused, and I laugh at him.

"How about Fuckstick? Aye, that'll do." He doesn't have a ward against me calling him the wrong name. I know it makes me a fecking arsehole, but he's a far sight more smug than I can stand. And besides, I have to carve off what wee slices of amusement I can from this situation. I'm pretty sure the First Law of Owen is about to enforce itself.

CHAPTER 3

Last week a vampire exploded in my bar in Warsaw. Not spontaneously: I unbound his undead ass because he came in to threaten me, and he went *sploosh* in spectacular fashion. People screamed and panicked. One of my regulars thought it was *so* metal, though, and he's become one of my favorite people. I give him free shots of Żubrówka with his beers now. Much of the vampire's remains landed in his pudding and kind of ruined his nice leather jacket, but he just snapped pictures of the gore for his Instagram.

Since Atticus and Owen are in Tasmania helping out the elemental there, I'm pretty much on my own—at least during the day—enforcing the treaty with the vampires. Specifically the part where it says all vampires need to be out of Poland in order to keep a promise Atticus made to the Sisters of the Three Auroras. A vampire older than Leif Helgarson by the name of Kacper Glowa emerged in Krakow and said he wasn't going to leave, and neither were the rest of the vampires, so he's thumbing his pale boogerless nose at both the Druids and at Leif.

I don't know: Do vampires have boogers? Leif finally admitted that they sorta-kinda poop—or, more accurately, *excrete* in the most disgusting fashion possible—but maybe I'm assuming too much on the booger front.

Leif is helping me with the problem, and we did clear out a nest in Krakow, taking out twelve of those suckers. But Glowa wasn't among them, even though it was his property. Leif thinks if we take out old Kacper the rest will fall in line and leave the country. All we have to do is find him. Which is proving difficult because you can't divine the dead, and he's old and rich and very, very good at hiding.

So I am back at work at Browar Szóstej Dzielnicy in Warsaw, even though I was shot in that nest raid a few days ago, because we're hoping he'll try to come after me or at least send a minion we can hopefully trace back to him.

Who comes to visit me instead? A decidedly dejected member of the Tuatha Dé Danann, looking out of place in hunting leathers with a bow strapped to her back. She sits down at the bar next to my metal regular, Maciej, drawing stares from pretty much everyone since she appears to be cosplaying for a Renaissance festival. Well, that, and she's a red-haired goddess renowned for her sexual appetites. She kind of projects an irresistible vibe, and the stares are mostly of the wanton and lusty sort.

Maciej is too startled to feel much else but surprise, however. "Oh, hey!" he says in Polish, which I'm pretty sure Flidais doesn't speak. "You have tattoos like Granuaile has. Or used to have."

The Polish word for tattoos is almost identical to English, and that, combined with his pointing to her Druidic tats and then my arm, is enough for Flidais to piece it together.

"Yes, hello, my tattoos are like hers," she says in English, then her eyes turn to me. "Hello, Granuaile. Would you—wait, what happened to your tattoos?"

I don't respond in English because it wouldn't do to have Maciej hear. I use Old Irish instead. "Welcome, Flidais. I still have them.

They're just under a nice magical cloak that the Sisters of the Three Auroras gave me. I got too many comments about them and it was distracting."

"You two could be sisters," Maciej says, switching to his accented English. "Are you sisters?" I can see Flidais getting annoyed and think perhaps I should defuse that before she acts on the violence in her head.

"Pardon me a moment, Flidais?" I say to her. "I'm just going to explain who you are." I switch to Polish for Maciej's benefit and also so I can speak frankly to him about the mortal peril he's in. He needs to know that Flidais is not my sister and she will most likely mess somebody up, and I don't want him to be on the receiving end. I hope my grasp of the language is up to the task; it's much improved but I'm not sure it's solid.

"*Wyglądamy podobnie, ale nie jest moją siostrą. Ma na imię Flidais i jest naprawdę niebezpieczna, mówię serio. Zobaczysz— potrafi naprawdę zepsuć człowiekowi dzień, kiedy ktoś ją wkurzy. Nie chcę tylko, żebyś to był ty, dobra?*"

Maciej agrees but asks for clarification. "*Dobra. Więc mam z nią w ogóle nie gadać?*"

I confirm that for him, continuing in Polish: "It's safer if you don't say anything. Enjoy your drink—it's on me, all right? And let someone else make the mistake. Just tell her right now it's an honor to meet her—because it is—and ask her to forgive your interruption. Trust me."

Maciej nods quickly, his long hair flowing around his head like he's rocking out to Trivium or HammerFall. He does trust me, and I like to think it's not just because I give him free booze sometimes. He turns to the Irish goddess of the hunt and speaks slowly in his best English. "Is an honor to meet you, Flidais. Please pardon my interruption."

Flidais's expression mellows from hostility to only mild disdain. "I appreciate your courtesy, mortal."

"Mortal?"

I shake my head at Maciej vehemently and he gets the message not to pursue that. Flidais ignores his question, fortunately, and just talks right over him.

"Please pardon me while I talk to Granuaile for a while."

"Of course," Maciej says. "Please."

Flidais awards him a brilliant smile for his compliance, and I beam at him also. He blushes a little bit and then looks down politely. I breathe a sigh of relief. That could have gone wrong so quickly for him.

"What can I get for you, Flidais?" I ask.

"Whatever you have that's closest to something Goibhniu would have brewed," she says.

I almost ask her, "Short or tall?" but catch myself just in time. She's an Irish goddess. If I give her a tiny glass of beer she will hurt me. Instead, I merely nod and pull her a true imperial pint of my favorite local brew, a thick oatmeal stout with chocolate notes and a clever bit of mint thrown in.

"There we are," I say, and set it down on top of a coaster. "It's great to see you. To what do I owe the honor?"

"I have a message for you from Brighid, but that can wait. This can't." She picks up the twenty ounces of stout and chugs the whole thing in one go. By the end of it, both Maciej and I have our mouths open in awe. "Ahhhh," Flidais says, thunking the empty glass down on the bar, a thin mustache of foam on her upper lip. "That was surprisingly satisfactory. Another." She meets my green eyes with hers, and I recognize the expression from the mirror whenever I feel like I could kill something.

Oh, shit. Something's up. I take her glass, place it in the sink, and fetch her a fresh chilled one, pulling another pint. She quaffs it just like the first and demands a third. Maciej looks like he might be falling in love just a little bit.

If it were anyone else, I would have said no. I would have been *required* to say no; forty ounces of beer in two minutes was going to hit her hard pretty soon—and it's not like this was some watered-down, mass-produced American swill. That stout has a beefy 11.2 percent ABV. But, like me, Flidais can heal the poison of alcohol anytime she wishes. She must, therefore, be drinking for a purpose, and has come to me to help her achieve it. My duty is clear. But drunken deities are rather infamous for collateral damage. I don't want to see Maciej—or anyone, really—get hurt over whatever's bothering her. And that could be almost anything these days, what with the turmoil going on in the Fae planes.

Normally Flidais is a hardcore soldier type, based both on what I've seen and what Atticus has told me. She's intensely loyal to Brighid, even taking Brighid's side against her own daughter, Fand. But she has a mercurial disposition, and any reading of her emotions you take in one instant can be null and void the next. Atticus says the thing about Flidais is you never know whether she's going to want to fight or fuck. Sometimes, he says, it's both. You simply have to tread carefully, mind your manners, and be prepared for either.

"So," I say to her as I put the third pint down and then switch languages again to Old Irish, so that we can talk in front of Maciej in complete privacy. If I had to guess, I'd say the two of us are currently the only speakers of that language in all of Poland. "Tell me in the old tongue, just between us Druids. If you are in the mood to share, that is. What troubles you?"

I count nine seconds of intense glaring before Flidais replies. "I will tell you, even though you are young and unprepared: Men. Are. Shit."

"Oh! Yes," I say, giving the empathetic bartender nod of acknowledgment, which is not actually the same as agreement, but people who drink a lot tend to miss the nuance. "I've actually heard that one before."

"Of course you have." Flidais chugs her third pint and demands another in an utterly sober voice, and it's at this point that Maciej starts to look a bit scared. I can see that part of him wants to leave, but his desire to see what happens next keeps him firmly planted in his seat.

Pint four. Flidais curls her hand around it, hunches over somewhat, and only now, it seems, will she nurse it and tell me what happened. But first she delivers a belch that's long and robust, supporting and sustaining the note from the diaphragm like a trained singer. Maciej nearly swoons.

"Perun broke up with me," she announces in English.

"What?" I'm truly stunned. Perun had been completely besotted with her. "When did this happen?"

"Couple days ago in Scotland. Some faery stole his thunder and I destroyed her with cold iron and he got mad and turned into an eagle and flew away and now it's done. All my fault too."

"No," I say. I have so many questions and I can see that Maciej does as well, but job number one here is reassurance, and I throw a warning look at my regular. If he opens his mouth now, it won't end well for him. "It can't be all your fault."

"Yes. Yes, it is. Because. You know. I betrayed him."

"You . . . did?"

"Yup. Uh-huh."

"How did you do that?"

"Well, that faery who stole his thunder, I knew she was going to do that. And I knew he was going to get it back! Because I'm a huntress. I hunt shite down, right? Including faeries. Perfectly safe. Kill her"—Flidais brings her fist down so hard on the bar that the wood splinters and Maciej flinches—"and he gets his thunder back. That's exactly what happened. I had a plan and that plan worked, mostly." She raises her fist and waggles a finger at me. "But see, I didn't tell him first."

"Oh."

"Oh is *right*. I didn't get his consent. I used him." She turns to Maciej and leers at him, switching from Old Irish to English. "Usually men like it when I use them."

Maciej gulps and slides his eyes over to me for a cue. I give him a tight nod.

"I can . . . see how they would," he manages to say in English. Flidais chuckles, her eyes appraising him, and I quickly step in before she can take it any further, pointedly using Old Irish.

"But Perun didn't like it, I guess?"

That draws her attention back to me. "No! He said he had a good time with me but now the time is over." She raises her left hand in the air and her fingers flutter in it. "He flew back to Russia or somewhere Slavic, I don't know. And it happened so fast I didn't even understand what I'd done wrong. I was still standing there, thinking I'd done the right thing because that faery had been violating treaties with the Scots, and it was only the result that mattered . . . but he was gone. I didn't have time to process it, to step outside my own stupid headspace and look at what I'd done from his perspective. I didn't . . . I didn't even get to say I was sorry."

Her voices catches at the end and I can see her eyes filling and I am struck by so many thoughts at once: Here is a truly ancient person feeling heartbroken and rejected and it's no different from the heartbreak someone would feel who was born twenty years ago; and, Oh, baby, you done fucked up bad; and, Oh, honey, at least you know it and you're going to be a better person from now on; and, Oh, shit, if I say the wrong thing right now, she will kill my ass. I should probably not say, for example, that if Atticus ever did something like that to me, I would most likely do the same thing as Perun. No matter what I say, though, she might pay me a visit later if she feels embarrassed about opening herself up to me, and I think Flidais is probably that sort. It had taken her sixty ounces of beer to relax the tight control she kept over herself, and once she sobered up, she might not want there to be any living witness to her moment of vulnerability. I need to bring my A game.

I lean over the bar, get as close as I can without touching her, and say, "If you still want to tell him you're sorry tomorrow or a hundred years from now, you're going to get that chance. Because you're going to be around. And maybe when you say it there will be forgiveness and it will be good. And if there isn't forgiveness, then it will *still* be good, because you will have done what's right: He deserves that apology. And in the meantime, there is beer and blood and the songs of bards, the great wide world to live in, and all the planes too."

Flidais nods, a tear escapes and runs down her cheek, and she raises her glass. "Beer," she says, and I rear back, horrified, while she chugs that fourth pint, swaying in her seat as she does so. I have made such an awful mistake. I flick my hand at Maciej and whisper at him urgently in Polish to run.

"Go, just go. Run! I'm serious!"

Thank the gods of all the pantheons he trusts me. Maciej slides off his stool and backs toward the door, keeping a wary eye on Flidais. And as he moves away and the goddess of the hunt puts down her glass unsteadily and it topples over, her motor skills deteriorating rapidly, some douchelord moves up on her left and offers to buy her another drink. He even puts a hand on her shoulder. Every word he says is in Polish, but that doesn't matter. His tone is condescending. He's clearly a predator. And because I love poetry and alliteration and all the ways in which words can sound delightful when strung together, I had unthinkingly given Flidais the worst possible advice.

"Blood," she says, and she promptly spills his by smashing her fist into his nose, a sharp left-handed backhand like she was signaling a right-hand turn on a bicycle. It's casual so she doesn't kill him, but he's knocked out and bleeding on the floor and there are plenty of witnesses. It's pretty clear I'm going to be fired and quite possibly sued for serving so much alcohol to a customer so quickly.

Flidais frowns at the man sprawled on the floor. "That was disappointing," she says. "I was hoping for a spirited fracas."

"If you'll forgive me, I think we should have discussed your goals a bit earlier. I was hoping not to have a fracas at all. I'm going to have to change the sign in the back to DAYS WITHOUT A FRACAS: 0."

Flidais hears me but does not care, because the man's friends have lurched from wherever they'd been watching to hurl some choice Polish epithets at her. She can't understand them—I'm not sure I understand half of them myself—but she can read their aggressive postures well enough. She smiles, sets herself, and beckons them forward. There are three of them, none especially in shape, and I think at least one of them is aware of it. But two charge forward, unable to resist a good goad, and my pleading shouts to stop go ignored. Flidais purposely stops them with a flurry of quick jabs to the face, and when they raise their hands, she sternly rebukes their groins with a powerful fist to the junk. They wilt like cabbage in boiling water and collapse on top of their unconscious friend. The third one prudently decides to preserve his procreative package and backpedals into the bar crowd, which is now aghast and staring.

"Flidais? Flidais. Let's talk in the back, okay? Come on."

Nope. Too late. The bouncer has come over to bounce Flidais, and she drops him even harder since he's fairly skilled and able to get at least a single punch through her drunken defenses.

"Okay, really now, let's talk. We need to go before the police get here."

"The modern police? The ones with guns?"

"Yes. Your shenanigans will bring them for sure."

"Very well. I'm finished drinking anyway."

She half-staggers around as I raise the bar flip-top and let her pass through into the back. Maciej is at the door, staring wide-eyed through the glass pane set in the middle of it, and he mouths a thank-you to me for saving him. I give him a salute and follow Flidais into the kitchen area. I guide her to the back, where the employee lockers are and a sign hanging on the walls says in Polish: DAYS SINCE A WORKPLACE ACCIDENT. It has the number 173 underneath it, but I pointedly change it to 0.

"Half a year since the last fracas, Flidais, and you ruined it."

"I dishagree." Flidais sways as she hooks a thumb over her shoulder. "Man ruined it."

"Your speech is deteriorating. Will you please heal yourself of alcohol poisoning? We're going to need clear heads to get out of this."

Flidais delivers a spluttery sigh, like an impatient horse. "Fff-fine."

Piotr Skrobiszewski, the manager of the pub, storms into the kitchen at that point, shouting in Polish. "Where is she? Where the hell is she?"

"Pardon me," I tell Flidais. I dart around her, find the manager, and sweep his legs. He knows English, so I pounce on top of him, pin his arms, and shout in his face, "Hi! I quit! I'm leaving in two minutes. The woman who knocked out three men in the bar will kill anyone, including you, without a second thought. I'm trying to get her out of here before anyone actually dies. So just let us go and you'll all see the sunrise, okay?" I slap his face companionably a couple of times. "Thanks for letting me work here a while, Piotr. You're a good guy."

I launch myself off my stunned former employer and wave at the slack-jawed line cook as I return to the goddess of the hunt.

"Feeling better yet?" I ask her as I move to my locker and spin the combination on my padlock.

"Yes. A moment," she replies, her eyes closed.

The tumblers click, I yank open the door, unbind my staff from the back of the locker, and pluck it out. "Let's go, please. We really can't stay."

Thank the gods of all the pantheons, she follows me out the back door into a dank alleyway. We hear sirens approaching and I lead Flidais to Pole Mokotowskie, the large park in the center of Warsaw where we can find plenty of privacy and a bound tree if necessary. She laughs when we hit the turf of it, feeling safe again with the earth underneath her feet.

"That was not a fair fight," she admits, "but I do feel better somehow."

"I hope you have an excellent reason for coming into my bar and getting me fired."

"Fired? You quit. I heard you."

"I had to quit because of what you did."

"Oh. Why were you working there anyway?"

"For many reasons. To learn Polish. To make money. To lure vampires in so that I may unbind them."

"Vampires?"

"That's what I said, yes. They made a treaty with us and were supposed to be out of Poland by now. But they have refused to leave because of one Kacper Glowa."

"He is also a vampire?"

"Yes."

"You should hunt him down and unbind him."

"I agree. I would love to do that. I'm not very good at the hunting bit, though, which is why I was working in the pub, hoping he or one of his associates would show up. One of them had appeared there before."

"I will hunt him for you. Where was he last seen?"

"I've never seen him, but I can take you to one of his nests. May I ask what brought you to my bar tonight? Something about a message from Brighid?"

Flidias waves that away. "Later. Let's hunt a vampire."

"He may be many miles away."

"I could use a good hunt."

There's a bound black poplar tree in the park that we use to shift to a wooded hill above Krakow, and I feel a grin spread across my face as the two of us jog to one of Kacper Glowa's safe houses. There were four of them scattered around a block, each one with a concealed stairway leading to an impressive subterranean complex. There is nothing dull about being a Druid. The study period is long and intense, but the payoff is tremendous: Earlier I was pouring beers, and now I'm hunting vampires with a goddess.

We break into the abandoned house, step past the bloodstains to the staircase, and descend into the dark. At the bottom I find a light switch on the wall and flick it on, gratified to see the electricity still works.

"There were twelve of them down here?" Flidais asks.

"Yes. Thralls too, and room for more. Glowa owns all this but wasn't here himself when we raided it."

"All right. We need to pick up his trace somehow. Let us see what can be found."

I follow her through the complex, moving from room to room, some of them riddled with bullet holes or smeared with blood on the walls. Flidais grunts periodically but says nothing as she inspects it all. Finally she unslings her bow and removes her quiver, placing them carefully on the ground.

"Normally I have my own hounds to help me with this," she says, pulling off her vest, "but in this case I will have to do the thing itself."

She strips to the skin and shifts her shape into her predator form, the tattoo for which looks similar to Atticus's but turns out to be a breed of hound that doesn't properly exist anymore. Hounds have changed quite a bit since Flidais was first bound to Gaia; she's not far away from a red wolf, and if I had to settle on a species, that's what I'd call her since her coat is somewhat tawny.

The huntress takes another circuit of the compound, her nose down and snuffling as she goes. She has to sneeze several times. I imagine the dusty skin cells of the undead have to be irritating to the nose. I certainly do not want to shift to a jaguar to find out.

She spends an inordinately long time in one particular room, which serves as a library. Dark cherrywood bookcases line the walls, some of them now splattered with blood. Rich leather upholstered armchairs squat next to varnished tables. They used to have vintage Tiffany lamps on them, but these are now shattered on the floor, colorful shards of the past. I do appreciate the smell of the room with my unenhanced human senses: pipe tobacco and old paper.

I check some of the titles they have on the shelves, and it's not long before my jaw drops. They have first editions of Poland's finest. I hesitate to touch the four-volume *Chłopi* by Władysław Reymont, who won the Nobel Prize in 1924, but not for too long: I can't resist. And once I flip to the title page of volume one and see that it's signed, my head swims with the treasure and I'm overcome with the temptation to steal it. An old Jane's Addiction tune starts playing in my head.

"Do you think anyone would notice if I took this?" I ask, turning to Flidais. She looks up briefly, nods her wolf head slowly and deliberately, then trots out of the room, keeping eye contact with me. She expects me to follow, so I do after returning the book to its shelf, all the way to the spot where she left her clothes. She shifts back to human, puts a finger to her lips, and shakes her head to make doubly sure I know not to speak. I nod my understanding and plant myself in the hallway as she dresses, watching our trail from the library. There would be no reason to be quiet if someone were not here. No one comes, however, and I hear nothing.

Flidais collects her bow and quiver and gestures that we should return upstairs. She wants me to go first, however; she nocks an arrow in her bow and backs slowly up the stairs, watching our six. That gives me a shiver.

We emerge from the stairs and I say, "What—" but Flidais draws her hand across her throat to cut me off.

"Not yet," she whispers. I follow her outside and she takes us all the way down the block before she halts, kneels, and speaks in very low tones in Old Irish.

"How well did you search that compound?"

"We thought we were thorough. I'm sure Leif was too."

"So you searched the rooms behind the library?"

"What rooms?"

"There are passages behind the bookcases. Tremendous traffic through there, and scents of vampires that did not match the scents of the slain ones. The smells are recent too."

"Are you saying there are vampires in there right now? And they could hear us mucking around?"

"That is indeed what I'm saying. Especially if they have some modern surveillance devices installed, which I suspect may be the case. If we go back we may find they have emerged. Or else they will hear us approach and hide again."

"So there must be some kind of Scooby-Doo lever that opens up a secret passage."

"What is Scooby-Doo?"

"A long-running television show that demonstrated to everyone what a terrible idea it was to wear an ascot. The protagonists solved mysteries in old houses that frequently had secret passages behind bookcases, always activated by moving a particular book or a small knickknack or even a torch in a wall sconce. There has to be a way through."

"We can unbind the cellulose of the wood if nothing else."

"So we're doing this? We're going to go down there and slay the undead?"

"Is that not why we traveled here?"

"Okay. I'm up for it. But before we go, I'd really like to hear that message from Brighid."

"Oh, yes! I nearly forgot. Ragnarok is coming soon."

"What? How could you forget something like that?"

The goddess shrugs. "Because I am not to be involved in the primary fracas. Siodhachan and Eoghan will be engaged in the main battle, along with many others. But we have heard of a building disturbance on the other side of the planet, on an island named Taiwan. Are you familiar with it?"

"Yes."

"Apparently it is to be the origin of the second major front. So you and I are tasked with containing whatever emerges at the site of the smaller, secondary, and inevitably lesser fracas. This is to ensure I won't run into Perun, you see."

"That may indeed be the reason behind what they're doing, but it doesn't sound like light duty. It could be one heck of a major fracas. Just you and me against who knows what?"

"Well, somebody *does* know what, or at least is supposed to have a fair idea. We're going to go see him first. I've been given directions and passwords and a rare fruit from Manannan Mac Lir's Isle of Apples."

"Who is it we're seeing?"

"Some man named Sun Wukong."

"Holy shit. Flidais, you're not joking with me right now, are you?"

"I do not jest. That is whom we are supposed to see. Why, do you know him?"

"Only by reputation. Sun Wukong is the name of the Monkey King."

i returned to the sandstone buttes of the Navajo Nation, baked red and gold in the sun, and found a place to wait high above the arroyos cut by flash floods. I built a spare, smoky fire out of creosote branches, folded my legs underneath me, and communed with the elemental Colorado.

I waited most of the day, skin cooking slowly among the rocks, and wondered if I wasn't wasting my time. I'd already made a couple of other calls before coming, but it wasn't like I had no other preparations to make. I couldn't afford to wait past nightfall, and I had to heal from sunburn several times.

He arrived late in the afternoon, the hottest part of the day, dust-caked jeans and boots scuffing the rock, a simple black T-shirt tucked in and a cowboy hat resting on top of long black hair.

"Hello, Mr. Druid," Coyote said, trying to peer around my body, looking for something. "Where's your hound? I brought sausages." He held up a greasy bag and I winced in regret.

"Oh, he's going to be upset that he missed seeing you. He's in Oregon."

"Well, damn. I mostly came to see him."

"Thanks a lot."

"Don't act like it's news. He's always been your better half."

"I won't argue with you."

"Well, damn it all again. That's the only other reason I came. Guess I have no business being here."

"Coyote, please," I said as he turned away. "May I beg a few minutes? It could lead to a fine argument. You might even win."

He halted, pivoted with a grinding noise underneath his boot heels, and considered me with pursed lips. After a long silence of holding my eyes in a staring contest, he finally replied, "You know how to push my buttons, don't you, Mr. Druid? You know I can't resist arguing with a white man."

"You'd probably enjoy Twitter, then. But I wouldn't push if it weren't important."

Coyote tossed the bag down and settled himself across the fire from me, peering through curling vines of smoke. "All right, then. Bring it."

"I need your help."

"No." He snorted and flashed a grin. "That was quick."

"It's not just me, Coyote."

"Honestly, Mr. Druid, I don't care who you're representing here. Why should I help you instead of helping my own people?"

"Because there's a narcissist with a bunch of cronies who wants to burn down the whole world—your piece of it included—for no other reason than to stoke his own ego and profit besides."

"So, kinda like an American president, then."

I gaped for a second as I tried to make the connection, then closed my mouth. "Yeah, kinda like that."

"Well, I seen men like that before, Mr. Druid. I've survived them, and my people survived them too, and I'm pretty sure we'll outlast this new one. And before you say anything," he said, pointing a finger at me through the smoke, "let me remind you that you never lifted a dainty finger o' yours to help us fight off all o' them presidents. And not just us, but all the tribes. And, hey, I'll be a sweaty sack o' nuts if you ever helped with all them settlers and soldiers who did their best to wipe us out, never mind the presidents. Don't try to tell me you're in the same boat as us either. Ain't no way we coulda helped the Druids out against the coming of the Christians. But you coulda helped us and you chose not to."

"That's not true. I couldn't help. I was hiding from Aenghus Óg and had to limit my magic usage."

"Well, I understand that, Mr. Druid, I surely do. So I hope you'll understand when I say we gotta limit our dying for white man's causes."

"But you don't die."

"Oh, I die, all right. I thought I made that clear before. The fact that I keep coming back doesn't mean I don't die. My people die too. But still we endure. Getting involved in this thing you're talkin' about doesn't sound like the best way to keep doing that. I figure the best thing to do, since y'all have mostly forgotten about us, is let you fight it out and we'll enjoy the peace afterward."

I deflated for a moment, defeated.

"Okay. Fair enough. I don't think you'll be left alone or that there will be a lot of peace afterward if we don't stop him, but I do see that you've done more than your fair share of fighting dudes who think the world is theirs to take. That's legit."

"Oh, well, thank you so much for validating my feelings, Mr. Druid. I was really hoping you would. Gonna sleep real well tonight. Normally I have to pop melatonin pills down my throat like candy, you know, because some white man hasn't told me I'm right recently."

"Sorry. That obviously didn't come across as I intended. I'm trying to agree with you. But this guy can probably take the world if anyone can. I'm talking about Loki of the Norse pantheon. He's going to bring a legion of the undead, a good number of fire and frost giants, and who knows what other allies with him. You might be safe here for a while on this side of the world, but if he's not stopped on the other side, by the time he gets here there will be no stopping him." I shook my head at the scale of what was about to be unleashed. If Loki wasn't stopped before he could build momentum, it would be because I failed to stop him. It would be because I had been stopped. "This is going to start day after tomorrow, probably, somewhere in Scandinavia. If you want to help, that's where to show up."

"What kinda help do you think I can give, Mr. Druid? I ain't some mighty warrior who's gonna come in there and rally the troops to charge or whatever."

"I know. You're not gonna pucker up and blow the horn of Helm Hammerhand. I want you to do something that you're uniquely qualified to do. I want you to assassinate Hel."

"What? Are you talkin' 'bout that half-dead woman who showed up to recruit you here that one time and because of her Frank Chischilly summoned Monster Slayer?"

"That's the one. She's the Norse goddess of the underworld, the daughter of Loki. And she can raise the dead. So once they start killing some folks, she can add them into their army, and you can see how that's going to quickly grow out of control. Removing Hel's the key to keeping the fight manageable, if just barely."

"If she can raise the dead, then can't she raise herself if I kill her?"

"Well, no. Because she has to be alive to do that, and in this hypothetical, thanks to you, she'd be dead." She would still be ruler of the underworld and she would have an existence there, but, like the Morrigan, she would be a shadow of her former self. She wouldn't be able to manifest on Midgard again in time to make any difference in Ragnarok.

"Huh. Is she going to be stomping around all twelve feet tall and stanky like raw chicken gone bad?"

"She might be, but she might be in disguise too. You can see through those, right?"

Coyote smirked. "Yeah, I know a thing or two about disguises, Mr. Druid."

"Well, I hope you'll consider it. Because she has been here before and she won't forget about you if they make it to this side of the world."

The trickster sniffed, hawked something up, and spat in the fire. "Sure. I'll consider it."

"Good."

"I imagine you have other places to be, other folks to see."

"I do."

"Fires to put out and whatnot. Don't worry about this one here. I'll take care of it."

I got to my feet, slapped the red dust off my ass, and nodded to Coyote. "Thanks. See you around."

"Maybe, Mr. Druid. But probably not. Tell your dog I said hi, though."

CHAPTER 5

a fen is not really a synonym for a bog, though it is rather wet and something of a mire. Its chemistry is different, though, so ye get a different set of plants growing there. Mostly grasses and the occasional scraggly tree, thin and fragile things. Ye might think it's a handsome plain, until ye step in it and the mud hugs your foot like a hungry python.

The Morrigan's Fen looks fine, just fine, until Coriander and I step away from the bound tree and see we have to cross it to get to the structure where Fand and Manannan Mac Lir must be hiding. I don't rightly know what to call it: It's not a castle or a manor or even a house, more of a gothic nightmare of architecture, like if the Morrigan had found a mason wandering in an opium haze and said, "Make it all foreboding and ominous, maybe a splash of drooling madness and a dollop of gibbering batshit." Dark and writhing shapes in some bits, pointy parts in others, and sometimes the black shines with a high gloss, and sometimes it lies flat like old standing coffee ready to grow a layer of mold on top. The low gray sky doesn't help to cheer it up any. Nor do the croaking crows.

It's just me that has to wade through the fen, it turns out. Coriander floats above it, and he does so just a wee smidge ahead of me so that I can see how easy it is for him. I mutter curses at him and he smirks, enjoying it.

Halfway across, me legs all slimed and squidgy, I see some upright lads with wild hair approaching in the distance. A bit closer and I see they're not lads. They have swords and dead eyes. Bark instead of skin. A mobile set of roots instead of feet, poling them across the fen like so many stilts. Yewmen.

I put on the brass knuckles Creidhne gave me, fully charged with energy. They let me shatter stone; should work just fine on a hardwood. That is, if I can get close enough to punch them without being sliced into cutlets. The Morrigan's yewmen aren't fooled by camouflage, and I'm not going to be terribly speedy in a fen.

"Go sic 'em, Fuckstick," I says to the Herald Extraordinary.

"I can do no more than accost them, sir. I am incapable of instigating violence."

"Give yourself some credit, lad. Just go talk to them and I bet they try to kill ye."

The Herald Extraordinary rolls his eyes at me and sighs like a phantom squeezing out a vengeful fart, but he floats toward the yewmen without fear. Once he reaches them and starts talking, they treat him like an obstacle in the landscape—that is, they don't engage, they just go around him. Coriander floats back, plants himself in front of one or the other, but they know the score. Just patiently flank him and keep advancing to the target. Me.

"That's not working, damn it!" I holler at him. "Get back here, Fuckstick. I have a better idea!"

He speeds back to me, frowning in disapproval, and the yewmen keep coming at their measured pace. "I really must protest your abusive language, sir—"

"I know, I'm a right bastard. But like I said, save me arse and I'll take the trouble to use four syllables. I want ye to float right in front of me, hear? Just a bit to me left, though, because it looks like they're right-handed. We're going to let ye take their hits and I'll counterpunch. Speed up with me now, we're flanking to their left, make them adjust . . . aye."

I move to the right and the yewmen have to respond. There's no way I can allow them to surround me; I won't have a defense against blades coming from all directions. If I move and strike and move again, I should be able to survive and outrun them once I'm past. I'd simply shift to a kite and fly over them were it not that three in the back have bows, waiting for just that. I'll have to make sure the herald covers me arse if I make it past the phalanx here.

For about six seconds I think maybe I'll outrun them. And then they find another gear somewhere, or just have no trouble in the muck like I do, and they take a good angle. They're going to have a shot at me.

The leader whips one of his long arm-like branches out in front of me low to the ground, and it's a fine gambit: Trip me up in this muck and I'm probably not going to get up again. But I see it coming and hang back just a wee bit, letting Coriander float into it first, and those kinetic wards of his do the trick. The branch rebounds off them and spins the yewman away. But reducing me speed like that has its cost.

The second yewman thrusts his branch around the back of Coriander, and I duck just in time. It opens a searing lash of pain across me shoulder blades and I curse the faery for being an incompetent shield.

"Do ye know how angry Brighid's gonna be if ye let me die?" I say, trying to keep up my speed.

"It is difficult to quantify, sir. Mildly vexed at the short-term inconvenience, for sure. But life is long, and her anger, like her fires, tends to die out after a while."

That response chills me guts five degrees or so. He really could let the yewmen have me and shrug it off. It's not like the yewmen don't have a reputation for being damn fine murderers; he'd have no trouble suggesting that they were more than a match for the two of us.

As he's talking, though, two of the yewmen make incidental contact with Coriander while trying to get to me, and they are both blown back like a hurricane uprooted them.

The one that sliced up me back is going to try again, but I'm watching the bastard and waiting. Let Coriander deal with the lads out front trying to trip me; I can handle this one who's hoping to pull off a deadly reach-around.

That thick branching arm of his with sharp stick fingers whips out again and I lurch to a halt, letting it pass in front of me. A claw scrapes across me chest and a flight of arrows from the archers passes in front of where I was going to be, two of them flying through and one rebounding off Coriander. I grab the yewman's woody wrist with me right hand and then punch straight through the bough with the knuckles on me left, splinters gouging me arm. Yewmen are silent, but I can tell he feels it. He stops the chase and I pick up speed again, taking his hand with me. One more yewman is denied in his attempt to trip me and he's spun out of the pursuit, leaving one that we haven't passed yet plus the archers, and I'm careful to put Coriander between us now.

This lad wants to take a swipe at me with his sword. His right arm visibly lengthens as he matches speeds with us, his arm trailing behind, his plan plain to see.

"Watch that shite," I say. "He's going to whip that around back."

"I am aware, sir," the herald replies, his manner calm and unruffled as he floats above the fen and I churn me legs through it.

It's a crafty strategy the yewman's chosen. To counter it, Coriander will have to stop, and that will do two things: allow the lads we've passed to catch up a bit, and leave me exposed to a volley from the archers if I don't stop in time. I peek around at the archers and see they're all ready and waiting for me to break cover again. Fecking hells.

This yewman's arm isn't tough and woody like the other one; it's limber and flexible and meant to bend instead of snap, so even when it runs into Coriander's wards, that arm and sword are going to keep whipping around my way.

Bollocks.

The branch yaws back and around, building all the tension it can with the sword clutched at the end, and then it releases and Coriander halts to meet it. I'm immediately exposed and the archers let fly. Nothing for it: I dive headfirst into the fen, stretching out and ready for the sting of foul water in me wounds. The arrows pass over me head and so does the curl of the sword, but all me momentum's gone and I'm covered in muck and I may have squashed an unlucky frog.

The yewman's arm whips away and I can see the archers reloading. A glance over me shoulder confirms the others are trying to make up that lost ground.

"Come on, Coriander, while me arse is still attached," I says, giving him the four syllables he wanted. I lurch up out of the sucking mud and stagger forward, trying to build up speed again. Coriander screens me from the next volley of arrows and then we're past, moving too quickly for the yewmen to catch up. Not that they stop trying. We just have to keep going and hope we don't run into some booby trap ahead.

A mist rolls in from the Morrigan's gothic horror show of a house, and I can tell by the way it behaves it's not natural, nor is it a mere binding: It's Manannan's Cloak of Mists, which means I'm about to be lost in the fog shortly before being pounded into stew meat. I shout into it as it envelops me.

"I'm here to talk, damn it, not fight! I'm here with a herald! Put your cloak away, Manannan, and let's spill some whiskey instead of blood!"

The mist halts, then retreats like it's being sucked down a drain, and when it's gone, there's a long-bearded man standing there in a white tunic, his blue eyes cold.

Manannan looks tired. Aged too; there's some gray in his beard, methinks, which wasn't there before. I think those magic youth-restoring hogs of his are still back in Tír na nÓg. Or perhaps his disposition isn't suited to being a rebel. Or perhaps it's my imagination and it's the dreary atmosphere of the fen that makes him look so weary and chewed up.

"Can we talk, Manannan? I've come with this Coriander lad, who's supposed to be well known, and I bring an offer from the First among the Fae."

A single eyebrow quirks up at that news. "An offer? Or terms of surrender?"

"Definitely an offer. No surrender involved, for you or Fand."

Manannan's eyes shift behind me shoulder and he raises a hand to halt the yewmen. "Stop. My last order is rescinded."

I turn and see the yewmen there, approaching from behind. They halt a safe distance away, and Manannan dismisses them.

"Our selection of whiskeys may not be so rare as the last time we dined," he tells me, "but you're welcome at our table, Eoghan Ó Cinnéide, and you as well, Coriander. We'll hear this offer."

"That's very kind of ye, Manannan." We draw close and I see that it's not me imagination: The face of the god of the sea looks like someone crumpled it up and then tried to stretch it flat again, lines of stress all over it. He made a hard choice when Fand rebelled, and had he chosen Brighid's side over his wife's, I don't think he'd look any different. He'd be miserable regardless, and I think I can empathize. Or is it sympathize? I fecking hate English. But whatever the proper word is, I see a smidgen of his problem. I am caught between Greta and Siodhachan and hope I never have to choose between the two. Luckily they are merely estranged and not actively trying to destroy each other.

Which reminds me: I owe the herald some kindness, and I pay him while we walk. "Coriander, lad, that was some fine saving of me arse ye did back there. Thank ye for keeping me alive to this point. I know I can be an angry hollering tit and—well, I just wanted ye to know I'm not that way all the fecking time."

The herald raises one corner of his mouth. "Indeed? And for

how much time, sir, shall I expect you to be . . . so mild and genteel?"

"Honestly, this half a minute might be it. Savor it while ye can. Greta—that's me girlfriend—says I might need years of therapy."

"She sounds like a wise and caring companion, if I may say so."

"That she is, and ye may." Manannan has nothing to add. He keeps his head down and gives no indication he wishes to speak or be spoken to. We slog in silence most of the way to the Morrigan's nightmarish warren or nest or whatever she used to call it. I speak up before we walk in, though, once the ground firms up and dries out a wee bit.

"Forgive me for askin', Manannan, but are ye well? I've seen ye lookin' better."

He stops, considers, then looks up when he has an answer. "I am well physically. But I have essentially been confined to this plane for a while now and I miss the ocean. I miss the sense of harmony I once felt. Both were more important to my happiness than I realized."

"Fair enough. I hope me offer will allow ye to find that harmony again."

"Let us hope together. Please, enter and be welcome."

In Fae circles, that's about as clear a guarantee of safety as one can expect. I step past the threshold and behold a room covered in bones. Not the floor, but all four walls plus the ceiling. It's a whole lot of dead people's remains, shellacked and burnished and fitted together, set off by the occasional skull grinning gumless at ye from the other side of the veil.

"Well," I says, "it's a bold look, an' that's no lie. Definitely a statement. Maybe not a statement of actual welcome, but it's a statement."

"Do excuse the décor," Manannan says. "The Morrigan had unusual tastes, and we have not had time to remodel."

He leads me through the next room, which contains a clear, narrow pool fed by three gurgling waterfalls. There's a chorus of eerie voices singing in a minor key, and it's the opposite of relaxing. I'm about to ask what fresh shite is this when Manannan offers an explanation.

"The Morrigan would use this pool to cleanse blood from her body after she returned from her exertions. We don't know where the singing is coming from, and our efforts to make it stop have thus far been unsuccessful."

"Ah. Very practical of her," I says. "That's thinking ahead, that is. Now that I see it, I can't understand why more homes don't have a room like this."

Coriander snorts softly and Manannan grunts, enjoying the dry commentary. "Refreshing bloodbaths, haunted by the voices of people you've slain. Blood rooms instead of mud rooms. Yes. They will soon be in the suburban homes of mortals everywhere."

"I could probably use a bath, to be honest. I'm a mess, wearing half the fen on me front."

Manannan waves at the pool. "By all means. I will have clothing brought to you here."

I strip and wade in and it's a cool pool, but not cold. It would be refreshing if not for the haunted cries wailing about the room. I do me best to wash off the wounds I've collected and use the energy in me knuckles to heal. Apart from that, I don't linger, because it's a mite creepy, and some Fae bring me a towel and some fresh clothes straightaway.

The next room is a long one, rather like the dimensions of a mead hall, full of helmets mounted on the wall, organized from oldest to newest. It would be a grand history of armor, I suppose, fit for any museum, except that the helmets still have skulls inside them.

"Trophies," Manannan says. "Men who dared to give her insult over the centuries."

The helmets give way to hats as the wars in Europe subsided, though I do spy an actual motorcycle helmet at the end and some ball caps, plus a couple of fedoras.

After that is the first genuinely pleasant room I've seen. There are two red upholstered chairs in front of a stone hearth, a wool rug spread out to buffer the feet from the cold floor, and gilt-framed paintings on the bone-free walls, illuminated by candles resting in sconces. Sure, the paintings are all of battlefields and feature crows feasting on the staring eyes of the slain, but they're masterfully done.

Our reception by the rebellious Queen of the Faeries waits beyond, in a dining hall that's fair-sized but by no means large, since the Morrigan never expected to play hostess for more than a few.

Fand, in contrast to Manannan, is fecking resplendent. She's wreathed in frippery and fancy doodads and whatnots and she radiates health and power. Maybe she's doing yoga or had a superfood for breakfast. Greta says science cranks out miraculous solutions to aging every week, so many that ye could spend your whole extended life trying them all out. But kale is worse than old man balls, she says, though I don't rightly know what kale is, or why she hates it so much, or even when old man balls became a superfood. That whole conversation confused me and I let it slide past, like much of the nonsense this modern age throws me way. Maybe Fand has been eating kale or something else to make her look so fine. More likely she's simply glamoured, but if I peek in the magical spectrum she'll know and be insulted. Better to just accept her magnificence at face value.

"Welcome, Coriander," she says, her voice warm and sweet like honey in summer. But when she turns to me, her voice is furry with hoarfrost. "Hello, Jailor."

Ah. She hasn't forgotten that bit, then. I give her a shallow nod—less than her due—and force a friendly smile. "Fand. I appreciate ye seeing me."

She offers no reply to this but waves at the spare table, set with a couple of cheese boards and some bottles of whiskey and wine. The room lacks anything fancy: Simple wood chairs, sunlight streaming through high windows providing some weak light instead of candles, no tapestries or sculptures or seashell motifs like I saw in their place in Tír na nÓg. Stone walls and floors, no rugs. It's a different aesthetic from Manannan's estate, for sure. Minimalist, methinks it's called. Or miserable. I think the words may be related. Only Fand and Coriander stand out in this gloom.

We sit and Manannan pours me some whiskey that's been aged in stout beer barrels. It's a fine medley of flavors and I feel it mellowing me bones almost immediately. Manannan pours a glass for himself and says, "Sláinte," but Fand reaches for wine, and Coriander follows her lead. I wonder if there's anything to that—is it merely his preference, or is there some message there? Is he being diplomatic, or is he trying to signal to Fand that his sympathies lie with her? Me skills with nuances are often limited to being just aware enough of their existence to know that I'm probably missing them.

Bloody nuances.

Fand asks Coriander how the Fae are faring in Tír na nÓg and asks him to convey her fond regard. He agrees, and an awkward silence falls until Manannan asks about me grove of apprentices.

"Ah, they're grand. Fast learners and pure hearts. They'll serve Gaia well." I remembered suddenly that I did have one icebreaker at me disposal that hadn't failed yet. "Speaking of apprentices, did I ever tell ye the totally true story about Siodhachan, the Roman skirt, and the goat?"

Fand frowns at the mention of his name, but a minute later she's snorting into her wineglass and peals of laughter bounce off the walls. Manannan throws his head back to roar out loud with such force that he topples over in his chair and crashes to the floor. Coriander's face turns the color of a tomato as he laughs hoarsely and tries to catch his breath. That story has done me more good winning people to me side than any bottle ever has, though the spirits no doubt help to loosen them up. They are all in a much better mood, then, when I give them Brighid's offer.

"Ireland's at risk due to this Ragnarok business. Word is it's coming in a few days."

Fand nods. I'm not surprising her with anything.

"I'm not the sort to be fancy with me words, so I'll say it plain: Brighid wants your help and then she'd like to welcome ye home. Fight in Ragnarok. Save some lives to make up for the ones ye took. Restore balance, gain honor and renown the way the Tuatha Dé Danann are used to, on the field of battle, and be welcome in Tír na nÓg again."

"Under her rule? The Iron Throne?"

"Aye."

"Absolutely not."

I catch a flash of disappointment on Manannan's face. He'd like to take the deal, no doubt. So it's Fand that needs convincing.

"Allow me to ask for clarification on one thing: Do ye object more to Brighid's rule or that she's doing it from the Iron Throne?"

"The throne, of course!" she spits, and the surprise on me face must have encouraged her to explain in more even tones. "It's that iron in the face of the Fae every day that makes her insufferable. It's both a threat and an insult. We *know* she's mastered iron and we're unlikely to forget it; there's no need to terrorize the Fae with it at Court every second."

I swing around to Coriander, Brighid's Herald Extraordinary, to see if he agrees with this assessment. He winces and sucks at his teeth and I have no idea if he's agreeing or what.

"Be plain, lad, don't just scrunch up yer face at me like some swollen, pouty anus!"

He flinches and then says, "Were we in private, I would agree with Fand's assessment."

"I'm not going to tell. I just need to know the truth of things, since I've obviously been away, so thank ye." I turn back to Fand. "I had no idea what Brighid sat on was such a thorny issue. Have ye communicated this to her before?"

"We have, on many occasions. She refuses to even consider scrapping it."

"And when was the last time?"

Fand defers to Coriander to answer that.

"I believe it was as recently as the 1960s, by human reckoning, when the Fae became upset at the existence of a mortal band called Iron Butterfly and renewed their plea to rid the Court of the scourge of iron."

"The Fae got upset over a band name? Never mind, of course they did—a better question is why ye think sixty years or more qualifies as recent? Plenty has changed since then. Especially right now. Ye may have some leverage ye didn't have before. So let me pose a hypothetical, Fand: If I can get Brighid to agree to ditch the Iron Throne, will ye fight in Ragnarok, then go home again to live in peace? She'd still be First among the Fae, mind, but you'd also have won something for them, wouldn't ye? And all would be forgiven. Manannan would have his ocean again." I gesture at the forlorn god of the sea, and Fand glances his way, seeing how desperately unhappy he is. I press on: "Ye wouldn't be stuck in this fen surrounded by bones and cold stone walls. Sounds like the closest thing to harmony you're going to get."

"Hmm. What say you, husband?" Fand asks.

"I say it's a way back," he replies. "And I think both the price and the reward are fair."

Fand leans forward, selects a cube of Irish cheddar, and pops it gracefully into her mouth. She chews as she thinks it over, demonstrating that it is in fact possible to eat cheese beautifully. I'm thinking that the Beautiful Cheese Eaters is a far better band name than Iron Butterfly when Fand gives me an answer.

"I am not so sure about the price. She gets rid of some furniture and in return gets an army. Still, it is, as you say, Manannan, a way back. Very well, Eoghan. Speaking only for myself and the Fae host: If—and only if—Brighid agrees to remove the Iron Throne from Court, we will fight in Ragnarok for Ireland and then return to Tír na nÓg, our rebellion forgiven, our possessions returned, and agree that Brighid is First among the Fae, to live in harmony again."

"Very good. Manannan?" I ask.

"Aye," he says. "I too agree to this."

"Coriander, do ye witness this?"

"I do."

"Well, then. If ye will excuse me, I have some more talking to do. I hope to have an answer for ye soon."

I have plenty of hopes, in fact, as I leave that fen. So many that I think maybe this qualifies as an example of the Second Law of Owen: Sometimes, ye can clean up the shite.

CHAPTER 6

i am so pumped full of adrenaline by the time we make it back
to Kacper Glowa's house that my hands are shaking as we
enter. I had shifted to Flagstaff briefly to pick up the special stakes
that Creidhne had given us to use in Rome, where merely breaking
the skin anywhere would unbind the vampire in question. We had
given them all to Owen for safekeeping and to help the werewolves
defend against any vampires that might show up at the site of the
grove. Owen and his grove weren't there, so it was simple enough
to sneak in, take a pair of stakes, and sneak out again. Now I have
one in my left hand as I descend into the vampire bunker, and Flidais has another; I carry my staff, Scáthmhaide, in my right hand,
and Flidais carries her bow. We each turn invisible by prior arrangement as we enter the bunker proper and pause to listen. Nothing.

We creep down to the library in silence and find it just as we left
it. I'm tasked with finding the Scooby-Doo lever on the bookcase,
and it takes me only moments because it's painfully obvious: Pull
on the Polish translation of Bram Stoker's *Dracula*, and a click and
scrape moves the bookcase aside. We're confronted with a hallway

paneled in hardwoods and a floor covered in a plush burgundy carpet. Neither of us moves; we wait.

"Hello?" A voice calls after a few moments, and then repeats it with a note of impatience. "Hello!"

We remain in place. Opening the door was our move; the next one was theirs.

A clear sigh of frustration meets our ears and then some mumbled curses as the unseen guard or receptionist comes to investigate. It's a mustached man who carries himself like a fighter, but he's not prepared for an invisible ambush. Flidais plunges a stake into his throat and he gurgles once before falling to his knees, clutching at the stake as blood wells around its circumference. He remains solid as he dies; a human thrall, then, and not a vampire. I figured there would be one or more guarding the place, and it's difficult for me to summon any sympathy for them since they would not be thralls if they did not wish to prey on other humans.

We wait a few moments more and then Flidais hisses quietly at me to follow. I can't see her, but once I'm in the hallway I see a desk with monitors behind it to the left. It's the thrall's security station. I go that way and run into Flidais by accident.

"I'm rubbish at this," she murmurs to me in Old Irish. "How do we proceed?"

I duck around the desk and look at the banks of monitors and keyboards and so on. Everything's labeled in Polish.

"A moment," I say, trying to decipher what I'm looking at. There are views of multiple rooms, each filled with many men and women lounging in chairs and talking over tables, but there is no way to tell which are vampires, which are thralls, and which are intended to be food.

One room is stacked floor to ceiling with coffins on shelves—strange vampire bunk beds, I suppose, but obviously in a more secure location than the few coffins we found in the rest of the facility. There are two buttons with biometric pads underneath them: one marked LIBRARY, and one marked SANCTUM.

"We're going to need the body over here," I tell Flidais, and soon I can see the guard being hauled by an unseen force back to the station.

There are several buttons and switches under the general heading of ALARM, but I don't know what they do. I'm afraid if I push any of them I'll sound the alarm rather than disable it.

There's nothing else around the station—no exits of any kind—so the door to the sanctum must lie at the opposite end of the hall.

"What do you want with him?" Flidais whispers.

"Lug him around here," I say. She does so and I grab his right hand, extending the thumb toward the data pad marked SANCTUM.

I point down the hall with my free hand. "There should be a door down there somewhere. I'm going to open it from here and follow you in."

"Understood," Flidais says. "Wait for my signal."

After a few moments I hear a hiss from down the hall. I punch the SANCTUM button then press the guard's finger onto the data pad and am rewarded with a soft chime of mechanical satisfaction. There's significant movement on one of the monitors, and I look up to see a black-and-white movie of vampires exploding as Flidais moves among them, alternately using her stake and her own unbindings to take them apart. I let the guard's body go, collect my weapons, and vault over the station, heading for the SANCTUM door. It's just sliding closed as I arrive and I squeak through, hoping there's a way to open it from the inside.

The room is painted in violent splashes of red and littered with viscera. Much of it begins to bubble and smoke, decomposing rapidly in the absence of the magic that kept the vampire functioning as a biological entity. Flidais has already moved on to the next room, pressing her advantage of surprise, so I hurry to catch up.

There's no scream quite like a vampire scream, unhinged from human restraints and allowed to be the thing it is—a sound of distilled rage, poured into the air and swirled in the ears like a fine vintage of malevolence. Of distinct benefit to me, however, is an overwhelming urge to kill the source upon hearing it.

So many screams. The vampires could hear us and smell us as we came into the room, but they couldn't see us, and by the time they'd gotten some idea of our whereabouts we had already staked them or unbound them with our words.

I do keep count and try to stake them in nonfatal places in case they're humans. That happens twice, where I sink my stake into the joint of their shoulder and chest and watch them cry out but remain whole. I kick them aside and tell them to stay out of the way.

Flidais has no such scruples. She kills indiscriminately, and we tear through the rooms together, leaving a red wake until we get to the last door, and it's a locked, armored one. It must be the true sanctum, the room with all the coffins, protected like no other. There's a bio-data pad on the side. I doubt the thrall's thumbprint would open it. I dimly hear the metal ratchet of guns loading rounds into the chamber. There's a different kind of fight on the other side of that door.

It's just as well that we're forced to slow down. We have them trapped anyway, so we can take time to ponder and take stock of what's been done.

I count forty-five dead vampires, about seven human thralls or meals that Flidais killed, and the two other humans I wounded. I wish I'd been able to save more of them or ask Flidais to have a care; I didn't think there would be so many. I see to the living, letting go of my invisibility and binding their pant legs together so they can't move, before healing them as best I can, stopping the bleeding at least and binding the flesh back together.

One of them, a blond pale woman with ice in her eyes, is unsociable and taciturn and says nothing. The other, an athletic man with dark hair and cool brown skin, breathes heavily and looks at me with undisguised fear.

"You just . . . just destroyed them!" he says in Polish. "What are you?"

"I'm a Druid. Sorry about stabbing you. I was only here for the vampires. Hold still, I'm trying to help. I'm going to close that up."

"But, like, I didn't see you until now."

"Nope, you sure didn't. So are you a thrall or what?" He has bite marks on his neck, but that doesn't signify his status.

"No, I'm just a bloodbag to them. They've been snacking on me for weeks, keeping me here with that hypnosis thing they do, whatever it is—"

"They call it charming."

"Yeah, that. Thought I'd never get out of here. Did you say you were a Druid?"

"Yep."

"I thought they just had sex rituals and burned people up in wicker men."

I blink a couple of times. "I guess we've diversified a bit," I say, after a pause.

"Oh, shit. Sorry. I don't know what I'm saying. Shock and all that. I mean, thank you for saving me. I should have said that first and then not said anything else."

"You're welcome. What's your name?"

"Andrzej Kasprowicz."

"Nice to meet you, Andrzej. Can you tell me anything about that last room back there?"

"That's where they sleep."

"How do they get in?"

"Oh, the scary one uses his thumbprint on the little pad thingie on the side."

"Describe the scary one for me," I say, thinking of an idea.

"He's short and pale and ugly, but he dresses better than anyone else. Expensive shoes. Actually wears a waistcoat and keeps a gold pocket watch in there."

"And none of the other vampires dress this way?"

"No—well, wait, his girlfriend does. Or wife or whatever she is. And some of the rest are hip but not like him. I think all his clothes are custom jobs. Bespoke, you know."

"So you've been here for how long?"

"I honestly don't know." His mouth dropped open in horror and he shook his head in an attempt to clear it. "Time kind of muddles together when you never see the sun."

"Fine. But in all that time, did you ever see any of the vampires pick their nose?"

"What? No. Why?"

"I'm just curious if vampires have boogers."

"I . . . I don't think so?"

"I bet they do, but they go to extraordinary measures to hide it."

"Is this . . . real? Am I dreaming right now? This conversation doesn't seem right."

"Yeah, it's the shock. Nobody would ever be interested in that, right? You just relax and recuperate and forget all about vampire boogers and we'll get you out of here safely, don't worry." I pat his arm a couple of times for comfort and rejoin Flidais, running my plan by her. She agrees that it should work and starts tearing up the carpet in the anteroom. I leave and wind my way through the bloodstained mausoleum we swept through to get back to the entrance. The sanctum door doesn't require a thumbprint to exit but rather operates on a simple push button. I walk around back to the security station and check the feed coming from that final, armored chamber. There are eight figures inside, all well dressed, but one of them has a telltale chain on a waistcoat leading to a pocket watch. That's the one Andrzej described.

I flick the intercom switch and speak into the microphone. "Kacper? I have a message for you, sir." The short, well-dressed man snarls and glares at the speaker mounted by the door.

"Who is this?"

"You wrote me a note. A rather unkind one. Sent your boy Bartosz down to my pub to get himself unbound."

"The Druid bitch."

"Ah, there's the unkindness I was talking about. I've been perfectly reasonable and generous with you. Gave you a month to leave Poland and live in peace, and you not only refused to take the offer, you taunted and threatened me. Said none of your vampires would leave Poland. Well, they all have now, excepting the ones cowering in that room with you right now. I just unbound the lot of them, and you're trapped. You're next, in fact."

"Come and get me, then!" he shouts. "Come in here and see what happens!"

"Oh, I will, Kacper. You've seen your last moonrise. Just wanted you to know, before I unbind you, that neither hell nor earth has fury like a Druid scorned. Because I am quite literally a force of nature, you know. You have precisely zero chance of survival. So make what peace you can with whatever gods you worshipped when you were alive, or just scream at the door. I don't care. Your end, and the end of all the vampires in your company, has come tonight."

I leave the intercom on and hear some inchoate screaming along with some choice curses as I employ the guard's thumbprint to open the SANCTUM door again. I leave the security station and jog back through the warren to the anteroom, waving at Andrzej as I pass. Flidais had, in my absence, torn through the carpet and unbound the cement foundation to get to raw, native earth.

"How goes it?"

"She will be here momentarily."

"Does she have a name?"

"I have never given her one. She seems content without it."

"Oh." I wonder what it would be like to have so little sense of self that one doesn't care for a name. Perhaps she has one and simply hasn't shared it with Flidais. But I will not interfere. Though it's my idea, it's Flidais's contact.

A few minutes of silence pass and then a dark, roiling mass comes bubbling out of the hole in which Flidais stands. It's a colony of dark furry whiskers made of iron. It undulates immediately for the armored door and, once it reaches it, slithers up the side, creates an eye slot in the middle of the door where there wasn't one before, and pours through into the room. We can clearly hear exclamations of surprise and dismay and some angry shouted questions.

"What is that thing?"

"Kill it!"

"Where do I shoot? Gaah!"

Shots are fired and there's more panic, but it doesn't matter; it's an iron elemental that Flidais has summoned, and she sent it into that room with the mission of eating up all the firearms and turning them into small, inert components of carbon and copper and anything that isn't iron. And while the vampires are busy dealing with the elemental—or utterly failing to deal with it—Flidais and I place our eyes to the slot and establish line of sight. We confirm that these are all vampires by checking out their auras and seeing the gray surrounding them with dull red pinpoints over the heart and head. And then we unbind them, mercilessly, preying upon these predators that had feasted on the people of Krakow for hundreds of years. Kacper Glowa's rebellion against the signatories of the Treaty of Rome ends in a messy splash of fluids, a ruined waistcoat, and a satiated iron elemental. I take some pictures of the gory aftermath to send to Leif Helgarson. He'll spread around what happens to vampires who violate the treaty and hopefully that will deter others from thinking they can ignore it.

Flidais remains behind to thank the elemental and dismiss it while I fetch the taciturn blonde, who I think might be a thrall. I show her the carnage in the sanctum, prove that Kacper's really gone, and she finally shows some emotion. She weeps.

"What am I supposed to do now?" she says through a sob.

"Be content with being human. Or become a thrall in some

other country, because all the vampires in Poland are now wiped out."

I lead her and Andrzej out to ground level and let them go. "Go see a doctor and don't come back here," I tell them. Then I give Leif a call.

"Yes?" His stiff, cultured voice always amuses me.

"Guess where our man was hiding? Underneath his house! The business is done. I'm going to send you some pictures to spread around, but you should come here to take his records and whatnot."

"I should. I will be there shortly," he says. "Thank you, Granuaile."

I can't leave fast enough; I don't need to wait for him. I just head back down once more to liberate the signed copy of *Chłopi* and tell Flidais I'll meet her in Taiwan the next day, after I go home to clean up and get some sleep. Then I head up the hill, shift out of Krakow, and arrive home to six more hounds than I was ready for.

It's the mental chatter between the hounds that tells me what's happened. *Orlaith! You had your puppies!* I say through our mental link.

<I did! You're home now! I wished you were here.>

Oh, me too! I'm so sorry I missed it!

<It was legendary. Earnest said most wolfhounds only have two or three puppies, but I have six! Did you know that's five plus one?>

Six perfect puppies! Oh, my goodness! May I come say hello? I promise not to touch them until you say it's okay.

<Yes, we are in a corner of the living room. Oberon and Starbuck are keeping watch.>

Everybody's helping—that's great!

When I enter the cabin, there is much attention to be paid to the men. Oberon and Starbuck, and Earnest as well, are very excited to tell me what I already know, and they are all as proud of announcing it as if they'd somehow managed to give birth themselves.

But once I assure them all that they did a fantastic job, I'm allowed to visit Orlaith and see her puppies all nestled against her belly, nursing.

"Oh, my goodness, they're so adorable!" I tell her. "How on earth did you ever manage six?"

<I was well fortified. Earnest did not neglect to feed us. But I've already started to worry what will happen to them all.>

I switch to our private line. *What? Why are you worried? There's no need. They'll all be taken care of.*

<But not with you and Atticus, right? Because you don't need that many hounds. So where will they go?>

I'd been giving some thought to this during her pregnancy, because six extra hounds *was* quite a bit more than we could handle.

Well, how would you feel about them being the hounds of other Druids?

<What other Druids?>

Owen has six apprentices. They're all young humans, so your puppies could grow up with them.

<Oh, yeah! I forgot!>

Maybe they would appreciate having hounds. I will make sure to ask. In any case, we have a few months before we need to make any decisions. You just do your thing and let me know if there is anything I can get for you, okay? Do you need anything?

<I'm fine right now. I just ate and drank before lying down here, and then you came home.>

Okay.

<Maybe you could stay here and tell me what you did today, though, because I'm pretty sure I smell blood. And give my ears a scratch or two?>

I would like nothing better.

Orlaith's pups are three and three, just like their parents: Three gray-coated boys, and three cream-coated girls. Or wheaten, I suppose, is the proper term. They make tiny puppy noises every so often as they're nursing, and it makes my heart all gooey.

You know what? I'm going to go grab myself a pillow and a blanket so I can sleep next to you. I do need to leave in the morning, but while I'm here I just want to snuggle.

<Sounds good to me!>

It's difficult to leave Orlaith and the pups in the morning, but I must. Oberon understands and sympathizes, because Atticus had to leave him behind too.

<Sometimes you just have to do your duty,> he says. <It's like we have a duty to chase after squirrels. You may not understand why, and we may not understand why you do the things you have to do, but we do understand duty.>

Thank you, Oberon. I give them all a hug, wave farewell to Earnest and the pups, and head for the bound tree behind the cabin, near the bank of the McKenzie River.

The bound tree in Taiwan turns out to be a Formosan gum tree, native to the island. It's a bit elderly, indicating that no Druids or Fae have shifted here in quite some time, and I think it might be wise to bind a younger tree soon. Flidais is waiting there for me and says as much, noticing my regard.

"We should bind a stronger tree."

We do just that, finding a younger specimen in the same area, which Flidais tells me is Yangmingshan National Park, near Taipei. My stomach audibly groans at the end of the binding, a long, hollow cry of dolor like that of a woebegone cetacean adrift in an empty sea. Flidais comments as if I had spoken a recognizable language.

"I hunger too. I know where to get really good beef noodles within a short jog out of the park, and then we can take an invention called the metro into the densely packed city, thereby avoiding a run of many miles. Have you heard of this invention? It transports many people at a time in these metal boxes that move on rails."

I stifle a smile. "Yes, I have. Please lead the way. But tell me, how do you know this place so well?"

"Mandarin is one of my headspaces," she says. "And Taipei is one of my favorite cities to visit."

We travel west from the bound tree out of Yangmingshan, past hot springs and Beitou Park, onto Daye Road, where we enter an establishment called Wu's Beef Noodles. I've never had them before and quickly discover that I've been missing out. It's similar to phở in that you have noodles in a beef broth along with thinly shaved slices of beef, but the similarities end there. They aren't rice noodles, for one thing, and the broth is different, as are the sauces arrayed on the side. Deeply satisfying and fortifying. I make a note to bring Orlaith here for a short break from the puppies.

The bill arrives and I experience a brief moment of panic: I have nothing resembling legal tender on me. But Flidais came prepared. She throws down Taiwanese bills and we exit, belching softly.

She leads me to the Beitou Station after that, and we ride the metro south to the Zhongshan Station in the middle of the city, and I gawk out the window like the tourist I suppose I am while I can; the Red Line is an elevated ride for half the distance before it goes underground and functions as a subway.

Like most big cities, Taipei offers the sublime alongside some truly worrisome signs for the planet's future. The soaring tower of Taipei 101 is a marvel of modern architecture, and everyone I meet is unfailingly polite and gracious. And while it doesn't have the apocalyptic pollution of China, where people often need to wear masks if they go outside, the air still punches the lungs with every breath, delivering a fistful of engine exhaust to the alveoli along with other assorted toxins. That's due, no doubt, to the bewildering number of scooters on the road, which vastly outnumber cars and are not renowned for their efficient engines. People in the West think Rome has a lot of scooters—and it does—but it pales in comparison to the number in Taipei. They are everywhere, clogging the roads and parked on sidewalks.

And foot massages appear to be popular here. Not that I can read Mandarin, but I certainly can see neon footprint signs all over the place and make an inference. These aren't relaxing massages, I'm guessing, or the kind of foot massages that Jules and Vincent Vega thought would cause Marsellus Wallace to defenestrate Tony Rocky Horror in *Pulp Fiction*, but rather intense sessions where pressure points on the foot are plied to improve all manner of health issues, redirecting chi.

I see so many places I want to visit and explore on the way: The Grand Hotel on my left, perched on a hilltop, looking like a beautiful red and gold palace. The Taipei Expo, an old football stadium that's now a park and gardens. There are some boutique clothing shops and some open-air markets down certain streets hawking everything from fresh fruit to lightning chargers, but I also see large malls full of clothing stores displaying brands from America, Britain, and Australia. Huge posters of Hollywood movies drape over buildings with Mandarin characters on them, and I love it. I think I want to learn Mandarin next after I'm finished learning Polish. Perhaps a nice collection of poets from one of the dynasties would provide a decent headspace.

We exit the train at Zhongshan Station, an underground stop, and I grin at the people teeming around me. There's a big bookstore down there and I want to browse, even though I can't read the language yet. "I see why you like it here," I tell Flidais. "Where next?"

"Time to see Sun Wukong."

"Is he far away, meditating at the top of a mountain or something?"

"No, he runs a bubble tea shop in Twatutia."

"I beg your pardon?"

"It's the oldest part of Taipei, in the Datong District."

"No, I mean, the bubble tea thing. What is a Buddha like the Monkey King doing there?"

Flidais shrugs. "I assume he must truly enjoy it," she says, climbing the stairs out of the station. "Immortals do things like this sometimes. Back in the late eighteenth century, I secretly ran a pub in Dublin with Goibhniu for nine months, until a mortal tasked with policing our treaty pointed out that the Tuatha Dé Danann were supposed to remain in Tír na nÓg. It was an amusing occupation while it lasted. I would guess the Monkey King seeks to keep himself busy by bringing a bit of enlightenment to the mortals. Eternity is a long time to spend doing nothing, after all."

We start to jog down Nanjing West Road, taking deep stinging breaths every few steps, but quickly discover that too many beef noodles are sloshing around in our stomachs, so we slow to a walk and enjoy the bustle of the city. I am nearly run over by a scooter at one point and am so glad I wasn't. Easy to laugh about it now, but that would have been a stupid way to die.

Twatutia, once we get there, is a marvelous meld of old and new, the architecture of different eras on display on every street, the juxtaposition of the ultramodern with nineteenth-century buildings, structures from the Japanese occupation, and post–World War II growth. The Monkey King's bubble tea shop is in an older building, accessed via an alley off Dihua Street, and we find it because there's a line snaking out to the main thoroughfare. We join the line and wait patiently as it inches forward.

The temperature noticeably drops once we get into the shaded valley between buildings. They're old stone, half blackened by carbon and soot, and the alley smells like alleys everywhere, redolent of rot and unpleasant emissions.

"So is he actually making the bubble tea?"

"No, his employees do that. He runs the register and welcomes people."

"Are his employees . . . human?"

Flidais favors me with a grin. "I suggest you inspect them in the magical spectrum. Just to make sure there aren't any shenanigans. Careful looking at the Monkey King that way, though. It can be intense."

Forewarned and intensely curious, I take in everything I can once I enter the shop—which appears to be little more than a widened hallway or corridor. It's a clean, well-lit place with absolutely no seating, and it's a one-way operation. Customers enter one door and exit at another down the hall, because there's no room to turn around. It's a single-file line in front of the register and counter, with a menu of bubble tea flavors and a small selection of cookies and pastries. It must have been a storage or shipping area at one time for some other business in the building, now plumbed and operating as a tiny to-go shop—a very popular one.

The man at the register is just slightly off somehow. Cheerful and smiling, he takes orders and exchanges money, his dark whiskers growing down his jaw to the sides of his mouth but his chin and upper lip shaved clean. According to Flidais, I'm looking at Sun Wukong, the Monkey King in disguise. He almost palpably exudes peace and contentment, and I wonder if people are coming here for that feeling as much as for the bubble tea.

He wasn't always so serene, if any of his early adventures in *Journey to the West* have a shred of truth about them, and I'm sure they do. He was contentious and grasping and a consummate narcissist in his early years, causing all manner of trouble on earth and in the heavens, but gradually came to serve the Buddha, until he became one himself.

He greets us with a beatific smile when we get to the register and says something in Mandarin—a request for our order, I'm assuming. Flidais responds and holds up her right forearm in front of her, showing him the back of her hand, where the healing triskele is. I do the same, and his smile fades. He asks something else, Flidais answers, and he punches the register before extending his hand. Flidais drops some money into it along with the apple from Manannan's Isle, Emhain Ablach, that she mentioned before, and he gives us a tight nod. We move along down the line, seeming to have accomplished nothing but a bubble tea purchase.

"What happened?" I ask the huntress.

"I ordered some Immortal Peach tea. That was the code, along with our tattoos, and the apple was a gift."

"Immortal—oh, because of that time he ate almost all of them." That had been quite the episode in *Journey to the West*, one of the last straws that brought the full force of the heavens down on Sun Wukong.

"Precisely. He'll meet us after we get our tea here at the end."

"We're getting Immortal Peach bubble tea?"

"No, just regular milk tea. He's going to get one of his employees to take over and then we'll be able to speak in private."

A stream of words from the register causes all the employees to look up, and one of them moves in that direction. They are dressed in brown uniforms with golden monkey heads embroidered on the left breast. Carefully keeping my eyes pointed away from Sun Wukong, I switch my vision to the magical spectrum to check them out.

They are, in fact, monkeys passing as humans. They're sitting on the prep counter instead of actually standing, as it appears to human eyes. Peripherally, I sense a blinding light to my right, where the Monkey King stands.

"Do they talk?" I whisper to Flidais, but one of the employees hears me and snorts.

"Of course we talk," he says in English. "More than one language too."

"Of course," I reply. "Sorry."

"The time to be sorry is not now," the monkey tells me. "But that time will come for you soon enough."

"Pardon me?"

"Come on," Flidais says, tugging me away from the smirking monkey. A flash of light warns me that Sun Wukong is entering my vision, and I dismiss the binding, returning the veil so that I see merely humans serving up bubble tea and pastries. I blink away the spots dancing in my eyes and collect my bubble tea at the end of the counter, where Sun Wukong awaits. He gestures to the exit and we take it into the alley. He follows us out and then points to a fire escape ladder ahead.

"Let's talk on the roof," he says in perfect English, and then he scrambles up it so quickly that Flidais and I are left agape at his speed. Flidais shrugs and discards her tea into a nearby bin, but I hold on to mine as I awkwardly make the climb up to the roof, tea in one hand and Scáthmhaide in the other, grasping the rungs by mere fingertips. This bubble tea was made for me by a talking monkey, and I feel like I should at least try it.

When I get to the roof, Sun Wukong has discarded his human disguise and stands resplendent, glowing, and serene, tricked out in red and gold finery.

"Welcome to Taiwan, honored Druids," he says. "I am Sun Wukong, and I am very grateful for your aid and your timely arrival. There is no easy task before us. This Norse god Loki has been busy stirring up much trouble. We have reason to believe most of the Yama Kings of Diyu will rise with the very worst souls of the damned to plague us."

"How many is *most*?" Flidais asks.

"Eight of the ten. King Yanluo and King Zhuanlun have refused—it is because of them we know this is coming."

"They can't convince the other eight to forgo this?"

"Their arguments have proven ineffective so far."

"When are these eight Yama Kings going to rise, and where?" I ask.

A thunderous boom shakes the sky as it darkens to the northeast of our position. We whirl around and see what looks, from a distance, like a black swarm of insects fountaining up into the firmament.

"Now, and over there," Sun Wukong replies. "They have chosen to erupt from Seven Star Mountain in Yangmingshan National Park."

That's near where we shifted in to the island. "Guess I'm not going to be enjoying my bubble tea."

"Nonsense," the Monkey King says, producing the apple Flidais gave him and taking a hearty bite. "Enjoy; take your time." He plucks a tuft of hair from his chest and tosses it into the air, which somehow forms a full-sized copy of himself, and more copies keep appearing—hundreds in mere seconds. As they materialize, the clones surge to the north to meet the swarm building over Seven Star Mountain. "That'll keep them busy for a while."

CHAPTER 7

there is so much fashion happening at the Fae Court I begin
to wonder if me own aversion to such frippery is a character
flaw. If so, I suppose I can just add it to the infinite list o' them.

I should rather go ahead and admit that fashion intimidates me.
It's like people are speaking a language all around and I'm missing
every word. I'm conscious that something is going on, at least, but
I don't know what it is. That faery has a flared collar and it probably means something. That other one has pointy tips on the end of
her shoes and that probably means something too. Sparkly buttons, lace sleeves, codpieces, jewelry, and studded belts, all of them
packed to bursting with meaning, like that one item of carry-on
luggage ye take with ye to avoid baggage fees.

Brighid is wearing something like fancy working leathers when
I arrive, and I'm sure that's fraught with meaning as well, especially
when contrasted with all the finery on display by the courtiers. It's
definitely not something a common lad would wear, because the
leathers are tooled and studded beyond belief, but for all its ex-
pense, it remains a practical outfit, unlike what most rulers tend to
wear. She's sitting on the Iron Throne and immediately dismisses

whomever she's talking to when she spies Coriander floating off to one side of me. We're summoned forth and she demands a report. I'm not one for throwing around sugary words, so I get right to it:

"Fand will accept your offer if ye first agree to destroy the Iron Throne."

Brighid takes this news mighty cool, raising a single red eyebrow. The assembled courtiers aren't cool about it at all. They set to whispering and tittering and gabbling about what it might mean or what Brighid will do and I want to shout at them all to shut it, but I grit me teeth and try to ride out the wave of me blood pressure rising to high tide in silence.

"Thank ye, Eoghan," Brighid says. "Coriander."

"Yes, Brighid?" the Herald Extraordinary replies.

"Report in summary the results of your meeting, including Fand's words regarding the agreement, so that all may hear."

Coriander bows, turns halfway to the assembled Fae Court without turning his back on Brighid, and announces the terms of the offer and Fand's conditional acceptance. When he's done, the excitement among the Fae is quite nearly raucous, because it's all news to them, and there're some spirited wagers being laid over how Brighid will respond. Brighid hears some of that, gives a tiny smirk, and lets it proceed for a full minute. Then she stands from the Iron Throne and projects her voice in three registers at once, which she only does on rare occasions. She cannot lie in that voice, and whatever she says during such times becomes the law.

"Hear me," she says, and the Court quiets immediately. "I hereby accept and ratify the terms of the agreement on two conditions: First, that once the Iron Throne is destroyed, the Fae will undertake to build me a new throne, reflective of their finest skill, which they will have no trouble honoring henceforward; and second, that once we have prevailed in Ragnarok, Fand and all Fae will immediately pledge their fealty to me anew as First among the Fae, here, regardless of whether the new throne is completed or not, and together we will enjoy a new age of harmony. Fand shall accept my conditions by showing up on the field of battle against the forces of Loki and Hel. However!" she says, holding up a hand to forestall applause. "I need not wait on Fand's acceptance to behave with honor and goodwill. To demonstrate both, I shall destroy the Iron Throne now. Let us celebrate that together."

The fecking Fae damn near destroy me ears after that. It's one hell of a roar of approval, and I clap me hands to the sides of me head for protection. Brighid smiles and summons a huge two-handed hammer from somewhere.

"Behold!" she cries out, and she swings it down right on the seat with a mighty clang, visibly denting the throne, and the roar swells anew. She swings again and again, and I turn to behold the Fae Court in all its joy, because the noise has turned odd somehow.

I quickly see why. It's such a momentous occasion for the Fae that they've decided there's nothing they'd rather do than have sex to remember it by. They're flinging off their fancy clothes and banging away at each other as Brighid bangs away at the Iron Throne. An entire generation of Fae babies are going to be told that they were conceived during the destruction of the Iron Throne. And, yes, they'll be thanking Fand for it. But they'll be loyal to Brighid too.

Those working leathers make sense now, and I realize Brighid had been ready for this. Yes, she's made a concession she'd never made before, but her obvious preparation signals that she was waiting for it, that she wanted it, and so it's really no concession at all.

It's about three seconds until I start to feel intensely uncomfortable. What am I supposed to be doing, then? Stand there and watch the Fae feck themselves sideways or watch Brighid work while I do nothing? I elect to silently get the hell out, because the last thing I want to do is interrupt anyone at that point. I assume that Coriander will communicate Brighid's words and deeds, and my part in all this is done. I shift back to the tree Brighid bound in Tasmania, hoping to catch Greta and the apprentices, but the elemental informs me that they all elected to fly back to the United States in me absence.

They'll be in the air for most of a day, and I feel a bit lost without them. I suppose I could simply catch up on me sleep, but instead I ask the elemental to contact Siodhachan and let him know I'd like to talk. Soon enough I'm answered: Me old apprentice wants me to shift out to his place in Oregon, and he'll meet me there. When I point out I haven't actually visited it yet, he says he'll meet me at the Fae Court and then lead me to the proper bound tree, which makes me chuckle. I can't wait to see his face when he sees what's going on there right now.

It's priceless. Just a gaping maw of horror as he takes in the whole field of writhing bodies, some of them flying and fornicating in midair.

"What do ye think they'll call this, later on?" I asks him. "The Great Iron Orgy? The Demolition Sex Festival? The Carnal Cornucopia?"

"Let's just go," he says, and he shows me which tether is his. I follow him and arrive in a blessedly quiet place, save for the soft gurgle of a river, under a canopy of evergreens. It's nighttime, wherever we are.

"Welcome," he tells me, and in the dim illumination from his back porch light I see his eyebrows shoot up. "Oh!"

"What is it?"

"Apparently Orlaith has had puppies. And we missed seeing Granuaile."

"How do ye—" And before I get me question out, that hound of Siodhachan's bursts from the house along with a smaller dog, and I realize they must have told him as much. I know we're not going to get much talking done until they settle down, so I remind myself to be patient and follow along into the house, where we must go to admire the new litter of hounds. They're cute and healthy looking, that's for certain, and after Siodhachan speaks with them and distributes scratches all around, he turns to me.

"Orlaith has a question she'd like to ask you," he says. "Go ahead and bind with her."

I reach out in the magical spectrum and tie my consciousness to hers.

Hello?

<Hello, Archdruid!>

Ye can call me Owen. Hello, Orlaith.

<Hello! I have a question, and you can think about it before answering. I was just wondering, since I have six puppies and you have six apprentices, if you think your apprentices would like wolfhound companions like all the best Druids have?>

All the best Druids, eh?

<Well, all the modern ones, you know. Irish wolfhounds are the perfect companion for any Druid and encourage the development of extra headspaces.>

I'm not sure how safe they'd be. I mean, we're living with werewolves, after all. Me apprentices all have werewolves for parents.

<But Druids can train wolfhounds so easily and explain the dangers clearly! I am sure the puppies would be safe with your apprentices.>

Well, let me think on it, will ye? It's not a decision I can make on me own. There are others to consider.

<I understand! Thank you, Owen! But I think you should consider getting a wolfhound companion also. It would suit you.>

Are ye sure? I turn into a great big bear pretty often.

<Oh, I know! But Oberon and I have learned to appreciate some bears now. There's you, of course, and we recently met one named Suluk Black, and she was very nice, told us what great hounds we are.>

"Is that so?" I turn to Siodhachan. "Who's this bear she's talking about named Suluk Black?"

"Oh, that's the daughter of Kodiak Black. It's a bit of a story, if you want to hear it."

"Sure. I have some time to kill."

"I don't have a lot, but I can tell you while I whip us up something to eat."

There's a British man in the living room named Earnest Goggins-Smythe, who's been looking after the hounds for them as a sort of live-in dogsitter, and after introductions, he just nods at me once before returning to work on his computer. He has a couple of dogs in there with him, a poodle and some other breed I don't know yet. They're lying down underneath his chair, and they watch me pass by but don't move. Siodhachan fixes up some burgers and bacon while telling me about Suluk Black and this squirrel on a train to Portland that got the hounds all excited and involved in solving murders. We're having a beer afterward and cooling our toes in the river behind his cabin when he gets around to discussing what comes next.

"Look, it's about time. It's eleven p.m. here and Ireland's eight hours ahead of us. I'm off to fight Jörmungandr. Part of a deal I made with the Norse to try to atone for my actions."

"Right, I remember ye telling me something about that. But what about Granuaile?"

"She's off fighting different battles in Taiwan. Probably in the thick of it already."

"Well, bollocks," I says. "What do ye think I should be doing, then? I didn't sign up for this battle, but I figure I may as well sign up now before I'm drawn into it anyways."

"You can ask the elementals where they need help. I'm sure something will flare up somewhere and require a Druid's attention. Stay out of Scandinavia and Taiwan and look after everything else."

"Ah, you and your girlfriend and the entire Fae host get all the glory, then, while I go get ye some coffee?"

Siodhachan frowns. "I don't know what you mean. You're not going to be doing anything less important. Wherever Gaia asks for your aid, it will be needed, you can be sure. You know the elementals do not make idle requests of us, because you taught me that. But be prepared for fire."

"Why's that?"

"It was part of the last prophecy the sirens spoke to Odysseus, which appears to finally be coming true here. It didn't mention the wrath of the World Serpent or the terrible attack of a Norse god, but it did specifically say the world will burn. I don't know how that's going to come about, or how badly, but the world is an awfully big place and almost all the Druids will be in Scandinavia, if you count the Tuatha Dé Danann, with the others in the Far East. You'll have an awful lot of ground to cover."

"Huh. I guess I will. I mean, I've looked at these globes and maps and such, and Ireland is such a wee place compared to the rest of it. I've traveled to some far distant lands but don't think I've seen much at all compared to you. How do I know what's worth pursuing? I mean, if the whole world will be on fire, what's the priority?"

Siodhachan shrugs. "I wouldn't presume to say, but if I were in your shoes, I'd ask the elementals where gods or monsters are mucking about and go stick my nose in."

I grunt at him. "Sounds like as good a plan as any." An owl hoots in the night, spooky as five hells and a jar of creamy peanut butter—that shite's unnatural. The owl seems like a pretty dire warning, but that's all right. At least it's not the Battle Crow. Still, methinks if there was ever a time for a careful word, it's now.

"Ye take measures, now, to keep your arse free of bite marks, ye hear? We still have all those devils to cure in Tasmania, and don't be thinkin' I'd rather have the whole job to meself."

"Wouldn't dream of it," he says. "I fully plan to cure more Tasmanian devils than you and all your apprentices combined."

"Ah, is that a wager you're proposin', then?"

"Aye, if the terms interest me."

"If I win, then I want to go with ye to a televised baseball game."

"Oh, that sounds great."

"Shut your gob, I'm not finished. While we're there, during the bottom of the seventh inning, I want ye to streak naked on the field for a full fifteen minutes, using the earth's power to make sure the cops never catch ye."

"Isn't that a frivolous use of power?"

"It's for the benefit of humanity."

"They'll tase me eventually."

"What's that? I don't know that word."

"They'll use electrical weapons to shock me into unconsciousness."

"Will they now?" I chuckle at the thought. "I would find that a satisfactory alternative to a full fifteen minutes."

"I'm sure you would. All right, I'll agree to those stakes if you agree to mine."

"What's that?"

"If I win, you will solemnly swear never to tell that unfortunate story about me and that goat again, and if someone you've already told ever brings it up, you'll disavow it."

"Shite, lad, I don't know if I want to give that up. People fall over laughing every time I tell it. You're getting serious."

"Well, you suggested fifteen minutes of serious public nudity and possible tasing and prison, so, yes, it's that serious."

"Ha! Well, then."

He extends his hand for me to shake. "Wager taken?"

I grip his hand and shake it. "Aye, lad. Tasmania wins either way."

"Indeed she does." He surprises me then and pulls me into a hug. "Thank you for taking me on as an apprentice all those years ago. I've seen both horrors and wonders, but I can't deny I've had a full life."

"Nonsense, lad. Thank ye for making me proud and keeping Druidry alive all this time."

He pounds me on the back a few times and I do the same, and

then we part. It's going to be hours before things start, so I remain at the riverside while he says farewell to his hounds. It's a bit slobbery and mushy and I hear some of it by accident, until I break the binding to give them some privacy. But I did hear Oberon wanting to go with Siodhachan and me apprentice being firm that the hound must stay behind for this caper. Which says to me that his expectations must be bleaker than a frog's hope for humidity in the desert, as I'm pretty sure he's taken that hound into some dangerous situations before.

It makes me wonder if he hasn't maneuvered me to the sidelines here, to make sure that I won't be leaving Greta and the apprentices alone. Methinks it would be like the daffy bastard to do something like that, out of guilt over the deaths of Gunnar and Hal, however much he was or wasn't responsible. He's probably thinking he's the one who's cocked everything up and it's his responsibility, so I shouldn't help or even want to. But of course I want to help—the fecking planet's on the line. I wonder if he knows that for all me bluster and shite, I'm really on his side and always have been.

I wonder, in fact, if I'll ever see him again, and if I shouldn't say something suitably sentimental so that we're both bawling and leaking a decaliter of snot on each other's shoulders. But then I think he probably doesn't need that right now. He needs me confidence in him and bollocks the size of basketballs, metaphorically speaking. And on top o' that, I can't properly think of what to say when he comes back outside and waves to me before shifting off to wherever he's going.

I do hope to catch that baseball game with him someday soon.

CHAPTER 8

i t has been so very long since I've been able to enjoy Ireland. A few brief, fraught visits aside—always under the threat of discovery by the Fae—the place of my birth has been essentially off limits to me ever since I fled with Fragarach almost two thousand years ago. With Aenghus Óg gone it's not so bad, but I've never felt welcome. I wonder if I ever will again. Perhaps, should I survive to see the other side of this mess I've created, there will be a path to a garden of sorts, and if I tend it, forgiveness will grow there.

Right. And perhaps Owen will stop telling that story about me and the goat out of kindness. There's no way I can heal more devils by myself than he and all his apprentices working together, so it looks like I have some public embarrassment in my future, if I have much of one left.

But I do want to spend more time in Ireland. I've missed the Emerald Isle; it's not the same as every other island in the North Atlantic. It has its own smells and sounds and natural rhythms that sing to me of home, even when I'm not precisely in the area where I grew up.

Thanks to Mekera's tyromancy, I came to the southern coast

south of Skibbereen, where there's an old fort on a hill overlooking a pasture of sheep. It was with a good measure of relief that I saw no shepherd tending the flock, and the few farmhouses in the area were set back a good distance from the coast. With luck, there would be no witnesses.

My brilliant plan to deal with Jörmungandr arrived in a rental car some minutes later and unfolded herself from the driver's seat, beaming at me. Her presence was the result of another call I'd made before heading out to see Coyote.

She looked resplendent in a red and yellow sari and a familiar gold necklace set with a stunning ruby in the center.

"Hello, Atticus."

"Laksha. Thank you for coming."

"I was grateful for the invitation."

"I hope you're well? Or that your host is well? Or both? Sorry, I'm a bit rubbish at figuring out how to fit your situation into established patterns of polite discourse."

She moved in close and gave me a brief hug, feeling especially warm, I supposed. She nodded in answer to my question. "Mhathini is doing very well. So well, in fact, that I think she's ready to resume her life with her full faculties. We've been working hard."

"That's excellent news!" I said, genuinely pleased. Mhathini had suffered brain damage as a result of a car wreck and Laksha had taken up residence in her head some months ago, pledging herself to repairing the damage in return for hitching a ride in Mhathini's skull. Granuaile didn't think her domestic situation back in India was the best, but I had little doubt Laksha had been working on that as well.

"You will promise to take care of her afterward?" Laksha asked.

"Of course. I'll see to whatever she needs."

"Good. So this is where it will happen?"

"Yep." I pointed out to the shore, visible from where we stood. A light breeze blew our hair around our faces. "Right off the coast there."

"What will it look like?"

"I'm not sure, really. All known portraits of the World Serpent are fabrications by the artists who produced them. I figure it's the kind of thing where you'll know it when you see it."

Laksha snorted, her mouth turning up at one end. "A fair prediction." She squinted out at the sea. "This is a strange place to start the end of the world, isn't it? It's so peaceful and quiet. And there's really nothing here."

"It's the perfect place to start, in Loki's mind. Ireland has few defenses, and Jörmungandr needs to grow quickly. By which I mean he needs to feed. Ireland's sheep and cattle and, yes, its people will be a fortifying snack on Jörmungandr's way to becoming truly monstrous and unstoppable. And it has the benefit of crippling the Tuatha Dé Danann at the outset by robbing them of the majority of their believers."

"Where are the Tuatha Dé Danann right now?"

"In Sweden, where Loki wants them to be. That's the main event, where everyone's supposed to be looking. This was supposed to be his stealthy strike. And I'm being stealthy in return. He can't divine me, so he doesn't know I'm here."

A flicker of worry tensed the muscles around Laksha's eyes and mouth. "And he doesn't know about me either, right?"

"No, he wouldn't know to worry about you."

Her face relaxed. "I have been a quiet if deadly witch, haven't I?"

"You have."

She sighed happily. "And now I can be quiet and deadly one last time. But on behalf of everyone else instead of myself. There is a balance to the idea. I hope there will be a balance in karma as well. How many people will I be saving in Ireland alone?"

I shrugged. "Somewhere between four and a half and five million."

"Ah! Much more than I ever got around to killing, then. I like this arithmetic."

"Is it merely arithmetic, you think, that decides your next life?"

"No, of course not."

"I'm glad. Because my ledger isn't that great either."

Our faces drooped and a silence lengthened as we both considered the personal accounts of our long lives. I didn't think either of us could definitively say we had done more good than harm, though I had certainly tried. Laksha eventually tore her eyes away from the sea to stare at me. "What is it you want, Atticus?"

"Hmm? To win, of course. To survive."

"I meant long term, if there is one."

"Oh. Right. Well, a somewhat normal life would be nice. Where I can start a family and not have to abandon them because Aenghus Óg found me. Where I can teach them all to be Druids and not have to worry about being hunted. A future where I don't have to be the *Iron* Druid anymore, just the Druid, like the elementals call me."

"I see. You seek peace as well. A different definition of it than mine, but peace all the same."

"Indeed."

"I hope you find it."

"You as well, Laksha."

We lapsed into silence again, and perhaps Laksha, like me, was contemplating what peace might feel like. My desire to be stable and to experience life without the feeling of being hunted was real, but realistically I knew that starting a family was not in the cards or even the deck I was currently playing, because Granuaile was on a path that diverged from mine—a vital one that she needed to walk, building headspaces and wrestling with her power—and that meant I either needed to wait or move on. I figured she was worth waiting for and that I could afford to be patient and that the time would not go dully by. All assuming, of course, that we enjoyed any time after today.

The distant cry of ovine terror drew our eyes back to the shore, where something long and glistening had erupted from the ocean to eat a woolly lunch.

Jörmungandr, the World Serpent, spawn of Loki and a giantess, had come out of hiding and was growing fast, sharing his father's talent for shape-shifting. There would be an upper limit to his growth without fuel, but with it, he could continue to swell to the genuinely mythic proportions that the Old Norse had assigned to him. And he appeared to be fueling himself quickly, gulping down a couple of sheep with his head pointed at the sky and then striking quickly to scoop up more. He was a beautiful sort of terrifying, purple and blue and green scales winking in the morning sun. I remembered the tale of Väinämöinen, who spoke of a smaller version of Jörmungandr he met off the coast of Iceland, an innocent serpent with a curious mind. Thor had come to destroy it as a sort of warmup exercise for Ragnarok, even though it had done nothing to humans and bore them no malice. Thor thought the murder justified, perhaps, since it was his destiny to meet death in battle with Jörmungandr, but instead he met his death at the blade of Moralltach, wielded by a vampire with an ancient grudge. I think Odin may have meant for me to meet my destiny with Jörmungandr in Thor's place, but I had other ideas. And so did Laksha.

"This is it," Laksha said, finding my hand and squeezing it. "After preying on humanity for so very long, I am hopeful and grateful and determined to do some final good. I do not know what suffering awaits me, but I accept it and go to it willingly."

"Farewell, Laksha. May your next life be a good one."

"Farewell."

The body of Mhathini Palanichamy slumped abruptly, and I caught her before she could hit her head on the ground. But once she was safely lying down, I turned my gaze back to Jörmungandr, grown even larger in those few seconds than any dinosaur or creature of fable. It was just finishing its second round of whole sheep and was eyeing a third strike from the sea but probably realized it would need to come ashore if it wanted any more mutton, since the herd was pelting away from the ocean as fast as it could. Its decision made, the massive gills on the sides of its neck flared one last time and then sealed up as Jörmungandr transformed itself into an air breather. It leaned forward and then abruptly flinched, as if punched by a titan's fist. A strangled shriek erupted from its mouth, and it shuddered from its head all down its sinuous length before going still and rigid and falling backward into the sea like strange, scaled timber. The surviving sheep bleated the ovine equivalent of "Did you see that shit just now? I'm never going near the ocean again, no ma-a-atter how green the grass is," and the sea sloshed and hissed as the World Serpent disappeared beneath the waves.

"Yes!" That deserved a fist pump, for Laksha had succeeded. She had left Mhathini's mind, shot through the ether, and executed a hostile takeover of Jörmungandr's brain. She had, no doubt, simply shoved its spirit out entirely, as she did in her earliest years whenever she felt like using a new body. To prevent Jörmungandr from settling back in, however, she'd have to occupy that brain and defend it until it died. And once it died in the water, she'd die too. Creatures of the ether don't do well in the water.

But Laksha had just willingly sacrificed herself to save Ireland, minus a few sheep, and she went with a lighter heart and soul than I had ever known her to possess. It was one hell of a good deed, and a counter to Loki's plans he could not have anticipated. That it also happened to save my own personal potatoes was beside the point: I'd be putting it all on the line before the day was through. And like Jörmungandr, I fully expected to exit this life via the unexpected, and people would find my body as they find so many others, staring at eternity in surprise. I felt prepared for most everything I could think of, but what kept my mind racing at night was worrying about what I hadn't thought of. Because just as I had managed a quick and abrupt removal of a key chess piece from Loki's board, the god of mischief and lies had no doubt prepared some surprises for our side. He had never expected someone like Laksha to get involved, and I had only vague ideas of what to expect when I got to Sweden.

But if I am honest, I did feel a bit giddy and self-congratulatory in that moment for thinking of a solution to Jörmungandr's rise that would benefit everyone. I might have even succumbed to the urge to quote some Shakespeare.

I squatted down next to Mhathini, entirely too pleased with myself. "Ligarius said in *Julius Caesar*, *Now bid me run, And I will strive with things impossible; Yea, get the better of them*. But he never did anything like that, did he?"

"Mmmh?" Mhathini stirred, and her next words were not in English but Hindi. Fortunately, that was a language I knew, though I'd had few reasons to speak it in recent years.

"Where am I? Ireland?"

"Yes. Welcome."

"Who are you?" She frowned and her whole body tensed.

"You can call me Atticus or Connor, whichever you prefer."

She breathed out in relief and relaxed. "Good. Laksha said you'd help me."

"And so I will."

Mhathini sat up. Her voice, while obviously using the same set of vocal cords that Laksha had used, possessed a slightly different timbre. A softer edge to it. Or perhaps it was the different language we were speaking, I'm not sure.

"Laksha said she was trying to prevent the end of the world but it might still happen in spite of her. Is that true?"

"Yes. Both things are true. She did her part, but it still might happen."

"I see." She looked down at Laksha's ruby necklace around her neck and brought her slim fingers to it, considering, or perhaps silently praying. I let her take all the time she needed, and it was only a couple of minutes before her fingers dropped away and she looked up at me. "Well, thank you for being here. I didn't ever think I'd get to see the sun again, and even if it's only for a little while, I'm glad I have this time. It's good to have a friend at the end of the world."

CHAPTER 9

i spare a worried glance at the swarming cloud of demons erupting from Seven Star Mountain and then look at my bubble tea,
which the Monkey King insists I must enjoy right now.

"I don't know, Wukong. Maybe the demons are more important? I can always try bubble tea later."

"Nonsense. Live in the present, Granuaile. Presently my copies
can take care of the first wave, and your bubble tea should be at its
peak deliciousness."

The Monkey King had sent an impressive number of clones to
join battle, and he seemed unworried. But his eagerness for me to
try this tea is making me worried in turn.

"Is there something in my tea?"

"Yes!" He flashes his teeth at me in triumph, excited that I have
finally figured out something important. "Little pearls of tapioca!"

"It's just a bit weird that you want me to drink it so badly."

"It is merely pride in my work. And it is the right action to take
in this moment."

I am not sure I agree with his priorities. But then, looking again
as the red-and-gold clones meet the swarm and immediately have a

visible impact, even from this distance, I doubt my participation in the fight would make much difference.

"Why am I here?"

Wukong chuckles, throwing his head back in unrestrained glee. "A philosophical question! The answer is simple: to learn and to grow."

"No, I mean, why am I here right now?"

The Buddha cocks his head at me and shrugs. "The answer is the same, and will remain the same days and months and years hence."

Flidais catches my eye. "Learn well, Granuaile. I must leave you now."

"What? I thought you said you had to be here—"

"I had to bring *you* here, and I have. I am needed in Japan. Farewell."

"Okay, yeah—" Flidais doesn't wait around. She's climbing down the fire escape before I can finish saying goodbye, leaving me with Sun Wukong. He waggles a bushy eyebrow at me and grins, nodding at my bubble tea. "Oh, fine, whatever! I'm trying it, okay? Look."

I take a sip through the almost absurdly thick orange straw and it's slightly sweet, slightly floral tea with milk in it. Light and lovely and—whoa. One of the tapioca bubbles rockets into my mouth, and it's mildly chewy and a perfect complement to the tea.

"Eh? Huh?" The Monkey King smiles as he watches my face. He so clearly wishes me to flatter him that I smile back.

"It's good, Wukong."

"Yes. It is good. And it can be enjoyed in so many different ways. That is the basic tea you have there. So much else for you to try."

"I suppose—"

"Good." Sun Wukong reaches a finger up to his ear and plucks at it. Something like a small toothpick grows and spins in his hand until it's a long golden staff. He crouches down and holds the staff in both hands. "Now we fight."

"What?" is all I can manage, because I didn't realize before that moment that tea could be a prelude to battle.

His only answer is to launch himself toward me, staff held high to crush me from above. I throw the bubble tea at him and he spins in midair to avoid it while I bring my staff up crosswise over my head to block his strike. The impact shudders through my arms to the sockets of my shoulders, and I stagger back. The Monkey King lands and promptly ducks under my counterstrike as he tries to sweep my legs. I hop over that and lash out with a kick, but he somersaults away. I pursue because the one rule of fighting someone this powerful is that if they start something, you need to be the one finishing it and doing so quickly, because the longer you delay the less chance you have of winning.

Sun Wukong cackles as he tumbles and somehow deflects every one of my strikes with his staff. When we run out of roof, he finds his feet and launches himself over my head, knocking away my thrust at his abdomen, and sticks the landing behind me as I whirl around to face him.

"My turn," he says, and then he's on the attack. I manage to parry the first five strikes or so, but after that he gets through my guard every other strike and lightly taps me instead of destroying me, a masterly show of control.

He backs away, leaving me flustered, and smiles again as he stands next to his staff, held upright in his right hand and resting on the rooftop. "Bubble tea is good. But as I mentioned, there is more than the basic flavor. Would you like to learn more?"

"Yes. I am always ready to learn more."

"Good. You have the right mind. Very well. You have been trained in techniques that date back a thousand years and you also have some modern moves." I nod once, because that's accurate—Atticus came to China in the eleventh century and received the bulk of his Eastern martial arts training then, which he passed on to me. "You are in fact a master by any mortal measure. I do not intend to demean your skill in any way. That must be understood."

"I understand."

He nods in acknowledgment before continuing. "But there are older techniques. Some newer ones. And some that are my own invention." He flicks a finger to the north. "What you see happening at Yangmingshan right now is the work of only the first and weakest of the Yama Kings. It hardly requires my attention. But there will be seven more, each deadlier than the last, and you need to be prepared if you are to survive and fulfill your purpose."

So many questions churn in my head—primarily the question of what he thought my purpose was here, but other things too, like what kinds of horrors we would be fighting and if I was going to fight an actual Yama King or merely hundreds of his minions—yet none of these is important next to the fundamental truth of his statement, so I quash the questions and store them for later.

"I agree," I tell him.

"So, if you are willing, let us begin your advanced training. From now on, you will call me Sifu Sun."

I bow to him. "I am willing, Sifu Sun."

CHAPTER 10

Once Siodhachan leaves, I get out of the river and dry off me feet, because that water is fecking cold. Colder than the welcome of a night club bouncer on a Friday night—which reminds me, I still owe an arse-kicking to that lad in Kilkenny who threw me out of the pub.

I go sit on the edge of the back porch, feet resting on the turf, and let the elemental know I'm available to help should I be needed anywhere. Starbuck the Boston terrier comes out and sits next to me, his mouth open and tongue lolling out. I connect to his mind so I can hear if he answers me and say, "You're a good lad, aren't ye?"

<Yes food,> he says.

"Ah. Still learning your language, then?"

<Yes food. Play?>

"Maybe. That word can mean different things, I've learned. What do you consider to be play?"

<Stay,> he says, and disappears through the plastic flap in the side of the house that Siodhachan says is a doggie door. He bursts through it a moment later with a knotted piece of rope. He drops it

by my side and looks up at me with his tongue out. <Throw please. Yes food.>

"Throw it, ye say?" It seems like a strange request, but I don't see the harm in it. Dogs like Starbuck didn't exist in me own time, so he's a new creature to me, and I'm interested in what he will do next. I pick up the rope and chuck it a good distance toward the river, taking care not to actually throw it in there. The wee lad springs off the back porch faster than I expect.

<No squirrel!> he practically shouts in me head, and for a moment I worry he's gone daft, but once he reaches the rope he picks it up and shakes it before galloping back to me with it in his mouth, and then I understand. He's practicing his squirrel slaying, and that's play for him.

<Good human,> he says as he drops it by me side again. <Throw please.>

I can't help but chuckle at that. "Ye know how to train humans already, don't ye?"

<Yes food. Throw please.>

I oblige him and think while he's off to fetch that maybe an animal companion wouldn't be so bad, if the werewolves would be okay with it. Before Starbuck can return for another go, a shudder runs up me leg, as the elemental speaks to me through my contact with the earth.

//Avenging Druid needed / Bavarian Alps / Urgent//

Elementals didn't used to talk to Druids like this. The earth hadn't been so fecking cocked up before, so I'd never had occasion to hear what elementals called me until I came forward in time. And I didn't really like that name, because it referred to an episode in me early years with a dodgy man in a bog and I didn't want to be reminded of it.

//Harmony// I reply, but then add, //Except for name / Please call me Ancient Druid//

//No / You are Avenging Druid / Hurry / Bavarian Alps//

Bollocks. //I go// I says, and hop to me feet.

I have to go inside and ask the British lad where in the world the Bavarian Alps are. Once he pulls up a map on his computer and shows me, I figure I can shift to something tethered there and then ask what trouble's brewing in the teakettle.

Sorry I can't play anymore, I tell the wee Starbuck mind-to-mind. *I've been called away to serve Gaia. Play later?*

<Yes food. Good human.>

I sprint out to the bound tree, shift planes to Tír na nÓg, and then spend a while trying to figure out which tethers lead to the Bavarian Alps. There are about ten of them, I reckon, and right as I settle upon one it disappears, snapping out of existence. Then the one next to it does the same thing. Something horrible must be happening there to disrupt the tethers. I choose the one that's farthest from the destroyed ones and pull meself along the tether, arriving with a bit of panic in me mind, afraid the tether will snap mid-transit. I don't rightly know what would happen to me if it did, but I don't want to find out. I do make it through, though, and soon find out what's been causing all the ruckus: The earth shakes underneath me, and it's no mild temblor either. It's a serious shake-up in progress, and it's going to ripple out to populated areas soon and disrupt far more than a few tethered trees.

But the trees and these mountains—gods below, they're gorgeous. I wish I would have visited before there was a fecking earthquake in progress, because it's a stunningly beautiful place I've come to. If I didn't know better, I'd say the landscape was trying to have some soft hot sex with me eyes, it's that seductive. Tuya, one of me apprentices, loves trees especially; she'd find this place so magical that the corners of her eyes would leak happy tears. Best be about preserving it, then.

//Druid here to help// I tell the elemental Bavaria. Its reply is less than polite.

//You are not Druid / He is elsewhere / You are Avenging Druid//

I blink a few times. This elemental is in the throes of an earthquake where all its living things are in crisis and it's quibbling over names?

//Query: Emergency?//

//Creatures disrupt earth / I will create path / Slay them//

That's straightforward enough. //Query: What creatures?//

//Follow and slay// is all the answer I'm given before a fissure opens before me—not an accident of the earthquake but rather something with a purposeful floor to it, with walls and a ceiling that remain sturdy even if they shift; no matter how violent the earthquake gets, Bavaria won't let it crush me while I'm on my way to do its bidding. The tunnel delves quickly and I have to cast night vision to see. I also put on me brass knuckles and remember that even though I've been given a mission, I can't use a direct binding to kill anything. It's the law of Gaia herself: She judges no deaths so long as one never uses her power to accomplish it. Druids have been doing her dirty work for millennia now—or Siodhachan has, anyway. Mostly it was demons from this hell or that, but occasionally something Fae or more sinister would require his attention.

It's not too long before I can't see a fecking thing, even with night vision cast. Ye have to have at least a wee bit of light to operate, and underground it's darker than the inky anus of a sleeping octopus. I let Bavaria know.

//Continue// it says. //There will be light soon//

I stagger on, a hand outstretched to keep track of the wall, and stumble a couple of times since I can't see the ground shifting and it surprises me. But I don't want to fail in this, whatever it is.

The light shows up soon enough. A dim orange glow and some heat along with it, and a sulfurous odor punching me lungs: That light source is lava. A bit more dangerous way to light up a space than those fancy twisty light bulbs ye see these days.

And it really shouldn't be this close to the surface. The Alps aren't a range of dormant volcanoes; they were formed by the collision of tectonic plates. Which means something nasty is bringing this up on purpose.

I hear it before I see it. Cruel laughter mixed in with throaty chanting in a language I don't recognize. And it's pretty clear I'm spotted first, because I have to duck a red glowing rock thrown at me head. It still glances off me left shoulder and sears a groove there, singeing hair and cooking an ear as it passes. I trace back where it must have come from, and there's a wee shadowy thing standing in a rivulet of lava like it's nothing but a cool stream. It looks like it's practically chiseled out of coal or volcanic basalt, all sharp edges even though it has a humanoid form. In the darkness it's just another slice of shadow until it moves, and it's moving to scoop up another lava bomb.

It has a face like someone took an angry shite and placed it on top of a neck. Or maybe that's just me own anger I'm projecting on to it. I know what this thing is now, attaching it to a description Siodhachan gave me: It's a fecking kobold, but the bloody dangerous kind and not the weak things I've seen when Sam and Ty, the leaders of Greta's pack, are playing this video game they like. In the game, kobolds are weak creatures with a wee knife, easily slain. But that's not the kind of creature that spawned horror stories from German miners hundreds of years ago. If you're a brave lad tunneling through a mountain, you're not going to be terrified of something with a knife when you have a pickaxe. No, those miners had reason to be afraid, because kobolds can move the earth and collapse a mine, or pick up handfuls of magma to hurl at Druids' heads.

I cast camouflage and wink from his sight just as he looks up to target me again. Then I speed up, watching me feet so I don't step in that lava stream, and feed him a fist of brass knuckles between the teeth. I half expect it to take his head clean off, but kobolds are as rugged as the mountains they live under. Some of his teeth chip and shatter and he's definitely knocked senseless, but it doesn't kill him. Ye can't handle the heat and pressure of the earth's crust without being a tough bastard, I guess.

Still, he drops that handful of molten rock and falls backward to the opposite side of the lava flow. Me job's not done: Bavaria wants these things dead, and I know there have to be more because the quake continues, so I have to figure out how to punch through something with natural defenses like rock. It's neither practical nor efficient. I hop over the lava flow and stand next to the kobold's head, kneeling down to take a closer look. His eyes are not impregnable, I see. Deep set and wee, but they're still eyes made of blood and jelly nestled in a socket with a hole at the back. I take off me clothes, shape-shift into a red kite, and place a taloned, brass-coated foot on his face and squeeze, punching into his brain through his right eye. He twitches a couple of times and goes still again. I shift quickly back to human because the heat's getting to me feathers. I'm going to need a better way.

I tell Bavaria that's one down but I need something to help it go faster. I picture what I need and it wells up from the earth at me feet in a matter of seconds: a foot-long spike of smooth, polished stone.

//Lead me to the next// I tell Bavaria as I pick it up. I leave me clothes behind since I may need to shape-shift again soon. The tunnel, I notice, has stabilized quite a bit since I took out the first kobold. But as I continue on and draw closer to the next target, it begins to shift and buck again, and I fall twice because the light is still none too good. I also start drawing power to heal me burnt shoulder because it's screaming like ten seagulls fighting over one fish.

The tunnel Bavaria's creating breaks through into a new cavern, and a fresh gust of sulfur fumes slithers down me gob like all the ghosts of me bad ideas. I cough and wheeze and tumble down into a roll as I enter, just in case there's an ambush waiting for me head. It's a good thing too, for a few hunks of rock that qualify as boulders sail over me and crash behind. I find the kobold responsible standing in front of a wall of lava. Me face is already baked dry like those fecking nuts they give ye on airplanes with a sad thimbleful of water, but I'm going to have to charge him and that wall to end this. And unlike the first lad, he's not chucking those boulders with his hand: This is a big boy in the world of kobolds and he's moving that weight with his own magic. Earth-based blighters, they are. And he knows *something* has to be here, even if he can't see me, because otherwise what opened that nice symmetrical hole in the wall down the way? And if he has any sense of the presence or energy of other kobolds, he probably knows one of them abruptly got snuffed a few minutes ago. So he's not taking any chances. He didn't hear a death scream or see any blood splatter, so he's going to throw more at me. I can see him clenching his fingers and the wall of lava bubbling and swelling behind him. This is going to be bad. I put the spike between me teeth and shift to a ram, the brass of me knuckles flowing up to the horns and coating them, making them unbreakable. Then I lower me head and charge straight at the kobold with all I've got, just as he sends a wide spray of molten rocks and lava in my direction. There's no avoiding it or dodging; it's like a net of fire backed with stone.

Me horns slam into the leading edge, breaking it apart, and that provides a sort of cone of protection, keeping it out of me eyes at least, but that doesn't mean I pass through unscathed. I get pretty fecking scathed, in fact, especially down me back above the tail; I'm pretty sure it's just on fire and I'm melting, but I have a target to hit first.

He sees the flare of my passage through his salvo, the fire burning on the outline of something indistinct, but he's still not sure what I am except coming for him. He tries to move, but I'm both watching and much faster and I adjust me course. I take him in the ribs, launching him off his feet and propelling him right into that wall of lava. Neither my hit nor the lava will kill him, but his advantage is all gone now: He can't stand there and throw fiery rocks at me.

I skitter to the side, clear of the lava's edge, and shift back to human, rolling around and away from the fire on me arse. I draw heavily on Bavaria's energy to heal me burning skin and let the spike drop into me hand, then I wait.

It's less than a minute before the lava erupts into the cavern, and had I still been standing in front of it I would have been completely coated, beyond the help of healing. The kobold steps forth from the fire, roaring his defiance, and when nothing comes to slap him, he chuckles, assuming me dead. Well, not yet, ye smug shite. I'm hurt and I could be consumed by fire at any moment, but I'm not out of the fight yet.

Except the lava now covering the cavern floor does present a problem. I ask Bavaria for help once more in fashioning something useful far more quickly than I could bind it together meself: makeshift stone sandal platforms that I bind directly to the skin of me soles, which will hopefully allow me to walk across the lava and sneak up on the rogue. That done, I check on the kobold; I'm off to his left, perhaps a tad behind his shoulder. He takes a couple of steps forward, obviously scanning the cavern for some sign of me corpse. The rumble and quake of the earth covers my whispered binding as I target a boulder across the cavern and take me first step onto the lava: hot all around, but the stone holds. All I have to do is not trip and fall over into the slag.

I step with more confidence and complete the binding, yanking that boulder on the far side right toward the lava. It begins to drag itself in that direction and the kobold turns to face it, which means his back is to me. It's nothing but a distraction. I'm wondering if I should tap him on the shoulder to get him to face me when I realize that the eye sockets are not the only path to the brain. The kobold's ears are wee, but the left one serves: I stab the spike inside, pierce the eardrum, and scramble his brain but good. He topples over and I back up gingerly, trying not to fall over meself and fail at winning. The shuddering of the cavern subsides, and once I'm on safe ground again I remove the stone shields from my feet and let Bavaria know it's done.

//No / Three more//

"Fecking hells," I mutter, and some of that sentiment must have leaked through, because Bavaria adds, //Smaller ones / You will win//

I'm not so sure. The burns are pretty bad, and me lungs feel permanently polluted. I can't get a proper breath, to be honest.

//Need clean air// I say, and the response comes quickly.

//Follow//

The earth behind me moves, a new tunnel boring through the crust. Once I stagger down it a few steps, Bavaria closes off the cavern, shutting out all that sulfur. The tunnel slopes upward after that until we get near enough to the surface for some sunlight and fresh air to rain down from a hole.

//Rest and heal// Bavaria says, and I give my thanks as I take big lungfuls of fresh air and feel the pain of me burns recede somewhat. The elemental's pouring huge resources into this, which must mean it stands to lose much more if the kobolds are allowed to continue. And they *are* continuing; the ground beneath me own feet might be steady, but there's still shaking going on nearby. And the longer I rest, the worse off this area will be—especially if any of that lava makes it to the surface.

I take one more deep breath and tell Bavaria I'm ready.

//Harmony// comes the reply, and the ground beneath me swells, pushing me up through the hole until I'm on the surface again. There's a buck standing there, and for a moment I think it might be Siodhachan, but Bavaria puts that notion to rest quickly. //Follow animal to next tunnel site//

The buck turns and bounds through the forest to the south. I can't keep up as a human, and me wounded shoulder would hamper me if I tried to fly as a kite, so I shape-shift back to a ram and put the stake between my lips, try me best to keep pace, and wince as the burns throb anew.

Makes sense to have me do this if it's going to be a goodly distance, and it is—it's miles, in fact, and there's no use spending energy to create a tunnel for me in that situation. The ground doesn't stop rumbling the whole time, and I hope Bavaria will be able to recover quickly from all this strain. I also hope no one has been hurt wherever people might be living around here. I don't think there are any huge cities in the area, but there are probably wee villages and some isolated cabins and farms, things like that, buildings that weren't designed to withstand earthquakes.

We run long enough for the burns to calm down to smoldering coals, relatively speaking, and for me lungs to feel like they're free and clear again. But the earthquake is getting worse—honestly, they're never supposed to last this long. The ram form is a bit steadier than I would be on two legs, but even so, keeping upright is a challenge.

//Hurry// Bavaria tells me. //Almost there//

That's a truth. A tunnel opens up less than a hundred yards from me, and once I get there I shift to human and cast camouflage, alert for ambushes. But the kobold I'm ushered to is not as paranoid as the others—he's too deeply involved in manipulating the earth—and he's easy to dispatch as a result. The earthquake subsides almost immediately afterward, and the last two I'm forced to chase are simply running away when I find them, because they must have figured out that their brothers all met bad ends. I would have said they learned their lesson and let them go, but Bavaria insists that I hunt them down, and I can't say no. It wants the kobolds to know that there will be no mercy for messing with the earth like that. But I have to pursue them underneath the mountains to their hidey-holes.

Hours later, when it's done and I emerge from my subterranean shenanigans on the side of some peak, I have no desire to go spelunking anymore or even try a subway. I'd rather see the sky, meself. I collapse and stretch out, bathing in the sun and enjoying the fields of treetops and meadows rolling beneath me, all bonny and blithe.

//You are beautiful// I tell Bavaria.

//Gratitude / Please visit at length / Enjoy my lands//

//Harmony// I says, and I think to meself I'd work to exhaustion every day for a view like this. There is peace to be found in unspoiled land.

I don't know how unspoiled it will remain. I imagine that we're getting quite close to the world's biggest demonstration of the First Law of Owen, and I worry about Greta and me apprentices, even though they should be safe in Flagstaff soon. For the first time, I wish I had one of those fecking cell phones, just to check on them.

And the next time I see Sam and Ty fighting kobolds on a screen, I'm going to tell them their video game monsters are shite.

CHAPTER 11

mhathini turned out to be a completely sweet person who'd rather do anything in the world than see her father or brother again. She did have a passport and Laksha had left her all her financial information, essentially transferring many lifetimes of wealth to Mhathini's care, so she was also abruptly wealthy, unbeknownst to her family. But she had no idea how to remain in Ireland legally for more than a few months or indeed if she even wanted to remain there.

We hopped into Laksha's rental and I drove her to Cork.

"I think you will find that money is the ultimate freedom," I said, "while the lack of it is often a prison."

"Yes, I can see the truth of that. I was dependent on my family and they were . . . unpleasant to live with. I felt trapped." Her face tightened in frustration before she muttered, "But I guess I'm free now."

"Indeed you are. You can fly anywhere, rent a place for a few months, and move on. I lived that way for centuries. Your family will never find you unless you wish it; minimize your online footprint and always use an alias for everything. Whenever you feel the least bit nervous, fly away to the next place. And when you find someplace you wish to stay, then you can take the time to arrange for a visa or permanent resident status."

I took her to a bank to make sure she could successfully wire funds and remain flush for a while, then I gave her my contact information, bid her farewell, and returned the rental car. There was a television screen blaring in the rental car office with news of strange eruptions in Taiwan, Japan, the Bavarian Alps, and elsewhere. No solid numbers on injuries or fatalities; just unprecedented seismic activity with no warning. Seismologists and geologists were baffled. Rumors were trickling in of other wild phenomena occurring around the globe, but nothing verified yet.

I wondered if these news organizations would send reporters to the scene to get live footage from the sites—and as soon as I asked myself the question, I knew the answer was yes. People sitting at home or in pubs or airports or even car rental agencies would soon be able to watch some hapless journalist planted in front of howling madness saying, "As you can see from the utter batshit unfolding behind me, the situation is pretty dire, and I can't believe my boss sent me into the middle of this insanity. That's it. I bloody quit."

Well, if they thought that was unusual, wait until they saw what was going to happen next in Scandinavia. It would be far more dark and dire than any Swedish crime drama.

When I'd made my first ill-fated shift to the Norse planes, I learned that the primary tether to the World Tree, Yggdrasil, was located in Sweden, "to the east" of Norway as it was set down in the *Eddas,* but not all that far east, relatively speaking. That tether point—or I suppose I should say that root of the World Tree—led straight down to the spring of Hvergelmir, and it was from that spot in Sweden where, if Mekera's tyromancy was correct, the host of Hel would emerge and Ragnarok would begin in earnest.

Mekera's divination had yet to fail me. I hoped she had called Fiyori by now.

The tethered tree was on the shore of a small pond near Skoghall, Sweden, on the northern shore of Lake Vänern. As soon as I shifted in, I scanned the area in the magical spectrum and saw a big glowing glob of juju off to the south. That's the direction I headed, and I soon discovered it was the mustering grounds of the Fae host—and it was also a swanky eighteen-hole golf course. It must have been here before, when Granuaile and I had plunged through the surface of the pond with Freyja and it turned out to be a portal down to Niflheim, but we'd sailed over it in the night and I never realized. The pond wasn't one of the water traps of the course; it was off the course itself, just to the north of it, and probably had some kind of stream connecting it to Lake Vänern.

The Fae hadn't used the same bound tree as I had; there was another one on the golf course, newly tethered, near where they were massed, and as I drew closer, I saw more and more of the Fae shifting in and sorting themselves into ranks. I had no idea if they were sent by Brighid or by Fand; Fand's presence would mean that Owen's mission had at least partially succeeded, but until she fought on Brighid's behalf and at her request, nothing was certain.

I veered off to one side as I neared the host. I was still the Iron Druid, after all, and not welcome among them. My aura would destroy them on touch. I did wave to the nearest one, however, and beckon her to come forward, signaling via drawn knots in the air that I promised safety.

The flying faery inched forward cautiously, and once I felt she was in shouting distance, I held up a hand to allow her to stop in safety and listen.

"Please inform the host I am here to fight alongside the Fae, for Ireland, Tír na nÓg, and all the Fae planes!"

She nodded and flitted away, and that would suffice. Word would spread quickly, and hopefully I wouldn't have to stare down a volley of arrows at any point.

I settled down to wait. The unfortunate reality was that we could only react to whatever Loki manifested at this point; we couldn't plan for anything, except to be ready for his arrival, since both he and Hel were protected from divination. Which meant Loki and Hel might not show up here at all; it was only the vast host of Hel and her uncountable *draugar* that would appear for certain. Nothing else about the prophesied sequence of Ragnarok could be assured. I had made sure of that when I killed the Norns. And Fenris the wolf, and Jörmungandr.

It was certainly a much larger show already than the original Norse conception. As I sat on the putting green of one of the holes, my meditative consultation with the elemental confirmed as much. In the African countries that comprised Yorubaland, the Orishas, led by Shango, were fighting the Ajogun. Ganesha and the Hindu pantheon manifested in India to beat back the surge of rakshasas and other demons there. Flidais was in Japan, fighting alongside the Shinto deities against a floodtide of oni. Granuaile was fighting alongside Sun Wukong against the Yama Kings in Taiwan. And there were many more such conflicts, some of them arranged by Loki but others arising because someone with a chaotic streak in their personality saw an opportunity.

My meditations were interrupted by a small but extraordinary delegation from the Fae host. Fand, Manannan Mac Lir, and five large white-furred creatures hailed me and approached from the fairway leading to my green. I was pretty sure I knew who the furry folk were, but I was entirely surprised that Fand was willing to appear with them.

"Siodhachan. Well met," Manannan said.

I rose to my feet and smiled. "Manannan. How pleasant to see you again. And you, Fand."

The Queen of the Faeries gave me the barest nod of acknowledgment but said nothing. Her eyes did not meet mine but rather fixated below my chin at the cold iron amulet around my neck. Even that much civility from her was probably a remarkable concession.

The god of the sea said, "I've come to introduce you to my children, the yeti." These were clearly not Fand's children, but her expression was blank. "They wanted to meet you."

"They did? The honor's mine."

Manannan and Fand stepped to one side and he introduced the tallest of the yeti, with extraordinary braids and silver threads worked into his facial hair. "This is the eldest, Erlendr."

The yeti broke into a wide grin and extended a huge furred hand for me to shake. I took it, and it was not unlike wrapping one's fist around an ice cube covered in felt.

"Oh, Master Siodhachan, it is such a pleasure! We are great friends of your apprentice, Granuaile, and wanted to thank you for sending her to us!"

"She speaks very highly of you as well."

Erlendr took over the responsibility of introductions, and rarely have I seen or felt such joy in a meeting. Granuaile had told me how wonderful the yeti were, but in person I discovered they were not the sort of beings to which words can do justice. They were unique, their magic combining the elemental talents of their frost giant heritage with the binding skill of Druidry.

Hildr, the second eldest, immediately asked me a question: "Did Granuaile tell you about the hockey rink she made for us?"

"Yes, she did." The way their expressions lit up, it was clear that Hildr had broached a favorite subject.

"It's fantastic! We dream of playing in a proper game with humans someday. Perhaps we could rival the professionals of the NHL! Do you play hockey, Master Druid?"

"Sadly not. But I do enjoy watching the games live and making fun of the Toronto Maple Leafs, who manage to lose all the time in spite of having an enormous budget. And please, call me Atticus, no honorifics."

Each of them had more to share about Granuaile in the most friendly, hairy, animated terms, and before long my face began to hurt from smiling so much. Skúfr asked me to relay that the ice sculpture of Jon Snow—"he who knows nothing"—was still standing in the Himalayas, and as far as they could tell he still knew nothing. Ísólfr hoped that he could share more of his poetry with her soon. And Oddrún, the youngest and smallest of them—but still far taller than me—asked about the whirling blade they made for her.

"Is it serving her satisfactorily? We all worked on it together."

"Oh. Yes, well. Unfortunately, it was stolen from her by Loki."

"Loki? The same one who is responsible for this thing we are here to stop?"

"The very same. He may have it on his person."

The yeti did something with their fur, an involuntary reaction, perhaps; it fluffed out and then flattened, their expressions turning dour.

"That is most unfortunate news," Erlendr said.

"I agree."

Beneath me, the earth rumbled. We all looked north to the pond and saw that it was bubbling away, boiling into nothing. In short order it exploded, a gout of flame rising from the center of an ever-expanding cloud of steam, and the yellow-orange center of it kept building and building as a mountain formed where a lake used to dwell, boulder-sized chunks of granite and basalt falling and oozing as a volcano formed before our eyes. But it was unaccompanied by the standard payload of ash; it was all rock and flame, the sort of clear, pure eruption Eddie Van Halen played once, the sky remaining crystal clear, a sunny day for an apocalypse in Scandinavia.

Atop the rising cone a form took shape in the flame, a monstrous humanoid the height of skyscrapers, and once it solidified, a head and molten shoulders with arms of stone and a heart of bottomless rage, it erupted anew, fountains of flame rocketing into the sky and spreading in all directions.

The fire giant Surt, long confined to Muspellheim, had finally come to Midgard, and he had come to burn it all. Wounded, seething, and petty, he vented his long-pent-up fury upon the world, and his fire arced like missiles to far-distant lands, careless of what joy it burned down or what ruin it brought to innocent souls.

The heat of him singed my face, even from such a distance, and I knew my iron amulet would be no protection against his flame should it be directed at me. Right now, however, Surt's fire was spreading vast distances, and we were standing underneath an expanding molten umbrella.

So this was how the prophecy of the sirens would come true. Surt's long-simmering tantrum would set the world alight, and there would be no scientific explanation possible except for the sudden eruption of a volcano where no seismic activity previously existed. Satellites would reveal the epicenter of the fire, but only we at ground level could see the figure standing in the flames.

The yeti sighed collectively, at once awed and dismayed by the power Surt displayed.

"I think that's our cue," Oddrún said, and her elder siblings grunted in agreement. The youngest yeti turned to Manannan Mac Lir. "We love you, Father."

"And I love you. All of you." He embraced each of them in turn, told them of his pride and hope for their safety, assured them of his confidence that they could save the world from all-consuming flames. And then the yeti stepped away, puffed out their fur again, sparkling with new crystals of frost, and froze the ground beneath their feet. They skated together toward the fire on a ribbon of ice.

They were quite literally beneath Surt's notice until the last second, when their single track split into five and each yeti crystallized their own shining path to a different part of Surt.

Erlendr rose highest on a pillar of rapidly melting ice toward Surt's face, and once he reached the height of his collarbone he let loose with a tremendous blast of icicles aimed directly at the giant's eyes. That provoked a violent reaction. The gouts of flame ceased erupting upward and exploded outward instead, over our heads into Lake Vänern and beyond, and the sky turned into a burning sheet of orange and black. The net result was that Erlendr simply disappeared behind a wall of orange, and both Hildr and Skúfr were consumed by globs of magma. Ísólfr, skating toward a knee, toppled from his ice sheet by a glancing blow but formed a ramp down to save himself like a downhill skier.

It was Oddrún, skating just above ground level, that Surt failed to notice until it was too late, distracted as he was by her siblings. Using her whirling blade, she pricked one of his massive toes—an exercise of stabbing it into the edge of a lava flow—and the effect was immediate and catastrophic, even if it was too late to save the other yeti. The towering form of Surt screeched as its soul was detached from its frame and sucked into the blade's reservoir of energy. The limbs wobbled, destabilized, and then the entire body began to come apart like orange gelatin, raining down on the mountain. Both Ísólfr and Oddrún raced to escape the umbrellas of it, ice tracks melting behind them almost as soon as they passed. They did manage to clear the ruin, but their fur was blackened and singed in places. Surt did burn the world, fulfilling the prophecy of the sirens, but the yeti made sure he didn't have time to burn it all down.

A cautious, ragged cheer rose up among the Fae host, but it didn't last long. The portal to the Norse plane opened again, and this time the eruption was of a different kind: The undead, phantasmal *draugar* boiled out of Hel, armored and fearless, a horde intent on razing all that stood before them.

CHAPTER 12

Sifu Sun grips his staff so that it points at me but rests against his left hip, a stance I've seen only a couple of times before, very briefly, from Atticus, as a throwaway demonstration: "There is a style of fighting that uses this stance with a very long and heavy staff," he said, "but that's an impractical weapon to carry around with you, so we'll skip that and focus on forms using the shorter staff you possess." The Monkey King apparently wanted me to use Scáthmhaide in that style of fighting, and I ask him if my staff will be sufficient. He shakes his head at me.

"Wrong question. Throw away your assumptions about the coming battle. You are not going to be fighting humans. These creatures will be stronger, and you will need to use your center of gravity and the strength in your hips to move them. Because they will move differently. The defenses you know will only be partially effective against them."

"What sort of creatures are we talking about?"

"Elongated arms, and more than two. Razor wings. Some have tongues like frogs but not sticky: They are stiff and pointed at the end, and they use them to pierce your body."

"Lovely. Are these Buddhist demons?"

"Some. Only some. The hells of the ten Yama Kings are a blended realm."

I squint at him, imagining a chunky demon puree. "How do you mean, blended?"

He cocks his head at me, scratches his chin. "Ah. My words fail. Take me as an example: I learned many of my tricks and skills from Taoist masters. Gradually I came to Buddhism and embraced that, but without rejecting my Taoist teachings. And many people in Taiwan, Hong Kong, and China also harbor beliefs from Confucianism. All three living in the same house, in harmony. Many shrines reflect this. You have an English word for this that escapes me now. This blending of faiths without conflict."

"Does Sifu Sun perhaps refer to religious syncretism?"

"He does! I mean, I do. This might be strange to you from the West, where people think you must believe only one thing, but in the East we have no problem with this."

"I have no problem either, Sifu. I am a student of religion and philosophy."

"Excellent. So as it is in the shrines and the heavens, so it is in the hells."

"As above, so below?"

"Precisely. You will encounter Taoist monsters and Buddhist demons as well. You may encounter hybrids of the two. And they will not fight like anything you have seen before. So you must fight like them, a blending of styles, ignoring adherence to this form or that and focusing instead on the pure expression of battle demanded by your shifting opponents. We will begin with this stance but flow into other forms from here and return."

"I understand now, Sifu."

"Begin. Attack and let me demonstrate the advantages of this stance."

He establishes a pattern of having me attack first from different positions while he displays the defense and counterattack, then switching roles so that I must learn and execute the moves flawlessly as he attacks. We do this while the battle rages over Yangmingshan. He pauses when Seven Star Mountain erupts anew with an entirely different horde. It looks . . . chunkier. Larger demons, perhaps. But mixed with smaller bodies that may be human.

"The second Yama King has come," he says, and pulls out another tuft of hair, making even more copies of himself. They immediately launch themselves through the air to join battle in the north.

I hear some exclamations and raised voices floating up from the streets below. People in the city are becoming aware that something untoward is happening.

"I'm worried about widespread panic as much as the demons," I tell him. "There will be traffic accidents and tramplings and who knows what else before the demons ever get to the population."

"Yes. That is the way of people who are not at peace. But we will try to keep the demons confined to Yangmingshan and minimize the loss of life."

"And if we cannot?"

"Then a great many people will be moving on to Samsara, the Great Wheel."

"Sifu, I have a question. I am able to make myself invisible due to the bindings on my staff. Will that not render these defenses pointless, since my opponents will not be able to see me?"

"You will be as plain to them as the sun in the sky. Your binding will not matter to them. They will not be using human eyes to look at you, after all. These creatures from the hells can pierce all veils."

"Oh."

"Now, concentrate. The same sequence again. Show me you have mastered it." And he launches himself at me in a blistering fury of strikes from both low and high angles that I must defend from my middle.

My instruction continues until the third Yama King arrives and the Monkey King sends out even more clones. I'm exhausted and my fingers are blistered and chapped from my staff. I've had no

contact with the earth in all these hours, and my energy is danger-
ously low. I don't know how much use I'll be without some time to
heal and recharge.

"That is all," Sifu Sun says after his third batch of clones de-
parts. "I can extend myself no more. And you are tired. Also, the
time grows short. Let us return to the shop."

"Thank you for the instruction, Sifu."

"You are welcome. But I am no longer your teacher, so you may
call me Wukong again."

The shop is cleared of customers when we get down there. There
are only a few employees left, arguing loudly in Mandarin about
something. Wukong's voice cuts through theirs and ends it. He dismisses them and they exit out the entrance, still in their human
guises, to go who knows where to enjoy the apocalypse. Wukong
locks the door behind them, displays a sign that I assume means
CLOSED in Mandarin, and pulls down blinds so that no one can see
us through the windows. Then he turns and grins at me. "Ready
for some bubble tea?"

"Seriously?"

"A different flavor this time. Something special."

"All right. Then what?"

"Then we go to fight at Yangmingshan, and we live or we die."

"*Can* you die?"

The Monkey King laughs as he moves around to the tea-making
station. "I admit the odds are in my favor. But I suppose it is possible. And if it does happen, well, I have a pretty good idea that my
afterlife will not be so bad. How about you?"

"You're asking what I expect in my afterlife? My karma points,
or whatever?"

"Yes. I speak of karma."

"Well, I never put my seat back when I'm flying coach and
thereby invade the space of the person behind me."

"I am not sure what flying coach means," Wukong says, "but I
am glad to hear that you do not invade the space of others."

"Yes! I have long thought that reclining your seat on an airplane is a sure sign of moral turpitude! Unless of course there is a spinal or other medical condition involved. Uh . . . what are you doing there?"

Sun Wukong slaps the wall with his knuckles in a sequence that's clearly designed, and once he completes it, a panel slides to the left and reveals a hidden wall safe. He spins the dial and smirks at me over his shoulder. "I am getting the special ingredients for your tea."

"You have some kind of food in a safe? Is that, uh . . . safe?"

"Yes. You may relax and depend on my methods of preservation."

"Of course. Yes."

A click and a twist of the handle and the safe swings open to reveal a glass container with a lid on it. No bearer bonds. No blocks of illicit drugs. Just a covered bowl of fruit, which Wukong removes with reverence. "Ahh. Do they not look marvelous?"

I am not sure what I'm looking at. Slices or wedges of pale yellow fruit. "Are those mangoes? Papaya?"

"No. These are Immortal Peaches."

I blink and look up at him, then back at the fruit, and back at him. "Immortal Peaches. Like the ones you stole thousands of years ago to extend your life. Upsetting the heavens."

"The very same. But taken with permission this time."

"And you're going to make bubble tea out of those?"

"Precisely!"

"For me?"

"Indeed!" He puts the bowl down on the prep area and uncovers it, and the most exquisite smell of peaches wafts about the room. I close my eyes and simply smell it. Divine.

Some blending happens after that. Some sloshing noises and the crisp snap of a plastic lid on top of a cup.

"Here you are," Wukong finally says. I open my eyes and behold a yellow-orange liquid. "Your original order: Immortal Peach bubble tea."

"Oh, my goodness. Thank you."

I take it carefully and bow to him and he nods in return. He offers me a straw and I stick it through the little hole in the lid and sip. It is the most exquisite taste to ever roll across my tongue. I know I shall forever eat peaches hoping to taste the memory of this drink, and they will never compare.

And it is not simply the taste of the tea that is sensational: It has a clear, immediate effect on my body. My exhaustion disappears and my muscles feel strong and ready again.

"I wish I had the words to express how wonderful this is," I tell Wukong. "It deserves its own poetry."

"You enjoy poetry?"

"I do! I'm memorizing Polish poetry right now for my next headspace. I think I would like to study Mandarin afterward, though."

"Oh, there are many fine poets in that language, especially from the Tang Dynasty. Have you heard of Wang Wei?"

"No, I haven't."

"He writes of nature quite often, so I expect you would appreciate him. Let me see—perhaps I can translate a couple of lines you might like?" His voice deepens and rolls across my eardrums like thunder in the prelude to a summer storm.

*"Look! I make no plans for the future
but to go back to my forest home again."*

Its brevity surprises me, but I do find it evocative and the sort of plan I would always have for myself, no matter my age. I suddenly miss Orlaith and her puppies, and Atticus and Oberon, and marvel again at the power of a few words to evoke emotion within us. "That sounds lovely."

"It is," Wukong agreed. "And it was. Let us hope we have both a future and a forest after this."

CHAPTER 13

i rather thought that business with the kobolds was enough riskin' of me life for the day, but almost as soon as I think it and make plans to catch up with me grove, I get a request to investigate some mess back in North America.

I'm starkers, and it's something that happens so frequently for both of us that Greta set up a clothing cache in the forest near her cabin next to the bound tree, just an old bureau she found at a thrift shop. It's far enough away from the house that me apprentices wouldn't see me appear, though that's not a concern since they're still on that very long flight home. I shift there long enough to get a fresh pair of jeans and a shirt before following the call of the elemental to the northern United States.

The Lewis Range of the Rocky Mountains, which runs north and south over the border between Montana and Alberta, had a portal open up a wee while ago and temperatures in the region began dropping all out of proportion to what could be called normal. On the Montana side it's part of Glacier National Park, which I've heard tell of before. Mostly I've heard that it used to contain glaciers, but in the last century they've melted away like Popsicles in an oven.

Once I shift to the area, I ask the elemental what's the problem.

//Unknown / Source of cold to the north / Find and report//

All right, reconnaissance is easy enough. But I'm feeling the chill already—it's cold enough for me nipples to be used as diamond saws. It's still dark here and I cast night vision to see better, but even with the elevation and time of day, it shouldn't be quite so cold. With a sigh of resignation, I strip off the clothes I just put on and bind me shape to a red kite, taking wing into the freezing air. Curiously, once I get a few hundred feet above the mountaintops, the air actually gets warmer. Not balmy by any means—it's still fecking cold—but there's a noticeable difference, and it's not the natural sort. Normally ye get colder, not warmer, as ye climb higher.

I point meself north and am awestruck by what I see: These Rocky Mountains are beautiful, even in the frigid blue tones of night. I never saw the like before; the Bavarian Alps were fine, make no mistake, but I didn't get to admire them from above. I surely never got to see such things in Ireland or on me few trips to the European continent in the old days. I saw some grand cliffs and some fantastic hills, but nothing like these mountains. I could see a Druid falling in love with land like this.

The air gets even warmer as I head north, and eventually I'm able to see why: There's a pack of frost giants on the mountains, actively sucking the cold out of the air and leaving only heat behind, bizarrely creating something close to a thermal updraft. And they're taking all that cold and moisture and making themselves a bit of a shelter out of ice. They have a lot of bags and parcels scattered around them, and one of them is using a shovel to dig a fire pit—though maybe that's wishful thinking on my part. I sure could go for a cozy fire.

Watching actual ice and snow crystallize from their outstretched hands to form frozen walls is what identifies them; otherwise I would have thought them nothing more than tall lads with powder blue skin, maybe some kind of Fae. But what are frost giants from the Norse stories doing here? The portal that brought them, at least, seems to have closed—but who opened it?

I begin to circle them, counting on the night and the tendency of people not to look up to keep me concealed, and work through what I know.

The original stories of Ragnarok suggested it was to begin with years of cold, to soften up the human plane—Midgard, they call it—and make it ripe for conquering. Perhaps that's still a part of the plan, except they're going to try it on a different continent. Maybe Loki figures once he gets the other hemisphere under control, this one will fall easily later on if it's frozen out just as spring begins. North America will lose a growing season, and suddenly you'll have famine conditions in the land of plenty. Weak folks put up a weak fight.

Maybe that's it. But they don't look like they are any sort of military force. They have a couple of wee ones with them. Giant kids. These are families.

Bright movement in the sky attracts me gaze eastward. There are streaks of orange in the dark, like a meteor shower passing by so close ye should be screaming, and while many of them pass high overhead in the upper reaches of the atmosphere, heading to points west, methinks some will be landing nearby.

One of them indeed plows into the ground short of our position, maybe a kilometer or more to the east, landing on the side of the mountain in a stand of timber, which immediately ignites a full acre or so—the opposite of a cozy fire. These things are fireballs, not meteors. Landing on a patch of forest like that, where there's no easy way to fight the fire, means it's going to burn for days, unless of course these frost giants decide to do something about it.

And they do. There's some angry grunting and pointing at the sky, then four of the giants break off from the group and take long, loping strides toward the site where the fireball hit. Must mean that the fire giant Surt has emerged from Muspellheim; there're going to be fires all over the world, and I wonder if any of them will make it down to the Flagstaff area. There's a whole lot of dry pine around there. Lot of trees everywhere, really. These fires are going to ravage the planet.

I drift away from the frost giants working on the shelter and follow the ones heading for the fire. They have some rough terrain to navigate, but those long legs help them scramble down; it's probably twenty minutes until they can make it there, and by that time the fire's not only caught on, it's spreading. They combine their talents and start throwing snow at the flames, lifting it right off the ground and smothering the tree trunks and branches with it.

It's going to take them some time, but they'll have this fire contained and extinguished in an hour, I'm guessing. And that kind of behavior doesn't fit with them being agents of Loki. If they're on the same side, they should be laughing about that fire, rubbing their hands together like villains and muttering darkly about how the world will soon be theirs. The shelter they're building is above the tree line, so they wouldn't be threatened by it, unless they're wanting to preserve the habitat here for animals. That's a different kind of long-term thinking, that is. That's the sort of thing ye do if ye want to stay. That's what ye do if ye want to protect your neighborhood.

I circle back around to where the group is working on their shelter and take a closer look. It's not a bunker or barracks that's forming up there. That's a home. Two of the giants—a man and a woman—are putting some decorative touches on the front pillars, little whorls and blossoms in ice. They're smiling at each other and saying, "Graah," whatever that means. I wish I could talk to them, but they speak Old Norse, a language I never picked up.

But add it all up—the kind of shelters, the makeup of the group, the baggage—and these are most likely refugees. These families don't want any part of Ragnarok or Loki's shenanigans. They want a safe place to raise their kids, and this particular slice of the Rockies has few humans running around. Siodhachan told me about the national park; it only has a couple of roads and they're closed off for the winter and much of the spring. The frost giants' only true chance of running into somebody would be mountain climbers in the summer, and if they kept this peak covered in snow and ice throughout—not difficult at these elevations—then even that would be unlikely.

I can't tell for certain, of course. Maybe they have some sinister agenda packed away in one of those bags, but they're not behaving like they want to destroy the world. They're acting like they want to hide in this one wee corner of it, bothering no one. Fact is, they're not doing anything now that's worth me putting on the knuckles. They opened a portal, and that raised an alarm with the elemental, but now it's closed, and so far they've done nothing else but make a cold place a bit colder, build an ice house, and put out a fire. Seems like this could be a noncrisis.

I spiral down to the north of them all to report to the elemental.

//Twelve frost giants / Building shelter / Plans unknown// I say, then add that the portal is closed, though the elemental surely knows that already.

//Very well / Watch and wait// the elemental says, and I decide it's best to shape-shift into a bear on the spot. There's no use for me to freeze if this is going to take a while, and bears can handle the cold a bit better.

I pad through the snow and find a place where I can watch the frost giants from a distance. They have that cozy fire going now in the pit, and they're starting work on a second house. The couple who were decorating that first house, they're taking a moment to stand back and admire it and smile. The man spreads his arms, closes his eyes, and takes a deep breath as he turns in place. He grunts and nods, and the woman says, "Graah," and nods back. They like it here—and what's not to like? It's fecking beautiful, and if I liked the freezing cold I'd want to stay too.

How they got here—who opened the portal and closed it

again—is something I'd like to know. But it doesn't appear to be an urgent matter requiring me attention. These folks have demonstrated by their actions that they're here to build and preserve rather than destroy. Meanwhile, I know right well there's plenty of destruction happening elsewhere. Those fireballs are most likely going to do damage wherever they land, excepting perhaps the ocean, but the elementals seem content to let those burn or let someone else take care of them. Plant life can come back from fires. It's tougher to come back from the drains and death that portals cause.

Watching the frost giants build their wee hamlet, I'm wondering if we might not work with them if they're going to be staying here a while. I might be able to bind tons of carbon to the ice if they are going to rebuild the glaciers. Could be good for the region and good for the world. I'd need Siodhachan to talk to them, though. I hope he's managing all right.

The frost giants who'd left to fight the fire eventually return and help build the houses. It's a bit after dawn when they figure they've done enough and disappear inside them for some rest. I let the elemental know that they're harmless, and I'm glad to see that.

She gives me permission to leave and get some rest in one instant—and then takes it back the next. She relays a distress call from near the equator. Something horrible is happening in Peru.

CHAPTER 14

after the fire I expected the ice. The frost giants were, by all accounts, on Loki's side and eager to transform the world. But for some reason, only a few emerged from the Norse plane to cool down the area where Surt had stood and smooth the way for the horde. And it was indeed a horde of *draugar*, the spirit-filled undead from Hel, that bubbled up out of the volcano's cone. That spirit inside them prevented me from unbinding them like vampires, and they were tough to kill otherwise. They had to be decapitated or somehow have their brains scrambled to be defeated, and they had a couple of squiffy dodges that made even that rough: They could swell up or shrink fairly easily and were also semi-corporeal. They could pass through solids—or let solids pass through them—if they wanted. Sort of like those spooky twins from the second *Matrix* movie, except a smidge slower and without a sense of humor or fabulous hair extensions.

They had very little going for them in the way of fashion. They did have swords, shields, and helmets, but everything else pretty much was left to hang out. And I'm not just talking about naughty bits. I'm talking intestines and organs, their manifestations looking an awful lot like Hel herself, except the various bits of *draugr* flesh were largely gray and bloodless. They were dead meat wagons for the saddest of spirits, and rather unappetizing meat at that, like nine steps down from fast-food roast beef.

Behind us—a couple of putting greens away—the darkened sky thundered and a rainbow descended from the sky to earth. It was yet another portal to the Norse plane, but this time originating from Asgard. Troops marched down ten wide on the Bifrost Bridge, far better armored and looking far less dead, even though in practical terms they were the same as the *draugar,* spirits riding around in manifested flesh. They were the Einherjar, the valorous dead selected by the Valkyries to live in Valhalla and dine with Odin, practicing for this final battle every day for centuries. They had to train vigorously and get really good at the killing bit because the valorous dead were far less numerous than all the other dead. They sure did look fancy, marching in ranks and with their spangenhelms all buffed and polished up, their wooden shields brightly painted. But they were going to be vastly outnumbered.

The Norse did have some gods on their side to even things out. Behind the Einherjar, Odin rode on a magnificent if rather ordinary horse—I was the reason he wasn't riding Sleipnir. I was the reason any of this was happening, in fact.

Valkyries circled above Odin on white winged horses. Frigg rode next to him, and behind him, in a chariot pulled by flying cats, rode Freyja. More of the Æsir followed behind, as did many of the Vanir, dwarfs from Nidavellir, and elves from Álfheim, but I still doubted we would prevail without more help.

More help soon arrived, before the rainbow bridge was finished offloading its troops. Yet another portal opened to my left, and at first I thought it was another fire giant rising from Muspellheim but quickly saw my mistake. It was Brighid in her battle dress, rising on a pillar of flame. And behind her came not only her own Fae host but another army we had coaxed to our side: the dark elves from Svartálfheim. Now it was starting to look like we had a prayer.

Brighid noted the *draugr* hordes mustering under a banner and moved toward me to parley. Her eyes flicked to the large Fae host and noted Fand and Manannan waiting to receive her, but she did not acknowledge them yet. Instead, she dropped to the earth in a scorched circle, extinguished her flames, and removed her helmet.

"Siodhachan. Why are you standing here by yourself?"

"I am less than popular with pretty much everyone I'm to fight alongside today."

"Including the Olympians, eh?"

"Olympians? Where?"

Brighid pointed over my shoulder. There, behind me and to my left, were many of the Greco–Roman deities. Zeus, Jupiter, Hermes, and Mercury floated in midair above the others. As before when I had met him in England, Zeus had a visible erection underneath his toga, because the prospect of violence excited him so. The Apollos were there, as were Ares and Mars and Athena and Minerva. I had never seen the latter four in person, and I did not want to get into a fight with any of them. The gods of war appeared to be comfortably wearing enough steel for a heavy-duty truck and gripped huge weapons and shields. The goddesses of wisdom were a bit more sensibly armored but looked no less deadly. Athena's owl was perched on her left shoulder; Minerva's flew lazy circles around the Olympians from above. I was relieved to note the absence of Bacchus and Diana, since either or both of them would enjoy filleting me and feeding me to their dogs.

We waved to them, and the Olympians gave us curt nods in return. Zeus's toga twitched.

"Has Hel or Loki emerged yet?" Brighid asked, her gaze turning to the volcano's slopes, which still poured out more and more *draugar*.

"Not visibly. They may have, though. Either could be wearing a disguise and watching us right now."

"Hmm." Brighid considered and shook her head. "Perhaps that would be true of Hel. She has the same blackened heart but does not have the bloated ego of her father. Loki will reveal himself, I feel sure. His constitution demands it. He must preen and be seen to be powerful. He may be part of the horde now, but eventually he will make himself a target."

"That sounds quite likely to me. When he does, though—is there already a plan that you know of to take him out? Because he is immune to both fire and lightning."

"Lightning?" Brighid scowled. "Didn't Thor used to punish him with that?"

"Perhaps so, in the past. But Perun sent multiple bolts at Loki since he escaped, and he was unaffected."

"Well. He is not immune to steel. And we have plenty of that to go around." Brighid's eyes slid left and right to make sure no one else was in listening range and then she lowered her voice. "In fact, we have a little wager afoot on who's going to get him. My money's on Ares. You want in?"

"Sure. Who's available?"

"You are, for one."

"I am? Nobody thinks I'll be the one to get him?"

"Not so far. The gods of war and the thunder gods are taken, as are the Apollos and all the Norse gods. So am I, plus Fand and Manannan."

"Well, what if I do get him and nobody's bet on me?"

"Then you win everything. The one to get him gets half the winnings, and whoever bet on that person gets the other half."

"Nobody's taken the goddesses of wisdom?"

"They're free."

"Then give me twenty on Athena."

Brighid scowled. "When I said 'money' I was speaking metaphorically. I did not mean we are using modern systems of payment."

"Then what's the buy-in? Not favors to be named later, I hope."

"No, it's . . ." She paused, sighed, and rolled her eyes. "It wasn't my idea, all right? Odin insisted, and it's all your fault."

"Of course it is. Everything's my fault."

"We're using Girl Scout Cookies. One thousand boxes, winner chooses what kind."

"Are you joking with me right now?"

"I am not. Odin is obsessed with them, ever since that time you gave him Samoas."

"Then a thousand boxes of Girl Scout Cookies on Athena."

"Fine."

"Out of curiosity, who did Odin pick?"

"Freyja. Now if you will excuse me, I must greet Manannan and Fand."

I was abruptly alone again and hyperaware that I may have as many enemies on my side as against the forces of Hel. The Olympians did not come over to say hi, nor did the Fae or the dark elves. I might have to watch my back every bit as much as my front—though except for the dark elves and some of the Fae, I did not think of the forces on our side as backstabbers. Certainly not any of the deities.

Though there was one I was hoping to see precisely because of his backstabbing ability but didn't see yet: Coyote hadn't shown up, and he'd left me little hope that he would.

I was pretty sure we'd get some interference from normal folks soon, however: "mere mortals," as the Olympians might call them. Every scientific instrument they had pointed in this general direction must be going bonkers. So far, three different portals had opened near here, and there'd been an unheralded eruption to boot. Add to that the atmospheric disturbances that Zeus and Jupiter were no doubt causing by floating there, and we could expect all kinds of investigation soon from the Swedish government, and probably other governments as well, at least via satellite. The amount of fodder this would provide the tinfoil-hat crew would last for decades.

I wished I could joke with Oberon about it. He'd make me laugh and calm me down. But at the same time, I was glad he wasn't here.

The likelihood of him surviving such a battle as this would be small. My own chances looked fairly dismal.

The *draugar* continued to pour out of the mountain and sort themselves on its slope and its base, facing our own mustered forces. Once the flow finally trickled to a stop, the mountain convulsed near the top, but what erupted was not lava. I groaned and got to my feet.

It was a massive gray hound, much bigger than Oberon, and its name was Garm, the hound of Hel. And Hel came with him.

There are few motifs more tiresome in history than the power-mad guy who wants to shape the world to suit his desires. Sometimes the power-mad guy spawns hellish offspring that are just as bad or worse, though, wee monsters that grow up to be big monsters, bereft of empathy or much in the way of soul that is not a small, starved, mewling thing. Loki and his children were cut from that cloth.

Hel stepped out of the caldera and kept growing, half of her a gray-skinned corpse and half of her exposed bone and flesh and pulsing organs. Behind her, the bright fiery hair of Loki rose. The god of mischief grinned madly as he emerged, swelling to gargantuan proportions. They towered over the field using their shape-shifting ability, standing sixty meters tall or more, like some giant mecha suit from an apocalyptic anime. Loki held a flaming sword that I recognized, though it too was much larger than it used to be, and he pointed it in our general direction. His voice boomed across the fields like thunder.

"Kill them all," he said. "Scourge them from the plane of Midgard." The much larger army of *draugar* surged forward to meet ours, outnumbering us four or five to one.

Someone on our side blew a horn high up in the air, and it came from behind me, to the right, where the Bifrost Bridge had settled. I turned to see who had signaled the charge, expecting to see Odin, but it wasn't him at all. There was a latecomer to the party: a chariot floating in the air, drawn by two goats, and a red-haired, heavily muscled figure standing in it.

"No, it can't be," I mumbled, but he let the horn fall away from his bearded face and held up a hammer to the sky. Lightning coalesced around it and he redirected it to strike amongst the oncoming horde, a pointless gesture since the *draugar* were unaffected by the electricity, allowing the bolts to pass through their phantasmal flesh. He'd have to hammer them into oblivion if he wanted to make them go away, because Loki and Hel would not let something so elementary as lightning thwart them now. But the stark fact of his presence was proof that he'd never gone away when I thought he had.

"They suckered me somehow," I breathed. "That's bloody Thor."

CHAPTER 15

Seven Star Mountain explodes again. It is a howling, ravenous force with which I am unprepared to deal. This is a battle meant for gods, not a woman from Kansas by way of Arizona.

"Wukong," I say, "I still do not know why I am here."

"And the answer still remains: to learn and grow." The grin he flashes me is mischievous. He knows full well how annoying he's being right now.

"To learn what, though? To grow in what way? I am willing to do both and to work for whatever goal you set before me, but what you have said so far is too vague for me to understand."

"Do you think you were brought here to fight the hordes of the Yama Kings? To fight perhaps the Yama Kings themselves?"

"No. I do not. That is the source of my doubt. You cannot possibly expect me to fight them."

"Oh, but I do. But they are not the true fight. They will kill you if you do not strive your utmost—do not mistake my words—but defeating them is not your true purpose. You must defeat something else."

"What? My secret desire to live on nothing but breakfast pastries? My growing addiction to anime?"

"Your comfortable assumptions. Your habits of thought. They are not merely ruts in the road keeping you on the path you're following, they are like blindfolds, preventing you from even seeing that there are other paths."

"I know that there are other paths."

The Monkey King smirked. "You feel comfortable saying that, don't you?"

I bite back a heated reply. For while I am aware that there are other paths, there must be some specific kind that Wukong is referring to and he knows I'm not seeing it. And he's not suggesting some kind of Yoda deal here, where I must unlearn what I have learned. He's acknowledged that I'm on a pretty high plateau of martial skill; he wants me to ascend above that somehow.

Or he might be speaking of a completely different path, unrelated to martial arts. For all I know, he might actually want me to watch better anime series than I'm currently watching. I appreciate the value of ambiguity in some situations, but it's damn infuriating when it's the guardian of a gateway to a deeper knowledge of the self.

And I *know* the purpose of it: The ambiguity forces the student out of established patterns of thinking, and the subconscious begins to chew at the problem like a tough, day-old bagel, even when the conscious mind is otherwise occupied. But knowing the purpose doesn't help; I'm still faced with a mental obstacle course obscured by fog.

Regardless, we are through speaking and training. The Monkey King grasps his staff in his left hand and reaches out his furred right hand to me. "Come, Granuaile. It is time to defend humanity, to live or die in the moment. If they win free of Yangmingshan Park, the loss of life will be vast."

I don't know what he intends to do here, so I hold tightly to

Scáthmhaide and put my left hand in his right. Sun Wukong grins at me.

"Sometimes humans soil themselves when I soar the clouds with them. Do please try not to do that."

"What?"

He cackles, shakes, crouches, and then I am yanked bodily into the air by his power, swept along in a massive jump toward the boiling, apocalyptic mess of Yangmingshan. In *Journey to the West*, it is said he can travel one hundred eight thousand miles in a single leap—enough to circle the globe four times, essentially no different from flying, so this comparatively brief hop to Yangmingshan from Old Taipei is nothing to him but a breathtaking and indeed a possibly pants-shitting experience for me. If it were not for my background flying as a peregrine falcon, I think I might well have had an accident of one kind or another, for as a human it is terrifying to be aloft without visible support.

And what we're flying into is terrifying as well. The Monkey King controls our descent to the base of the mountain; we must both bat away skyborne mouths ravening for our flesh along the way, and on the ground a few figures clear a space for us because together we make a strange silhouette.

Once there, I'm not sure how to feel about what I'm facing. Some of them are clearly demons of unusual physiognomy and have never been anything but horrid creatures that take delight in the pain of others. But some of what I see are maddened human figures, both male and female, charred or bearing scars of some kind, confused as much as anything else. They are souls working off their bad karma in hell until they can be reincarnated, and they're as worried as I am about what will happen if I kill them like this. Will they immediately be reincarnated, or will they return to their purgatorial hell for centuries more of purification? But there's a certain fatalism to them as well, these wretched creatures who died who knows how long ago: They know full well they cannot stroll into Taipei and resume their lives as is, being shades of their former selves. They must instead please whatever Yama King is in charge of their hell, and right now their Yama King wants them to slay whatever's in front of them. There's a moment in their faces, a flicker of curiosity in their expressions at why there's suddenly a red-haired white woman here, and then a palpable shrug when they realize it can't matter in their particular scheme of things, right before they lunge at me with sharpened fingernails and feral teeth in mouths gaping wide. The blunt end of my staff thrust between their eyes, or a blow to the temple or back of the head, ends them quickly. They are unarmed and unskilled and offer no serious threat to me, and I'm saddened by the necessity to hurt them to defend myself. I suppose I'm defending plenty of people back in Taipei, but I don't feel that; instead, I feel like some sort of monster for taking advantage of their weakness.

That is, until a serious demon comes my way, blue-skinned and borne aloft by brightly colored wings akin to peacock feathers, with red glimmering eyes in a black-toothed visage. He wields a mace dangling on the end of a chain rope, and I know he's a dude because he wears nothing.

"Uh, Wukong?" I glance over my shoulder and see that he is already otherwise engaged. This one's all mine, apparently. Some lord of a hell upset that I'm plowing through his forces so quickly.

"Have no mercy," Wukong calls over his shoulder. "Do not hesitate."

Taking his advice to heart, I pull out a throwing knife from my belt and bullseye the demon in his junk. He shrieks and curls around the shaft buried in his shaft, and I brain him with Scáthmhaide while he's mourning his nads. That makes the damned pull back from me a bit, and I pause as well.

"No," Wukong says. "Continue, Granuaile! They must all be sent back, you see? These souls must continue their punishment until they can be reborn again. You do nothing wrong by your violence here. You are both protecting the living and helping these souls on their journey."

That wrenches my head around to a different paradigm. I'm not really killing the innocent, or anyone; this is a cleanup operation. Sanitation, even. As evidenced by the fact that soon after these vessels "die," they melt away much like demons from the Christian hells do, but thankfully these don't smell as bad.

"Just think," the Monkey King said, "after another thousand years or whatever debt their soul has taken on, these people can be reborn and experience bubble tea."

That's a mighty strange thing to think about in combat while shattering skulls. What shall I say to them right before they die again? "Try the kiwi watermelon flavor when you get a chance," or something like that? Would such words even hold meaning for them? Would they hold on to the idea throughout their purgatorial suffering and then through rebirth? Would they even understand a single word of my language, or might I be communicating to them somehow my personal regret and hope for them? I certainly hope better things for them than mere bubble tea. Their expressions are desperate to simply get through whatever this is—me, hell, whatever—so that they can reach a better place.

"Am I helping them to learn and grow?" I ask as more of the damned flood down the mountain and our staffs whirl and thunk against heads, caving in temples and crowns.

"Probably a measure of mercy," Wukong replies. "We are both giving them quicker deaths than anything they receive from the Yama Kings."

I don't know how merciful it is to send these people right back to be tortured for—did the Monkey King say a thousand years? How does one do so much evil in a human lifetime to deserve that much punishment? I imagine someone like a dictator or a serial killer could manage it, but I'm sure all these people weren't such. They were millers who cheated farmers, perhaps, or farmers who didn't take care of their horses, or petty local officials, or terrible grandmothers, but not spirits that could do anything in seventy years to earn a thousand years of punishment, right?

I try to shake away the thought, because attempting to judge systems of judgment is how one winds up with a head full of batshit. Pick a system—any system, legal or ecclesiastical—and you'll start to wonder at how anyone could think it was fair. And then you'll realize it was never meant to be fair but rather was intended to protect the interests of the powerful, and then you're wading through a swamp of cynicism and your day's ruined.

What I like about being a Druid in service to Gaia is that Gaia doesn't judge much at all—just the theft of her own life force to kill some other part of her. That's why she prohibits us from using our powers to directly harm others. Otherwise, she's going to let us sort out judgment for ourselves.

Why should Gaia care precisely how people once behaved in Taiwan, or about the spiritual life of a mayfly in Connecticut, or about the deviant proclivities of an alley cat in Kathmandu? She will endure so long as the life upon her keeps reproducing. The violent tides of creatures eating, shitting, and fucking each other are what keep her alive. She's not going to impose morality on that.

It is why I have kept my Druidic moral code as simple as possible: If you're doing some kind of large-scale harm to Gaia's ecosystems, I'll probably do something to stop you and make you regret doing it. The punishment will be swift and short term. You'll have the chance to be kind to the earth afterward (or not) and be judged according to some other system (or not) when you die. You might even die in a fight over whose system of judgment is better—but of course that's not something you can ever know, even in death, because you'll only be judged according to one of the systems, if at all. I'll be long out of your personal picture by that time, and your elements will return to Gaia, perhaps to be reused by some other spirit that needs a flesh cart to walk around in some distant day in the future.

Three lines of fire open up down my side, deep scratches from some clawed, hissing creature that slipped inside my guard. My response is to bat his head off his neck like a melon on a stump and draw power to heal. Wukong is right: They will indeed kill me if they can. I need to keep my headspaces firmly separate if I want to ponder questions of judgment in the midst of battle. Though I am not sure why I should—wasn't I trying to shake off such thoughts moments ago?

I compartmentalize the battle in my Latin headspace—*pugnā diabulōs!*—and retreat to English to consider something new: Perhaps it is my comfortable assumptions about judgment I'm supposed to challenge? The Monkey King and these damned souls certainly have me thinking about it, and I'm at least clear-sighted enough to see I haven't examined my assumptions thoroughly. I can spy room to grow here, even if it is not what Wukong intended.

I think my instinctive rejection of judgment comes from meeting too many people who say on the one hand that their chosen deity shall judge us all but then they judge me anyway, rather than leaving it up to the deity they profess to believe in and trust. That's using religion to cudgel people into conformity, and it grinds my gears.

But Laksha recently pointed out to me that I had been judging her decisions in a similar way—not via religion, but via my cultural or even personal views of patriarchy. I do regret judging her, but I don't regret my views. Which, I suppose, is how lots of folks feel about their faiths or deeply held beliefs. That allows me to understand, at least, how easy it can be to slip into a robe of righteousness and comfortably judge others, even if I don't understand or agree with the viewpoints others are coming from.

I suppose what I'd really like to understand is our collective urge to focus on differences rather than similarities. I know our brains sort and categorize by default because that's a survival mechanism—that mushroom's good to eat, that one will kill you, that one will have you seeing wacky shit like mangoes and papayas complaining to pineapples that millennials are killing the fruit-juice industry. But despite this hardwiring, there has to be a way of thinking that will allow us to see nonlethal differences and celebrate them rather than point at them and judge them unworthy. For we seem to be ever running toward dystopias rather than the other way.

The Polish poet whose work I'm absorbing as a headspace, Wisława Szymborska, wrote about the loneliness of Utopia and how utterly bereft it is of actual people: *As if all you can do here is leave / and plunge, never to return, in the depths. / Into unfathomable life.*

It's an apt metaphor. I often feel that I am swimming in a vast ocean, a lonely mackerel who's lost her school and is trying to find her way back or else find some other bunch of fish that will let her swim along with them. Meanwhile, Utopia is above the surface somewhere and I have no clue. Is that what the Monkey King was talking about? A path to peace I'm incapable of seeing? How do I know . . . Wait.

"Wukong?" I say, looking around briefly to make sure he's still close enough to hear me. He's not far, but I repeat myself a bit louder in case he didn't hear me in the din.

"Yes?"

"How do I know if I have good judgment?"

He barks out a few simian laughs. "Do you like bubble tea?"

That seems like an inconsequential detail, but perhaps even my judgment of that is suspect. Still, it's a bit of a no-brainer, because it's delicious. "Yes," I tell him.

"And what do you think of this fellow coming our way down the mountain, tall and armored and wielding a sword that looks longer than you stretched out on the ground?"

He chucks his chin uphill, and I try to steal a glance up there while making sure none of the damned take advantage of my distraction. The figure he's talking about is impossible to miss, the plates of golden armor gleaming and etched and tied on top of red leathers, his malevolence and power distorting the air around him like heat bouncing off asphalt in the summer.

"I think he looks dangerous."

"Then I think your judgment is sound. That is Wuguan, the Fourth Yama King of Yingian."

"I don't suppose there's a chance of us hugging this out?"

Wuguan utters a death-metal grunt that vibrates in my bones and raises his sword, his mad eyes locked firmly on me rather than on Wukong. His muscles bunch, and I can see he's going to charge or—I don't know, something aggressive.

"Wukong, none of my assumptions about this guy are comfortable right now. Does that make you happy?"

"Let's talk afterward if you beat him," the Monkey King says, and Wuguan roars, leaping into the air with his sword held high.

CHAPTER 16

i've heard of the Amazon, o' course, but it's not something I can really comprehend, a vast river spanning a continent that's the breadth of nine fecking Irelands or something like that. We have lots of bonny water on the Emerald Isle but not concentrated in a river that bloody wide or long. And it doesn't hide alligators and piranhas and the like either, or huge great snakes that have somehow become euphemisms for a man's mickey. I'll tell ye what, lads: The day I see a mickey that can wrap itself around a full-grown man and squeeze him to death is the day I stop even trying to have sex.

The tree I use to shift in is right by the bank of the Amazon, near a city in Peru called Iquitos. I don't realize it when I get there, but later I find out that ye can't get to this city by car. Ye have to either fly in or float in on the river. Or shift in, like me, using a tethered tree. They have local transport in the city, roads and such, but the roads don't cut through the forest otherwise. Still, it's not a wee town. It's half a million people, and it smells like they've been here for a while.

Siodhachan told me that most of this continent got colonized by the Spanish and Portuguese. Those were a couple of the big colonial powers, along with the British, French, and Dutch, who used gunpowder and disease to make the world such a European bollocks.

"The Irish," he says to me during that history lesson, "were among the first to be colonized."

I shan't lie to ye, that sticks in me arse like a toothpick shoved in sideways. Can't blame anyone who's resentful of those colonial powers or the destructive swath they cut through the world. Whole peoples have been erased by them, others enslaved by them. But it goes further than the human cost, as far as the earth's concerned. Gaia herself has paid a huge price for such arrogance.

Here in Peru, for example, the Incas had four hundred different kinds of potatoes, and the Spanish wiped almost all of them out. They brought a few kinds back to Europe, and that became a huge staple food for the Irish, which is why Siodhachan bothered to tell me about it, but the diversity was gone. There used to be a whole bunch of bananas too, if ye will pardon me pun, but now ye have just a few kinds left and some plantains. Siodhachan says he regrets not saving some of those in a seed bank or something like that, but he didn't realize it was happening, because potatoes and bananas don't have death screams. Extinctions are sad, lonesome exits by the last few specimens, often silent and always tragic. And they're still happening.

Something around Iquitos is fed up with that. It's decided humans are the problem, and much like Bavaria told me to take out the problematic kobolds, it's taking out humans in this isolated city surrounded by the jungle.

Except it's no single thing doing the damage. That's the true problem here.

A swarm of wasps swoops down on an auto-rickshaw—a noisy three-wheeled open-air machine—and proceeds to sting everyone inside to a screaming death. Clouds of mosquitoes settle on others like a bloodsucking horror show. Monkeys have come out of the trees to throw rocks and anything they can find at people's heads from the rooftops. Birds of all kinds dive and peck at eyes, but the harpy eagles are especially deadly. There's a jaguar chasing people down and tearing out throats. The best thing for everyone right now would be to get indoors and stay there, but I would not be surprised to learn that people are getting attacked by their own pets. I greet the Amazon elemental and hope she might be able to help me figure this out.

//Query: What is source of this attack?//

//Nature goddess//

That part was at least partially expected—the disturbance here could hardly be organized by anything else—but it sure does pluck the string labeled *wrong* on me personal harp. It doesn't make sense that a nature deity would join Loki under any circumstances, if he could even communicate with one. I mean, as soon as a nature deity heard Loki say, "First we're going to burn everything," it should have kicked his gibbering arse for opening his gob. So I think this must be a reaction to the chaos erupting elsewhere. Nature's having a rough go of it thanks to Loki's shenanigans, and the deity here is thinking globally but acting locally, blaming humans for the mess.

//Query: Where do I find her?//

//Unknown//

Bollocks.

//Query: Name of deity?//

//Unknown//

Hairy bollocks, damn it. Sweaty ones that smell like dodgy cottage cheese. I need to know more if I'm going to figure out how to deal with this.

A red-furred monkey scampers above me head and I reach out to him, binding me mind to his, and ask who sent him. I get a mental shrug, a shriek, and a rock thrown at me head in reply.

I duck into a place that looks like a restaurant, advertising something called tacacho. "Who speaks English?" I ask the room, and a few hands go up, including the lad behind the register. I approach him and tell him thanks. "Do ye have a nature goddess people pray to around here?"

My question is heard by several people, and they all respond the same way: "Pachamama," they say. They exchange glances and trade tiny smiles and nods, recognizing fellow worshippers.

"Ah, good. What does she look like?"

That gets me some confusion. "You look for art?" the lad behind the register says. He's young, probably not old enough to drink yet.

"No, no. I don't want art. I'm not a tourist. I want to know what *you* think she looks like."

Because if this deity has manifested anywhere near here, she's going to look something like what her worshippers envision in their minds.

"Big?" The register lad throws his hands wide, like he's describing the fish he caught yesterday.

"No, no," one of the patrons says, his mouth full of whatever tacacho is. A bit of it spits out as he tries to talk around it. "Long hair. Many colors. Healthy size, not big or small. Made of plants and animals."

"What? No, she looks human and has normal brown skin!" someone else says.

"She is mother of all," the eating fellow says. "Not just humans. She is not confined to human form."

I can see why Amazon had difficulty identifying where she might be. Judging by these varying descriptions, she could manifest as nearly anything.

"What is she like? Does she have a temper?"

"No, no, she is gentle and loving," the boy at the register says, and the others agree.

That doesn't fit with the wrath going on outside, and the patrons here seem largely unaware that it's happening. That changes when an auto-rickshaw crashes through the huge front windowpane and a fecking plague of something flying comes with it. I've never seen people fill their pants with shite so fast.

When the first thing stings me I understand why, because it

bloody hurts. I realize I'm a target as is, but there's a simple solution: Cease being human. I shape-shift to a red kite and let me clothes fall off, emerging through the neck of me shirt and flying right out the window past all the stinging insects, which only want to sting humans. I spiral higher and higher and then circle the borders of the city, looking for something that might qualify as a nature goddess stomping around. Off to the east, near what I later find out is the Belén district, I think I see something worth investigating. Treetops not quite treelike, moving against the prevailing wind.

I ride up on a thermal, gaining more altitude, and see that there's a river there—the Itaya, in fact, a tributary to the Amazon. The housing, especially on the other side, is the most basic shelter, built on stilts to allow for seasonal flooding; the people there are living crowded together in awful conditions. And I worry they may already be dead, for what I see peeking over the treetops across the river is a creature of wrath, and the swarms are flowing from that direction to the city.

I don't want to try to fly against that, so I angle around to land on the bank to the south, flanking it, and once on the ground I shift into a bear. If a jaguar wants to take me on, I figure I'll give it a proper fight that way; I doubt these jungles have any bigger predators than that, apart from the swarms of this ant or that hornet.

There's no time to be cautious after that. People are dying and I need to figure out how to stop it. I rumble north along the eastern bank of the Itaya until I arrive at what is unmistakably a manifestation of Pachamama. Once I get a good look I understand why the Amazon elemental couldn't figure out where she was, for she is not any one thing distinct unto herself. She is a collection—no, there's a fancy-arsed word for it—an *amalgamation* of plants and animals, all forming the shape of a human woman twenty feet tall or so. She's made of vines and monkeys and saplings and beeswax and every fecking thing in the jungle. She is both terrifying and beautiful. I don't know half of what I'm looking at, since I'm not from around here and lots of these species are new to me. I have two apprentices, though, Luiz and Ozcar, who come from different ends of the Amazon. Ozcar is from Peru, but Luiz, from Brazil, is undoubtedly the biggest animal lover of me whole grove; either one of them could probably tell me what I'm looking at in great detail. All I can tell is that it's a seething mass of mammals and birds and insects around a skeleton of wood and vines, and it's powerful mad and a right glory all at once, staring at the human city across the river with churning eyeballs made of fiery-red army ants and bending all her will to destroying everyone living there. Should Gaia ever choose to manifest herself, I imagine she might look something like this, but on the scale of mountains.

Figuring out how to talk to her is going to be the problem. She's manifested from local belief and they speak Spanish around here, which means that's probably what she speaks. That's not one I've picked up yet, apart from a few words.

I can't even tackle that, however, until I figure out where she's keeping her consciousness for this manifestation. She has so many critters hanging out in her skull that I can't find hers. It's a frustrating search in the magical spectrum—I even look around the chest cavity for something special, thinking perhaps she'd be keeping herself where the heart should be, but all I can pick up is an overall glow suffusing her constructed body, which does have hair of many colors, the strands made up of vines covered in various furred and feathered animals.

I grunt a bear's equivalent of "Oh, shite!" when the answer is precisely that overall glow—Pachamama is a manifestation of nature, so her identity is not separate from that body but rather shared among everything in it. She is the sum of those many parts—which is why Amazon could not locate her specifically. She is a distributed consciousness. Or maybe the proper word would be *diffused*? I still fecking hate English.

But it gives me an idea. If I bind with any animal that's part of her, that should be a way in. I choose a somewhat goofy-looking creature hanging on to a knotted bole around her ankle. It has a smile on its face, very long arms, and three enormous claws on each hand. A three-toed sloth, I learn later. Luiz would love it.

I've had frequent practice with the binding of minds thanks to Siodhachan's hounds, and it's a quick process now. Not sure how quick the speaking bit will go, but fortunately once the binding's made a whole lot can be communicated through emotion, imagery, and intent rather than spoken words. Rendering it into mere sentences later is like hitting a dartboard's outer rings instead of the bullseye, but at least it counts toward some kind of understanding.

<Hello,> I says, <I'm a Druid of Gaia. May I speak to Pachamama?>

The creature slowly looks around at the animals teeming around it on the ankle and foot of the giant goddess. Her mental voice is affable and kind.

<Who said that in my head? Or did I eat some leaves with a trippy fungus on them again?>

<Me. Over here to your left. The big black furry thing. I look like a bear.>

<Wow. You're different! I haven't seen anything like you in the jungle before.>

<I'm not from around here. May I speak to Pachamama?>

<You're bigger than anything. Kinda blowing my mind. You probably spend all day eating stuff. Whoa. Hey, you won't eat me, will you?>

<No, I won't. Pachamama, please?>

<Oh, yeah. Who shall I say is speaking?>

<Owen Kennedy, Druid of Gaia.> That's not something I can really communicate with just images and emotions. It's a name couched in language, and she has a spot of trouble with it.

<Oaken, Drood of Guy?>

<Owen Kennedy, Druid of Gaia. The last part is the important bit to get right. I am representing Gaia, the whole earth, and her elementals, including Amazon.>

<Whoa. Is this really happening right now? It seems like a funky dream.>

<I promise it's real. Can you get Pachamama's attention for me?>

<Oh, yeah. I'll try, Oaken Druid of Gaia.>

I don't mind her messing up me name like that. I kind of like it, really. Maybe I can convince the elementals to call me Oaken Druid someday. There has to be some way to get them to change that.

It's almost a full minute before I get a response, but when I do, fecking hells, it nearly liquefies me brains.

<WHO ARE YOU?> The mental voice would be a pleasant alto if it weren't like a jackhammer in me skull. I can tell the sloth feels it too, because she closes her eyes, whimpers, and nearly falls off the branches she's clutching. Poor lass won't have a good day if that keeps up.

<I'm Owen Kennedy, a Druid of Gaia, sent to you at the request of the Amazon elemental. Thank you for speaking to me, Pachamama. But could ye maybe take that volume down a few notches? That hurt.>

The seething mass of creatures shifts its attention from the city across the river to me—all these eyes, compound and binocular, looking at me. I definitely have Pachamama's attention. Her answer is modulated to the loudish range of normal when she replies.

<A Druid of Gaia? There was one before who visited my forest from time to time. Human with red hair. You are not he.>

<No, that was me apprentice.>

<What do you want? I am busy.>

<I wanted to talk about why you're busy. You are a nurturing spirit. What has you so upset?>

<They rained fire down on my forest! Not to clear land to grow food, but to destroy!>

<Do you mean humans? That wasn't them.>

<There are no volcanoes here. This fire was unnatural, which

means humans were responsible. They cannot be allowed to continue.>

<It was a volcano in a sense, but far away from here. On the other side of the world, a fire giant from another plane came to earth and erupted. Fire has rained down all over the planet, not just here. And humans were not responsible.>

<I DON'T CARE,> she booms, and when both me and the sloth wince, she quiets, but the anger in her tone is unmistakable. <Do you not smell the poison in the air with every breath? Are you not aware of the trees they cut down, the animals they drive to extinction?>

<I am aware. But predation is part of nature.>

<This is not predation. It is excess. Gluttony. Exploitation.>

It's impossible for me to argue with that. Ever since Siodhachan brought me forward in time, me gob has been more than smacked, it's been practically obliterated by the ruin humans have wrought upon the world. It's not just coastlines that are going to disappear under the waves with these rising temperatures. Plenty of critters will vanish too, and they already are. Like the great extinctions of earlier epochs—except one, all of them were caused by warming global temperatures like this—the die-offs are going to accelerate and cascade without a massive correction to carbon emissions. If we survive this day of reckoning, we still have many more days ahead to reckon with. I plan to make sure the Druids are ready.

<When me apprentice visited—the red-haired human. Did he help the Amazon in any way? Improve the conditions here?>

<Yes. He was a rare human.>

<He still is! He's a Druid like me and he is fighting the giant that caused the fire, for your sake and everyone else's. He nurtures the earth like you. And I am training more Druids right now. One of them was born near here; his name is Ozcar. Another was born at the other end of the Amazon River, and his name is Luiz. And when their training is complete, I am sure one or both of them will wish to return here, to protect the creatures of this forest.>

<The creatures would not need protection if it were not for these humans. Ridding this place of humans will let the balance return.>

<No, it won't. It would be disaster.>

<How? They are the problem. Remove the problem and balance returns.>

<They have built systems that will inflict ruin on the rivers and forest here without maintenance.> I have no idea if that's true or not, but it sounds good.

<What systems? What ruin could be greater than what they have already inflicted?>

Ah, bollocks. I've gone and bent meself over for one of those Amazon snakes, haven't I? Siodhachan surpassed me in slinging shite long ago, but it's not like I never gave him any lessons in the fine art of prevarication. He just had some natural talent to add to me own legendary instruction.

<Their power and sanitation systems will release pollutants into the river.>

<They already do that.>

<But it could be so much worse,> and even I can hear how lame that sounds. So much for me legendary skills.

The problem with this is that I'm arguing with a force of nature. Humans have few redeeming qualities from nature's point of view. I can't appeal to Pachamama's appreciation of art or music or theatre when she's honestly not a fan of any of that. But perhaps I can appeal to her sense of self.

<I've come to ask ye to stop on behalf of the Amazon elemental, which is one of the elementals that supports you. Stop this slaughter and let me and the other Druids protect and improve the land. Stop and return to being the nurturing mother you are.>

The great head with colonies of army ants for eyes turns from me and looks back across the river. Her posture slumps, and she returns her gaze to me and pivots in my direction, placing her hands on her wide hips, everything still a boil of plants and chattering, squawking animals.

<You will protect me? Protect this land?>

<I will. And like I said, I have two apprentices who will most likely spend much of their time in this region when they're ready.>

<Then help me, Druid. Be faithful to your word. The fire is to the north, burning out the heart of me.>

<Will you stop killing the humans in the city?>

<It is done. I return to myself.> Her massive form contracts briefly and then the birds all leave it in an explosion of feathers. The monkeys climb down the sapling skeleton or leap into the tops of neighboring trees. Insects scurry down the boles or fly away. The sloth I'd bound me mind to slowly crawls off the ankle, rapidly outpaced by all the other animals returning to the forest. As the animals disperse, I can see them more clearly as individuals, and I'm overwhelmed by the variety of them. I see a capybara, an anteater, some giant fecking spiders that look like they could pull out me teeth with their chelicerae, and a procession of mantises intent on finding a quiet spot to mate and then snack on some heads. Looking closer, I realize quite a few of the animals are suddenly in a reproductive mood. I'm standing in the midst of an incipient orgy. Pachamama is reaffirming her commitment to life. A guilty reaction, perhaps, to what she had just done.

I don't think she'd ever dreamed of turning violent. She'd simply been pushed to believe she had no other choice, and when I pointed out that she still had one, she was only too glad to return to peace. She is beautiful and I tell her so. The sloth responds instead.

<Oh, hey. Thanks, man. I get people saying I'm cute sometimes, or slower than a snail hitching a ride on a tortoise, but never beautiful.>

<I was talking to Pachamama.>

<Oh! She's gone. Sorry.>

Even as she speaks, the skeleton of saplings falls in a controlled pattern to the forest floor.

<It's all right. You are beautiful too. Thanks for being our relay.>

<No problem,> she says, then amends that with a mental sigh. <Except for getting back to the tree I was munching on. That's going to take all day.>

<Is it that far?>

<No, I'm just that slow.>

<Why? It looks like you could move faster if you wanted.>

<Oh, I totally can. When that fireball hit near me, you can bet I moved faster than I ever have. But I have to conserve my energy. I eat rubbery leaves and it's a bit of a drag. I mean, they're delicious, don't get me wrong, but wow. They take forever to digest, and they don't leave me enough juice to be monkeying around.>

<You know where the fire is?>

<Yeah. For reals.>

<I need to go there. You can ride on my back if you will show me the way.>

<You sure? I have bugs and stuff living on me.>

<That's fine, they won't bother me. What's your name, anyway?>

<Slomonomobrodolie.>

<I'm Owen.>

<I thought you were Oaken Druid of Gaia?>

<Right, that too. But you can just call me Oaken if you want.>

<Awesome! Thanks, Oaken!>

<Would it be okay if I called you Slomo for short?>

<Sure!>

I move over next to her and she rises on her hind feet at roughly the pace of an advancing glacier. I fear I might need some more Immortali-Tea before we get anywhere.

<Listen, Slomo. I'm going to give you some energy. You won't need to conserve it and you can move faster.>

<How—>

<Druidry.>

<No, I was going to say, *how fast*? Like monkey fast? Because that would be a lot of energy.>

<We can try it.>

I arrange the bindings for both strength and speed because I'm curious to see what speed equates to for such a creature. I have to admit: She's fecking adorable up close. A white-furred face with a stripe of black fur across the eyes and some coarse, bushy brown fur at the top of her head and all over the rest of her. Black nose and muzzle, but the pattern of fur at the edges curls up a wee bit, giving her the appearance of wearing a perpetual soft smile. Her mental voice is kind of like that too, quietly amused. But gods below, she's got some long claws!

When the bindings hit her, Slomo's eyes pop wide and that smile becomes a genuine openmouthed grin.

<Wow, Oaken! This is some amazing juice! Watch out, I'm coming on board!>

I have to admit that when she spreads out those long arms with those claws of hers and leaps at me, it's damn hard to stand still, but I do, figuring I can heal if she does me any damage, and it's not bad at all. I grunt under the impact and the weight, but she's gentle and hugs me more with her arms and legs rather than digging in with those claws.

<Oh, wow, Oaken! This feels amazing. I feel like I can achieve true monkey velocity, swinging through the trees like I have always dreamed!>

<Ye really have a thing for monkeys, don't ye?>

<Well, they're so fast! I think it's because they can eat yellow tube fuel.>

<Ye mean bananas?>

<What? That's a terrible name for them. Makes no sense at all. Yellow tube fuel is more accurate. Go that way a little bit.> She extends her left arm out past me head and points, and I adjust course to match. <Good. So are all Oaken Druids big hairy things like you?>

<Nay. I'm not even a big hairy thing.>

<I'm pretty sure you are.>

<Right now I am bound to the shape of a black bear. Sometimes I'm a kite; sometimes I'm a ram or even a walrus. But normally I'm a human. An old human who looks like a middle-aged human.>

<These pictures in my head—these are real animals? I've never seen any of them before! Except humans. I've seen some of them, but mostly they have darker skin than you.>

<I have never seen an animal like you before. The world is a very big place. It's not all forest, you know.>

<It's not? What else is there?>

<Oceans full of fish. Deserts full of scorpions and cactus. Mountains covered in trees that have needles instead of leaves. Vast plains populated by buffalo and antelope. And so much more, really. I am still learning about it meself. Every day, it seems, I meet something new and wonderful.>

<That sounds great! It's all monkeys and leaves and birdbrains around here. Whoa, smell that smoke? We're getting close.>

<I smell it.>

<We're probably close enough, actually. I don't like fire, Oaken.>

<I don't either. I have to put it out, though, for Pachamama's sake and all the animals that live around here.>

<My tree is probably burned down now. I almost got hit when the fire came down from the sky.>

<You can find another tree, though, right?>

<Oh, sure. That was just going to be my tree for a while. I had named it Lopoyamalachamanowe and it said it liked that.>

<Trees talk to you?>

<Of course. Trees are always talking. But most creatures move too fast to hear them. Trees try to say hi to most everything that passes through their branches, because they're friendly like that and so happy when animals come to visit, but by the time they're finished saying hello the animals have usually already moved on. You have to be willing to hang around and really listen. That's my specialty.>

<You are full of surprises, Slomo. I have an apprentice named

Tuya who would really like to hear that and learn how to talk to trees. Okay, I need to shift to human and take care of the fire. Why don't ye hang out in one of the trees near here, and we can talk more later if ye like?>

<Okay, Oaken! That would be great! Can it be that tree right there?>

I head over to the right, where she's pointing, and stop next to the trunk. I don't even know what kind of tree it is, but I wonder already what she'll name it. <All right, ye have all that energy, so I want ye to scamper up that tree like a proper monkey, now. Pretend ye just ate some yellow tube fuel.>

Slomo scratches me a wee bit as she launches herself at the tree and scrambles up it with those claws, but it's totally worth it. She's fast like she's always dreamed, and her glee at being alive in the world is wonderful to hear right now when there's a gobshite trying to burn the whole thing down.

<Wa hoo hoo ho ho ho ho!> she cries out in me head, and she makes some noises like that with her vocal cords too. It might be actual words in Slothian language and not simply an exclamation, but I can't be sure. But I can be sure she's happy. She's having a grand old time, monkeying around like the monkeys do.

I shape-shift to human and warn her that the energy's about to run out, so she should get herself settled. She scampers higher up and dangles from a branch, surrounded by many leaves, all within easy reach.

<Okay, I'm ready to be a sloth again,> she tells me, and I dissolve the bindings.

Is that okay?

<Ahhh. It's quite a difference. But for a little while, I out-monkeyed a monkey. I sure hope this was all real and not some bad leaf trip.>

It's real. Do you get bad leaf trips often?

<I meant to say a *good* leaf trip. Hey. You're not big and hairy anymore. I mean, you're hairy but only in a few places.>

This is what I look like as a human.

<Most humans I've seen wear something to cover up their middle. Why do they do that? Is it because you have a smaller patch of fur there and a tiny snake living in it?>

That's not a tiny snake.

<Pretty sure it's not a big snake.>

It's not a snake at all! Look, never mind that. I'm glad you're safe now. I'll deal with the fire and return.

Dealing with the fire isn't even a little bit of fun. It's hot and smoky and a fecking shame, because a lot of plants and animals died here. But for some reason I'm smiling the whole time I'm crafting bindings, smothering the flames with dirt.

The reason is Slomo. She makes me laugh. And she's seeing the world in a way that's fresh to me old eyes. I suppose because she's seen even less of it than I have.

But she sees it with a sense of wonder, like me apprentices do. I think it's good for me to see that; it renews me own sense of wonder. When ye get old, ye can get tricked into thinking there's nothing new to enjoy in the world, because ye slow down, ye don't see much except the same few things, and ye think, feckin' hells, why don't I just lie down tits up and give up the ghost? I'm bored with eating soft foods and watching game shows and getting dressed, because clothes are all shite and scratchy.

There's no doubt that having me youth restored has gone a long way to renewing me love for the world. And seeing so much of it recently has renewed me willingness to fight for it—not that I've ever been unwilling to fight. It's just that I'm starting to feel more zealous about fighting to defend Gaia. Perhaps Granuaile's attitude is rubbing off on me. Or perhaps, when ye know what the world once was like and ye see what humans have done to it, ye just get fightin' mad as a matter o' course.

When the fire's finally out, I can feel the forest relax. I've kept me word and Pachamama can return to nurturing all.

I'm relieved that she listened to me and stopped what she was doing without a fight. Perhaps she stopped because she saw that I'm on her side, but I'm sure she knew that the true fight is going to rage for quite a while, and I'm going to be the one fighting it for her.

I let Amazon know the work is done and I'll be up a tree for a while, then I shift to a red kite and fly back to where Slomonomo-brodolie is hanging out, chewing on a rubbery leaf.

<How's me favorite sloth?> I ask her.

<Whoa. Oaken, is that you?>

<It is.>

<I hear you in my head, but I'm not sure where you are.>

<I'm the bird perched on the branch above you. A red kite, to be specific.>

<Wow! You have wings! You can fly! I bet you feel really good about that!>

<I do.>

<You're magic, Oaken.>

<Nah, it's not me so much but the earth that's magical.>

<I'm pretty sure you're magic.>

<Tell me more about yourself, Slomo. What's it like to live here? I'd like to hear some of your adventures.>

<Is it okay that most of them begin with me dangling upside down like this?>

<O' course! An adventure without dangling is no adventure at all.>

<Whoa! Really? That means practically my whole life is an adventure! I never realized!>

<That's okay, love. Few people do.>

CHAPTER 17

t he Thor I'd met in the past—and watched die under the blade of Moralltach—had worn blond hair, which was different from the *Eddas*, where he had bright red or even orange hair, but it wasn't a detail I had worried about at the time. People can have whatever color hair they want, so I imagined gods could figure out some way to do the same. Everything else had matched the old stories: He drove a chariot pulled by flying goats, he wielded Mjöllnir, and he had the ability to sling lightning around like a painter applying gouache to a canvas. So was this Thor re-manifested due to the significant number of pagans who still worshipped him around the world, or had this been the real Thor all along, and Leif had slain some other, convincing manifestation? Either way, I'd been played, and when my eyes slid to Odin I saw him staring back at me with a huge grin on his face. He laughed openly at my expression. Freyja caught it and she looked my way as well, and her smile was anything but friendly.

I don't often get a cold, squirmy feeling of fear in the pit of my stomach, but when I do, it's because I realize I'm surrounded by enemies on all sides and I'm most likely not going to survive the day. Or maybe I'm going to suffer something worse than death. The assembled deities were rather famous for doling out such punishments, and Jesus had warned me on more than one occasion I would suffer more pain than I had ever known as a result of my invasion of Asgard. It was a debt he'd made clear I would one day have to pay, and every instinct I had told me I should flee the field now, because that day had come. The Æsir had the Fae, the dark elves, and some significant Greco–Roman assistance ready to meet Loki and Hel. Chances were I wasn't going to sway the battle all by myself. I'd already taken care of Jörmungandr—or, rather, Laksha had—but eliminating him had been the specific request Odin had made of me in lieu of a blood price for Thor's (supposed) death. My oath was fulfilled—though it was apparently extracted from me based on a lie. My obligations were quite thoroughly discharged.

Except for the greater obligation I had to Gaia. Should Loki's forces break through, the destruction they would wreak on the world—the lives lost—would be incalculable. And just as I believed Jesus when he said I had a whole lot of pain coming my way, I also believed him when he said I was one of the few who could minimize the destructive consequences of this mess. By taking out Jörmungandr, Laksha had certainly saved many people and plenty of livestock. The yeti had saved more by stopping Surt before he could erupt for more than a few minutes. If I could save anyone by staying, I had to do it.

Surprising everyone, Fand sounded the charge first and led the Fae into battle with Manannan Mac Lir by her side, winged pixies and sprites floating above a motley horde of boggarts, barghests, spriggans, and other creatures. Brighid followed close behind with her host, almost indistinguishable from Fand's except in proportions of this type of faerie or that. I followed close behind them, figuring they were a safer bet for me than joining any portion of the Æsir forces. A wedge of *draugar* advanced to meet them from the volcano's slopes, and I realized after a few seconds that it was proportional. But whereas the combined Fae host was a significant chunk of our forces, it was only a sliver of theirs. The scale of what we faced sank in, and that cold tremor in my stomach shivered and solidified into a block of ice.

Speaking of which, the two surviving yeti marched with Manannan, whirling blades at the ready since their frost magic would be minimally effective against the *draugar*. I didn't like them being at the front; they had already sacrificed enough, and I didn't want the yeti to be erased from the earth. There was also a small forest of yewmen—good call bringing them along. They were hard to kill.

I had to break into a slow jog to keep up. The charge was not a full-speed plunge into clashing weapons just yet, but it would build.

Casting a glance over my shoulder, I saw Odin nod to the Olympians. Zeus ordered them to fall in behind us and he led the way, gliding obscenely above the field with his battle boner, a savage grin peeking through his beard. Thunderheads roiled above us now: With Zeus, Jupiter, and Thor on the field, there would be plenty of thunder and lightning. I wondered where Perun was, thinking that his friendly, hairy personage would be a welcome addition to this battle, but he was no doubt occupied elsewhere with troubles in his Slavic lands. It would be a certainty that the Sisters of the Three Auroras were protecting people in Poland.

We kept closing the distance, and I periodically checked behind to see how the armies would deploy; they were obviously deferring to Odin, and I wondered why I never got that memo or a nice outline of the battle plan, highlighted in neon colors and annotated in red pen.

Had Fand's charge been the plan all along, or was Odin improvising according to developments on the field? At least he wasn't smiling at me in mockery anymore. With any luck I had not deployed as he expected, though I'm sure that whatever Odin had planned for me, he had already thought through multiple scenarios.

The Svartálfar did not fall in behind but rather advanced on the left to flank, and that would require a response at some point from the *draugar*. The Álfar spread out to the right flank—yes, probably wise to keep them away from the Svartálfar. The dwarfs with their rune-carved weapons reinforced the middle, the Vanir behind them, and then finally the tightly packed ranks of the Einherjar advanced, shields and axes ready.

I pumped myself up with bindings for strength and speed and then cast camouflage as well, even though it was an energy hog. If there was ever a time not to hold back, this was it. I needed every advantage Gaia was willing to give me.

The Fae host began to move faster, a roar of defiant voices Doppler-shifting louder and louder, venting their rage and stress, as all living creatures asked themselves why they were rushing toward their probable deaths and struggled to come up with a reason that was worth it. Mere orders don't really cut it, not when you have time to think about what's coming, and not once you realize you're probably going to get cut down but you'd be cut down for deserting as well. The only way out is through, and that's where battle cries come from: an abyss of desperation and sheer, utter rage that someone is standing in the way of your own safety and the safety of those you love.

I didn't see the actual first clash of the armies, since I was somewhat to the rear of the initial action, but I heard the clang of metal and the death grunts and smelled the spray of blood, saw the lines of fighters in front of me crumple together like an accordion, saw the pixies surge forward in pairs, razor wire held between them as they flew on either side of the *draugar* and clotheslined them at the throat, neatly slicing through them so that their heads toppled off like unbalanced watermelons. It took all their strength to do that, though, so they had to ascend rapidly and loop around after each kill to build up speed again. Some of them didn't climb fast enough and got cut down. Some of the *draugar* saw them coming and became incorporeal in time so that the wire passed through them harmlessly, which meant the pixies could continue forward or try to come around for another pass, and when one pixie opted for one thing and the other didn't, it ruined the attack, one or more of the pixies died, and the razor wire got dropped. Which is not to say they made no difference. They did. They must have cut through close to a third of the necks they set out to sever, and that eased the first crush just enough to keep from getting overwhelmed, though it was a close thing.

We knew the weakness of the *draugar,* and they knew it too: They were prepared to parry a swipe at their heads and then they got to counterstrike anywhere, because their opponents were vulnerable everywhere. The *draugar* were brutal, strong, and effective warriors, if not especially creative. They absorbed any damage to their bodies and simply kept coming, death rattles quaking in the air as they took joy in slaying without consequences—for they could suffer no fate worse than they had already suffered in Hel, and returning there would be returning home now.

The helmets were proving problematic for most of the Fae. They were providing just enough protection to keep the *draugar* standing after the first blow, and they rarely had to absorb a second. Many of the Fae were falling as a result and I felt ineffective. I couldn't very well go through the middle of the Fae lines without potentially doing them harm with my cold iron aura, so I sprinted around to the right flank, where the Álfar were advancing, keeping the Fae between me and the dark elves on the left. There I could finally join battle myself and be grateful once again to the ancient enchantment on Fragarach's blade that allowed it to cut through any armor. The *draugar* had no protection against my sword, and it cut through necks or crunched through skulls quite well. I could at least hold my own against them, even if their endless numbers meant I could not advance.

The Fae did not enjoy any such advantages. They were getting cut down as often as not, a one-to-one ratio that didn't favor our side when we were already so outnumbered. We could hope for reinforcements—the Norse and Olympian gods had yet to wade into the mêlée—but they would need to do far better.

The Álfar and Svartálfar pinched in from either side, and while both had a visible impact, it was the dark elves that proved to be far more effective. Their ability to become incorporeal served them well against similar abilities of the *draugar*. They dissolved into smoke, using the discipline they called *Sigr af Reykr*, and then materialized inside the guards of their targets, thrusting black blades up underneath the chin and into the brain. The left side of the field began to visibly wilt under that onslaught, just as the Fae line visibly crumpled before the *draugar*. The Álfar, to my mind, were doing very little to reduce the *draugar* numbers. They had shields and terrific armor that protected them against the *draugars'* strikes but made few killing blows of their own. They earned a biscuit for suffering few losses and containing the enemy, I supposed, but they weren't winning the battle so much as not losing.

And then Hel got involved, unseen somewhere in the back, having shrunk, along with Loki, to normal size. But her influence on the battle was outsized in proportion: She took control of the fallen Fae—those that still had their heads, anyway—and raised their corpses from the dead to turn and fight against their former comrades. Pixies and pumpkinheads, spriggans and sprites, all rose from the field and turned on their erstwhile friends, thrusting bronze swords and spears into living bodies, faces lit with surprised expressions as they died.

Since Fand and Manannan were at the front, they were among the first to be attacked, and Manannan didn't care. He just kept with the hewing and cleaving; he was wielding Moralltach, the blade that spread necrosis through the body with a single cut and that Leif Helgarson had used to slay whatever iteration of Thor that had been. Against *draugar* it worked well, surprisingly, since they were already dead. But part of their flesh must still have responded to nerve impulses, and Moralltach's infection made sure they couldn't, so they collapsed, doubly dead without being beheaded. The Fae fell to its iron content as much as to its enchantment, and Manannan put them down for good.

But Fand wasn't able to defend herself against her own beloved Fae. Or perhaps she would have, given time enough to think it through. What happened instead was that she froze, confronted with a reanimated spriggan she quite probably knew by name and had seen fall moments before, and it did not hesitate to take advantage of her hesitation. Its wooden digits already lengthened and sharpened into claws, it closed in, heedless of its own defense, and I saw Fand's mouth drop open in shock, then widen further along with her eyes as the spriggan's deadly claws punched through a gap in her armor and pierced something vital. She must have cried out, though I couldn't hear it, and the light winked out in her eyes as she slumped, already dead before she hit the ground.

Being in camouflage allowed me a bit of time to pick and choose my targets, since the *draugar* in front of me were uncertain what seemed to be killing all their buddies. They came in slowly but they kept coming, and I hacked a few more down in panic, because I had a horrible premonition of what would happen next. Fand and I had never gotten along, but she was deeply loved by the Fae and by Manannan Mac Lir—and Manannan was someone I did admire and respect and with whom I'd enjoyed a long history, even friendship. I hurt for him instantly and felt hot tears watering the corners of my eyes. I had to take care of two more *draugar* before I could glance over again, and that's when Manannan realized that his wife had fallen, because the same spriggan who'd killed her tried to take him out too. The strike on his right side failed to penetrate his armor, and the bite of Moralltach put the spriggan down, but he realized he shouldn't have taken an attack from that side unless Fand was no longer protecting it. He looked down, saw her still and beyond care, and he fell to his knees beside her, throwing his sword away to gather her up in his arms and scream her name to bring her spirit back to this side of the veil. That was precisely what I'd feared. The undead Fae and the *draugar* didn't stop to let him mourn. They kept coming, as they kept coming at me. I beheaded another *draugr,* flicked my eyes briefly to the left, and saw multiple attackers cut down the grief-stricken Manannan Mac Lir, one of the eldest and most noble of the Tuatha Dé Danann, far more a god of love in his behavior than Aenghus Óg ever was, a man capable of loving and giving to all, and he would never have come to this end if it weren't for me. I went on a bit of a tear after that, hacking through these confused spirits in long-dead husks who had no particular motivation to press on except to escape Hel for a while.

"I'm so sorry, Manannan," I said, wondering if those words would ever reach his ears, somewhere in Tír na nÓg on the other side of the veil. When I was next able to look over, the Fae host was in full retreat, demoralized completely by the deaths of their leaders and the realization that should they die, their corpses would rise to fight those who remained. A maddening, amplified laugh bubbled up from the vicinity of the volcano: Loki was amused.

Some of the Fae rallied to Brighid's fire—she was again airborne on a pillar of flame, looking invincible in that armor she'd forged herself—but most of Fand's army was broken, streaking back to the point where they'd shifted into the plane.

The lone bright spot was the yeti, Oddrún and Ísólfr, who could not be overwhelmed and whose whirling blades were devastating against the *draugar*. They slowed and disoriented attackers with sprays of frost to the face, then stabbed them with the tip of those blades that drank the soul within—no decapitation necessary. When they saw Manannan fall, they rallied to his side and beat back the swarm of undead Fae even as the living Fae broke into a retreat. Then Ísólfr held off multiple attackers while Oddrún encased her father and Fand together in a block of ice to prevent them from being reanimated by Hel. She pushed them along a slick track of ice she created toward Brighid's forces, with Ísólfr and then the yewmen covering their retreat. I rather hoped the yeti would simply continue to the south and leave the field, for both their victories and their losses already exceeded anyone else's.

I had no illusions that the Fae who joined with Brighid's forces to fight in the second wave represented anything but a few individual triumphs; in the first clash, we'd been routed, gods had fallen, and the forces of Loki and Hel had only been strengthened by fresh meat for the necromancer's commands. The dark elves were already tiring, and the Álfar were doing little but maintaining the right flank—and they were themselves in danger of being flanked by the remainder of Hel's army.

We would need to do much better or the people of Sweden would never see the sunrise. Nor, for that matter, would much of Europe.

CHAPTER 18

Yama King Wuguan looks like the sort of fighter that relies on brute strength to win the day. He'll gladly take some hits so long as he gets in a good one on you, because he thinks one is all it will take. And maybe he's right. Even if he doesn't finish me like One-Punch Man—an anime hero I've been enjoying recently—he'll probably do enough damage that he can administer the coup de grâce with little resistance. So it's probably best that I get out of the way of his leap. I can't engage his sword when it's way above my head.

And I feel that this is a test somehow. Wukong clearly wishes to see if I can defeat Wuguan before he teaches me anything else, and I suppose it's fair. If we're supposed to fight eight progressively tougher Yama Kings, I should be able to defeat the guy at the halfway point if I expect to stick around until the end.

Is it perhaps a test for Wuguan as well? Is he trying to move up in the hierarchy of Diyu or perhaps escape it entirely for a cushier job in one of the heavens? I know nothing about him or what must be his very long history, other than what I see.

It occurs to me as I scramble to my right—Wuguan's left—that

I've been fighting alongside beings that are older than Atticus, and that's the sort of realization that can make you feel pretty small when you're only in your thirties. Especially since I've gradually gotten a sense of the scale that such a lifetime represents after listening to Atticus's stories. He lived nineteen centuries or so without access to plumbing, for example, which makes me cringe. The few times I've had to go without a toilet were unhappy and uncomfortable and I kept thinking about what could bite me. He must think we're all pampered hedonists.

I take nothing for granted regarding Wuguan's leaps, because if he could skate around in the air like the Monkey King, then normal physics would not apply. I automatically execute a blocking maneuver for an attack that isn't there yet but abruptly arrives a moment later. The impact nearly rips Scáthmhaide from my hand. He *does* have those abilities, he's as strong as I feared, and he is much faster than his bulk would suggest.

The battle continues to rage around us, but a space is cleared somehow for our duel; the damned must have received some signal—there must be plenty riding on this for both of us. The Monkey King and his clones are still fighting the rest of the demons and the damned all around the mountain, protecting the people of Taipei and not simply watching the duel, except in brief glances. I don't understand why I was singled out for this, but I doubt Wuguan will pause to explain. And I doubt I will have much time to win; if he's in Wukong's class as a fighter, then he outclasses me.

Wukong pointed out on the roof of his shop that my fighting patterns are recognizable and easily countered. They are essentially Chinese methods that Atticus taught me, after all, and old ones at that—so old that they're almost new again. But Wuguan knows them as Wukong does. I show him something he's going to recognize and counter, then mix in something he doesn't: My staff whirls around in my right and he expects it to land in my left hand, so he slaps it away, expecting me to be open to counterstrike—and I will be. Except that I've palmed a knife and thrown it at his right eye while his arm and sword were out of position, a gamble that pays off as it sinks home. His reflexive flinch ruins his counterstrike, but he surprises me with a stiff kick to the midsection as I try to close in, covering his retreat. He's annoyed to be feeling pain instead of dealing it, and I'm out of breath and on my ass, my diaphragm bruised and a couple of ribs cracked. He yanks the knife out of his eye and tosses it at me, and I'm able to roll in time to have it sink into my left upper arm instead of my own eye. I pull it out and crank the healing on high.

We both take time to reset after that. He presents his left side, sword held defensively, so that he can keep his remaining eye on me. I roll to my feet and wonder how I'm going to surprise him now that he's wary. He still has a tremendous advantage in strength and reach. In the plus column, he won't want to be taking those huge leaps anymore, for fear I'll get around to his blind side. In the minus column, that armor means he's not vulnerable anywhere else to a knife throw and now he's going to be guarding that weakness intensely.

Which . . . might be good? I check to confirm that I have two throwing knives left. I palm one in my right hand and twirl it. That's right, big guy. Lookit the shiny knifey.

A couple of twirls with the staff in my left while I'm still twirling the knife in my right, and I'm watching how his eye tracks this. He flickers to the staff but keeps his eye on my knife and also on my hips to watch for telltales there. Good. Movements with my left arm and wrist he won't be watching—or he's confident he knows what I'll be doing there. That's where I need to surprise him. I lunge forward with a conventional attack and throw the knife to see what he does. He blocks the staff and ducks the knife, then slashes at me with a damn fast cut that would have taken off my beard if I had one. Good to know.

I pluck out my last knife and make the same throwing motion but don't release. He buys the feint and I do a double-tap with Scáthmhaide wielded in my left hand: once on the flat of his blade, knocking it aside, then thrusting forward into the space where I think his cheek will be as he ducks my phantom throw, and it connects hard. He howls and staggers back, that left eye now instinctively closed, and he can't see until he opens it again. I throw the knife for real this time and it sinks into his throat. He's losing blood and is unable to breathe in addition to having trouble seeing, so he's not at the top of his game when I come in to finish him. I tee off on his face and he falls backward, his head a shattered mess inside his helmet. Fare thee well, Wuguan.

His death—or, rather, his melting away—has the curious effect of destroying all his minions a minute later. They converged on me after the duel but then exploded into goo before I could engage more than two of them. The mountain is clear and I'm expecting the Monkey King to give me some approval at this point, but instead when I look at him he leans on his staff and frowns.

"You could have let that go on a little longer," he says.

That makes absolutely no sense to me and I say as much. "What? Why would I increase my risk that way?"

"You defeated him so quickly that he lost face and recalled all his souls."

"But that's good, right? We won! People are safe."

Wukong shakes his head and waggles his hand at me. "Four more Yama Kings to go. And now that you've humiliated one of them, they'll be coming for you. Not Taipei. Not the mainland. You."

"Oh, well, that's just great. You could have warned me ahead of time that in addition to my own life or death, I'd have to worry about fragile egos too."

"I didn't think it would be necessary. Fragile egos are at the root of almost every conflict. My ego is certainly what motivated me in my younger years. Did you know that I once demanded to be called the Great Sage, Equal to Heaven?"

I throw up a hand to stifle a laugh and try to turn it into a cough. "I may have read some stories that mentioned that."

He's not fooled. "You may laugh. I deserve it. But I am no longer of that mind, and I have a different name now."

"Yes, I've heard. The Buddha Victorious in Strife. May I ask . . ."

"Of course."

"Why is a Buddha spending his time serving bubble tea?"

He shrugs. "It is a simple pleasure that tends to make people happy. And when they see that they can be made happy by something so simple, then all their other grand desires seem silly by comparison—for indeed they are. A Buddhist wishes to point out that desires are what prevent people from achieving happiness, that materialism is the cause of discord. The simple pleasure of bubble tea gets them to a receptive place to hear that message. Or to reinforce that message, if they've already heard it."

I suddenly cannot keep myself from smiling as I mentally take note of what I'm doing: I am talking to the Monkey King in Taiwan about Buddhism. My life has become far more dangerous since becoming a Druid, but at the same time, I get to talk to living legends.

It's at that point that Seven Star Mountain explodes again.

CHAPTER 19

Slomo tells me of the birds she likes and the birds she doesn't.
The insects who bite and who leave her alone. The monkeys,
screeching and leaping around her, eating yellow tube fuel. The
colorful moths and butterflies snapped up by croaking frogs. The
thrilling quiet that settles in the forest when the jaguars pass
through. Her occasional, half-hearted yearnings to find a mate, but
even yearning was more energy than she wanted to expend.

<Mostly you have to have perspective. Is anything—short of
teeth coming at my face—worth burning more than the basic calories I need to eat and not fall out of the tree? The answer is no.
Except for swinging around like a monkey. That was totally worth
the calories. Because I didn't have to burn them. They were free.
Like sunshine.>

<What about things that make ye happy? Aren't those things
worth burning some calories for?>

<Well, sure, but what makes me happy is not moving very
much.>

<How can ye say that? Ye just said you've never been happier
than when ye moved like a monkey.>

\<I'm complicated. There's a lot of nuance you're missing here.\>

\<I can handle nuance. Bring me the nuance.\>

\<Okay, you asked for it.\> And then me mind is bombarded by images and emotions, all relating to a sliding scale of satisfaction with staying still through a wide range of environmental factors. Bearing witness to frenetic activity while remaining almost motionless gives Slomo great pleasure, but she can visualize and imagine things so well. When I ask her why that is, she replies, \<Well, you have to imagine quite a bit when you're incapable of moving very fast or doing all the things other creatures do.\>

\<Would ye like to see more of the world, move fast like ye did, more often?\> I ask her.

\<Sure. But wishing won't make it so.\>

\<Ye don't have to wish for it. Ye can come with me. I'll show you a few places.\>

\<Places where those buffalo things roam?\>

\<If ye like. Deserts. Oceans. Mountains.\>

\<But aren't those far away?\>

\<Yes, but I can move very fast.\>

\<Won't they have a disturbing lack of leaves?\>

\<We can bring some with us. Or just come back quickly before ye get hungry again.\>

Slomonomobrodolie chews on the idea along with a leaf, slowly enough that I can hear the exquisite crunch and grind of her teeth and perhaps the churning of metaphorical gears in her head. When she finishes, her eyes refocus on me and she nods, upside down.

\<Okay, Oaken. I'd like to see some of those things.\>

\<Great! I have some questions first. How old are you?\>

She answers and I continue to ask, absorbing as many basic facts as I can and combining them with a fluid understanding of her personality so that I'll be able to shift with her safely. And in truth there is no hurry until I'm asked to be somewhere again. A couple of hours pass with her sharing her life with me in pictures and feelings, and I can sense I'm getting attached to the lass. She doesn't like toucans, for example, because they have wee beady eyes of death and huge beaks.

<The large, colorful beaks,> she explains, <are there to distract you from the eyes. If you look into a toucan's eyes you will know the heart of evil, and what's more, you will know they'd like to eat you.>

<What, they're meat eaters?>

<I don't really think so. I'm not sure! But the eyes, Owen, you have to listen to what the eyes are telling you! They always say that even though they don't normally enjoy meat, they would make an exception *just for you* and snap your flesh away from your bones with terrible little toucan beak-clacking sounds.>

<Well, I kind of hope I don't meet any now. That sounds worse than garnishing your cocktail glass with a log of shite instead of a nice lime wedge.>

<What are cocktails?>

<I'll have to get you one,> I promise her, and then the elemental summons me. I'm needed somewhere in Europe because some daft donkey cock has gone and messed with powers he shouldn't have. <Time to go,> I says to Slomo. <Ready to see the world?>

<Sure, Oaken! I'll start moving now and we can probably leave before the sun comes up.>

The sun wasn't down yet, so that's an alarming estimate. I shoot her some more juice and her eyes pop wide.

<Bollocks to that. We have to scurry now. Climb down and drape yourself on me back. I'm going to shift to human.>

<I've never scurried before! This is exciting!>

I float down to the forest floor and shift to human, and Slomo is ready to hop on after a few seconds. *Careful with those claws, now. Wrap your arms around me neck and I'll catch ye.*

She leaps and lands with a grunt, and I grunt as well. She's a bit prickly, not as soft as she might look, because that fur is matted and filthy. My skin begins to tickle; she wasn't lying about the bugs living on her, which I guess are now having a look around at this new thing she's hanging on that isn't a tree. I take time to reach their tiny brains—nothing more than a few nerves—and tell them to stay on Slomo. Not sure they're going to make the shift, honestly, but they might, as Slomo considers them to be a part of her.

I have to jog through the brush and get used to the weight, and it's bouncy for both of us.

<Is this a scurry?>

A bit. It's also called riding piggyback, though I don't know why. Never seen a single feckin' pig do this. Language is strange.

<I hope I get to learn your language. I can teach you Slothian words if you want.>

I'd like that. Okay. Here we are. This tree is special. We can use it to shift to Tír na nÓg and from there to practically any other place on the planet. But I need ye to put one of your hands on that tree.

<Whoa, what's Tír na nÓg? There were a lot of images with that.>

It's many things. Mostly magic and bollocks, but not magical bollocks, if ye take my meaning.

<I don't think I do.>

Just hold on.

We shift through, pulling along the tether, and I hold the wonder of Slomonomobrodolie in me second headspace, hoping I don't cock it up, for it would be a tragedy if I brought her to any harm. I pause on the other side to check on her.

How was that?

<Whoa! I mean, wow, Oaken, that was—I don't know. My stomachs are doing flippy-floppy monkey business. It's possible I might—>

A hot juicy something lands on me shoulder and drips down me chest.

<—Be sick. Yeah. Uuaagh. It's a sure thing, actually. Sorry. Those were good leaves too. You know, I think I recognize one of

them! I guess I didn't chew that very well because I was so excited about how delicious it looked.>

How are your bugs?

<My bugs? I imagine they're fine. I still feel them and stuff.>

Great. This is Tír na nÓg. Full of trees, but not the kind you're used to eating. We're going to do that one more time, so hold on to your stomachs.

I shift to the tether point that Gaia wants me to use, though I'm not sure precisely where it is. Somewhere to the north and east of where I was before—in Europe, certainly, but north of the mountains and east of Germany. I might actually be in Poland—I'm not sure where the modern borders are drawn. All I know is that it's quiet enough to hear Slomo barf wetly on me shoulder again.

<Urrrgh. Sorry, Oaken.>

It's okay, lass, I tell her, brushing it away. *Maybe ye will get used to it. And maybe we won't shift very much from now on.*

<I like that second idea. So where are we?>

On the other side of the world from your jungle. This is across an ocean or two.

<It's drier here. I mean, I can feel the air is dry.>

Wait until you feel a desert. Okay. I have to find out from the elemental what we're here to do, and then there may be some action.

<More action? I have already experienced more today than I have in my whole life!>

This might be the kind of action where ye have to defend yourself. You've done that before, haven't ye?

<Once or twice. So much energy, though!>

Don't worry about energy. I'm going to give ye all ye need. Just make sure whatever ye see goes down instead of you. Those claws of yours can do some real damage if ye put some muscle behind it. Move fast as ye can and don't give anything the chance to hurt ye.

<What are we going to fight?>

We'll find out soon enough.

The elemental tells me where to go: It's a decent jog of a couple of miles, because there aren't any tethered trees closer than that, but after only a wee while Slomo asks if she can follow along in the trees. We're running through some woods that are close enough to allow swinging in the branches, and she argues that it will probably be a smoother ride for both of us. I agree, and the weight soon lifts from me back and she hoots as she takes to the branches, her long arms propelling her from tree to tree.

Have fun but try to do it quietly, I says. *We don't want to announce that we're coming.*

The objective, I'm told, is to close a portal to the Christian hell that someone has managed to open. Hell was supposed to stay out of this fight, I thought, but some gobshite didn't get that particular memo. Which means I have to deal not only with whatever's coming out of that portal but with whatever sorcerer had the moxie to open it.

Perhaps I'll get lucky and find that the sorcerer got eaten by what came out of hell. Siodhachan's stories about it suggest that happens as often as not.

<There are lights and grunty fighty sounds ahead, Oaken,> Slomo tells me.

Oh, aye? After a moment I see and hear them too. *I'm glad you're in the trees. Stay up there unless ye have good reason to come down.*

I'm a bit more worried about her being here than I was before, because Siodhachan's stories about hell are flooding back and they're not the shiny happy sort. I've never had to deal with the Christian hell meself, because that whole religion came along and flourished while I was stuck on that Time Island. The day Siodhachan told me that Christians drove the Druids out of Ireland and then the Irish wound up killing one another over different versions of Christianity centuries later was an especially dark stretch of a dark feckin' day. A notable detail about the religion is how much effort is spent on imagining eternal punishments after death. Plenty of faiths have richly imagined hells, Siodhachan assures me, but apparently the Christian one deserves the biggest slice of bread pudding at the end of the night. So many demons and devils eager to torture souls—so eager, in fact, that they want to trade for them and are willing to deal with sorcerers to get what they want: more deaths, more corrupted souls. And should they be set loose on this plane, they will never hesitate to kill anything living in hopes that it might increase their own power, especially since it reinforces the idea that they *are* hellish and to be feared, a circular thought pattern within the faith that they exploit. It's no place for a sloth to be dangling around.

I come to a small clearing in the forest that's been turned into a battlefield with multiple light sources. One of them is the moon and stars above. There's an orange-red glow coming from the open portal to hell, which is rapidly draining the elemental's energy—the entire reason I've been called. But there are also other lights, purple cones surrounding thirteen women as they battle the horrors coming out of hell and the white light of whips they're using like scourges to banish the horrors from this plane.

I have to stop to take it all in, because it's as intense and alarming as a chopped ghost-pepper poultice applied directly to the genitals—with forethought, and malice.

What I'm seeing fits with stories Siodhachan has told me before. These must be the Polish witches he told me about, the Sisters of the Three Auroras, who derive their powers from goddesses called the Zoryas. The purple cones surrounding them are protective wards, and those weapons they're lashing around are hellwhips. And that smell is entirely from hell.

<Oaken, something smells really bad. Like even worse than jaguar poots,> Slomo says, <and in case you didn't know, there is no poot in the world worse than a jaguar poot.>

I file that information away to share later with Granuaile.

That's the demons. Stay away from them, all right? If any come near, I want ye to get away if ye can, take off their heads if ye can't.

<Which are the demons?>

The ones that smell bad and try to kill ye.

<Got it.>

The sorcerer is on the far side of the portal: Some sad scabby punk of a lad who thinks the world owes him something, and he's come to collect. I put on me brass knuckles and call out the name I remember from Siodhachan's stories—the leader of the coven, if I'm not mistaken. "Malina! Can I help?"

Most of the witches do not react, but one of them looks in my direction after finishing off some monstrosity that looks like an ambulatory slime mold with eyes.

"Who are you?" she shouts, backing up and flailing the hell-whip around in front of her in a defensive pattern. She has long straight blond hair falling over her shoulders, most likely the finest hair I've ever seen in me whole life, and like the rest of her coven, she's dressed in something black that I suspect must be fashionable these days. I don't know how to describe it in modern terms, but basically, if I were a wee lass, I would look at Malina and want to grow up to be her someday, and even as a grown man I'm more than a bit sad that I will never, ever look as good as she does destroying evil. Kind of glad, actually, that me young apprentices aren't here to see this, or else they might not want to be Druids anymore.

"Owen Kennedy, Druid of Gaia. The man who taught that O'Sullivan lad!"

She squints at me for a moment, probably confirming that I have the requisite tattoos and am bound to the earth, and then she nods. "If you can take out the sorcerer, that would be helpful."

Helpful, she says! That would end the whole fecking game, the way I see it, but it's not the sort of thing to raise a fuss about. I'm here to close that portal, and everything else is a distant second to

that. I just don't want to get mistaken for an enemy in this blood-
bath and get lashed with one of their hellwhips.

I circle around to the left, running clockwise, as they say, and
plow me fist through the face of something orange and toothy that
tries to stop me. It explodes under the knuckles and falls over in a
shower of its own ichor, but that only draws the attention of four
more horrors. I realize that none of them are flying and I might be
able to avoid some messy bollocks by shifting shapes. I strip off me
shirt and shift to a red kite, soaring above the demons and circling
around behind the sorcerer. The clever bindings Creidhne worked
into the knuckles mean the brass has flowed down to me talons,
and I'm thinkin' as I glide behind the sorcerer that it's going to be
so easy to simply latch on to his neck from behind, clutch, and tear
away his throat. Easiest mission of the whole day, and on top o'
that, I get to look cool in front of the cool kids of the coven.

Except it doesn't work out that way. Nope.

Instead, I run into an invisible wall like a fecking dumbass spar-
row assaulting a glass door and flail in a mess o' feathers, head
buzzing from the impact, until I hit the dirt outside a ring of salt.

Ah, the protective ring. That's what happened to me. When I'm
shape-shifted, I'm precisely the sort of thing the sorcerer's wards
are designed to keep out. The ring detects the magical aura of my
bound shape and denies me access. Well, lad, good on you. But I
can shift back to human and obliterate your fecking salt, can't I?

I perform the shift and grunt, and he hears it. He whirls around
and it's a face of blue-eyed madness I see, paranoid testosterone
that's been let out of the barn. Some young punk who's either never
had the shite beat out of him, so he doesn't understand that there
will be consequences for his actions, or who's been beaten so much
and so badly he doesn't give a blistered tit what happens to him
next. He's poxy as a baby swaddled in poison ivy and as incensed
about it as ye might expect. He shouts something at me—in Polish,
I suppose—and I don't understand a word of it but I sure feel whatever it is he casts my way. His hand thrashes and clutches and I

suddenly feel like all me muscles are clenching at once except for me arse, which is relaxing at precisely the wrong time. It hurts more than anything is rightfully supposed to and I can't think of what to do except to cast healing on meself before he kills me. I'm spraying shite around the forest, thinking this is not the way I wanted to die, and also that maybe Siodhachan had a point about the uses of cold iron, when something savage bugles above me head. I throw up a forearm, hoping to protect meself from whatever it is, but it turns out that it's not some hellspawn come to snack on me spleen. I'm not even the target—that would be the poxy sad sack who's draining Gaia with his festering hellhole.

It's Slomonomobrodolie, leaping down from high up a tree to grasp on to the lad with one long arm around the back of the neck while she plunges the three long claws of her right hand directly into the blackguard's throat. She rips up and out, screaming in his face, and he manages a panicked gurgle and a surprised pair of eyes before he topples backward, ruining his salt circle and breaking who knows how many concurrently running spells. I guess the binding I used to give Slomo her energy wasn't enough magic to trigger his protective ward. All I know for sure is that I'm grateful to get control of me own arse again while the rest o' me relaxes. The lad was keeping the portal open through force of his own will, and with that gone, the portal closes on its own.

That doesn't mean it's all over, though. There are still plenty of hellspawn out there, and the sudden scent of spilled blood in the air has drawn them in our direction rather than toward the unspilled blood of the witches. Malina and some of the others snag a few of them, but that still leaves at least three pelting toward the body of the sorcerer, and me favorite killer sloth is sitting right on top of him.

Slomo! Back to the trees, fast! Climb high, hurry! I quite nearly shite meself again out of fear that I may have placed her in harm's way. I haven't even had time to properly appreciate that she just saved me ancient bones, and here she is in peril as a result. One of the things coming at her is mostly teeth and stomach, propelled by four legs underneath that look like an insect's, bending up and out and clawed at the feet. Another is a slimy red glob of a thing oozing far too quickly our way, with a tongue questing for fresh meat to wrap up and pull into its dark, moist mouth. The last demon looks like an angry avocado that's sworn to get revenge for all the world's guacamole, and it's moving the fastest. I scramble to me feet to intercept it as Slomo leaps to the nearest tree trunk. She's digging in with those claws and doing the best she can, but the damn avocado has zeroed in on her. It realizes at the last second that I'm not racing to beat it to the meal on the tree but am racing to pound its lumpy face instead. It tries a hiss and snarl to intimidate me, but I'm not the type that responds well to that bollocks.

When I plow me fist between its eyes, I discover that it's nothing like an avocado at all. It's more like a bag of something caustic that latches on to me skin and burns, and even though it falls over and melts into goo, I'm left with something burning away at me arm. I holler about it as the tongue from the other horror wraps around me midsection and yanks me through the air to its mouth. I make sure it gets a taste of me burning, slime-covered arm first, and when everything goes hot and wet and dark, I shape-shift to a bear and start lashing about with me claws. It can't barf me out fast enough, and I wind up clawing me way out of something dead and melting around me. These demons don't last long on this plane once you've destroyed what little shred of force is keeping them bound together. That's probably why those hellwhips of the witches are so effective. Malina demonstrates by lashing through the stomach of the toothy thing that's snacking on the remains of the sorcerer; it screams and dissolves into a mess on top of him, and I check to see that Slomo is safe before assessing what other threats might be around.

<Ye did good, lass. Are ye hurt?>

<I'm fine, Oaken! A bit shocked at how mad I got when that human was trying to hurt you but otherwise okay. Are you all right?>

<Nothing wrong with me that can't heal eventually,> I says, and in truth I already have that in progress, as much to test for damage as anything else. Whatever's burning me hasn't damaged the integrity of my tattoos, thank the gods below. <Where'd you learn to take someone down like that?> I ask Slomo.

<Oh. Watching jaguars hunt. They either leap on something and just bite through the head into the brain, because their jaws are really that strong, or they go for the throat. Quickest way to end it.>

I turn to see if there's anything else to worry about, but there's not so much as an angry gnat around. The portal's closed and harmony's restored. The witches have taken care of the rest of the hellspawn, but they're sure giving me the doubtful glare, muscles tense and weapons at the ready in case I turn on them. Probably because of the bear thing. I get that a lot.

Shifting back to human, I wave me uninjured hand at them to show them I'm friendly. I sure can't be hiding any weapons in me clothes, because I don't have any. They don't seem concerned with that at all; I think they're more interested in the ease of the shift itself than in what I've shifted to. I do notice that they're keeping their wards up.

"Owen Kennedy," I call to them, because no doubt several of them missed it when I first arrived. "Druid of Gaia. I was called here to close the portal, so that's done. Thanks for your help."

"Malina Sokołowska," the blond woman says with a charming accent, "leader of the Sisters of the Three Auroras. May I ask what killed the sorcerer? I was occupied and didn't see clearly."

"Oh, that was a sloth."

"A sloth? You have to be joking. There are no sloths around here, and they don't move that fast."

"She came with me, and they can move that fast when you give them enough energy."

One of the other witches titters. She has long blond hair as well, but it's pulled back and bundled up on top of her head. She also wears a pair of enormous eyeglasses. Malina turns to see what's so funny and the witch says, "We did see something in the divination that hinted at unexpected aid. I think a pumped-up murder sloth qualifies as unexpected." The whole coven either smiles or chuckles at this.

"Divination, eh? Is that what has ye out here in the woods?" I ask.

"It is. We're aware something truly frightening is going on in Sweden, but we wanted to address local threats. We've been keeping an eye on that guy for a while," she says, flicking a finger at the body, "and we saw that he planned to take advantage of the chaos elsewhere to further his own agenda."

"And what agenda would that be? Who was he?"

Malina shrugs. "Another man who wanted to climb to power on a ladder of violence."

"Well, I'm not one of those, if ye want to relax. I mean ye no harm."

She nods at me once and drops her wards. The others follow her lead, and one on the fringes holds up my shirt. "Your clothes are over here, if you want to get dressed."

I don't, especially; I'd rather dive into a lake somewhere and clean up, but methinks they want me to, so I jog over there and shove me shanks into the jeans and pull on the shirt.

"I appreciate what ye did here, taking care of all those beasties. That would have been a rough job to do by meself. So you're the coven Granuaile has been studying Polish with?"

"That's right," Malina says. "Would you be interested in learning the language also?"

"Perhaps someday, sure," I says. "But I'm still working on English at the moment."

She introduces the entire coven to me, and I'm subtly checking out auras as she does. They are no doubt assessing me as well. I've not had particularly good experiences with witches in the past; I've met more of the kind that behaved like the dead lad over there than the nurturing sort, but these don't have a trace of avarice or sullen resentment about them. Guile, sure. But they're confident and happy and clearly more interested in protecting their people than exploiting them. It wasn't always that way with this coven, according to Siodhachan, but even he admits that they've changed significantly since Malina took over. It reminds me how much awesome responsibility there is in being a leader and a teacher. And seeing them and how powerful they are together, it gives me hope for what me grove of young Druids could be one day. Of a sudden I feel a pang in me chest for them and wish for nothing so much but to catch up with them, wherever they are now, and teach them something new.

It's been one of me greatest pleasures, since I've come forward in time, to see the wonder light up their faces. And it's probably why I enjoy hanging out with Slomo too; she's seeing something new every moment she isn't dangling from a tree, and she loves it. Methinks I know why I find watching others learn to be so fulfilling now: Siodhachan let me know pretty clearly that I could have been a better teacher to him back in the old days. It wounded me pride, sure. There's nothing I can do to fix that now, but what I can do is be a better teacher for the grove—a far sight better—and so far I think I'm pulling it off.

"It's a pleasure to meet you all. Where am I, do ye mind me asking?"

"In the southeastern corner of Poland, near the border with Ukraine," Roksana tells me. She's the one with the glasses.

"Is there a lake nearby?"

"Lake Solina is only a few kilometers to the west. If you run that way, you can't miss it."

"Pretty big, eh?"

"Big enough for bath time, if that's what you have in mind."

"Aye, there's that, plus I want to show the sloth. She's never seen a lake, only rivers. Do ye need me to bury the body or anything before I go?"

"No, we'll take care of all this," Malina says, and I thank them again and say I look forward to meeting them in less dangerous circumstances before collecting Slomo from where she dangles and heading west a wee bit. As soon as we're out of sight, I strip again and shift to a bear, consigning those soiled clothes to history. Dawn is coming, the dark sky edging to gray, as Slomo climbs on me back. I give her a ride to the lake, which turns out to be a long, spidery thing that fills up some valleys by damming up a river on one side. Looks like lots of people enjoy boating on it, judging by all the moored craft I see along the shores. We pause while we're still a ways up a hillside so that Slomo can appreciate the sunrise hitting the surface and lighting up the hillsides opposite us.

<Wow, Oaken, that's pretty! Does all that water just sit there?>

<It has some circulation. It does drain at one end, somewhere. I want to go down there and have a swim. I have blood and shite and demon goo on me and I want it off. Want to come with me?>

<I don't like swimming,> she says, <but I'll go wash off the blood and stuff from my hands. I'm feeling a bit sad that I did that to him.>

<No need to feel sad. Ye saved me and the whole world a bunch of trouble. That lad wanted nothing but pain for everyone, and if ye had given him a chance he would have done the same to you.>

I start rambling downhill and Slomo is silent, taking it all in, I suppose, but I can tell she's thinking too. Finally she says, <He did seem to be pretty mad about stuff, which is strange because there's so much to be happy about. I mean, even when you figure in toucans, this huge world is pretty awesome. Maybe he's happier being dead in the sense that he's not angry about being alive?>

Slomo's attempts to rationalize the sorcerer's death fascinate me because she's focusing not on my safety or hers but rather on his happiness. I figure it's best to leave out the idea that his spirit is probably in the Christian hell now and he's unlikely to be happy there.

<No way to know for sure,> I says to her, <but I'm sure looking forward to getting clean, and I'm happy to be here with you.>

<Me too, Oaken! You know what's strange?>

<What's that?>

<I wouldn't be here looking at a lake or seeing any of the things that I've seen recently if that fireball hadn't almost killed me and awakened Pachamama. Strange how something so terrible can lead to something good afterward.>

<You're right, Slomo. I've been surprised by it too.> And that's no soft lie I'm telling her. Had Gaia not been placed in so much peril, I wouldn't have seen as much of her as I have recently and learned to love her even more, even as I'm beginning to grasp the scope of the work we have to do to bring her back to something close to balance. Siodhachan should take on a grove of apprentices like mine, and Granuaile too, when she feels ready. We need many more Druids.

Slomonomobrodolie climbs down off me back when we get to the shore. It's early enough that no one's around to marvel at the black bear and sloth on the shore. I wade on in and feel the insistent burn on me right forearm instantly cool down. Once I'm deep enough to feel me paws struggle to reach the bottom, I shift to human, take a startled gasp at the cold, and get meself all scrubbed.

Slomo is less than expert at washing herself. Those claws are great for climbing trees but do make softer tasks a bit troublesome. She's splashing around, rubbing her wrists awkwardly with the flat of her hands, but mostly she's getting frustrated.

Would ye like some help getting your claws and arms clean? My fingers might be able to handle the job.

<Oh, sure, Oaken, that would be great! I want to be clean, but I'm not very good at staying that way.>

Not to worry. Ye just described the fundamental state of being for most of us.

CHAPTER 20

Before Brighid's block of Fae can engage, the Olympians see room for sport between the flanks and swoop in to have their fun. And I do think they viewed it as fun—at least Zeus and Ares did, along with their Roman counterparts. The thunder gods flew down and hurled their gods of war at the mass of *draugar,* which had no immediate effect since the *draugar* allowed the armored bodies to pass through and roll on by. Ares and Mars came to a stop and began swinging huge maces around, sending some *draugar* flying through the air but not really ending any of them. They thought it all entertaining, depending on their armor to stop whatever attacks might get through their defenses. They were laughing. It was recreational for them, since they felt they had nothing to lose. They couldn't die, really; once their injuries became catastrophic, they would vacate their flesh and regenerate upon Olympus.

Zeus and Jupiter didn't deign to land and get involved. They just floated out of reach and smiled at Ares and Mars playing around. Athena and Minerva had not come to play, however, and neither had the Apollos. They went to work behind the others. The goddesses worked with bronze-tipped spears and the gods with shields and swords, thrusting blades through *draugr* faces and cutting down reanimated Fae. They'd been brought to the front by Hermes and Mercury, who dropped them off and then sailed over the *draugar,* wearing some strange goggles, scouting ahead for something—presumably to find where Hel and Loki had hidden themselves in the horde. Perhaps that's what Zeus and Jupiter were waiting for—a true target worthy of battle. They wanted to skip the minions and proceed directly to the boss fight, because there were Girl Scout Cookies on the line. I'm not sure Hermes and Mercury were up to the task, though. Maybe those goggles would allow them to see through illusions and maybe not. The Romans had used something like that to deconstruct camouflage and find the Druids in the old days—some invention of Minerva's. But seared into the flesh of both Loki and Hel was his mark, some sort of runic protection from divination that had obviously kept them hidden very well to this point, and Loki was a master of disguise. I doubted Minerva had come up with something to pierce his protections— unless those goggles showed them the magical spectrum. That would be the key to finding them both, but neither the Norse nor the Olympians were renowned for magical sight—Odin typically needed to be seated on Hlidskjálf, the silver throne, to see all. Of those remaining on the field, only Brighid and I had the ability to use it—unless there were other members of the Tuatha Dé Danann in her army somewhere. My guess was that she left some behind in case she didn't return.

I hadn't triggered my magical sight yet, because there was so much magic as well as actual gods flying around on the field that I figured it would be blinding. But it might also be the best way to end things: Taking out Hel would at least allow us to make significant progress against the horde. Some of the slain Álfar were beginning to rise from the dead, and since I was near them I needed to keep an eye out now for that as well as for *draugar*.

I backed away from the fight somewhat before I switched my

vision over. Being on the fringe and camouflaged allowed me that space. I triggered the charm on my necklace to the magical spectrum and had to blink and squint to filter through what I was seeing. The *draugar* had their own magic signature, and the Olympians were blinding white silhouettes off to the left. The Álfar, meanwhile, had plenty of magic baked into their armor. Except one of them nearby—quite close by—had a whole lot of extra something going on. His was a shifting riot of colors, magically speaking, and I had only seen a signature like that once before.

"Coyote?" I said. "Is that you?"

The elf slid a spear neatly in and out of a *draugr*'s eye and then turned to me with a smirk that was familiar even on another face. He slipped out of formation and came over to stand next to me, even though I was practically invisible.

"Sure is, Mr. Druid. Took you long enough to notice."

"What are you doing?"

"Oh, just slayin' the undead like one o' them regular elves, lookin' down this long white nose at everybody, feelin' fancy. Kinda wonderin' what these fellers use to wash their hair." He looked down at the thick braid falling down his chest and sniffed. "Smells like pears or something."

"Maybe you could ask later. I was just going to try to find Hel."

"Oh, you were? Might be able to save you a bit of trouble." A *draugr* broke through the Álfar line and came after him, but he dodged the blow. I raised my blade and he said, "No, no, don't kill it! I need one alive for a few seconds. Can you hold on to it?"

"For maybe a second. They're strong and they can become incorporeal." Though in truth I had not tried to put one in a hammerlock yet. Perhaps my cold iron aura would interfere with its ability to go ghostly and would keep it solid.

"Try, will ya?"

I dropped and swept the *draugr*'s legs, a move it wasn't expecting at all, and it landed heavily on the ground. I stomped on the flat of its sword, pinning it to the ground to make sure it didn't go anywhere, and Coyote leaned over on the other side, grabbing the bony left hand as if he were going to help it get up. The *draugr* was clearly confused, since neither of us seemed ready to kill it, and its wonder grew as Coyote's appearance shifted and rippled from the hand, from that of an elf to . . . a *draugr* that looked exactly like the one we have on the ground. A perfect copy, down to the smell and the exposed innards kept in by a shredded curtain of muscle. The trickster even had the rusty chain armor and helmet, the ratty leather boots, and a scrap of something belted around the waist.

"Okay, Mr. Druid," Coyote's new voice rattled. "You can kill it now."

I shoved Fragarach into the thing's face and it twitched once and expired. An ambitious elf who saw the new *draugr* behind the lines came over to take care of him, but I cried a warning, dropped my camouflage, and stepped in front of Coyote. I had to block a strike and shout in Old Norse before the elf got the idea he should stand down.

"This one's on our side," I explained, leaving out that Coyote is not a *draugr* at all. "He's going to lead us to Hel and help us take her down so she doesn't keep raising the dead." I half-turned to Coyote and muttered in English, "Smile and nod so he knows you're friendly."

Coyote waved at the elf with a twinkle-fingered flutter and tried to smile with his ruined, half-rotted face.

We wound up employing the elf to get us back through the line. I cast camouflage again and put a left hand on Coyote's shoulder as the elf led us to the front and made sure we didn't get cut down by any other elves. We were expelled into the horde and the *draugar* ignored Coyote as one of their own, flowing around him and showing zero interest in why he was going the wrong way. I followed in his wake and asked him where we were going.

"Hel's up on the hill, where she can maintain a view. I can see her from here."

"You can?" To me it was still a wash of magic, nothing distinct.

"Sure."

"Is Loki nearby?"

"He was earlier, but I don't see him now. Say, Mr. Druid, I've been wondering: If one o' them purty elves back there eats a burrito and poots, you think it smells like buttercups or something?"

"That would require them to have floral agents in their intestines."

"You say that like they don't. I bet they take supplements—poot supplements—to make them smell good. I want some so I can poot on people and have 'em compliment me on how fine it smells."

"It's good to have goals, Coyote."

"Heck yes. Fresh Poot Supplements would be a revelation if you made them available to humans. Folks would just be rippin' poots in cars and elevators without fear of embarrassment, because it would smell so fine. They'd probably eat more sauerkraut and beans. It would change the world and its standards of etiquette. It might even become polite to poot on someone when you first meet them."

If that seemed like an odd conversation to have in the middle of a battle, it was because our progress against the tide of undead was less than swift. It gave Coyote time to share his theories about elf poots and gave me plenty of time to look around and see the battle from the enemy's perspective.

The forces defending humanity looked pitifully small. Odin had ordered the Vanir and Einherjar forward to reinforce the center and support the flanks as well, but it appeared that Thor was summoning mist around them to hide the gods from view. Why would he do that, unless the Norse had some way of seeing through it?

My answer came perhaps a couple of minutes later, after watching Brighid's army meet the *draugar* and do somewhat better. They were at least cutting down more *draugar* than the others: The yew-men had come to the front and were taking plenty of punishment, while other Fae thrust forward with spears in between to slay the *draugar*. Better tactics. Brighid herself was fighting among them.

The Olympians continued to run amok in the midst of the *draugar,* thinking themselves invincible, until Loki struck back.

Ares was the first to fall, with an impossibly well-placed arrow finding the eye slot in his helmet and piercing into his brain. Mars fell the same way seconds later, and that's when Zeus and Jupiter realized that this wasn't a playground. They scanned the slope of the volcano for the source of the arrows and I suppose they found it, after a fashion, since they fell out of the sky with arrows protruding from their skulls too. I wondered if, once they re-spawned back on Olympus, they would look back at their brief participation in this battle and recognize their hubris. They had done very little damage for having such great reputations.

And that's when I remembered that Loki had stolen the Lost Arrows of Vayu from Granuaile in India, though I supposed now they must now be considered the Found Arrows. Those were long-distance godslayers, each of them enchanted to find its target. Very similar to Odin's spear, Gungnir, which always hit its target, or Thor's hammer, Mjöllnir. Hermes and Mercury went down next, having never found where Hel and Loki were hiding in the mob.

At least the mist around the Norse gods made sense now. Loki couldn't target them if he couldn't see them. But neither could the Norse gods really let loose with the threat of those arrows out there. Loki had effectively neutralized them.

Though he had really pissed off the remaining Olympians. Athena, Minerva, and the Apollos sped up from their patient, workmanlike pace of battle to reckless abandon. If they were going to be taken down by arrows too, they wanted to leave some mark on the field. But no further shafts appeared in godly skulls. Loki must have a limited supply, and he was almost certainly saving one for Odin.

The ones he'd let fly, however, could be recovered and shot again. In the teeming mass of bodies, I couldn't see if any *draugar* were currently bent to the task of recovering arrows, but Loki would be a fool not to at least make the attempt. If one of the Apollos, for example, got hold of one of those arrows, it could be employed against him.

"Did you see where those arrows came from?" I asked Coyote.

"What arrows?" he rasped.

"The ones that killed the Olympians."

"What? I missed that."

"How could you miss that? He just removed six gods from the battlefield."

"Hey, it's real nice that you can just keep your hand on my shoulder and gawk at the show, Mr. Druid, but I'm tryin' to find a path forward and keep an eye on Hel, because I thought that's who we're after. Are you changin' the plan on me now?"

"No, no, you're right, sorry."

"Maybe you can give me a play-by-play," Coyote said. "We're going to be at this for a while."

I reviewed the deity body count for him and then took another look at the field to see how that was going.

"The Álfar are still essentially keeping it a stalemate on the right flank, but every time one falls, Hel raises it up. That doesn't appear to be the case with the dark elves on the left flank."

"No?"

"I don't see the dark elves shifting to smoke like they did at first. They've probably realized they don't have to. They're naturally faster than the *draugar*. But I have yet to see a dark elf raised from the dead. That would be interesting, wouldn't it, if they had a natural defense against necromancy?"

"It sure would. Sounds like the sort of thing you could bottle and sell. You'd make a fortune, and it would be the ultimate in late-stage capitalism. 'Protect yourself and your family from the apocalypse with Mr. Druid's Anti-Necromantic Tonic and Salubrious Elixir!' All o' them doomsday preppers would buy a bottle and store it in their bunkers, just in case. Huge part of the human economy is based on just in case, you know that? Insurance, condoms, diapers—it's all just in case."

I chuckled, because it's difficult not to like Coyote even when he might mess with you at any moment, and because I understood that he was nervous. Humor often shields the mind against fear. And we had plenty to fear ahead. The slope of the volcano was slowly coming into focus for me, and while I didn't see Hel yet, I felt sure Coyote was right about her being there, because Garm, her hound, was standing sentinel. She would be somewhere nearby, probably not right next to him but a few quick leaps away.

"That dog's gonna be a problem," Coyote said, saying aloud what I was already thinking. "That's the one that chased us all those years ago, am I right?"

"Yes. Through the planes of the Diné."

"So he knows our scent. He's gonna smell us before we get in range. Or smell you, anyway. I copied the scent of this undead asshole, and lemme tell you, Mr. Druid, I don't smell like pears and happiness no more."

"Yes, I've noticed that."

"More like prunes and despair," Coyote said.

"Well, which way is the wind blowing? Maybe he won't be able to pick me out of the crowd."

"Maybe. But once we do anything to Hel, he's gonna come runnin' regardless. We can deal with him before or after we attack Hel, but one way or another he's gotta be dealt with."

We moved in silence for a while, thinking, before I answered.

"I don't really like the idea of hurting a dog, even if it is a pretty mean one."

"I don't either."

"Is Hel to the left or right of the hound?"

"She's to the left, in the center of the slope."

We were on the right side of the field. "How do you feel about circling around that way, coming at her from the left?"

Coyote didn't reply for so long that I wondered if he'd heard me. But just as I was about to ask him again, he said, "Way I see it, that plan has its good points and its bad ones too. Might keep us from having to confront the dog right away. Might even allow us to get in and get out without confronting the dog at all. That's good."

"Agreed."

"But that's gonna take a long time. Already taking us a long time as it is going straight ahead. Lots more folk gonna die. Loki's reloading."

"What? Where?"

"I don't know where he is yet, still haven't spotted him. But off to the left, where you said those gods fell, there are *draugar* moving toward the mountain like we are now. Six of them. You said there were six gods that fell, right?"

"Yes."

"So we can follow them to Loki if you want, or keep doing what we're doing and deal with the dog somehow, or turn left and try to circle around."

I still thought taking out Hel was more important than taking out Loki. She was the one replenishing their numbers with the fallen and therefore winning by attrition. I wasn't sure how much control over the *draugar* Loki would have with her gone; if we were fantastically lucky, they would all return to her realm once she died.

I didn't really think we'd be that lucky, but removing Hel from the battlefield would mathematically improve our chances the most. Loki might have the Arrows of Vayu, but they were of such limited supply that he required a reload after six shots. Hel, on the other hand, could reanimate the flesh of nearly anyone who fell on the battlefield, as long as they still had a head or, apparently, weren't one of the Svartálfar.

"Let's keep heading down the highway to Hel, so to speak." I got no response to this, not even a groan, so I sighed and mourned the wasted reference to AC/DC.

"What? Was that a pun or something, Mr. Druid? If it was, I'm sure it was terrible."

It undeniably was, but terrible puns were my specialty.

Surviving was also my specialty—the sort of fact that's true until it abruptly isn't. If I wanted to survive this trip behind enemy lines, I should probably start worrying about my exit strategy. Because killing Hel would doubtless evoke a response from Loki.

A telltale chop to the air above drew my eyes to a couple of helicopters coming from the north. Either the military or police forces of Sweden were a mite curious about all this brouhaha. Right now that pilot was trying to process what he was seeing and report it in a way that wouldn't get him a psych evaluation.

The all-inclusive *hostiles,* I thought, would be the way to go. Tell 'em you see "multiple hostiles" of "unknown origin" fighting out there, and leave out the bit where there seem to be a whole lot of undead fighting against elves and dwarfs and possibly gods, that it might, in fact, be Ragnarok unfolding. Let them figure out those details for themselves when they send troops to join in. They couldn't fault the pilot for saying there were multiple hostiles.

But it did add another note of urgency to our mission. If humans joined in and got raised from the dead with all their modern weaponry, well, it could quickly spiral out of control. Not that we had any sort of real control at the moment.

"There, Mr. Druid. You see her?"

"What? No. Where is she?"

Coyote pointed with his spear a tiny bit west of north. "Near the base of the mountain, just a touch that way."

I scanned the horde and saw nothing in particular that stood out. It could mean that I was simply missing her. Or it could mean that Loki's mark was somehow disguising her even in the magical spectrum. Or it could mean that Coyote was messing with me for some reason. Not that he needed a reason, once I thought about it: Messing with me was reason enough for him to get out of bed in the morning.

"I don't see her."

"Are you shittin' me right now?"

"No. Are you shitting me?"

"Damn. Whatever, we'll keep going."

Movement off to the right drew my gaze. Garm, the hound of Hel, had just swung his head in our direction. He was staring right at us, it seemed, with those yellow eyes. His lip curled back from his teeth and he growled. His nostrils flared and he huffed a couple of times, then his growl built until a low, booming woof rippled across the field to me.

"You smell too good to him, Mr. Druid. Like coffee and bacon in the morning."

He had to be right. There was no one else on the field that he'd recognize by scent. His muscles tensed and he began an exploratory stride in our direction, nose twitching, trying to zero in on me.

I tried an old trick that had worked on the Fir Bolgs once: I had the earth soften and then tighten around his paws to keep him immobile. But it failed because the earth was almost completely drained of juice near the portal. The land was going dead and it didn't have the strength to hold on to Garm—but it did trip him, and he went down with a howl, crushing several *draugar* underneath him and perhaps getting stabbed with their weapons in the process. He'd be up in a moment, though, and pretty soon I'd be running out of juice to maintain my camouflage. I'd be visible and far away from any help in the middle of a sea of enemies.

"That got her attention," Coyote reported. "She's looking at her hound now."

"She is?"

Coyote pointed once again with his spear. "She's the ugly one looking toward the hound. All the rest are looking forward at the front lines."

Coyote's phrasing left me a bit at sea: If Hel was the ugly member of the undead, which was the beautiful? I still couldn't pick her out; his attempts to point to her were like waving at a colony of fire ants and saying, "That one!" But his assertion that she was interested in Garm gave me an idea. "Okay, I'm going to keep messing with the hound and you keep leading us to her. If she's not paying attention to us, you might be able to get a free shot."

"Okay. You try to keep us from getting eaten. I'll try not to lose sight of our target."

On the one hand, I didn't want to use any more of the earth's energy, but on the other, it was going to get used anyway and I also didn't want to die. Garm needed a distraction, so I gave him one. I bound a bunch of *draugr* armor to his coat—all the leather stuff, which was in many cases connected to metal stuff and to the *draugar* themselves. They could phase right out of it and probably would, but in a few seconds he had a lot of annoying extra weight on him, *draugar* being lifted toward his body and vice versa, a tug in both directions every time I completed a binding. Garm must have thought the *draugar* were attacking him, for he didn't take kindly to it, turning around and biting at them as if they were saucy jumbo fleas.

"Attaboy," Coyote said, and I thought he was talking to Garm at first, but then he added, "Keep that up. She's moving closer to him. We don't even have to change course."

I hoped he was right. I hoped we would be able to pull this off all sneaky, in and out, change the course of the battle, and—

"Uh-oh."

"What?"

"She's looking around. She can smell the shenanigans."

"Well, she can't see me," I said, just as all the earth went dead beneath my feet, its energy drained away, and my camouflage fizzled. I could recast it using stored energy from my bear charm, but I rather thought I'd need that for something else. I was quite visible and quite visibly alive in a sea of undead. And what's more, Hel spotted me right away and shrieked in recognition. That allowed me to finally locate her: She had taken the trouble to make herself look entirely rotted instead of only half-rotted, but her eyes held burning scleras and if they indicated emotional heat then she was ablaze. She'd once asked me to join her side for Ragnarok and I'd refused. She'd been alone and outnumbered that day and we chased her off. It would be safe to say that the circumstances had changed.

I shoved Coyote forward as I drew Fragarach and said, "You're not with me now!" hoping he'd get the idea that he should blend in. I kicked the *draugr* to my right to clear some space and expected to be overwhelmed shortly from all sides, but instead the *draugar* pulled away from me, and Coyote followed suit—because Hel was coming straight at me, charging down the mountain. Her assumed form of a *draugr* melted and shifted until she was the deity I had seen and smelled before, half living and half skinless putrid corpse. She grew as she approached, taking longer and longer strides, topping ten feet easily, and I had to rapidly reassess how I was going to fight someone that huge. The reach she now had far exceeded mine, and she had drawn her knife, Famine, out of her rib cage. Unlike Loki's sword, Famine did not grow in proportion to the rest of Hel—probably because Loki was casting an illusion there—but her knife was a significant piece of cutlery regardless.

Hel's stench arrived in advance of her actual person, and it was enough to make me wistful for the smell of pears in braided elf hair. I blinked and coughed, trying to keep my wits, and took a tiny step back even as Hel grunted and her eyes widened. Her hands splayed out in a desperate bid for balance, but it was too late. Physics had asserted its mastery over her person, because Coyote had expertly tripped her with the shaft of his spear as she passed him. She'd never expected to be tripped by one of her own *draugar*. And I hadn't expected that either. The net result was that I scrambled away from her knife hand but couldn't avoid being flattened by the other one as she crashed to the ground. It knocked the wind out of me and I remained still too long. A giant hand—Hel's flesh-covered one—wrapped itself around my body and picked me up, trapping my arm against my side so that Fragarach was useless. She was still prone, so she didn't raise me too high, but she slammed me back to earth again and it was less than gentle on my head. I saw lights blinking in my vision and felt nauseous—probably because she was bringing me up to her face and I got a lungful of her death breath. The side of her face that was exposed tissue and bone had wee maggots writhing in her cheek meat, and I first thought that those had to be distracting and then wondered madly why she hadn't taken time to remove them on her big day.

"Druid," she rasped. "Die now." She wasn't into small talk. Just enough gloating for me to appreciate my own defeat. Her other hand, the bony one with Famine in it, approached blade-first. I felt the cold steel press against the warm flesh of my throat and then slide across, sawing me open. Blood and air escaped and I silently triggered my healing charm as soon as she withdrew the blade, having no trouble at all relaying my panic in gurgles and wheezes. Because I'd only bought myself a little bit of time. When the blood stopped flowing, she'd have at it again and perhaps not content herself with merely slitting my throat. I had no options to retaliate, and she grinned with blackened teeth as my blood spilled onto her hand.

Abruptly her entire body jerked—including the hand with me in it—and her expression altered to one of surprise and then scrunched into a wince of pain. She began to shrink, and her hand could no longer wrap itself around my body. I flopped to the ground with all the grace of a stunned cod and hoped I'd be able to breathe and function again soon. But I saw a *draugr* atop Hel's back, with its spear sunk into her torso. He was twisting it around like a swizzle stick, tearing up her organs with the bladed tip.

"Hey there, Mr. Druid!" Coyote called in his gravelly rasp. "This has been fun, but I expect I'll be dying shortly. Looks like you will too. She got your throat, eh? Well, at least I won't have to hear any more of your puns. And my people should be safe now."

Coyote will never gain a reputation for kind farewells, but at least he had his priorities straight. The Norse goddess of death expired with a hoarse rattle and one final spasm, and the entire army of *draugar* flinched as one—at least, all of them that I could see surrounding me. I don't know if they flinched at the front lines. But they didn't melt away or explode in a puff of ash either. They looked around as if waking from sustained somnambulism, bereft of Hel's guidance, and decided they weren't really eager to march forward to face an army intent on destroying them. They started looking around for exits. And they were not interested at all in me or Coyote or the lifeless stank of Hel.

"What's this, now?" Coyote said. "None of these fellers cares what I did? Whipped me up a batch of heart and lung marmalade right in front of them using one hundred percent rotten-goddess ingredients and they ain't even the least bit mad?"

They wouldn't be. They had no loyalty to Hel. Her realm was where no one wanted to go, and she had never treated them well. A howl tearing through the sky reminded us that at least one creature was loyal to Hel, however.

"Oh, shit," Coyote said, which was what I was thinking but couldn't say. Garm had freed himself of most if not all of the *draugar* and become aware that Hel was no more. He was a biggun, as they say, twelve feet tall, and even at a distance he could clearly see Coyote and me next to Hel's body.

My throat closed up and my neck shortly thereafter, and I could breathe again and get some oxygen to my brain. I had enough juice for maybe one trick and that was it.

"You got a plan, Mr. Druid?" Coyote said. Garm showed his teeth and barked, his hackles raising.

I gasped once and said, "Run. Change your scent!"

"Don't gotta tell me twice. Bye!" Coyote left his spear behind and hopped off the still form of Hel, streaking right into the confused mass of *draugar*. Garm watched him go but didn't watch for long. He turned to stare directly at me and growled. Mine was the scent he already knew, the one that had gotten away once upon a time. And now that he saw me next to the dead body of his mistress, he wasn't going to let me get away again. He sprang forward, scattering *draugar* and knocking over any that didn't get out of the way in time. I had two choices: fight or run.

If I stood and fought, it would be in a weakened state, with little to no magic at my disposal to boost speed or strength, and unless I got the proverbial "critical hit" right from the start, my long life would end as a chew toy for a hellhound with a legitimate grudge. There was basically only one way to escape him, and it was by no means a safe option but it involved a sacrifice as well. The odds of surviving were slightly higher, however, so I didn't hesitate. Using the last of my magic, I shape-shifted to a great horned owl and took wing directly away from Garm, rising to what I hoped was just above the height of a spear thrust. I didn't want to rise too high and make myself a clear target for Loki's bow or anyone else's.

And though it hurt, I left Fragarach behind, to be found and picked up by anyone. Because I needed to achieve the full air-speed velocity of an unladen owl. That's about forty miles per hour, and I'd never make it if I had to lug an awkward few pounds in my talons. As it was, I couldn't reach that speed right away. There was a whole lot of flapping that had to happen first, and there were no magical bursts. Garm had a head start on getting up to speed, and an aggressive woof told me he'd seen me take flight and was on my literal tail now. And he was closing the distance between us, rather than me opening it up. I might be snatched out of the air, a nice snack for him. There was nothing for me to do but to keep calm and flap on—a phrase that is not emblazoned across T-shirts everywhere for good reason.

Noise grew behind me as Garm drew closer—hoarse cries of undead surprise as the *draugar* were mowed down, the baying of Garm himself as he tried to catch up, and the crunch and clatter of collisions. The *draugar* were slowing him down at least a little bit, preventing him from reaching top speed, but he was still getting closer. I could feel it. And then I realized that the *draugar* could probably help me out quite a bit. Most of them were in retreat, heading around the base of the volcano to see what was on the other side. As a result, Garm was running into their flank. If I turned in to the *draugar*, though, and flew toward the Fae and the Norse and others, I might be able to capitalize on their instinct.

Garm's breath blew hot and snotty on my tail feathers, and that's when I banked sharply left, directly over the heads of the retreating *draugar*. They're not trained fighters necessarily, like the Einherjar, but when something is coming at you and you have a sharp stick to poke at it, chances are you're going to use it if you can't get out of the way in time. That's what I was counting on.

Garm overshot me on the sharp turn and I gained some ground, but he halted and came after me. And in so doing, he encountered some fierce resistance. The *draugar* weren't obeying Hel now, so they gave her hound no breaks. They saw a big dog and they didn't want to get run over, so, with the tips of their spears, they tried to discourage him from doing that. Since he wasn't paying attention to the *draugar*, he ran right into more than a few of those spear tips. It slowed him down and he yelped a couple of times, eventually giving up to attend to his many wounds. I banked to the right, heading for the far side of the battlefield again. I needed to get clear and find a place to replenish. I hoped Coyote was doing the same thing.

The *draugar* continued to retreat, but those that Hel had raised from the dead fought on. Whatever she had done to them did not require her constant control. At least she wouldn't be raising any more.

Not that there weren't still huge problems to solve. The *draugar* might have no stomach to fight the armies ready for them, but they weren't popping back through the portal to the gloomy realm of Hel either. They were going around the lake to the north, toward human settlements, where maybe a handful of people had a few things ready "just in case" of a zombie apocalypse but the rest were woefully unprepared. And then there was the issue of what had happened to Loki—

A thunderous roar shook the air. Loki had found the body of

Hel. "Where are you going?" he boomed in Old Norse, and I thought at first he meant me, but it turned out he was talking to the *draugar*. "You must fight and win if you want any peace! Fight!"

I don't know what he was talking about there, what lie or promise he had made them, but it worked. The *draugar* spun around and fought much more viciously than before, and the sudden reversal was devastating to the pursuing troops, who had broken ranks. Brighid still stood, but the Fae host was much reduced. The remaining Olympians continued to fight well. The Einherjar and the dwarfs were engaged, but the Álfar and Svartálfar both took heavy losses on the reversal. I saw no sign of the yeti, and the Norse pantheon still hid behind a dark cloud of Thor's making, though it had advanced somewhat on the right. I imagined that anything that walked into that cloud would not be walking out. In the meantime, Loki could not target them. And they, likewise, could not seem to find him; I would have expected Odin's spear or Thor's hammer to have flown by now, but they held back.

Loki's voice rolled across the field again. "Druid! I have your sword! I know it was you!"

I cleared the edge of the battle and dropped to the earth a safe distance away, behind the Svartálfar troops. I felt a tiny trickle of the earth's magic there, fading but still available. I shifted to a hound so I'd have some speed and some teeth if I needed them and then refilled my bear charm and resumed healing.

So Loki had found Fragarach. I was ready to let him have it, for all the good it would do him. I should go straight to the nearest bound tree and exit. I'd helped take out Hel, got my throat cut, and almost become a doggie treat. That was enough. No reason to stay, except maybe to root for Athena to win me a thousand boxes of Girl Scout Cookies.

Off to my left, a *draugr* staggered out past the dark elves and transformed in front of me into a coyote. It was, in fact, Coyote himself, who'd crossed the field successfully. He let his tongue hang out as he trotted up to me, and I thought he was going to stop, but

he merely bobbed his head and kept on going. I chuffed in laughter.
I couldn't blame him, and I took a few steps after him, thinking I'd
go with him and buy him a few beers somewhere. But Loki's voice
called out again.

"Come on, Druid. You've killed all my children. Come and face
me now. You know where I am. Come and face me."

I stopped, and so did Coyote. He turned around and sat, waiting to see what I would do. I tilted my head at him and he mirrored
the action. Smartass.

Loki was under a misapprehension. I hadn't actually killed any
of his children—not really. Granuaile and Freyja had both played
major roles in killing Fenris. I had only witnessed the death of Jörmungandr. And if Loki would simply think clearly for a moment,
he would realize that my sword on the ground next to Hel was not,
in fact, the spear stuck in her back. I was not the cause of death.

I still didn't need to face him. I didn't think I could take him,
honestly—not without Fragarach and a whole lot of luck. But I did
know where Hel's body was, and I could lead others there. With
Loki out of the picture it would be over; the Norse could handle
things from there. Wouldn't it be worth it, then, to do at least that
much?

I raised a paw to Coyote and then pointed my body back to the
battle, keeping an eye on him. Coyote shook his head and turned
tail, trotting away. I was on my own for this one.

Fair enough. I'd get myself some armor and a sword from the
field and find Brighid. She could fight Loki's fire with her own fire.
And feeling the land go dead beneath me again, I knew Loki needed
to go sooner rather than later.

CHAPTER 21

the eruption is different this time. The previous ones happened while I was on the rooftop with Wukong, but this one I can feel through the soles of my feet. And through the tattoo on my right heel, I can feel the paroxysm of pain that the elemental is experiencing, the profound drain that's occurring due to this portal opening and closing repeatedly. The land near here will die, like the land in Arizona around the portal Aenghus Óg made. That was high chaparral desert, and this is subtropical forest. Obviously not a worry for the Yama Kings, who'd like to do far worse, but it's the sort of thing that ignites my ire, and I have no qualms about judging the situation. This should not be allowed.

I try to communicate with the elemental Taiwan, whose voice already sounds tired. //Query: Who opens the portal?//

//Local deities// she says.

Taiwan must mean the Yama Kings. //Query: Can I stop them?//

//No / Portal opened from other side//

It would have to be voluntarily closed by the one who opened it or, as with the others, by the actual defeat of the Yama King in question. It occurs to me that perhaps I should rephrase the question. //Query: Can I prevent next one from opening?//

//Yes / Slay deity first//

In other words, if I want to end this, I need to skip this fight, go to the next hell, and kill the Yama King there on his own turf.

"Wukong: Which Yama King is this?"

"The sixth. King Biancheng. The fifth is staying out of this mess." The demons and the damned begin to land on the slopes, and Wukong's clones engage some of them. More stream in our direction.

"So who's the seventh?"

"He is called King Taishan."

"What's he look like?"

"Why do you ask?"

"If I take him out ahead of time, can we end this early? Will the other Yama Kings keep coming if they know King Taishan never even made it here?"

"You mean go to the seventh court and kill him there?"

"Yes."

"That's—"

"Please don't say it's dangerous. So is being on this mountain right now. Just tell me if killing him will stop the others."

"I think it might. Why would the others risk such a preemptive defeat? And I was going to say that's unexpected. Are you perhaps looking at things differently?"

"No, I think I'm still in the same frame of mind. I just want to protect Gaia. What's King Taishan look like?"

"He wears a judge's cap, like all the Yama Kings. His robes are blue because of the cold hell he watches over, Utpala, which turns the skin of all the damned blue. But he also rules a fiery hell called Tapana."

"All right. Let me see if this is even possible." The damned reached us and I had to separate headspaces to continue the conversation, but this time I battled in Whitman's English headspace so that I would have the Latin one to speak to the elemental.

//Query: Where is tether to seventh hell of Diyu?//

//No Druidic tether exists / Must be escorted by deity of pantheon//

Balls. I hadn't tried out my Polish headspace yet because it wasn't technically complete. I still had some poems to absorb and some fluency to achieve in Polish, but perhaps I could use it well enough to fight the damned. These from the sixth court of Biancheng had different wounds and marks on them than the ones from the fourth; they had been pierced and sliced with steel and some of them still had spikes poking out of their flesh, but Scáthmhaide caved their heads in just as easily.

No time like the present to see if I could juggle three headspaces. I would need to if I ever wanted to shift planes with more than just Orlaith.

I switched my battle to the Polish headspace and gave it some time and some lines from Szymborska's "Soliloquy for Cassandra" to make sure it was established. A fitting poem, since Cassandra kept telling people something terrible was about to happen and was never believed:

> To ja, Kasandra.
> A to jest moje miasto pod popiołem.
> A to jest moja laska i wstążki prorockie.
> A to jest moja głowa pełna wątpliwości.

I kept that going in my head while I fought, then flipped on the English for conversation. "Wukong. The elemental says I need a deity from your pantheon to escort me to hell and back. There are no Druidic tethers to that plane."

He did not answer right away, and for a time it was just the sounds of battle, crunches and screams and grunts. But eventually he said, "There is one who can do this. He will be here soon."

"Who?"

"The immortal warrior, Erlang Shen. Do you know him?"

"I know *of* him, sure! Wasn't he the one from the stories that subdued you so long ago?"

The Monkey King laughs even as his iron rod destroys the damned and sends them back to Mahāraurava, one of the hells over which King Biancheng presides. "Yes, I remember well. He is the one who defeated me in battle in the days I was rebellious against heaven. But now we are on the same side. His arrival was already planned to come at the emergence of King Biancheng."

And when the warrior does come, some minutes later, he is a riot of colors and a pageant of death. His hound accompanies him—very similar to a wolfhound, in fact, but far more used to battle than Orlaith is or will ever be if I have anything to say about it. Together they cut a swath through the hordes of the damned as they move to join us at the base of Seven Star Mountain.

The Monkey King is glorious and impressive, to be sure, but as Erlang Shen descends from the heavens, I think he could practically slay people with how badass he looks, a mixture of flowing red and white silks and hardened-leather armor inlaid with gold and accents of jade. Steel armor is not necessary for him, since even without a stitch on he is practically impervious to weapons. His chosen weapon is sort of like a spear, except the head is three-tipped and double-bladed. Rumor has it that the weapon functions much like Fragarach and can cut or punch through armor as if it were cotton. It certainly seems to have no trouble slicing through the damned as if they were cucumbers instead of flesh and bone.

And once he lands and introductions are made and the plan is revealed to him, I am brought forcefully to the question once again: Why am I here? Because Erlang Shen and the Monkey King can obviously take care of this on their own. Both are more skilled and powerful than I and would easily be able to defeat King Taishan without my help. I am not even needed for them to shift planes— it's in fact they who must shift me to the seventh court! So for what purpose have I been sent here by Brighid? I worry about her motivation more than these Buddhist deities, because the First among the Fae didn't get that title granted to her. She earned it by being stronger and smarter than everyone else. And it has to be something significant, doesn't it, if she's gotten the Monkey King to agree to her scheme? It can't be simply to help Taipei by battling these poor souls. I mean, I'm sure she'd want me to minimize the damage here as much as possible, but if that were all, there would be no need to have Flidais bring me here with code phrases and magic apples and have Sun Wukong lay down mystic riddles on my brow. She could have simply said to minimize the damage and I would have done it.

It's an uncomfortable feeling, knowing that gods are playing a game with you as a prominent piece but you're not able to see the board or even know the rules.

And then the puzzle turns and clicks into place for me like a Rubik's Cube—or at least a part of it does. I have not been viewing events from the proper perspective. I've been a Sunday-afternoon sports spectator, looking at all the action from my couch and involved in what I'm watching, unaware that people can watch me in turn from the kitchen or hallway or even outside and laugh because I am so engrossed by minor happenings in my narrow vision and cannot see the bigger picture.

This is not about Taiwan. I've certainly not been sent to save it, because it's in perfectly capable hands. This is about whether I can step outside my own exquisite narcissism and serve a greater cause. This is about my field of vision. About my judgment. About how someone obviously felt I wasn't able to judge for myself where my talents would best serve Gaia, so I was sent here to be safe—oh, my. That's it!

I've been packed off on a milk run, faced with just enough danger to make me feel like it was something real. No wonder Flidais didn't feel like there was any hurry to tell me about this caper; she knew she was essentially escorting me to the kiddie pool to splash around in shallow waters. And she knew that's what she would be doing in Japan too. The Shinto deities would need us no more than the Taoist or Buddhist ones. The question becomes, why would Brighid do this to us?

To save Druidry. An obvious answer once I ask the question. In case everything goes wrong in Sweden and Loki's forces prevail, I'll still be around, as will Flidais and whoever else they've sequestered in undisclosed locations. Owen, perhaps—where's he, I wonder? Keeping his grove safe, I hope.

The two immortals have stopped fighting, I notice, and Wukong's clones have circled around us to provide a sphere of protection. Apparently I've spaced out a bit and they're waiting for me to come around.

"Wukong." He merely raises a bushy eyebrow at me. "Did Brighid ask you to keep me occupied during Ragnarok?" His eyes slide over to Erlang Shen and they share a tiny smile. They'd either been waiting on this or they had a bet going as to whether I'd figure it out.

"I think perhaps our American friend is finally challenging her assumptions," he says to Erlang Shen, which is not precisely an answer but confirms my suspicion.

"Damn it. Then you don't need me here? I can go help somewhere else and you can end this on your own?"

"Of course."

"But you'll shut down King Taishan and the others soon? The earth is being harmed every time the portal opens."

"We will," Wukong assures me. "But are you finished learning, then?"

Oh, shit. I've missed something important or he wouldn't prompt me like that. I look around and see nothing obvious—so it must be that I have made yet another assumption.

"Wait. When Brighid made this arrangement with you, did she say why?"

"I'm afraid I'm not allowed to recall."

"Not allowed?" Brighid must have extracted a promise not to reveal any details of their conversation. But there was clearly something to reveal that Wukong thought I should know. I shudder at a sudden suspicion, a thrill of cold fear coursing down my spine. "Did someone put her up to it?"

The Monkey King shrugs, helpless.

"Wukong is bound by oath not to answer. But I am not," Erlang Shen replies. "Brighid made these arrangements with us at the urging of Siodhachan Ó Suileabháin."

I gasp audibly, shocked and saddened to have my suspicion confirmed. I didn't want it to be true. But he knew when Ragnarok was going to begin. He had advance warning and time to set this up. And he probably thought he was doing the right thing. That's when heat flushes my cheeks.

"Of all the bullshit patriarchal moves he could pull—well. He and I are going to have a talk. Perhaps even a spirited fracas," I add, after thinking that this is precisely the sort of thing that got Flidais in trouble with Perun. You don't make plans for someone else and not consult them.

Which is not to say I haven't enjoyed my time here. I feel like I *have* learned and grown, and I was led to it in a much different way than I'm used to. And as much as I was frustrated by the leading questions and the vague statements at first, I can appreciate with hindsight how effective they were. It's a way of thinking I should cultivate.

"Sifu Sun," I say, bowing to the Monkey King, "may I return at a later date to learn more?"

"What is it you wish to learn?"

"Whatever you wish to teach me. How to make perfect bubble tea, more about Buddhism, how to fight. But I also wish to learn Mandarin. I am nearly ready to add another headspace."

Sun Wukong smiles at me. "Very well. You know where my shop is. I will be there when you are ready."

"Thank you. And I am very grateful for the training you've already given me."

"Do not let it go to waste."

"I won't." I bow again, and also to Erlang Shen before taking my leave, fighting through the damned to get to the bound tree. True to the Monkey King's word, King Biancheng lands a short distance away, armor shining and face snarling, eager to have a go at the Druid who killed King Wuguan. He draws his weapons and advances, but I put my hand on the bound tree and shift away, leaving him to Erlang Shen. There's a fight going on in Sweden, and once I get there, I don't know if I'll go after Loki or Atticus first.

CHAPTER 22

i'm so fecking tired after the swim that I might need to try one of those superfoods modern humans are always on about. Thinking I might try kale, even if Greta's right and it's somehow worse than old man balls. Or maybe I'll be set right by some pancakes drizzled with maple syrup and a hot mug of coffee. Sounds less risky to me, more of a sure thing.

The elementals tell me I have applied the Second Law of Owen as much as Gaia requires: There are still all sorts of fires to put out, but others are seeing to it, and the primary shite festival in Sweden is still happening, but that's not a fight for me own fists. I hope Siodhachan and Granuaile are all right, but all I can get from the elementals is an assurance that they're still alive. I'm given leave to return to Flagstaff and a rare gift: In return for saving Bavaria and Amazon and more, the elementals ask what I'd like to be called from now on instead of Avenging Druid, and I tell them Oaken Druid would suit me fine.

//Oaken Druid it is / Harmony//

//Harmony// I says, and ask Slomo if she'd like to visit me home before returning to her jungle in Peru. I give her a mental picture of what the trees look like there, the Ponderosa pines and the alligator junipers and the white-barked aspens.

<Sure, Oaken!> she says. <Would I be the first sloth to ever dangle from those trees?>

I think so.

<Securing the First Dangle is a great honor among sloths. Let's go!>

I shift to a bear once more and give Slomo a ride out of the lake area. Some people are starting to appear on the shores, and I'm afraid they're going to notice us soon. I'm pretty sure they would have some questions about why there's a Peruvian sloth in Poland. After we shift to the bound tree on Greta's property, where it's late evening of the night before, Slomo drops off me back to barf quietly on the forest ground. She staggers a bit to the right afterward. <Oh, Oaken, I feel woozy. It's super dry here too.>

I give her a bit of energy from the earth. <How's that?>

<Better, thanks,> she says, <but I should probably eat some leaves soon.>

<I'll fetch ye some. Stay here; I'll be gone for just a wee while.>

It's only a few minutes' work to shift back to Peru, gather some leaves from those trees she likes, and return.

<Oh, wow! Those look delicious! Thanks!>

<Crawl up on me back and ye can eat while we go down to meet me girlfriend and apprentices. They'll be delighted to meet ye, I promise.>

And they are. They've all switched out their spheres from Tasmania in their lockets with Colorado's sandstone, so they're able to communicate with Slomo much like me, in images and feelings. Everyone is delighted. Slomo establishes First Dangle on an aspen near the house and eats leaves while the kids laugh and talk with her. A couple of parents stay behind while I go inside with Greta and the rest of the pack to fill them in on what's been going on with me, and they catch me up with what happened in Tasmania after I left.

"We obviously decided to return home since we didn't know how long you'd be gone." Greta speaks from the kitchen because she's trying to make my dream of pancakes come true. It was time for breakfast in Poland, but it's bedtime in Flagstaff, and I realize with a yawn that I don't properly know what day it is or when I last slept for more than a couple of hours.

Sam and Ty, the co-leaders of the Flagstaff pack, arrive after a few minutes and look mighty pleased to have me back, since it probably means we can resume tearing the hell out of each other in sparring matches. They don't often get to unload against anyone who can challenge them, and they like it. Truth is, I do too. Sometimes I win and sometimes they do. It's good to have some mates who will beat the shite out of ye in the friendliest manner possible and don't get sore when ye beat the shite out of them. And those lads are an example of how to be lovers. They've been together more than a hundred years and they still think the man they married is the best man on earth. But after we catch up, they start talking about wine for some reason, and that's a subject about which I know very little. In fact, I don't know Jack Shite.

That's an expression Siodhachan taught me, but I don't rightly understand it. I have so many questions. Sometimes people leave off the surname and say, "Ye don't know Jack," but everyone knows you're not talking about Jack Black or Jack Daniel's or Jack Be Nimble—nay! When someone says, "Ye don't know Jack," it's automatically understood that they're talking about Jack Shite. But it makes ye wonder why anyone would walk around this world with the surname of Shite. If ye have such an awful name, wouldn't that be a fine excuse to change it to Jones or something common and boring and unrelated to feces? And what's really confusing to me is whether we *should* know a lad named Jack Shite or not. Sometimes people say, "Ye don't know Jack Shite," and ye can tell by their tone that you're practically the only person that doesn't. But sometimes people sneer at ye and say, "You know *Jack Shite*," and the scorn in their voice lets ye know that ye should have never been introduced to him, even by accident. Well, I don't know Jack Shite yet, and I'm mighty conflicted about whether I want to meet him or not. He's a controversial figure. I'm wondering if Sam and Ty know Jack Shite and I realize they must because they know so much about wine, so I don't ask them out loud.

The conversations fade until Greta shouts me name and I startle straight up. "Eh? What?"

"You need to go to bed," she says. "You've drifted off twice now."

"I have? When was . . . first time?"

"Just go. You've been mumbling about not knowing Jack Shite."

"But Slomo—"

"She'll be fine. The kids will let us know if she needs anything, and if she does, we'll wake you. She probably needs to sleep too, and there's nothing out here that will mess with her."

"No, ye definitely don't want to mess with her," I says.

Greta asks Thandi's dad, Sonkwe, to finish up the pancakes and store them while she pulls me from my seat and escorts me to the bedroom. Me limbs feel like lead weights and me vision's all blurry. Me brain knows I'm somewhere safe and it just wants to shut down and recover.

"Don't want to mess with me either," Greta says, which is all too true. Once I collapse on the bed, I feel her lips press against mine briefly. "Thanks for coming back safe to me, Teddy Bear."

"Oaken," I mumble, on the edge of slumber.

"What?"

"'M Oaken now."

"All right, Oaken Teddy Bear."

Something about that isn't quite right, but it's not worth climbing back to consciousness to figure it out. I have a wee space to meself to enjoy some peace and I'm going to wallow in it as long as I'm allowed, because after that, we have so much fecking work to do. And puppies to raise. Can't forget Orlaith's puppies. Me grove will be so pleased . . .

for the record, and at risk of stating the obvious: Looting corpses is nothing like the way it's presented in video games. You click, get a little sound effect and a tiny hit of serotonin, and coins are automatically put in your purse and items go into your giant bag of holding, possibly to be equipped, possibly to be sold later to an NPC for meager ducats. It's fast, bloodless, and carries little risk of disease or septicemia. No interaction with an actual corpse is necessary. Which is true of every aspect of games—there's no actual *anything*. But looting has always been a casual pastime in games, one of the fun parts, and I guess I wish it wasn't, because it turns us into vultures.

If you want to loot a corpse, make sure you know from the start that it's going to be literal deadweight and that you might pull a muscle. There's going to be blood and there's going to be shit—not the mere stink of shit, but actual shit. Might be some brains lying around too. It's going to take far longer than a mouse click to get the job done, and when you finally get the armor that you need off the corpse, you will probably find it doesn't fit well. And the weapon won't be a legendary blade like Fragarach either.

So it was that I searched several Fae corpses for adequate replacements. I settled for the third, finding a sleeveless shirt to wear under a cuirass and some basic breeches, over which I secured a hardened leather skirt to protect the legs, fastened by a belt. Boots that fit took another three tries. I did find a sword with a whiff of magic about it, and a look at the bindings in the magical spectrum revealed that it was an unbreakable blade. I picked up a shield too. Considering myself to be at least partially protected, I sought out Brighid.

I couldn't wait to finish this, to bring an end to the danger I'd put everyone in by making two disastrous trips to Asgard years ago. The people fighting Surt's fires around the world or who may have perished in them—that was on me. Everyone who'd fallen here, or who fell elsewhere in some battle provoked by Loki's allies—that was on me too. Fand and Manannan and the three yeti and so many more. There was really no way I could ethically walk away from this, despite my attempts to rationalize doing just that. To be fair, I should be facing Ragnarok all alone. I was the one who killed the Norns and set this snowball rolling, so I should be the one who stood in the path of the avalanche.

It took some time to make my way to the front without killing any of the Fae with my iron aura. The yewmen had no such vulnerabilities, however, and it was they who protected Brighid on either flank as she swung her sword at the necks of *draugar* and let her armor take the occasional hit. On her immediate left, however, was a curious figure in green and silver livery, one of the Fae, who held no weapon nor tried to attack. He simply existed and had some incredible kinetic wards. Every time the *draugar* tried to attack him, their force was returned upon them with degrees of magnitude. I came around to Brighid's right to make sure I didn't disturb him.

"Brighid! It's Siodhachan!" I had to repeat this several times to get through to her, but once she spared a glance my way, she pulled back and let the yewmen close up the gap.

"Siodhachan. What has happened? Why does Loki have your sword?"

"I had to leave it where we killed Hel."

"Ah. I wondered if he spoke true when his voice rolled across the field and said you'd killed his children. But who are 'we'?"

"One of the Native American Coyotes helped me. He's the forward-looking sort, didn't want this mess coming to his continent. He's had enough of being invaded."

"I see. Is he still here?"

"No, he's decided he's done enough. Did you also hear Loki's challenge to me?"

"Everyone heard it."

"I know where he is and can lead you to him. Do you want your shot at winning the Girl Scout Cookies?"

Brighid shrugged. "I want the victory and honor more than the cookies." At a sudden thought, she frowned at me. "But why help me? You bet on Athena."

"Yes, but Athena will get fried almost instantly. You won't. And I bet you have wards that will deflect those arrows he's letting loose."

The goddess of poetry, fire, and the forge smiled. "Yes. He has already attempted to slay me with one from afar."

"Excellent. Shall I usher you, then, to a fight worthy of your skill, which will burnish your reputation and live on in the songs of bards?"

"Absolutely, Siodhachan. Usher away. Let us form a detail."

Her eyes slid away from me for a moment and she smiled over my right shoulder, but when I looked behind me all I saw was a tightly packed throng of Fae, keeping their distance. When I looked back she had turned to shout orders at the yewmen and the Fae lad in livery, whom she called Coriander. They formed a sphere of protection around us, with Coriander at the point, and rather than hold the line, we pushed forward into the throng of *draugar* and began a slow jog, the yewmen batting aside the undead instead of trying to decapitate them and Coriander plowing through them like a cowcatcher on the front of a train. We were not trying to win by attrition now; we had a destination in mind. I directed them straight ahead until we got to the base of the volcano, which was essentially the edge of the former lake, and then we turned right. I did not see Garm anywhere, and even though he'd tried to eat me on two separate occasions, I hoped he was okay and recovering.

I cast my eyes back to the front; Coyote and I had basically advanced straight forward from the Álfar position, and we were approaching it now.

"Should be coming up soon," I told Brighid, "somewhere slightly uphill from us. Loki will use fire at some point and probably shape-shift, so beware."

"Remain in my shadow," Brighid replied, "and you will be safe from the fire."

I wasn't sure any of us would be safe. After throwing a horde at us, Loki had to be confident of being able to face down Odin and Thor and the rest of them if he wanted to win this thing. He'd been planning for this a long time and wouldn't have called me to fight him if he wasn't confident of the outcome. My calculation was twofold: I had it coming, and whatever happened to us, the rest of the assembled gods would see it and know where Loki was. Engaging with us would paint a big target on his back. Or face. Whatever.

And both Brighid and I had backups. She'd kept Ogma behind in Tír na nÓg somewhere to lead the Fae should she fall, and Flidais was in Japan. Granuaile and Owen would continue Druidry if I fell—especially Owen, who had a fine grove going already. I imagined Granuaile would like to add a couple more headspaces before she took on any apprentices. And I hoped she was safe dealing with whatever threats emerged in Taiwan.

The first sign we were close came when an arrow struck the kinetic wards surrounding Coriander and its bladed tip shattered to pieces.

The second, unmistakable sign that we'd found Loki was when

he loomed out of the throng, growing to the size of a giant in seconds, and hosed us down with fire that he channeled from his sword—the bow and arrows were nowhere to be seen, nor was Fragarach. Coriander had some rudimentary protection against fire, but as the Arrows of Vayu had been no match for the kinetic ward, his protection was insufficient against the heat Loki was bringing. Likewise for the yewmen, whose only fear was fire. While they all flinched and cried out under the onslaught, Brighid shouted at Coriander to retreat behind her and she charged straight forward, arms spread out, gathering that flame to her and redirecting it to the *draugar* on either side of Loki. The lord of mischief had to stop soon afterward because Brighid leapt at him, her own sword ready to deliver a killing blow, and he had to deflect that. The metal of their swords screamed as they slid against each other and Loki twisted impossibly to let her pass by, and his push at the end forced her to tumble off balance. But now he had enemies on either side of him, and he couldn't abide that. He waved at the nearby *draugar* to either attack us or protect him, and the distinction mattered little. They rushed in from all sides, and that meant I'd have very little ability to attack Loki. He wanted to focus on Brighid, the clearest threat. Once she was out of the picture, he'd be able to fry us without interference.

His head turned away from us even as his left hand pulled out a knife that looked familiar—a cold blue ice knife with a red line along the top of the blade. It was one of the yeti whirling blades—the one he'd stolen from Granuaile in India.

"Oh, no, you fucking don't," a voice said behind me, but when I turned all I saw was yewmen, who cannot speak, and beyond them, *draugar*. But, then, I wouldn't have seen anything if that voice belonged to who I thought.

"Granuaile?" I said. "Are you here?"

"We'll talk later," her disembodied voice replied. "I have a score to settle."

"I thought you were in Taiwan."

"We're going to settle that too, believe me."

"What?" I got no answer. I got a face full of *draugar* instead. I fell into a defensive sphere with Coriander and the yewmen and missed Fragarach desperately. Swords that don't cut through armor can't compare. That was a fact Loki was finding out in his battle with Brighid. He kept shifting his shape as his blows came in, and Brighid couldn't react in time to them, so he landed both with his accustomed sword and with the whirling blade. But both were turned back by Brighid's armor. She disarmed his right hand soon afterward, managing to open up a wound along the inside of his forearm. In need of a new weapon and unable to pick up his old one without exposing himself to attack, he did what any infinitely malleable shape-shifter would do: He reached into his own body and pulled Fragarach out of there, slimed with Loki juices. He met Brighid's next attack with it and surprised me by being a far better fighter than I thought he'd be. He counterstruck but again slipped past Brighid's guard with a trick, and that's when Brighid learned whether the armor she'd forged specifically to withstand Fragarach worked or not.

It sort of did.

Normally, Fragarach treats armor like it's denim. There's some small resistance, in other words, but not enough to matter if you are striking well. Brighid had forged that armor at a time when she worried that Fragarach could fall into the hands of her enemies and be used against her. She'd never had it tested until now.

Loki's blow was a powerful one and it sank into the top of Brighid's left shoulder plate and the top of her chest, knocking her backward—but she took Fragarach with her, lodged in the armor. Perhaps the blade bit into her and perhaps it didn't; the armor wasn't perfect but it did the job, because that would have been a disabling or even killing blow against any other armor. Both Loki and Brighid appeared stunned by the outcome: Loki was once again disarmed, and Brighid had a sword stuck in her kit.

Before either could resume, however, Loki cried out as a sharp crack announced the shattering of his left ulna at the distal end—right at the wrist, in other words, which caused him to drop the whirling blade. He reared back, cradling his arm, his teeth bared in a hiss as he searched for the cause. Granuaile dismissed the binding on Scáthmhaide that kept her invisible, whirling blade in her left hand.

"Hi!" she shouted up at him. "Remember how you stole this from me?" She flashed the ice blade at him. "Ambushed me, broke most of my bones? Lured my father into a death trap?"

"You—"

"Yep, me. Just wanted you to know who gotcha."

"No!"

Fire bloomed on Loki's right fist and I hoped Brighid would stop him, control that fire before it could hit Granuaile, because she had no defense against it. But the fire snuffed out as Granuaile whipped the blade at Loki's thigh, mere feet from where she stood, and it plunged into the muscle above his knee. The vortex in the tip of the blade sucked the soul right out of him into that glowing reservoir, but his was no ordinary spirit. His was the soul of an old god, and it was too much for the whirling blade to contain. It quivered and then shattered into chunks of ice and mist, and the malignant spirit of Loki dispersed with it. Loki's body, meanwhile, shrank and ejected a number of weapons from his torso as it fell, including the Arrows of Vayu and the bow he'd been using to shoot them.

As when Hel had died, the *draugar* lost interest in fighting folks who fought back and began to drift away toward the human city. The Norse pantheon, which had bided its time until now, sprang into action. The cloud that had been hiding them from view grew and shifted perceptibly to enshroud the human helicopters, and only once they were screened did the Norse deities emerge, joining the armies in routing the *draugar*. Valkyries swooped down to sever necks with great axes. Mjöllnir plowed through them from above, crunching them into small craters, and returned to Thor's hand for another throw. Odin rode out with Hugin and Munin circling above him, Frigg and Freyja flanking either side.

I checked on the yewmen and Coriander: all singed but alive. I left them to see whether Brighid was all right. She'd gotten to her feet and was wrenching Fragarach out of her armor. She won it free as I got there and she offered it to me. There was no fresh blood on the blade. "I think you dropped this," she deadpanned. I tossed my looted sword aside as I took it from her.

"Yes, I did. I had a hound on my tail at the time." My head whipped around to the west. "I wonder what happened to him?" I didn't see him standing above the sea of *draugar*.

"He may yet live, and if he does, we will return him to Niflheim."

Grunts and punting noises drew our attention to Granuaile, who was kicking Loki's still form. "You evil fuck! Ugh! Victory is mine!" She stopped after that and stepped over him, to where the Arrows of Vayu lay on the ground. She scooped them up in her left hand and then glared in our direction, daring us to challenge her right to them. "I deserve to keep these. He tricked my father into going after them, and I suffered quite a bit to find them."

I nodded at her. "No argument here."

"Of course," Brighid agreed. She gestured at the body. "Well done. Whether you wanted a cookie for that or not, you're going to get thousands."

"How did things go in Taiwan?" I asked.

"I'm glad I went," she replied, "because Sun Wukong is an excellent teacher and Taipei is a wonderful city. I'm going to make Mandarin my next headspace. But I wasn't truly needed there. The masters of the heavens are more than a match for the lords of hell, and you knew that. You both made a decision for me as if I were a child, and I don't appreciate it. You might think the difference in our ages makes you wiser somehow, but I don't need to be thousands of years old to know you shouldn't treat someone like that."

Neither of us was able to respond, because a good chunk of the

Norse had arrived. Thor and Freyja landed first, each in their chariot, on either side of Loki's body. Odin and Frigg appeared soon after, escorted by Valkyries, and they set up a perimeter, making sure the retreating *draugar* streamed around and didn't interrupt—or interrupt us, anyway. I felt fairly certain they would be interrupting the citizens of Skoghall soon.

"Who slew him?" Odin demanded.

Granuaile raised her hand with the arrows clutched in them. "I did."

The Norse all blinked in surprise, clearly expecting Brighid to have done it. "The Druid? We didn't know you were here."

"Late arrival."

"Huh. You win all the cookies, then."

"Yeah, Brighid mentioned something like that."

"There is a more important matter to settle, Odin," Freyja said, descending from her chariot, sword in hand, "and you know it."

"I do, yes. Your pardon, Freyja. Druid," he said, and pointed to me so that there would be no question to whom he was speaking, "you have committed many crimes against the Æsir, for which you now need to answer."

"I've already answered," I said. "We made a deal in Oslo. I returned Gungnir. I helped destroy both Fenris and Jörmungandr, and I was instrumental in slaying both Hel and Loki."

"You never made a deal with *me*, Druid," Freyja said. "You killed the Norns and unleashed all of this. You killed Sleipnir, and your actions brought about the deaths of Ratatosk, my brother Freyr, Heimdall, Thor, and many Valkyries."

"First," I said, pointing to the thunder god, "looks to me like Thor's fine." The others she'd mentioned weren't fine, though. Or at least they weren't in attendance. Four figures muscled through the throng of *draugar* and passed between the Valkyries. It was the Olympians, Athena and Minerva and the two Apollos. Owls swooped down to land on the shoulders of the goddesses of wisdom. "And for the rest I have made recompense. You even helped us fight Fenris."

"Yes, at Odin's request, I agreed to defer my vengeance until a later date to accomplish a strategic goal. But that deferment has now ended. You have not answered for what you did to me personally, and Odin cannot bargain that away. And for that offense I call you out right now."

"Wait. What offense?" Granuaile said.

I closed my eyes and sighed. I knew Freyja would never forgive me, and I could not blame her.

"He recruited the frost giants to help him invade Asgard," Freyja explained. "And their promised payment . . . was me."

"What? Atticus, you never told me this."

"No, I didn't."

People tend not to volunteer what shames them the most. This was, as I'd feared, my personal judgment day, and I had so much to answer for: A discordant symphony of poor choices that accelerated and crescendoed from the moment I decided to fight Aenghus Óg. Boneheaded moves rooted in codes of honor and loyalty more than logic. Astounding dismissals of the warnings of two deities—one of them omniscient—who stated in plain terms that this wouldn't end well for me. And I am just honest enough with myself to realize that I would probably make those same decisions again, for that is how deeply flawed I am. My long life has not made me especially wise or some paragon of moral rectitude; it has just given me greater scope to cock everything up. Coyote's observation that all presidents were narcissists came back to me, for it struck me that I might be one such—not a politician, of course, but a person in power who made decisions in his own self-interest over the obvious interests of a great many other people.

I stepped away from Brighid on suddenly unsteady knees and faced the Norse goddess of war and beauty. Physically my knees should be fine—I'm still enjoying the ligaments and cartilage of a man in his early twenties—but such is the power of emotion over our bodies. "Freyja, I apologize. I never should have done that."

"I didn't come here for an apology." The grin on her face contained no scrap or hope of mercy. That same grin bloomed on the faces of the other Norse in attendance, and I remembered they had flashed such smiles before the battle too. This confrontation had been planned all along. They'd been looking forward to it.

"I know. I wanted to give you one anyway. It's sincere."

Freyja ignored this and bent her knees ever so slightly, raising her sword and her eyebrows. "So you will answer on your own? No pleas to Brighid or summoning the Morrigan to your side?"

"I will answer." I glanced at Granuaile and added, "On my own," to make sure she wouldn't intervene.

The land we stood on was dead, drained by the portal to the lower realms of the Norse. I was out of energy, my bear charm drained. I could not boost my strength or speed or perform the simplest binding without Gaia's energy. I was a mere human squaring off against a goddess who once held her own against the Morrigan and walked away—a trained fighter, sure, and with an excellent weapon, but still a mere human.

"Good," she said, crouching down to spring. I set myself in a defensive stance and felt the adrenaline begin to pump into my system. It didn't help much.

When Freyja attacked, she blurred with speed, and the only reason I got Fragarach up in time to block her blow was that she had some distance to cover and I guessed right about where the attack would come from. It came from above, just to the left of my head, and though I placed my blade in the perfect position, her strength was such that it simply knocked my blade down on contact while only slowing her strike somewhat. The edge hit my scavenged Fae armor between my neck and shoulder and it held, but I staggered back and she followed, kicking me in the chest to make sure I went down. That knocked me clean off my feet and I crashed into the flash-cooled volcanic earth, crunching my head onto something and seeing lights pop in my vision.

I heard some chuckles, maybe someone retching, but saw no incoming attack. She was waiting for me to get up again. Playing with me. And I felt the hot trickle of blood on my neck. I'd gashed my scalp and most likely earned a concussion. But when I got up I didn't feel like waiting for another beat-down. I charged and delivered the best flurry of attacks I could manage, but her speed and strength allowed her to deflect and parry and repel me. It was abundantly clear that I couldn't win and that she could end it whenever she wished, but she wasn't smiling anymore. Her expression was one of intense concentration. She was looking for something—but what was she after? She beckoned me forward, but I planted myself instead. I wasn't going to give her what she wanted.

"Fine," she growled. "I'll make you hurt first."

First before what? I wondered, but then she launched herself at me, and after my initial attempt to block, I was rocked by punishing blows to my body from both fists and feet. I took the pommel of her sword in my right temple, which stunned me until a tremendous impact chunked into the top of my right shoulder just outside the protection of the armor and it dawned on me, far too late, what she'd been after. I toppled over a few pounds lighter, my blood spraying onto the ground, and I let loose a single cry of horror and disbelief.

Freyja had cut off my right arm.

CHAPTER 24

turns out you can actually be sick with worry. I always thought it was just an expression, being worried sick. But I'm so stressed and fearful for Atticus as the duel begins that I throw up a little bit. Because without the earth's power at his call, he's so slow compared to Freyja. He doesn't have a chance and he's well aware and fighting anyway, and I'm sure that she's going to kill him, especially after that first blow—that's when I toss my cookies. But then she beats him down, hacks off his arm, kicks it away, and all I can think is that he's going to bleed to death because there's no way he can heal. I mean, apart from the fact that there is no power to draw upon, his healing triskele is now separated from his command. And so are his bound animal forms and his ability to shift planes.

I lunge forward and open my mouth to shout, "That's enough," but Freyja backs away and turns to the Norse, making it unnecessary. "It is done!" she crows, apparently agreeing that she has meted out sufficient justice. She spreads her arms wide, sword dripping Atticus's blood, enjoying the approval of the assembled deities and Valkyries, and I rush to his side and kneel next to him. His eyes are unfocused in shock already. I have a little bit of Gaia's energy remaining in the silver reservoir of Scáthmhaide, and I use it to close off those pumping arteries and prevent him from bleeding to death.

"Do the Olympians bear witness?" Freyja says, and it's such a strange question that I look up to see the Apollos nod, and then Athena and Minerva also.

Minerva's cool rich voice says, "I will tell Diana and Bacchus it is done."

Athena chimes in, "Artemis will be pleased."

Minerva adds, "Of course, Diana wishes to have her trophy."

"By all means. It is yours."

I don't know what kind of trophy they're expecting and I tense when Minerva comes forward, wondering if she's going to want his heart or something, but the goddess merely picks up Atticus's severed arm from the ground.

"Mercury was supposed to deliver this message," she says to Atticus, "but as he's not here I will deliver it in his stead. Diana and Bacchus now consider their grievances with you satisfactorily concluded. You need not fear anything from them so long as you do nothing else to awaken their wrath. I imagine it is the same with Artemis?" She looks up at Athena, and her counterpart nods.

"It is."

Minerva returns her gaze to Atticus. "Have you anything you wish me to say to them?"

Atticus shakes his head, his lips pressed tightly together as he takes deep breaths through his nose.

"Then fare thee well, Druid," she says, and walks off with his arm, leaving Atticus no chance of reattaching it.

I crane my head around to see how Brighid's taking this, and she is standing like an exhibit in the Hall of Armor at the Metropolitan Museum.

"Aren't you going to say anything?" I ask her.

"I said plenty to both the Norse and the Olympians earlier. They were not allowed, under any circumstances, to kill him."

"You *allowed* this?"

"I could hardly prevent it, Granuaile. They had serious grievances. Winning his life was the best victory I could expect."

Gods, these gods. Making decisions about our lives without our consent—they just kept doing it.

"Am I to suffer some kind of judgment and sentence too?"

"No, you're free to go," Brighid says. "In fact, you need to go."

"What? Why?" I turn back to where the Olympians had been standing and see that they've mounted the winged horses of some Valkyries, and they hold on as the Choosers of the Slain lift them above the hordes of *draugar*.

Freyja answers me as she wipes Atticus's blood off her sword using some rags she had in her chariot. "We have some words to trade with him in private. He will come to no further harm."

I have words I'd like to trade with her, but I bite them back. "Give me a moment, then?"

I get a scant nod, and then I turn to Atticus and try to pitch my words as low as possible, though it's probably a futile effort when one is surrounded by deities.

"I'm so sorry about your arm. Relieved you're still alive, though."

He only nods at me, says nothing. I think he's doing some stoic thing or simply trying to deny the Norse any satisfaction at hearing him in pain, and he's scared that if he makes any sound right now it'll come out as a scream. I know how that feels.

"We need to talk more," I tell him, "but this is not the time or place. I will go home and fetch whatever you need, because you can't shift—speaking of which, we need to get you out of here. Hold on." I rise to my feet and find the Allfather, calling out to him, "Odin, may I strike a bargain? My winnings to you—all the Girl Scout Cookies I'm owed—in return for taking Atticus wherever he wants to go on Bifrost and then bringing his hounds to him there directly afterward."

"Done!" Odin says, much quicker than I'd anticipated. He didn't even have to think about it. He might have been intending to grant that favor anyway. Or he had an unhealthy obsession for Girl Scout Cookies—Frigg's scowl at this development seemed to imply as much.

I squat down next to Atticus and lay a hand on his chest. "I will see you soon." He nods twice, teeth clenched against pain, and then I rise again and sweep my staff around, pointing to all the deities and reminding them of what Freyja said. "No further harm."

And then I run out of that circle of scheming immortals, race for the bound tree to the south, and let the tears I'd been holding back flow out and blur my vision. I counted that as a victory too: I had shed nothing—neither blood nor tears—in front of those inhuman creatures.

CHAPTER 25

i t's perfectly natural to scream when one loses an arm at the edge of a blade, but beyond the first cry of surprise and pain, I shunted all the screaming I wanted to do into a different headspace, because giving voice to it would only give the Norse pleasure. Since there was very little else I could deny them, I would at least deny them that. But there was plenty of woe going on in that space as I realized that removing my arm had been Freyja's goal all along. It wasn't just my sword arm: It was also my ability to heal, to shift planes, and to take animal forms. I'd still be able to perform free-form bindings and would retain the rest of my skills, but my effectiveness as a champion for Gaia was much reduced. And my life as I'd lived it for more than two millennia was over. I'd never fly as an owl or run as a hound again. I'd never be able to travel the globe as I used to.

Granuaile came over to administer what was probably lifesaving first aid, but then she requested that Odin bring my hounds to me wheresoever I chose to be deposited, as if I would never choose to go home to the cabin in Oregon. I might be thick about a great many things, but even I could tell what that meant. My day of judgment would soon grow worse, for it was pretty clear that in my love's eyes I had been found wanting.

I understood, finally, what Jesus meant when he warned me against going to Asgard, when he said I'd suffer pain like I'd never felt before. Because everything I felt right then—the great gnawing absence that nibbled at the edges of my will to live—wouldn't heal up after a few weeks of convalescence. The physical pain would fade with time, but the emotions associated with the loss would stay sharp and prick me anew each day. Every time I wanted to slip into a river and play around as an otter or take wing as a great horned owl, I'd have to remain awkwardly human and remember I had only myself to blame. Oh, there was plenty of anguish bubbling away in that headspace. But I brought Old Norse to the fore as Freyja approached. She picked up Fragarach from the ground and took a knee next to me.

"This sword will be my trophy. I personally think you should have been killed, because I am not persuaded that you have come close to balancing the scales, but Brighid and some others lobbied in your favor." She leaned closer. "I have to go clean up your mess now, because the *draugar* are entering Skoghall."

I flick my eyes to the mass of bodies streaming past us and realize it's the Einherjar and dwarfs, in pursuit of the *draugar*. "Wherever you choose to go after this, Druid, make sure it's far from here. You are not welcome in the lands of the Norse from this day forward. So long as you respect that condition, you have nothing to fear from us now."

I give her a nod and nothing more.

"I hope you forget that after some time passes," she murmured, low and menacing. "I hope you trespass and give me an excuse to finish this. Please do." She leaves, taking Fragarach with her, and Brighid comes over, her helmet off now that danger has passed.

"Ireland is safe and thus is Tír na nÓg. I know you do not feel it now and may resent my part in this, Siodhachan, but know this: I believe you have done much good today. If I may grant you a boon in the future, call on me." I saw her hesitate, on the verge of saying more, but she decided against it with a tiny shake of her head and said farewell.

With her exit I was left in a circle of Norse, and they simply stared at me. I rolled to my left and levered myself up to my feet. I felt a bit light-headed, and I paused a moment for the spinning in my head to subside before taking careful steps over to Thor and Odin. I nodded at them and they returned the gesture, waiting for me to say something. I started with the red-bearded thunder god.

"You're Thor?"

"Yes."

"So who was it that Leif Helgarson killed with Moralltach?"

Thor snorted in amusement. "Oh, that was me." He grinned briefly, and then it melted away, replaced by chagrin at the memory. "That was the old me, who had been bound by the prophecy of the Norns regarding Ragnarok. I lost my way while they lived; over the centuries I became corrupted, thinking that there would be no consequences for my behavior, until the day I met Jörmungandr. That is the true poison of prophecy and destiny, the implication that you are somehow not responsible for your actions. But I was wrong, for there were consequences, weren't there? Indeed, I was justly brought to account by those I had wronged. And do you know what is miraculous about that? I am glad. I am grateful. I am manifest again thanks to those who still worship me, and I find it is a new age of humanity, more hopeful than before. I'm remembering what it means to be good. I have this same hope for you, Druid. For now you are being brought to account, and it may serve to refresh your perspective."

"Or turn me bitter and vengeful."

Thor wagged his head, admitting the possibility, then chucked his chin at the still form of Loki. "He was bitter and vengeful."

"Point taken. What about Heimdall and Freyr and the others?"

"There is hope that they will receive enough worship to manifest again, but at present they remain memories. And for my part, I bear you no ill will. Odin does not agree, but I think you did me a favor. Perhaps in time you will see we have done you one."

"Perhaps."

"I'm glad we could talk. But there is still much for me to do, so if you will excuse me." He strode to his chariot and took off to the north after the *draugar,* leaving me with Odin and Frigg and the Valkyries. Odin watched him go and then his eye fixed on me.

"I am not of Thor's mind, Druid. I still bear you plenty of ill will. I rather hoped you would die in battle."

"Yes, you mentioned such a hope to me before." Frigg said nothing, but the expression on her face communicated plenty. She agreed with Odin.

"I will content myself with knowing that you are miserable. And hopefully far away from here. Where is it you wish to go?"

"The eastern coast of Tasmania, if you wouldn't mind, to the east of a town called Triabunna. Oakhampton Bay. I'd like my hounds brought to me there—Oberon and Starbuck."

"By all means. Let us go, for I have other work to do, but I want those cookies. You joined the pool, did you not?"

I ground my teeth. "I did."

"Excellent. I will let you know where to send the cookies here on Midgard. I want Samoas."

"Of course. I'll see to it."

We don't speak as I trail behind him and Frigg to the nearest piece of unspoiled land. They will need that to summon Bifrost. They were mounted but didn't offer me a ride. I saw Valkyries off to the right, capturing a wounded Garm in a net. He survived, then. Good.

Part of the golf course had withered and died from the drain of the portal, and I had to trudge across it.

"Is the portal to Hel still open?" I asked them, since I couldn't feel the earth's energy under my feet.

"No," Odin replied. "It closed once Loki died."

Perhaps Granuaile would see to mending the land. She would have to see to quite a bit, I supposed, without my help.

The reconnection of Gaia underneath my heel was all too brief, because Odin summoned Bifrost immediately, and then we traveled in a starry furred space between planes until Odin delivered me to the northern beach of Oakhampton Bay. I gave him instructions on how to find my cabin and which hounds were the ones to bring me, and then I was alone in the darkness. It was that oddly timeless time between midnight and dawn in Tasmania, when the absence of light and activity suggests that the world may have stopped moving.

I remained standing but reconnected with the Tasmanian elemental and asked for his aid in healing my stump. Granuaile had stopped the bleeding, but the wound was still open and susceptible to infection besides being quite painful. Relief washed over me in one sense, but in another the pain only increased as I felt the accelerated growth of new skin smoothing over the place where my arm used to be. I felt so off balance and unmoored. Alive, but unable to think what I should do next.

We seldom recognize where the chapters of our lives begin and end until we are gifted the benediction of hindsight. Our loves, our triumphs, our tragedies—they do not exist unless we endure long enough to label them so. I am not sure if I have accomplished much else, but I have at least survived long enough to exult and mourn, to cherish my victories and regret my mistakes.

Both are legion.

I think surviving Ragnarok and getting the gods to leave me alone should be counted somehow as a victory. It just doesn't feel like one right now, because by losing a large part of my connection to Gaia I've lost . . . well, too much.

Maybe that will change with time, but time has a way of passing slowly when you're suffering. I spent an uncounted span in the darkness, listening to the waves lap against the beach, and thought perhaps the night would never end, until the sky grayed with the

approaching dawn. That's when the light of Bifrost returned and
two dogs bounded off it to land on the beach. Odin did not descend
to chat, which suited me fine.

<Atticus! You made it!> Oberon shouted in my head as he gal-
loped my way.

<Hi, Atticus! Good human!> Starbuck added.

"Most of me made it, yeah," I said. "Careful, now, don't jump
on me; my balance isn't so good yet."

<Whoa, suffering cats, Atticus, what happened to your arm?>

"It's gone," I told him. "But the world is safe." At least for a little
while. At least from Loki. There were still literal fires to put out, no
doubt, and there would be plenty of questions asked by most of humanity and no satisfactory answers for them. They would have to
learn to live with the mystery and rebuild what was destroyed, while
I would have to solve the mystery of how to rebuild my life.

<Safe except from squirrels, you mean.>

"Right. Except from squirrels. That threat continues to hang
over us all."

<So what happened?>

I sighed. "Would it be all right if I shared that with you later? I
have a lot to process and . . . I think I want to write it all down.
With my left hand, which should be an adventure."

<Oh, sure. That would be fine. What do you want to do now?>

"I think I'd like to have something to eat and drink."

<You always have the best ideas, Atticus.>

<Yes food!> Starbuck said.

"Come on, then. Town's to the west. We live here now, even
though we don't have a place to live yet and we need to get ourselves situated. But first, as a matter of principle: breakfast."

<Yes! Principles are important.>

"Indeed they are. I think it's past time for me to examine mine,
but '*breakfast first*,' at least, is rock solid. Let's go."

Dogs, I think, might be more important than principles. They
provide love and loyalty when you need them the most.

CHAPTER 26

With the help of the Tasmanian elemental, I find Atticus at a teahouse in Triabunna, painted yellow with green trim and potted flowers all about the porch. He and the hounds are on that porch, though he's sitting on the edge of it with his bare feet resting in the dirt rather than sitting in their wicker outdoor seating. He still has plenty of healing to do and he looks rough. He's discarded the cuirass he'd scavenged from the field, but the shirt he wore underneath is torn and bloodstained down his right side. He's still wearing an armor skirt of hardened leather strips, though, and I'm sure he looks less than sane to modern eyes. I'm surprised the teahouse served him like that. He looks tired and miserable as I approach, and his face offers no smile of relief or welcome, but the hounds wag their tails.

I let the duffel bag I'm carrying slip off my shoulder. "Hi. I brought you some fresh clothes and things. New prepaid phone, your ID and credit cards, Aussie cash, that kind of thing."

"Thanks," he says. "Odin told you where I was?"

"Yeah."

"Mind grabbing a shirt out of the bag for me? Lady in the teahouse almost called an ambulance when she saw this."

"Sure." He peels his blood-soaked shirt off over his head and puts on the fresh one I hand him, and he does so with only a little awkwardness. He must have those nerve endings locked down tight.

I'm scared about what comes next as I sit down on the porch with him, feet in the dirt. "Sooo . . ."

"Hold on a second. Oberon, would you and Starbuck mind heading around to the back and investigating some shrubbery or something? We need to talk in private. Just holler if anyone gives you any trouble."

The hounds oblige him and trot around the corner of the house, and I grow suspicious. "You already know why I'm here?"

"Yes, but it wasn't any kind of divination, if that's what you're thinking. Telling Odin to drop me off anywhere but home was a pretty big hint. Bringing me my ID and some clothes was another."

I wince and suck my teeth; I hadn't realized I'd telegraphed it so plainly. "Oh, yeah. Sorry."

"But go ahead. Say it."

I take a deep breath and let it out. "Well, I want you to know I'd already made up my mind about this before we got interrupted by the Norse. I mean, obviously you're already having the worst day ever and I'm really not trying to pile on. But it won't be less true later, and after hearing what you did to Freyja—gods, Atticus, I know where she's coming from. I want to hit you myself. I can't believe you did that. It just confirms what I was already feeling: I think we should go our separate ways. Because you made a decision for me, sending me to Taiwan like that, and it doesn't matter if you thought it was for my own good. I can't live in this situation where I have to wonder if you're manipulating things behind my back. I know you're not the only one doing it either—obviously Brighid thinks it's fine, and Flidais too. Well, it's not. I am simply done with all that. I'm nobody's chess piece." My throat dries up suddenly as I see a tear leaking out of the edge of Atticus's eye, trailing toward his jaw. I continue in a calmer voice, since I'd gotten a little worked up. "I am obviously grateful for all you've done for me and I owe you everything. If you ever need me, I will be there. But this—us—it needs to end."

He nods and his voice is a tightly controlled rasp. "First, I am sorry, Granuaile. I was wrong. And second, I understand your decision and do not blame you. Clearly this is my time to go off to a corner of the world and think about what I've done. May I ask about your plans regarding the cabin?"

"Oh. Yes. Well, I really can't leave the cabin now, with Orlaith just having her pups. We need three months to get them weaned, and then we'll be out. Can you give me that?"

"Not a problem. I can give you longer if you want. But when you're ready to vacate, if you'd let me know, please . . . ? I'd like to sell it."

"Of course." He is making this easy for me. "Do you need me to bring you anything else?"

"No, the clothes and the basic needs of modern commerce are all here. Thanks. If I think of anything, I'll give you a call."

"Okay, then." I get to my feet, a bit disoriented to be walking away from someone who's been a huge part of my life to this point. It's necessary, though; there's an open road before me and I want to see where it goes. "Goodbye for now. I hope that after all of this . . . Well. May harmony find you."

He replies in kind and I take my leave, intending to return to the cabin in Oregon for some sleep and a cuddle with Orlaith. I hope harmony does find us both, though it will have to find us in different places for a while.

I will finish up my studies in Poland while Orlaith is nursing, and we'll find those puppies a good home somewhere—if not with Owen's grove, then with some other lucky people. I think Orlaith and I will go to Taiwan after that to discover how we may both learn and grow. I would first like to learn how that monkey in Wu-kong's shop knew my time to be sorry would be coming soon. For I *am* very sorry. This is not the future I'd been contemplating a month ago.

Perhaps Atticus and I will be together again and perhaps we won't, remaining nothing more than colleagues of a sort. I write this knowing full well he'll read it. He knows from experience that attraction is an alchemy of chemicals and circumstance and ever-shifting emotions, and they may or may not align and ignite again for us at some point in the future. We have a lot of it in front of us.

It's been good to review how we got here. All I can conclude, however, is that he's given me an extraordinary life and he's already lived one. Despite that, he remains a work in progress, and so do I. So do we all, for that matter.

In one regard I am eternally content: I know he and I will always love Gaia, both together and apart.

CHAPTER 27

"Owen? Owen, wake up. You have to see this."

"Hnngh? What? See what?"

Greta's standing over me and there's sunlight streaming through the window. "People trying to figure out what happened yesterday. The news is hilarious."

"News? Uggh."

"Plus your sloth looks like she's missing you, so get up."

"Oh, shite! Slomo!" That cleared me head quick. "Is she all right?"

"Seems like it, but it's hard to tell. Is she going to stick around?"

"I'm not sure. Hey, what do ye think of the apprentices having wolfhound puppies? Granuaile's hound had six and they'd like to give them to us. Would the pack be all right with that?"

Greta flinched. "That's a lot of number one and number two."

"We've got a lot of land and we can tell them to go outside. Instant training, the Druid way."

Me love considers it and shrugs. "Sure, why not? I mean, run it by the parents first. If one says no, then it's no for all of them. Can't have one being left out. But come on, now, you gotta see this."

The news isn't what I'd call hilarious. Earthquakes in Bavaria. Animals killing people in Peru. Bizarre sightings of demons and flying monkeys in Taiwan. Conflicts between strange figures in most every country, with eyewitnesses claiming to see gods and other supernatural creatures in the flesh. Lots of collateral damage. And over all of it, fires to put out around the world as a result of a singular explosion in Sweden. What Greta finds amusing is how they keep bringing on experts to say they don't know what's going on and nothing makes sense.

"We could have walked downtown and shifted into wolves right in front of everybody yesterday," she says, "and it wouldn't even have made the news today."

"Is there a fire near here?" I ask. "If there is, I'd like to help put it out." That might be the best use of the next few days or weeks—putting out fires, since they obviously do tremendous damage but can impact smaller ecosystems disproportionately.

"I'll switch to local news. And don't worry about the kids; they're out with their parents in town right now. Wanted to give you a chance to sleep."

"Thanks. I'll check in with Slomo." I pour a cup of coffee in the kitchen and then use that connection I forged yesterday to send messages of happiness and welcome and an inquiry into her health, the equivalent of smiling and asking, "*How's me favorite sloth this morning?*" Her answer comes quick and then I'm smiling for real as I step outside, steaming mug in hand.

<Hi, Oaken! I am kinda cold and dry and hungry for fresh leaves. But your tiny humans are great. They want to be Droods of Guy like you?>

Druids of Gaia, yes.

<Oh, yeah! I thought maybe I wasn't saying that right. Actual

words are hard. Pictures and feelings are better. Are you still in the house?>

Just came out to join ye.

<I am in a tree nearby, and did I mention it is cold and dry here?>

You did. We should probably get you back to your jungle and find ye a nice tree to dangle from. One that feels like having a nice long talk.

<That would be great! Except I wish you could dangle with me. We could watch monkeys play around and protect each other from toucans.>

I don't think toucans will ever bother ye, Slomo.

<They are waiting for their chance. We must be vigilant.>

I find her on the east side of the house, dangling upside down from a juniper branch and smiling at me.

All out of leaves, then?

<Yes, I ate them all.>

Ready to go home now?

<I am. It will be both happy and sad at the same time, though. The word for that in Slothian is *dolofabolo*. Do you have a human word for it?>

Oh, aye. Lots of words in lots of languages. The word for it in English is bittersweet. Come on, then, hop on me back. I'm gonna give ye some juice to move fast.

<Going home will be bittersweet,> Slomo says as she drops onto me back and wraps her arms around me neck.

Dolofabolo, love.

<I hope you don't misunderstand me, Oaken. I really like seeing new things and I want to see more. But I also need to rest and re-charge with familiar things.>

I understand completely, I say as I begin an easy jog to the bound tree located in our back acreage. *There's so much I want to see too, but ye can't just go all the time without a break. Ye need a quiet place to retreat and chew on life and take time to digest it.*

<Yes, that's it exactly!>

Shall we make a habit of taking little trips like this, going some-where new for a day and then coming home to talk it over with a tree?

<Yes! Now that I know there is a great big huge world outside the jungle, I want to see it all! But in small doses, please, and on Oakenback, like this.>

Ha! Ye like riding Oakenback, eh?

<I do. I can see things and you move at half the speed of a monkey—which is still super fast to me, but not too fast.>

When we shift back into the Amazon basin, the humidity smacks me face like a wet herring and just sticks there.

<Ahhh!> Slomo cries in relief. <That's more like it!> And then she barfs on me shoulder. Its heat and consistency are much like the Amazonian atmosphere. But I tell meself that this time, she tried to vomit affectionately. Or maybe it's me own affection that I'm pro-jecting.

Methinks I truly needed to meet her. This wonder she has for the world has reawakened me own; it's what the grove of appren-tices feels every day, and that's something I need to encourage. The danger of growing old is growing comfortable and complacent at the same time. We should seek out the new and strange and ap-plaud it and throw wild fecking parties whenever it walks into our lives. We should be building roads in and out of our own wee heads rather than erecting walls around them. And I had to be thrown forward two thousand years into the future to understand this, to have no retreat available to me before I saw what a dark mental well I had dug for meself. I was lucky to have Siodhachan lower down a rope to fetch me out, but I'd wager that a few billion people are in dark places like that and they're not even trying to escape; they're both snug and smug and content to stunt the growth of their own spirits.

I'll be a bucket o' beaver snot before I let meself shrink into the space of a small mind again. I don't want that for meself *or* me grove. These new Druids are going to learn how big Gaia truly is, that she's here for us all and we should be there for all of her.

We head north from the bound tree until Slomo points to what she calls "an ideal dangle." I can't see what makes it better than any other tree around, but that's why she's the expert. I make sure she has enough energy to climb it quickly and get herself situated, and then I promise I'll see her in a few days.

<What if I change trees?>

. . . Is that likely?

<Not really, no.>

Then I'll find ye, don't worry.

I'm going to see the world with that sloth. And I will love Greta and teach me apprentices and apply the Second Law of Owen wherever I can. So that's me road ahead all settled. I might even wind up knowing Jack Shite someday.

Siodhachan said Ragnarok could well be the end of the world, but I'm right glad he cocked that one up. If anything, it feels like a new beginning.

EPILOGUE

One of the great gifts that talking hounds give to Druids is that they don't allow you to drown yourself in alcohol. I know this because I tried to do it a few days later. After I bought a twelve-pack and drank four beers in the span of a few minutes, Oberon ran away with the rest of the pack in his mouth and tossed the box over the cliff I was lounging on at Oakhampton Bay. The bottles smashed on the rocks below.

"Oberon, what the hell were you thinking?"

<Remember Bingo the beagle, Atticus? He was worried about Dúghlas drinking so much and he had to save his human. I'm just doing the same thing here. Plus I'm worried about your bladder. It's so tiny,> he said.

"Well, that glass is going to hurt a fish or an anemone or something—"

<Glass? Let's pause for a moment to remember one of the greatest rhetorical questions ever asked, the one John McClane posed in *Die Hard*: "Who gives a shit about glass?" What you should be worried about right now is your state of mind. You should be doing

something to relax besides exploding your bladder. Yoga or bubble baths or recreational wombat chasing—>

Starbuck picked up on that and turned in tight circles of excitement, shouting, <Yes wombats!>

"Oberon."

<If you would just chase them with me, Atticus, you would see how relaxing it is! Every time I'm closing in on a wombat I'm thinking how incredibly relaxed I feel—>

"Oberon. I . . . I don't want to hear it."

<Fine. Then hear this: You still have two jobs.>

"I don't have any jobs. I'm invested in a solar company with Suluk Black that will keep me flush forever."

<Wrong. You have two jobs: Feed me and heal Tasmanian devils. Which means feed me and serve Gaia. And by feed me, I mean give me whatever I want. And since we're traveling around the countryside a lot looking for devils to heal, I want you to buy me a thermos and keep it filled with hot sausage gravy. I know people don't normally think of gravy as a thirst quencher, but it totally is. Gravy is both hydrating and fortifying, and professional athletes chug it during time-outs.>

"No, they don't."

<They will soon. They just haven't caught up with the science yet because it's difficult to achieve the right consistency for chugging. No—I mean the right *viscosity*. That's the word. Viscostitists are working on it right now, and I deserve a gravy thermos for telling you.>

"*Viscostitists?* That's not even a word."

<Viscostitologists, then.>

My diaphragm heaves in quick succession and I realize belatedly that I'm laughing. And once my slow-moving thoughts catch up and I hear both made-up words in my head and how silly they are, I laugh louder. And soon it's out of control, I've given up trying to stay upright, and both Oberon and Starbuck swoop in to lick my face and keep it going. It doesn't remove even a smidgen of my anguish, but it does remind me that there are other emotions to feel and I could stand to enjoy a dollop of joy in my dolor. He's right about my jobs. Regardless of how miserable I feel, I do need to feed my hounds and serve Gaia. Perhaps focusing on them will pull me through to a better place. Once I wind down from the laugh and attempt to give them both some scritches, one at a time, the two dogs snuggle up against me on that cliff top for a serious nap.

In Tír na nÓg you'd have your arm back, a voice whispers in my head.

"Morrigan?"

The Chooser of the Slain materializes in front of me, seated nude in a pub with a tall glass of dark brew in front of her. I'm seated across from her, also have a glass, and am also lacking a shred of clothing. Everyone else in the establishment is dressed but not paying any attention to us. It's going to be one of those dreams. Now that she's materialized, she speaks aloud instead of whispering in my head.

"The beer is great there too, Siodhachan. Goibhniu makes sure of that. The stresses of life—its cares and worries—are all gone."

"Well, yeah, because what you're talking about is me being dead, right? You're talking about Tír na nÓg as an afterlife, not the plane I pass through while I'm shifting."

"Yes. And it's quite the party here now. Manannan and Fand have arrived, and three yeti, and so many more. It's certainly superior to your current situation."

I reach out to my dream pint with my dream arm and take a delicious swallow. "I don't currently have any good beer or a right arm, that's correct, but I'm not ready to agree that having those things make death a better deal than life."

"You're tremendously unhappy."

"That's true. I'm depressed and heartbroken and wracked by guilt ferrets. But I'm not longing for death as an alternative."

"Why not? You've had a good run, as the mortals say."

"I've had a *long* run, certainly, but I don't think I can qualify it as a *good* one. I was hiding for most of it, fighting for my life for the rest of it, and I made plenty of bad decisions along the way. I'd like to try being good for a while, genuinely good for Gaia. Build up some karma points."

The Morrigan's eyes flashed red for the briefest second. "Karma is not a concept applied to Irish lives. I will not be judging you when you part the veil, nor will anyone. You know this."

"I do know that. But in judging myself I'd like to provide some balance to my life before I give it up."

The Morrigan smirked at first and tried to hide it by putting her glass up to her lips, but then it turned into a full smile and a chuckle and she gave up, placing the glass back down. "Do you know why I adore you, Siodhachan?"

"I don't, actually. It's a mystery."

"You often see the good you do as bad and just as often make terrible decisions in service to what you think is good. You are so wonderfully damaged."

The same could be said for the Morrigan, but I didn't think it politic to say so aloud. "Ah, and you think you can fix me up?"

"Why would I want to fix you? I like you this way."

"Well, thanks, I guess? Despite your acceptance of my many flaws, I'd like to work on some things for a while. And may I ask: Why are we naked?"

The Morrigan snorted and waved a dismissive hand. "I think it better to ask why these people are dressed. You have spent too long in the company of prudish mortals."

"That's a fair question. You're probably right."

"I'm right about a great many things. You would be happier with us in Tír na nÓg. With me."

I nodded to buy myself some time to choose my words carefully. "Most likely. But I don't feel I deserve such happiness yet. Let us stay in touch. Perhaps through these strange dreams you've visited me with a couple times now. Let us drink many more of these fabulous dream pints together, naked, in front of a congregation of strangers. In the waking hours I'll continue to observe the rites as I always have, of course, but those are one-sided affairs, not ideal for conversation. If you wish us to have a relationship deeper than what we've had thus far, then let us have a proper courtship. Perhaps something will grow from that."

"And if it doesn't?"

"Well, then, I suppose it doesn't. We still get to have fun together in the meantime. The thing is, Morrigan, I need some time. If I may—please forgive me, as I'm still processing quite a bit of this and sort of thinking aloud here—before you decided to face both Artemis and Diana in combat, you thought about it for a good while, yes? It wasn't an impulse of the moment?"

"No. Or yes. To be clear: My exit was planned. I had considered it for centuries."

"Centuries! Ah. Then consider that I have only begun to consider it in the past few days. I need to think it through. Set my many affairs in order. And perhaps write it all down. You know what the catalyst was that brought us here, to this moment in this dream? The day you flew into my shop in Tempe and told me that Aenghus Óg had found me."

The Morrigan tilted her head, her eyes edging toward red. "Is this . . . blame?"

"No, not a shred of blame. It's mere recognition of cause and effect. If there's any blame to be cast, be assured I'll cast it on myself. I am simply saying that I need time. There will be time, yes— I beg your pardon, but might you be familiar with the poet T. S. Eliot?"

"No. Was he Irish?"

"Alas, he was not. The British and the Americans both claim him. But our conversation reminded me of one of his poems, where he said there would be time: *Time for you and time for me, /And time yet for a hundred indecisions, /And for a hundred visions and revisions, /Before the taking of a toast and tea.* After all, you had thousands of years beyond mine to consider, am I correct?"

"I do hope, Siodhachan, that you are not asking me to specify my age."

"No, merely confirming that you lived longer than me, which should be obvious."

"Yes."

"That being given, I hope you will understand: I need a while to think this over. And it may be a good long while, just as you took a long while to make your decision."

"I do understand that, Siodhachan. I respect it and will do my best to be patient. But perhaps you are forgetting something: You have no reason to fear death. There is only pleasure awaiting you in Tír na nÓg. That is something I can guarantee."

"You can?"

"Yes, of course! Siodhachan . . . I love you."

Perhaps at another time, her plain speaking would have affected me differently. But after dwelling on the many manifest flaws that had caused me to be maimed and alone, I could not fathom how that could possibly be true. "Gods below, Morrigan, why?"

She shifted in her seat and fidgeted with her beer glass. "As one of the gods below that you just invoked, allow me to have my reasons. I am not . . . accustomed to sharing such sentiments."

"I understand and withdraw the question."

"Is your reluctance . . . because of Granuaile?" She held up a hand to forestall an early reply. "I am not jealous of her and have never been. I ask merely for information."

I sighed. "Perhaps that is a part of it. But it is by no means the sum. I have amends to make. Regrets I must own, and many seasons of peace I must sow and harvest. One day—I hope, anyway—we will feel the sadness peel away from our past and stand justified, knowing we could not, as imperfect beings, have made any other choices than the ones that haunt us in this moment. I know, intellectually, that this must be true. But my heart is incapable of feeling it right now. With sufficient time and the daily practice of kindness, I hope to stroll someday into that soft green glen where I can finally be free of my own wretched self. That's going to be a victory like nothing I've ever felt, and I want to make it to that space and live there a while. And I know that you will say I could spend that time in Tír na nÓg. But here I can spend that necessary time and still do some good for Gaia."

The Morrigan nodded slowly. "I too have much to work on. This suits me well. So I will wait. And we will, as you say, visit and drink and court."

The strangers dissolved into mist and the Morrigan melted into shadow. I woke up from my nap without an arm or a beer and with the same hollow dread for the future. But I got up and told the hounds it was time for me to get back to work.

I turned away from the ocean, intending to walk inland some distance before contacting the elemental about where to find the next den of Tasmanian devils, only to find a woman standing perhaps fifty yards away, clearly waiting for me.

I did not immediately recognize her. She appeared middle-aged, had tawny brown skin, and wore a navy blue dress, modestly cut, with a white headscarf to shield her from the sun. A pleasant smile on her face welcomed me as I approached, but she wasn't going to call out until I drew nearer. One could tell by her bearing that she was not the sort to raise her voice. She had her hands clasped loosely in front of her, and from her fingers dangled an ivory envelope.

"Hello, Siodhachan," she said once I was close enough to hear at a normal volume. "Do you know me?"

"I don't recognize you, sorry," I replied, shaking my head.

"I look different now." Her brown eyes gleamed above a generous nose, and there were laugh lines at the corners of her eyes. "The last time you saw me was in Arizona, and I was white because I manifested from the mind of Katie MacDonagh. I blessed some arrows for you."

That could be only one person. "Mary?"

She beamed at me. "You do remember!"

"Of course! It's wonderful to see you again. I hope nothing is wrong?"

"Oh, no, child, all is well, and Katie sends her love. I've come to give you a message from my son. A letter, in fact."

"Jesus wrote me a letter?"

"Yes, I thought it was a bit eccentric, for we haven't so much as a book of stamps in heaven, never mind a postal service, but he likes to keep us guessing, you know." She held out the letter to me and I took it.

"He does have a reputation for that. Thank you."

"Quite welcome, my child. I shall leave you to it; he's not expecting a reply, and there are some people in town who require my attention. But I am so glad to see you safe. Peace be with you."

"And also with you, Mary." I looked at the envelope, which bore my name on it without an address. "Ha! He wrote it in red ink?"

Mary tittered. "He thought it was funny and said you might appreciate the joke."

"I do. Please give him my best regards."

"I will. Farewell." She turned toward town, headscarf billowing gently in an afternoon breeze, and I turned my attention to the letter. There was a wax seal on the back in red, imprinted with the silhouette of a dove in flight. I pried open the seal, unfolded a single sheet, and began to read.

Dear Siodhachan,

Welcome to one of the timelines in which you survived. If you're wondering if there's one in which you're happy right now, the answer is no. You are universally miserable, and this is the moment where I could say I told you so, but we are friends and I wish to remain your friend. Instead, since you did not heed my advice earlier, I hope you will heed it now:

Live in peace. Do not pick up a sword again, and harmony will find you.

By the way, your fly is open. It was totally open in front of my mom, and yes, she saw.

Yours in joy and whiskey,

Jesus

I looked down to confirm and, yes, indeed, my fly was open. "Oh, crap!" I hurriedly zipped it and looked up at the sky. "Sorry," I mumbled, then flapped the letter a couple of times in the air. "And thanks for the advice. I'm ready to listen now and I will live in peace. If I don't die of embarrassment first."

Oberon, alert as ever, did not miss an opportunity to tease me. <Heh heh. Hey, Atticus, remember that time you flashed your junk at the mother of God? That was just now actually, but I didn't want you to forget.>

THE VERY LAST EPILOGUE

a week after the Morrigan's visitation and my mortifying faux pas in front of Mary, I sat under a swamp gum eucalyptus with Oberon and Starbuck, taking a modest lunch break from healing Tasmanian devils. Without my healing triskele tattoo it took a while longer to do the first healing, because I had to craft the bindings free-form, but once I created a macro for it the process worked just fine with Tasmania's help. We'd finished our salame and crackers and I was giving Oberon a lazy, distracted belly rub.

<I know this is going to sound selfish, Atticus, but I really miss your other hand. Belly rubs aren't quite the same.>

"I'm sorry, buddy."

<There has to be something we can do to fix it. Hey, wait!> My hound rolled over and sat up, his tail wagging, excited about whatever had just occurred to him. Starbuck leapt to his feet and crouched, in case Oberon was ready to play. <Atticus, what about that guy who owes you favors?>

"Which guy, Oberon?"

<I remember you told me some stories two centuries ago around the fire. It was when Clever Girl was in her training period, I think.

There was some pretty good stew, I recall, once you got rid of the carrots. But anyway, you told us a story about this god who wanted you to fetch some stuff out of a library but you wound up stealing a book full of some really loud cat sex, and another time that same god had you fetch a magic cauldron from a naughty necromancer in Wales.>

"Oh! You mean Ogma!"

<Yeah, that's who I mean. You said he would owe you a pretty big favor for both of those things, right?>

"Yes, that's right."

<Well, it's time to call in those favors, don't you think? I mean, when were you planning on using those? They didn't go bad, did they, like a cheesesteak left out in the sun? That would be . . . that would be so sad. I'm getting very sad just thinking about it. Why do people abandon their cheesesteaks, Atticus, *why*? Do they not have stomachs or taste buds or what? Help me understand!> He tilted back his head to howl mournfully and Starbuck joined in, albeit in a much higher register.

"Oberon, please—you made a good point and then you got sidetracked. I can't explain wanton cheesesteak abuse any more than I can explain why some people watch other people fishing on television. Those are inexplicable mysteries. But Ogma's favors do deserve some consideration. I put my life in jeopardy both times. That means they're pretty big favors."

<And *that* means I deserve a pretty big snack, right? Like a whale or something.>

"Whales are not snacks, Oberon."

<That was merely a suggestion based on the size of the favor I just did you. It's okay if you don't give me a whale. You could substitute a herd of cattle or buy me my own chicken-and-waffle restaurant. It would be called Oberon's Chicken and Waffles, because all the chicken and waffles would in fact be mine.>

"Well, let's see how it works out first. Let me think about this."

I called to the Morrigan that night, wondering if she would be willing to grant the favor. Her breathy whisper sounded pleased at first.

Siodhachan. I didn't expect to hear from you again so soon.

"I admit that I was hoping to get your help with a couple of favors that Ogma owes me."

I don't understand. You want me to repay favors that Ogma owes you or force Ogma to grant you the favors he owes?

"Neither. One of the favors requires him to find Miach, who was slain by his father, Dian Cecht, and learn from him how he performed the feat for which he is still famous."

I think I see. You are asking a favor of me so that Ogma can perform a favor for you.

"I'm not exactly asking in the binding contractual sense. I am wondering if you will do this for me without expecting to be paid later."

Why would I do that?

"Because it would demonstrate to me that you can behave in ways to which you're unaccustomed. It would be proof of your personal growth."

Perhaps it would demonstrate that. Or perhaps you are using my professed feelings against me to your advantage. Manipulating me.

"Perhaps. But you don't have to continue to think of every transaction or exchange as having a winner and a loser."

I only think of it that way because it's true.

"It's not true if you want to build a relationship based on trust with someone. Both people can and should win."

Is that so? How would I win in this case?

"I would be grateful and think of you fondly."

Are you saying you would love me?

"No, that's not what I said. But believing you will do something for me without payment in kind—that's a big step along that path. It's crucial, in fact."

And have you ever done something like that for me?

"I have worshipped you and observed your rites for more than two thousand years. I have prayed to you, honored you, and I took you to a baseball game once just to enjoy your company. Bought you a cute baseball cap and everything."

Ah, yes, I remember. The despair in the dugout was delicious. Very well. Have Ogma call me when he is ready and I will take him to the shade of Miach, expecting no favor in return.

"That's very kind, and I appreciate it."

Getting Ogma to visit me took several days of prayer and calling upon him and relayed requests through elementals. He hadn't participated in the fighting of Ragnarok, being one of the gods Brighid had decided to sequester, and he was not anxious to return from wherever he was. He appeared to be in a poor mood when he arrived. The hounds and I were finishing up an early dinner on the beach of the Mayfield Bay Conservation Area when he emerged from the eucalyptus forest. The undersides of clouds were lit in orange and magenta and bruised with purple higher up as the sun set. He pointedly crossed his arms, something I could no longer do.

"Hello, Ogma. I once retrieved the Dagda's cauldron for you and raided the library at Alexandria, both for favors to be named later."

"I'm aware. This is quite a bit later."

"The favors had no expiration dates. I'm ready to call them in now."

"I assumed as much. What are they?"

"First, I'd like you to contact the Morrigan and have her lead you to the shade of Miach, who healed the arm of Nuada, and learn from him how it was done."

"That's more than one favor."

"It's only one: Learn from Miach how he healed Nuada. I'm only suggesting you contact the Morrigan because you'll find him faster that way and she's already agreed to do this."

"And if he refuses to teach me?"

"You keep trying until he does, of course. Though I will note that the Morrigan can be very persuasive when she wishes."

Ogma grunted, looking at my stump. "I think I already know what the second favor is."

"Yes. Heal me the way Miach healed Nuada. Regrow flesh and bone so that I can be whole again and get my binding to the earth restored."

The god's lip curled in a snarl. "You'd better not ask me to complete that binding."

"I won't." I planned to ask Brighid to restore my bindings, should I be so fortunate to possess an arm again. She had said she would grant me a boon.

"Why are you even bothering? You've done enough. Granuaile and Owen will make sure Druidry endures. Go to Tír na nÓg and take your rest."

"I've lost a lot, Ogma, but not my will to live. Nor did I lose my sense of responsibility. I still have plenty of work to do on Gaia's behalf." And I had a bet with Owen that I wanted to win.

Ogma hawked up something gross from his throat and spat it on the beach, a nonverbal hint at what he thought of my reply. "This will take some time, if it can be done at all. Where will you be?"

"Somewhere on the island. I obviously won't be shifting around anytime soon. You can ask Tasmania where I am."

The god grimaced as if he'd just swallowed a mouthful of sour milk, but didn't say anything else. He couldn't simply kill me to make the problem go away—not without severe consequences. Dropping the Morrigan's name ensured that. And refusing the attempt or claiming it was impossible was equally unworkable. I have often thought the economy of favors-to-be-named-later is the shadow economy by which history is funded; nothing important would get done without such favors. He muttered a farewell and departed, and I didn't know if I'd see him again next week or next month or next year, or, indeed, ever again. The same could be said, I supposed, for Granuaile. There was no guarantee that anything would work out.

But at least I had some small hope of healing and a better hope of learning how to live differently, without having to hide from the Fae or the gods of various pantheons anymore. And in the darkness of time that stretched before me, I saw a small winking light that could be forgiveness. Perhaps it would be others forgiving me my trespasses, or me forgiving myself. I hoped I could make it there, regardless, to let it shine on me.

In the meantime, there was an entire planet to nurture and a couple of hounds who hadn't forgotten that I promised them a romp on the beach after dinner. And I realized with a start that there was no longer any reason for me to hang on to my American accent. I shed it and returned to my old Irish one, and it was like wrapping myself in a favorite blanket.

"What d'ye say, hounds o' mine? Ready for some sand and surf before we settle down for the night?"

Oberon and Starbuck didn't wait but immediately took off toward the wet sand in the day's last light, tongues flapping in the salty air like pink pennants. Oberon's mental voice floated back to me, taunting. <Last one to the water's an old Druid!>

I grinned as I chased them onto the beach. Yes, I am an old Druid. And I plan on getting much older. I have many, many years to go before I see my final sunset.

acknowledgments

egad, it's strange and wonderful and sad to come to the end of a series like this. Bittersweet. *Dolofabolo*, as Slomo would say.

I may return to this world later on with some adventures featuring Owen's apprentices, but the story of the Iron Druid, at least, is finished. Ye may assume that Atticus and Granuaile are still out there in the world somewhere, looking after Gaia, and that Oberon is still fond of sausage and poodles. (And Orlaith likes Newfoundlands, by the way. Dogs are not monogamous, so there's no need to worry about their relationship.)

In the meantime, I'm writing two new series. I'd be honored if you'd try *A Plague of Giants*, out now, and the soon-to-be-released *Kill the Farm Boy*, co-authored with Delilah S. Dawson.

I'll always be grateful to my agent, Evan Goldfried, and my editor, Tricia Narwani, for taking a chance on me. And I will always be grateful to you for reading, because without you buying the series and telling your friends and family about it, I never would have been able to finish it as I wished.

The following peeps were kind to group-source Polish translations for me: Loë, Bartosz Grabowski, Piotr Warzecha, Anna Pyrich, Edi Skrobiszewska, Anna Flasza-Szydlik, Dagna Korosacka, Miłosz Kasprowicz, Aleksander Glaz, and Andrzej Stępiński.

The two lines of Wang Wei's poem, "Reply to a Magistrate," were translated from Mandarin by Sam Hamill.

Many thanks to the folks on Twitter who helped me out with the two whole words of Latin that Granuaile spoke. Conjugating verbs is rough and I'm much obliged, and I also hope you know who you are since I don't.

Humongous thanks to Fang-Chin Chang of Gaea Books in Taipei, who was so gracious and helpful regarding my questions about the city. Any inaccuracies are of course mine and not hers. And more generally, thank you to the people of Taiwan for being so wonderful. I enjoyed my visit to Taipei in February of 2017 immensely.

Shoutout to my copy editor, Kathy Lord, who has saved me from many mistakes great and small and deserves all the whiskey.

High five to audiobook narrators Luke Daniels and Christopher Ragland, who have brought the series alive for so many listeners.

I'd also like to thank artist Gene Mollica and designer Dave Stevenson for the outstanding series covers. They've made plenty of folks pick up the books and they're very good at their jobs.

Much appreciation for Ryan Kearney, Julie Leung, David Moench, Keith Clayton, and Scott Shannon at Del Rey for the work they do getting the series out there.

I am always grateful for the love and support of my family, friends, and doggies. I'm also thankful to y'all for coming along on this ride. Hope you had as much fun as I did, and may harmony find you.

About the Type

This book was set in Sabon, a typeface designed by the well-known German typographer Jan Tschichold (1902–74). Sabon's design is based upon the original letter forms of sixteenth-century French type designer Claude Garamond and was created specifically to be used for three sources: foundry type for hand composition, Linotype, and Monotype. Tschichold named his typeface for the famous Frankfurt typefounder Jacques Sabon (c. 1520–80).

extras

www.orbitbooks.net

about the author

Kevin Hearne hugs trees, pets doggies, and rocks out to heavy metal. He also thinks tacos are a pretty nifty idea. He is the author of *A Plague of Giants* and the *New York Times* bestselling series the Iron Druid Chronicles.

kevinhearne.com
Facebook.com/authorkevin
Twitter: @KevinHearne

Find out more about Kevin Hearne and other Orbit authors by registering for the free monthly newsletter at www.orbitbooks.net.

if you enjoyed
SCOURGED

look out for

WASTELANDERS: BITE

by

K. S. Merbeth

MAD MAX, EAT YOUR HEART OUT.

Hungry and alone in the desert, Kid is picked up on the side of the road by Wolf, Dolly, Tank and Pretty Boy: a raider crew with a big, bad reputation and even bigger guns.

But as they journey across the wasteland, Kid learns that her saviours are hiding a terrible secret. In a world that's lost its humanity, how long will Kid stay hungry before she loses hers?

I
Show Your Teeth

'Need a ride?'

His grin looks more like an animal baring its teeth. His teeth are yellowed and chipped, with gaps between showing where others have been knocked out. There's something starkly predatory about him, which is the first reason I shouldn't say yes.

The second is I'm small, alone, and unarmed. Any of those could be a death sentence in a place like this.

And there we have the third reason: By 'a place like this,' I mean a torn-up, full-of-potholes road running through the middle of nowhere. It's the only thing marking the landscape for miles. There's nothing but empty desert and the ruins of old cities in every direction. Nuclear war can do that to a place, I guess. But the point is, there's no one around to hear if I scream. Plus, even if someone did hear, chances are they wouldn't give a shit.

The fourth reason is the creepy lady in the passenger seat, who has blue hair and an assault rifle in her lap.

The fifth reason is the red-stained sacks of something-or-other sitting in the backseat.

The sixth reason is . . . ah, hell. Need I go on?

I scratch my nose, sniff, and spit. The rumble of the jeep is the only sound in the stagnant air.

It's obvious that getting in this jeep is a terrible idea. A sixteen-year-old girl like me could provide a hell of a lot of entertainment for someone with a sick enough mind. I must look like easy prey, with my ragged clothes and skinny body.

So naturally, my answer is—

'Sure, why not?'

When it comes down to it, I've been walking for days. The soles of my boots are collecting holes. The sand burns my feet during the day, and the world is dark and frightening at night. The sun has left my skin raw and peeling, and when it sets it sucks all the warmth away. I'm down to one can of food and less than two days' worth of water – not enough to make it back to town even if I wanted to go. Lord knows how far I'd have to travel to find more.

This jeep and its driver are smelly, creepy, and very possibly dangerous, but they're my only ticket out of here.

The stranger shows his teeth again. His eyes are hidden behind a pair of goggles too big for his face.

'Hop in then, kid.'

I clamber into the backseat next to the reeking mystery bags, nearly tumbling onto them before I manage to squeeze myself into the tight space between the bags and the door. I place my backpack on my lap, my arms curling around it protectively. It doesn't hold much, just my canteen, one can of food, and a blanket my papa gave me, but it's all I have. I lean back with a sigh as the jeep starts moving. Sayonara, middle of nowhere! I might end up dead and dismembered in a ditch, but it'd be better than wandering aimlessly through this hellhole of a desert.

We pick up speed quickly, and I have to pull down on my beanie to stop it from flying off my head. A few strands of mousy hair poke out from underneath it, and I try to push them under again, but it's no use. I settle for holding the beanie with one hand and resting the other on the side of the jeep. The rank smell of the bags is getting stronger and stronger, making my eyes water. I blink it away and try to ignore it.

My attention shifts to the lady in the front seat, who still strikes me as pretty creepy. She was still and silent the whole time they waited for my answer, but now she turns around. It's impossible not to stare at her hair. It's very long, nearly waist-length, and oddly straight and sleek. I really don't understand how someone could have hair so perfect-looking, or how and *why* her hair is colored electric blue. The color is incredibly vivid in the dust-colored world around us.

She has dark eyes that reveal an Asian heritage, and small lips painted a vibrant red. She's pretty, with a noticeably ladylike figure despite the wasteland garb covering her quite modestly. Her red lips are mouthing something, but I can't make out any words with the wind whipping around me.

I squint my eyes, tilt my head to the side, and give her a vacant stare. She stares back at me for a moment before turning around.

She doesn't try to talk to me again, and neither does the feral man. Apparently they don't care enough to ask where I intend to go. I'm just along for the ride, and that's fine by me. Wherever I'm going has to be better than where I've been.

If I had any common sense at all I'd probably want to stay on edge. But, at this point, I'm already in the jeep. Either they want to kill me or they don't, and I won't get much of a choice in it either way. So I decide to nap. What can I say? It's been a long couple of days.

I wake up with my face pressed against the lumpy garbage bags, and *wow* do they smell. The scent is invading my nostrils, pillaging my throat, and violating my poor brain. I gag and recoil, pressing against the side of the car and frantically wiping my face with a hand that is probably even dirtier. I don't know what the hell is in there, but I don't want it on or near my face.

Once I determine I'm safe from any obscene-smelling substances, I realize the jeep is no longer moving, and my backpack is no longer on my lap. The man and young woman are standing a few yards away from the still vehicle, having a quiet conversation. Neither of them is paying attention to me.

I adjust my beanie and climb out of the car, stretching out my bony limbs one at a time. My back cracks and both of the strangers' heads jerk toward me.

'Err,' I say. The woman still has her assault rifle, and it's now pointed in my direction. I raise my hands and smile nervously. 'My bad.'

She relaxes when she sees it's just me, and the man displays that grin of his again. I notice my backpack in the dirt at his feet. In his hand is what I assume to be my last can of food. Unsurprisingly, it's beans. Despite how sick I am of goddamn beans, my stomach rumbles. But his other hand holds a really big knife that he must have used to pry the can open, so I decide not to comment.

'So you're awake,' the man says through a mouthful of food. He swallows, sighs with unabashed satisfaction, and continues. 'We were about to wake you up, but you looked pretty happy in there. You were drooling a little on the goods.'

I wipe my mouth and feel my cheeks grow hot. He laughs, a hearty and surprisingly genuine sound. He bends down to grab my backpack off the ground and tosses it over to me. I can't resist the urge to take a peek inside, just to make sure nothing else is missing. Once I'm certain that my canteen and my papa's blanket are still inside, I sling the bag over one shoulder and smile at him.

'We found a little town,' he says, jerking his thumb behind him. 'Decided it was as good a place as any to stop.'

'Oh, yeah, great,' I say sincerely. 'That works just fine. Thanks for the ride, mister.'

He laughs again, this time for no good reason I can decipher.

'Right, kid,' he says. 'Mind helping us carry this?'

I glance at the gross bags in the back of the jeep. The thought of lugging them around is far from pleasant. I don't know what's in them, and honestly I don't want to know. But he *did* give me a ride, so . . .

'Sure.'

'Good!' He grins again. 'Don't drop 'em or anything, we're selling this shit.'

I nod and wipe my sweaty palms on my jeans. Right, I can handle that. Probably.

The blue-haired Asian lady has been looking at me intently

this whole time, and it's starting to make me uncomfortable. She has a weird blankness about her. Not a hint of emotion ever crosses her face, and she has an incredibly unnerving stare. It's like looking into the eyes of a corpse. I try to ignore her, but looking at the guy with the savage grin isn't much better. At least the woman combs her hair. The man's is in long brown dreadlocks, and obviously hasn't been groomed in an awfully long time.

The two of them move over to the jeep and start unloading. They pack my arms full first, and I scrunch my nose and try not to inhale too deeply. Once we all have as much as we can carry, we head toward the town.

Or, rather, toward the pathetic collection of shambling buildings we call towns around here. Like most, it's built over the ruins of an old city, and made mostly of crumbling walls and scrap metal. People have patched up half-destroyed shells of rooms with blankets and plywood and whatever else they can find. From the looks of it, no more than a couple dozen townies live here. They peek out of doorways and windows as we pass through the outer limits of town. I see mostly men, a handful of women, and not a single child, which is not surprising. The end of the world didn't exactly encourage people to go making babies left and right, and half of the ones that do get born won't make it past their first year.

I've only ever seen pictures of the great old cities, but it's enough to make me appreciate the sadness of what they've become. I thought the town I left was small and run-down, but now I know the people back there had it pretty good. These people are dirty, thin, wrapped in rags.

Hollow eyes in hungry faces turn to watch us, but they

don't seem overly alarmed. Apparently this place is used to strangers, which is a bit odd. Most of these little towns can go months without seeing a new face. Three strangers arriving would've been a big old affair where I came from, and not a friendly one at that.

We walk for a few minutes, moving into what seems to be the heart of the town, an open space between some of the more well-kept buildings. The man dumps the bags he's carrying on the ground, and the woman and I follow suit. They produce wet thumps and small clouds of dust as they hit. I gratefully suck in fresh air while the other two survey the area. I'm not really sure what my plan is at this point, but these two seem to have some kind of goal, so I figure it can't hurt to stick with them for now.

'Where are they?' the woman asks. Her voice is nearly a whisper, and as flat and emotionless as her face.

'Not here,' the man says, 'which can't mean anything good.'

I eye them, but bite back my question as a townie approaches. He's a tall, wiry, dark-skinned man with a commanding presence and suspicious eyes. He folds his arms over his chest and spits a gob of yellowish saliva that narrowly misses my boot.

The dreadlocked man beside me shoves his hands into the pockets of his ratty jeans, assumes a relaxed posture, and grins.

'Name's Wolf,' he says. 'We've got some goods here. You have anything worth trading for? Gasoline, maybe?'

The townie says nothing. He looks at us, scrutinizes the bags, and looks at us again.

'Might,' he says finally. 'What've you got?' He nudges a bag with one shoe.

Again comes that cruel display of teeth.

'Meat,' Wolf says, overemphasizing the word.

The other man's eyebrows rise.

'Ain't seen that in a while,' he says. 'What's it from?'

'Couple o' wild hogs.'

'Hogs,' the townie repeats. He stares at the bags, his jaw working as if he's chewing on the information. 'Lot of meat for a couple hogs.'

'Fat ones,' Wolf says dryly. 'Look, you gonna trade or not?'

The man pauses.

'Let me think,' he says. He seems to be carefully weighing each word. 'I'll have to look at our stocks. Why don't you lot stay overnight? We'll talk in the mornin'.'

'Meat won't stay good forever,' Wolf says. It's hard to read his expression behind the goggles.

'Meat probably ain't good now,' the townie says, spitting again. I have to hop to the side to avoid this one. 'One more night won't hurt.'

'Fine,' Wolf says. He turns and jerks his head toward the woman. 'Dolly, you'll sleep with the jeep.'

'We ain't thieves,' the man says.

''Course not,' Wolf agrees enthusiastically, but shoots Dolly a meaningful look. 'Anyway, we should at least get our goods out of the sun.' The townie nods, saying nothing, and Wolf turns to me. 'How 'bout helping us with these bags again?'

Something tells me I should leave right now and pretend

I never had anything to do with a strange couple of travelers called Wolf and Dolly. Something tells me a man with a smile like his can only bring trouble. Maybe that something is what normal people call common sense.

But Papa always said I don't have a whole lot of that.

'Sure,' I say. 'Why not?'

II
The Strangers

Carrying the cargo is sweaty work, and by our second trip into town I think I'm starting to smell as bad as the bags. It doesn't help that Wolf is off bartering somewhere, leaving Dolly and me to handle it all ourselves. None of the townies offer to help. Instead they completely ignore our presence. Men rest on rocks or lean against nearby buildings in small clumps, carrying on conversations that fall silent when we get close. And it really is all men; the women have disappeared. So have the elderly, and the incapable. Every single person left lingering outside looks like they could give me a thorough ass-kicking if necessary. I can feel their eyes following me when I turn my back.

'This is weird,' I say in a low whisper. I glance over at Dolly, who keeps her eyes forward. 'Isn't it?'

She gives a minuscule shrug of her shoulders and says nothing. I guess that's as close to an answer as I'm going to get. I sigh and try to ignore the uneasiness creeping up on me. These people did invite us to stay in their town for the night. That alone makes them friendlier than the town I left. Wolf and Dolly would've been shot the second they got within ten paces of the place. These townies are just being reasonably wary of strangers. Probably.

'So, where are you and Wolf headed, anyway?' I ask, trying to distract myself from my nerves. Neither of them has told me anything about themselves or why they're here. They haven't asked about me, either. Come to think of it, I don't think they've even asked for my name. Maybe I'm supposed to assume those are the rules of our temporary relationship, but my curiosity is getting the better of me.

'Nowhere,' Dolly says. I frown.

'So you're just ... driving around randomly? Isn't that kind of ... ' Pointless? Dangerous? A waste of precious gas? I don't even know where to begin. 'Are you traders?' Traders are the only people I can think of who would have any reason to wander like that. Well, and myself, but I have my own reasons.

'No,' she says. I wait for her to continue. She doesn't.

'Okay,' I say. When I was young and my papa left me in our bomb shelter by myself, I used to play a game that involved bouncing a ball off the wall. It always just came bouncing back, but I would keep doing it like I expected something new to happen, or thought a friend might materialize. Trying to carry on a conversation with Dolly feels about as productive as that did.

I shut my mouth and keep walking. I should save my breath, anyway. Even though I'm only carrying half as much as Dolly, the bags are heavy, and the exertion is making me more aware of the hunger in my belly and the tired ache in my bones. Despite that, it's nice to feel helpful.

Back in my old town it was always *Get out of the way, girl* and *Don't you know how to do anything right?* One of the many reasons why braving the wastes alone sounded better than staying.

As we pass one of the rickety buildings, the door bangs open. A woman comes out, dragging a young boy behind her. I guess there are children here after all; they must just keep them hidden away when strangers are around. The woman stomps her way over to a group of men sitting on the hood of a rusted, broken-down vehicle. She speaks in hushed whispers to them, saying something that involves a lot of head shakes and hand gestures. She releases the hand of the boy as the conversation seems to grow more heated. The boy's gaze wanders over to us. As our eyes meet I shoot him a friendly smile.

My smile drops as the kid takes that as a sign to start walking over to us.

'Oh, no. No, no, no,' I mutter. As much as I like children, somehow I don't think this kid is supposed to be near us. I don't want to give the townies any other reason to distrust us. But it's not easy to wave him away with my hands full, and I don't want to raise my voice and draw attention.

I slow down as he gets closer. It's hard to see the kid around the bulky bags I'm carrying.

'Careful, little guy,' I say, stepping around him. 'This is heavy stuff.'

Apparently he's not the sharpest tool in the shed, because he moves away from me and steps directly into Dolly's path. He stares up at her with wide eyes and doesn't move. Dolly stops in her tracks.

'Can I touch your hair?' the boy asks.

'We're kind of busy here,' I say. Dolly doesn't seem like the kid-friendly type, and I don't want to see her go all ice queen on this poor kid. But instead, to my surprise, she drops her bags and crouches down, bringing herself to eye level with the young boy. With several inches between their faces, they scrutinize each other with an apparently shared sense of awe. He raises a hand and touches the ends of her hair with small, chubby fingers. I'm sure his hands are filthy, but Dolly doesn't pull back from his touch. I catch a glimpse of something oddly soft in her face, a crack in her blank expression. She almost looks sad for a moment.

'Mommy said you were bad people,' the boy says, 'but I think you're nice.' He smiles. His two front teeth are missing. Dolly leans close and whispers something in his ear.

A surprised expletive alerts me that the boy's mother has noticed his disappearance. She looks around frantically, homes in on us, and rushes over, her eyes wide and fearful.

'Jimmy,' she hisses, grabbing the boy by the hand and yanking him away. She pulls him behind her and backs away from us. Her suspicious eyes flit back and forth between Dolly and me. Once she's apparently decided we're not going to attack her, she turns her back and hurries away, tugging her son along. 'What did I tell you about talking to strangers?' she scolds him.

With another loud bang, she disappears into the building she came from. The men near the jeep are watching us with a renewed and obviously unfriendly interest. I frown, and glance at Dolly to see if the interaction bothered her, but her face is back to its usual blank slate. She stands up, takes her bags, and resumes walking. I hurriedly follow, trying to match her long strides.

'You like kids, Dolly?' I ask, not really expecting a response.

'Yes.' A straight answer, to my surprise, and when I turn to look at her there's a ghost of a smile on her lips. It disappears immediately when she notices me looking.

'Me, too!' Finally, some shared ground. I smile at her, but she doesn't seem to notice. 'What'd you say to him?'

'To listen to his mother.'

I nod slowly, automatically assuming it to be good advice before I remember what his mom said.

As the day grows later, the townies invite us to share a meal with them. It's good hospitality, especially for a place this small. The idea would have been laughable where I came from. Even after living there for a couple of years, I wouldn't get fed unless I got enough work done during the day.

I'm grateful for the generosity, and yet something about this place is definitely rubbing me the wrong way. Nobody says anything openly, but everyone gives us these weird sideways glances and dirty looks. It's gotten even worse since this morning. Part of me wonders if it's Wolf and Dolly specifically they're suspicious about, but since I arrived with them and have stuck with them since getting here, it's a little late for me to try to distance myself from them.

Since Dolly is watching the jeep, Wolf and I are alone. The townies light up trash can fire pits, place sheets of metal over the tops, and set aluminum cans of food on top of those. They cluster around the trash cans as the sun sets and the

Paisley Central Library
68 High Street, Paisley PA1 2BB
Renfrewshire Libraries Tel: 0300 300 1188

Borrowed Items 04/07/2018 10:25
XXXXX5703

Item Title	Due Date
* Scourged	01/08/2018
Besieged	19/07/2018

* Indicates items borrowed today

Thankyou for using this unit

The library is always open at
www.renfrewshirelibraries.co.uk

day's warmth slips away. Wolf and I stand apart from them. I can barely feel a hint of heat from this distance, and have to rub at my arms to keep from shivering. However, the smell of the meal cooking reaches us just fine, and my mouth waters at the distant memory of hot food. I haven't eaten anything but cold beans for days.

But the looks from the townies sour my stomach. They all look incredibly pissed off as soon as they catch me looking. I can read the accusations in those stares: *strangers, untrusted, unwelcome*. I'm particularly familiar with the latter. In the wastes, you have to fight for your right to exist.

'Are you sure we were invited?' I ask, turning to Wolf and trying to ignore the stares. My stomach churns with a familiar discomfort. I didn't leave my last town just to become an unwanted mouth to feed again. At least Wolf doesn't seem to mind my presence.

''Course I am.' He continues staring at the food. He pulled his goggles down around his neck when the sun set, and his eyes are sharp and intense without them. I shrug and look down at my boots.

As the townies start passing out cans, clumps of people shift into a messy line. I watch as Wolf walks up and completely ignores them, bypassing the line and snatching a can of food without a moment's hesitation. I attempt to follow in the wake of his bravado, but only make it two steps before someone bumps into me and sends me stumbling.

I look up to see a gaunt-faced townie scowling down at me. His eyes are hard, his lip curling derisively.

'Sorry,' I say automatically, as my brain tries to work out where the hell he came from. All of the other townies were by the fire pits, so why was this guy behind us? Was he watching us? My uneasiness deepens, and I swallow hard.

'You ain't supposed to be here,' he says.

'Huh? Wolf said—'

'Not him. *You*.' He jabs a finger into my chest. I back up, rubbing at the spot and staring at him. 'What are you doing with them?' he asks me.

'Umm, well, it's kind of a long story—'

'Scrawny little thing like you,' he says, stepping closer and bringing his face down to mine. I'm uncomfortably aware of how much bigger than me he is. Would the other townies step in if he tried to hurt me? I doubt it. 'Think you can just wander into town and help yourself to our food?'

'I thought—'

'You thought wrong.' He puts a hand on my chest and shoves, sending me stumbling right into Wolf.

'Is there a problem here?' he asks.

I never thought I'd be so happy to see his crazy grin. I scamper behind him and stay there, eager to have a shield from the townie. The man stares at Wolf for a long few seconds. Wolf barely looks at him; he's focused on the can of food in his hands, which he's slowly opening with a knife much too big and sharp for the task. Metal grates harshly on metal as he peels it open. The townie's jaw is clenched, a tic jumping in his cheek. He looks like he's dying to throw a punch. But just when the tension seems taut enough to snap, he shakes his head and walks away.

I let out a low whoosh of breath and step out from behind Wolf.

'Well, I'm sure glad I didn't show up here alone,' I say,

forcing a laugh. Wolf shrugs nonchalantly, raises his can to his mouth, and takes a big gulp. My mouth fills with drool at the sight, and I realize with a sad twist of my stomach that there's no way I'll be brave enough to get food for myself now. Wolf lowers the can and notices me staring.

'What?' he asks, wiping his mouth with the back of his hand. 'What is it? Why aren't you eating?'

'Oh, uh, I'm not that hungry,' I say. 'I just ate ... the day before yesterday.'

Wolf rolls his eyes.

'Do I gotta do *everything* for you?' he grumbles.

Before I can protest, he shoves his can into my hands.

'Let me show you somethin', kid,' he says. He walks over to the townies and casually cuts into the front of the line again. He grabs a can, grins at the man passing out food, and saunters back to me. 'See? It's that simple.'

Apparently he doesn't notice the death glares and murmurs that follow. Though, at this point, it's probably more accurate to say that he doesn't give a shit.

'Well, that's easy for you to say. You're—' I pause before the word *scary* leaves my mouth. 'Umm. You have a really big knife.'

'Oh, this?' He looks down at the knife, which he's currently using to pry open the second can of food, and chuckles. 'This ain't nothing. Now eat your damn beans before they get cold.'

Of course it had to be beans. I suppress a sigh and take a sludgy gulp of the familiar food. At least they're hot. I scarf them down as quickly as possible and swipe a finger around the can to collect the last remnants.

Once I'm done, I watch Wolf. He eats slowly, which is

Enter the monthly
Orbit sweepstakes at

www.orbitloot.com

With a different prize every month,
from advance copies of books by
your favourite authors to exclusive
merchandise packs,
**we think you'll find something
you love.**